Best Wishes!

S. O. Hosla

9/25/84

THE
HAWTHORN
CONSPIRACY

THE HAWTHORN CONSPIRACY

AN ADVENTURE NOVEL

by Stephen Hesla

DEMBNER BOOKS / NEW YORK

Dembner Books
Published by Red Dembner Enterprises Corp., 1841 Broadway,
New York, N.Y. 10023
Distributed by W. W. Norton & Company, Inc., 500 Fifth Avenue,
New York, N.Y. 10110

Library of Congress Cataloging in Publication Data

Hesla, Stephen.
    The Hawthorn conspiracy.

    I. Title.
PS3558.E7965H3   1984   813'.54   84-4985
ISBN 0-934878-39-0

For my sons,
whoever they may choose
to become

THE HAWTHORN CONSPIRACY

This book is a work of fiction, though many of the events described or referred to in it are true. British Guiana did go through a period of turmoil during the time this story takes place, and some names, dates, and political developments are taken from history. There is a Demerara River, and there is a bauxite mine north of the campsite, but there is not, to the writer's knowledge, a mud basin as described in the book.

The U.S.S. *Ticonderoga* was not off the coast of Korea during the last days of the Korean conflict, though other carriers were, and the account of Stephen Moffit's attack and subsequent internment is purely imaginary, though pilots who survived similar experiences may argue the point.

It is possible, perhaps even probable, that a plot such as the Globe project did exist, and that certain of its elements were in fact initiated. The people in this account come together in a time when corporate dirty tricks are only slightly more offensive than political chicanery. The writer, however, has invented the fabric that covers those thin bones in order to create a story that could have been true.

Part One

CHAPTER 1

July 1953.

The late afternoon shower had become an endless drizzle, cold and wet and gray as a softly swirling scud drifted across the city of Hamburg, toward the Baltic coast. Alan Drinkwater, a darkish mushroom stem under his black umbrella, stopped, peered over his spectacles, and then hurried in little, quick steps to the entryway of the old office building. At the foot of three short stairs he paused, slid his attaché case over his wrist, and fumbled with the umbrella catch until it collapsed with a wet slap. He shook it once, opened the door and stepped inside, waited a moment, then turned toward the dimly lit staircase that would lead him, thankfully for the last time, to his dreary office.

At the end of the first flight he paused again to catch his breath, then headed down the narrow yellow corridor, passing three naked doors on his right, four on his left. His was the last office in the hall, the one chamber that was in use after eight o'clock.

He stood before the door and wiped his glasses with a handkerchief, slipped them back onto his nose, found a latchkey in his coat pocket, and turned the lock. He glanced back down the hallway, then went inside and closed the door. An unshaded window filtered enough light through its sooty glass to see by, and he dropped the attaché case on a small desk, hung the umbrella and his raincoat on a corner clothes tree, and deposited his hat on a worn sofa as he took his usual inventory of the small room. He moved a leather side chair a few inches out of the way and crossed to his own wooden chair closer to the desk, fitting his knees into the small space that would afford some meager comfort against the damp air. Already he was beginning to smell the familiar fragrance of wet wool. It would remind him for the next hour that he was once again the misplaced English gentleman on another unhappy assignment.

He would not have described himself that way. Alan Drinkwater, Ph.D., O.B.E., Q.C., and others was a dedicated man, and dedicated men are seldom unhappy in the purest sense. He had asked for this duty and it had been granted him, possibly as a reward for the many other jobs he had done in the service of his King, and now his Queen. His was a strange business, a secret kind of business, a business that had occupied thirty-seven of his best years.

This would undoubtedly be his last assignment. He was sixty-three years old, his penetration was less brilliant than before, and his acumen, although still keen, was not as precise as it had to be in the face of new processes. But he was in charge of this project and it would be a noteworthy adventure, a perfectly adequate coda for his career.

Drinkwater reached across the desk and pulled the attaché case to his chest, got a key from his vest pocket, unlocked the zipper and opened it. He drew out five envelopes, and placing the case on the floor by his foot, wiped the desk dry with his sleeve and carefully arranged the envelopes in a row, one beside the other. He stared at them for several minutes, touching each with a pencil eraser. Slowly he moved them about, forming a tree, then a hexagon, then a V, deciding finally that the envelope marked "Sh" should be saved for last. The others, "T," "NJ," "BP," "Ge," he stacked, tucking the privileged envelope in a drawer. Then he turned and faced the window, frowning at the thought of holding this interview without a curtain. But since the only possible observer would have to be a mile away, across the Alster, he relaxed and turned on the green desk lamp, then sat back to wait for his visitor.

Alan Drinkwater was not a handsome man. His face gave the appearance of a narrow cantalope, textured and somewhat yellowish, with studs for eyes set deep into their sockets. His nose was bulbish, his mouth too small and his chin too quick, too sharp. A short-cut crop of white hair sat atop his head like a stiff old brush, giving him a vigorous, even a tough aspect. Still, for all of that, it was a respectable face. He had learned to show it with honesty and good humor.

The texture was from smallpox, biting cold, desert sun, and a long period of deprivation during the last war. He had been captured in civilian clothes crossing the border between Rumania and Yugoslavia, trying to pass as a Bulgarian worker. His escape from the Bratislava prison would have made a remarkable novel, for he was able to con himself across five countries in four languages, finally reaching Algiers the day the Allies moved in. His business was intelligence gathering, specifically intelligence pertaining to critical materials, and more specifically, petroleum.

Even then he was too old, too experienced a veteran for field apprenticeship, but there was the need for his service. His recognition came when it was all over, when the Council of Europe was formed after the Russian invasion of Czechoslovakia. Drinkwater was named as British advisor to the Council and later became a member of the secret International Commission on Petro-Politics. It was the Commission's work that brought him to Hamburg, to begin the process that would ultimately contain Russia's ambitions in the West. Tonight he would set the plan in motion.

Drinkwater folded his hands on the gray metal desk and sighed. He needed these minutes alone to gather his thoughts, to assemble them in a neat, orderly fashion for his meeting with the man who had been the subject of so much investigation, so much internal bickering and consternation. It wasn't so much a question of the man's abilities or his qualifications as it was his attitude toward big time business. To him, if one were to believe the reports that filled the man's dossier, to this brashly articulate American, it was all a game. If there was a flaw in the man's character, it was his willingness to gamble without considering the impact a possible loss might have on his fellows. He was a selfish man, Drinkwater supposed. He and the Commission members had considered that carefully. Could a selfish person do this unselfish job?

The Englishman reached under the desk and rubbed his knees, softly cursing at the terrible feeling of wet tweed on his bare skin. Well, perhaps the man was merely determined. In the end, the decision was to go with him in any case. The majors had given their opinions, the members had acquiesced, and Drinkwater, for all of his misgivings, agreed that Gregory Hawthorn should be their man.

With dusk, the gray sky turned an almost greenish color, like chiffon, with dark streaks of purple and deep red where the clouds still caught the last of the day's sun. The streets along the Alster were shiny, polished-looking, with pools of water dancing among the cobblestones as errant droplets, stragglers behind the earlier downpour, fell home.

Behind the broad, newly unveiled facade of the Atlantic Hotel, a formally dressed waiter carrying a silver tray hurried across the floor of the famed Alsterblick Restaurant. He stopped at the table near a great bay window, bowed, placed the check at the diner's left hand, and stepped back, smiling.

Gregory Hawthorn returned the smile and nodded, a gesture that was interpreted as a dismissal. The waiter bowed again and withdrew.

Hawthorn had finished his dinner as the darkness of the rain began to lighten and had been observing the color changes through the reflection of his window. Beyond his own face he saw the darker shadows of the low office buildings far across the lake. He sat quietly now, sipped his coffee, and allowed nightfall to come to Hamburg.

He had made no plans for this trip. It was as though a force, perhaps the same force that was responsible for his successful business ventures, had assumed the responsibility for his life and established the schedule of events that brought him to Germany. He had been summoned. That was the only term for it. He did not know why.

It was not a good time for him to be away. There was work to be done and there were critical path consultations in progress that bore heavily on his corporation's future. Hawthorn was in the process of consolidating recent gains, gathering up a dozen profitable but loosely organized divisions, and planting them all under one manager. All right; if consolidation was the objective, and if Henri Amont was the right man, then Amont would prove it now, or a year's worth of effort would be wasted. Gregory Hawthorn was willing to gamble on his people.

When had he learned that difficult lesson? In the war, certainly, as a B-17 pilot over France, Italy, Yugoslavia. Through twenty-seven missions, until a Messerschmitt found them low over the coast and shot their tail off, he had trusted his men and his squadron commander.

The restaurant was filling with people now, many of them foreigners or Germans with foreign guests, diplomats or contractors working deals under the Marshall Plan to rebuild Europe. Hawthorn's chair was placed so that he could watch them as they talked. The animated personality was the seller and the man chewing on a stick of celery was the buyer. Hawthorn let his eyes wander from table to table and observed the same interplay at each one. It was a familiar scene, one that should have made him feel at ease.

Yet, from the moment he stepped off the plane, he had felt instead a subsconscious tugging at his sense of balance, a subtle perception that he was somehow out of place here. His dark gray suit was too well pressed, his military cordovans were too polished, his tie and buttondown collar were Madison Avenue in the middle of a war zone. When he followed the very proper headwaiter to his table, he felt much taller than his six feet, broader across the shoulders, slimmer at the waist, an athlete among old or beaten men. And at the table, the few other guests who happened to meet his midnight blue eyes turned away quickly, perhaps intimidated by the tough honesty they saw there, an uncomfortable invasion of their privacy.

Hawthorn, at age forty-one, commanded the fastest-growing domestic oil production company in America. His was the leader among nearly two hundred drilling and transportation groups that fed the majors. He had started with a Mississippi barge operation that was left to him by his

6

father, used that small fleet of seven old boats to raise the money for an investment in a poorly ranked concession in Oklahoma, and struck oil at less than five thousand feet. By the end of the first six months he was pumping over one hundred thousand barrels a day and was ready to move on a rail contract. In seven years he had built a reputation as a smart, aggressive, and sometimes reckless business manager whose moves were bold, if not always squeaky clean.

He folded his napkin and looked again toward the low buildings across the lake. He glanced at his watch, then pushed his chair back and deposited a twenty-mark note on the silver tray.

At the front doors of the hotel he smiled at the doorman who helped him into a tan raincoat. He stepped down, crossed the street, and established a brisk pace that would take him across the Lombardsbruke in less than the thirty minutes he had allowed. His appointment with Dr. Alan Drinkwater was for nine-thirty.

The air smelled clean and fresh. It had brought the people out as though a truce had been declared. Couples, families, and small groups of students were walking, talking together, relaxing from the firm-jawed persistence that had carried them through the day. He wondered if some of them were still smelling the pungent phosphorous of the incendiary bombs that had turned Hamburg into a torch in 1943. At the end of the bridge he stopped. Behind him to his left, the huge Rathaus tower clock was still plodding on toward the half hour. Hawthorn had five minutes to kill. His meeting was in Number 23, the building across the street and to his right. He walked slowly toward the stone ledge that rose from the lapping waters of the Alster.

The first contact had been a month ago, a call from Senator Richard Short to meet him for lunch. Their light conversation lasted only a few minutes. Then came the salad, the soup, the sandwich, the coffee . . . and the questions. "Would you be interested in a gamble that might possibly concern the national interest?" "How much do you know about international shipping?" "Could your company handle a big overseas exploration project?" Hawthorn's reply to each of these had been a cautiously curious one. Senator Short promised to contact him again but made him agree to keep the conversation strictly confidential. Hawthorn was left to believe that the senator had a private little enterprise in mind.

A week later Hawthorn was summoned to Washington by a courier-delivered note, signed in the hand of J. Thomas Pointer, CINCLANT. One could not ignore an invitation delivered in such a manner from the commander in chief, Atlantic fleet. Hawthorn was in Pointer's office on the appointed day.

7

With them at that meeting was another man, G. Thompson Burt, chief executive officer of the giant Standard Oil Company of New Jersey. For less than half an hour, Hawthorn listened to them discuss between themselves the enormously difficult alternatives open to the West vis-à-vis Iran, British Petroleum, and a certain Dr. Mossadeq, whose Iranian nationalization program had upset the oil industry very considerably. The meeting ended there, and Gregory Hawthorn went back to Baton Rouge.

On July 24, Hawthorn received a note from Senator Short, instructing him to "show passport identification at the Pan American counter, La Guardia Airport, 7:00 A.M., 7-26-53." His impulsive reaction to that dictatorial command was to place a phone call to the senator to suggest a place where he might put that idea, but he couldn't reach him. So more out of curiosity than out of any sense of duty, Hawthorn made the trip to New York. When he showed his passport to a clerk behind the counter he was promptly handed an envelope. Inside was a ticket to Hamburg, Germany, and a typed note:

"Dr. Alan Drinkwater, Jul 26, 9:30P, Hamburg. Neuer Jungfernstieg 23, #16. You have been cleared for Top Secret. Treat this accordingly."

The note was signed by Admiral J. Thomas Pointer. The clerk who handed him the envelope was not dressed in a Pan Am uniform.

Hawthorn leaned over the lakefront rail and watched the small wavelets, now black in the night. He had the feeling that he had either done something very right, or very wrong, something related to his place in the petroleum industry, probably. But regardless of the outcome of this night's mysterious meeting, he felt confident that he had a choice. It was his decision, not someone else's, and as long as he kept that fact in mind, he was in control.

He turned away from the rail, crossed the street, and mounted the three entrance steps. Inside, an arrow pointed up another flight of wooden steps, directing him to numbers 9 through 16. A single naked bulb hung from a wire in the stairwell, giving shadowed corners and uncertain sounds a threatening character. It was not what he had expected. At the top he found number 9 on his right, continued down the corridor past the other doors until he stood before number 16. He unbuttoned his coat and knocked. He waited a moment.

The door opened and Alan Drinkwater, hand outstretched, welcomed Hawthorn into his office. He was smiling, his dark eyes squinting behind silver-rimmed spectacles.

"Mr. Hawthorn, I expect. Ah! Well, then! Come in. Come in!"

The older man took Hawthorn's coat and dropped it carefully on the sofa, then stood back and looked at Hawthorn for a long moment before returning to the door, shutting it quietly and turning the lock.

8

"Sit down, please." He motioned to the side chair near his desk. Hawthorn remained standing.

"You are Dr. Alan Drinkwater?"

"I am, sir. I am Dr. Drinkwater, I am indeed, sir. Please. Please sit down, Hawthorn," he invited again. This time, Hawthorn sat down, folded his hands in his lap, and crossed his legs.

"Stopped raining in time for your stroll, I see. Well, I wasn't that lucky. I'm still a sodden mess, I'm afraid." He paused. "Thank you for coming."

"You know I went for a stroll?"

"You had to come across the bridge, Mr. Hawthorn, or along the other side. You have a room at the Atlantic Hotel and there are no boats at night. Besides, I took the precaution of having someone keep you in his care."

"I've been followed, is that what you mean?"

"Observed, Mr. Hawthorn." Drinkwater pulled at his lapels and sniffed. "Speaking of which, I'm afraid I must ask you for some identification. A passport and a driver's registration will do for the moment."

Hawthorn reached inside his coat and handed a billfold to the Englishman. From another pocket he produced the passport.

"Should I ask for yours as well?"

"I think not," answered Drinkwater. He spoke like a bad actor doing a butler's part. "I am who I say I am or I would have no business being here. Besides, I am the one who will be doing the talking, not you. I will tell the secrets, not you." He was examining Hawthorn's documents.

"Here, then." He passed them back. "You were wearing a coat, a dark brown summer coat when you visited the admiral. When you left his office, did you find something in the pocket?"

Hawthorn remembered.

"Yes," he replied.

"What was it?"

"A clothespin."

"Excellent! A wooden clothespin! Excellent."

Hawthorn smiled. This was absurd, totally absurd.

"Which will certify that I am Gregory Hawthorn?"

"It will do for now. To tell you the truth, I have no doubt that you are. But we are not exactly tea salesmen in Chicago, are we? We must be rather delicate about these things. And I presume the crossing was satisfactory?"

"A DC-6, first class. Very nice. You paid for it, I presume?"

"Oh, well, someone did at any rate. It got you here, I see."

9

Drinkwater was standing near the window, scrutinizing Hawthorn. He sniffed and returned to his place behind the desk, moving the chair to an angle so that he was not so patently the senior supervisor counseling his younger worker. He moved the green shade a few inches to clear the line of sight and sat down.

"You came without much of a clue, then. As to why."

"No clue at all, sir."

"On faith, then."

"Faith. Curiosity." He paused. "A decent respect for authority perhaps, or maybe just for the adventure of it."

"Ah!" Drinkwater tapped the desk top with a finger. "You have said the magic words, Hawthorn, 'adventure' and 'authority.' One without the other is either illegal or it is dull. I promise you, sir, this shall be neither!"

For a long moment, Drinkwater stared at the handsome American, a war hero, a poster soldier grown to become a business general. He blinked.

"Gregory Hawthorn, middle name Busche, after your mother's maiden name." Drinkwater looked beyond his guest and concentrated on the dark wall over the sofa. He sat back and placed his hands in his lap, scratching the wool, then turning his thumbs around. "Born in Curaçao, June one, 1912, German parents. Moved to Minneapolis in 1919 where your father worked as a river barge operator. A brother died on the river in 1921 and a sister moved to Berlin in 1936 and was killed in the war. Mother and father both dead." Drinkwater shifted his glance to Hawthorn's face, then continued. "You enlisted in the Army Air Corps in 1942 and were assigned to a bomber squadron after flight training, B-17s I believe. A most cumbersome machine, I'm told."

Hawthorn sensed that he should say something, but he decided to let the Englishman deal with the uncomfortable pause.

"In 1945 you were discharged as a major, and you took over your father's business, eventually moving it to Louisiana. Through some creative manipulation and a good deal of raw luck, your business has prospered. I should imagine that is all essentially correct?"

Raw Luck. Hawthorn let it pass. "You've done some homework, sir. I suppose I should be flattered."

"Poof! A single sheet of paper, Hawthorn." Drinkwater stood and moved to the window, clasping his hands behind his back.

"Ruddy chill in this awful room!" he said. "Tell me." He turned quickly and faced Hawthorn, his head slightly inclined. "What did you think of Pointer and Burt, their little conference a few days ago?"

Hawthorn answered without hesitation. "It interrupted a very impor-

10

tant week, sir." He folded his arms across his chest. "I'll tell you what I thought of it, sir. It reminded me of something my father used to do when I was a youngster. If he had an important man in the house, I would be invited to sit quietly in a corner and listen. He thought it was good for my development."

"Ah, well. And I'm sure it was, sir. I'm sure it was! But I mean, what did you think of the problem itself, the Iranians and Mossadeq and the oil crunch and all that business?"

"It was disturbing."

"Disturbing, disturbing. Yes. That would describe it, I should think. To be held ransom by an idiot, a lunatic. I would call that very disturbing. But what do you think they were striving to tell you? What specific thing did they want you to hear?"

Hawthorn was getting irritated. He was being prodded, pricked, coached, given a line to say in a classroom.

"Frankly, Dr. Drinkwater, I don't know. Do you mind if I smoke?"

"No, good heavens, man. Smoke if you like. Here." He pushed the empty wastebasket toward Hawthorn with his foot and stepped back to the sofa, into the shadow. Hawthorn lit a cigarette and turned his head to follow the little man. He seemed to have gotten smaller in the darkness.

"Tell me this, then," said Drinkwater from the corner. "Didn't you think it odd to be called to Washington like that? What could you possibly have inferred from such a visit with two men in their position?"

"I was reasonably sure they were sizing me up for something, sir, but I have no idea what that might have been." He puffed on the cigarette. "I think I'm about to find out."

"Oh, yes indeed, sir. Yes, you are. But first I'll tell you why I wanted you to be there, to listen in on their private little prefabricated conversation." Drinkwater sniffed again, louder this time. "If I had called you here without their help and their benediction, 'cold turkey' as it were, I would have been faced with explanations and questions from your side that I could not possibly have managed under the circumstances. You would have demanded credentials that I am not privileged to show. Furthermore, had I gotten you here in spite of those difficulties, you would not have believed me."

Drinkwater stepped out of the shadow and approached the desk. "Because, Mr. Hawthorn," he continued, "what I have to tell you is really very extraordinary." He leaned forward and placed his face squarely in front of Hawthorn's.

"I am going to tell you a spy story."

His eyes were inches from Hawthorn's face, his narrow lips were

11

pursed tight; the sounds of air passing through his nostrils filled Hawthorn's ears. Slowly Drinkwater straightened, circled around to his side of the desk. He pulled his chair back with slow deliberation and sat down.

"Did you know that Iran was controlled jointly by Russia and Great Britain during the war, and that we had enormous difficulty easing the Russians out of that horrid country? Interesting information, but only peripherally vital for now. And did you know that there was only one oil concession in Iran at the time? Did you know that it was owned by British Petroleum?"

Drinkwater was lecturing, picking on a student again. This time he sensed his own lordly arrogance.

"Forgive me, sir," Drinkwater said. "Of course you know those things. It's your business to know them. Well then, I needn't remind you that in 1951 the Majlis, the Iranian parliament, elected that pajama-wearing fanatic, Dr. Mossadeq, to be their bloody prime minister. They were so taken in by his wild and frightful weeping in public places that they shot the incumbent and set Mossadeq in his place! Perhaps you did *not* know that he gained his popularity by demanding the expulsion of British Petroleum. Mossadeq's very first act as PM was to nationalize the industry, take it away from the British.

"That was in 1951, just two years ago, sir. A good deal has happened since then, of course. The American oil companies have stood in support of the British and have boycotted all Iranian oil. The country is drying up, sir. But the worst of it is, the free world's oil supply is drying up as well!"

Hawthorn was aware of the impending shortages. He was in fact counting on them for a temporary hardening of the market, sure to become soft and glutted with hundreds of new exploration projects already showing remarkable promise. Drinkwater dabbed at his brow and went on.

"Now, then. Everyone knows that the Shah of Iran is the rightful monarch of that country. At the present time the oil as well as the country is in the hands of Dr. Mossadeq, who is by all reasonable standards a wretched individual. You will know from the discussion in Washington how this all affects the western powers and how anxious they are to dispose of the problem." Drinkwater moved the envelopes with his hand, pushed them toward the lamp base. He leaned forward.

"In a matter of days, Mr. Hawthorn, the streets of Tehran will become a battleground and Mossadeq will disappear. The Shah will return and the oil will once again flow to the West."

Up to that point Hawthorn's face had remained impassive. Now his eyes opened slightly and he worked his jaw under the skin. He crushed

12

the cigarette under his heel, picked the butt from the wooden floor, inspected it and dropped it into the wastebasket. Slowly, he shoved the wastebasket toward Drinkwater with his toe.

"Now I'm going to ask how you come to know that."

"Because I planned it, dear boy." Drinkwater was smiling again.

Hawthorn chose to be still for the moment. Outside, there was a siren's high moaning, nothing more—in the room, only the sound of Drinkwater's breathing.

"I thought you would have been more impressed," Drinkwater finally said. "Perhaps you don't believe me after all."

Now Hawthorn uncrossed his legs and planted his shoes flat on the floor. He leaned forward and placed his hands on the desk top.

"I think you had better tell me why I'm here," he said.

"Yes. Perhaps I should do that. All right, Mr. Hawthorn." Alan Drinkwater pulled himself to his full sitting posture and articulated his startling announcement carefully.

"It has been decided that you and your company may be usefully expended in the service of the West against communism. You have been chosen to become the instrument that will totally confuse, confound, embarrass, and finally destroy the Soviet Union in the Caribbean basin."

CHAPTER 2

As though on cue, the distant siren began again, a dominant fifth sound rising and falling in a regular rhythm, punctuating the silence of the small office. Hawthorn allowed himself to sink down into the leather cushion, drew his hands back and let them rest on the shoddy arms of the chair. He had no idea what to say, was unsure if he had understood the Englishman, so he said nothing.

Drinkwater made a little tent with his hands and looked over it into the handsome American's face.

"Shall I go on?"

Hawthorn found himself staring at Drinkwater's hairline, at the green-tinted, wrinkled forehead. He averted his eyes, glanced momentarily at the window, then brought his attention back to Drinkwater's intense stare.

"I'm not at all sure I understood what you said, sir."

"Of course not! I really didn't expect you to grasp the entire proposition on the first go! But if you will allow me to continue . . ."

"I'm sorry, sir. Say it all again. Please."

Drinkwater spoke very softly, clearly.

"The Commission has decided that your company will be used by the West to undo, to disrupt . . ." He paused, sniffed. "Good heavens, man! I can't think of another way to put it . . . to sabotage, then, to sabotage the Russian invasion of the Caribbean basin. Is that better?"

"Which commission? Where? I want to know what that means."

Drinkwater wagged his head impatiently. "Of course you do. And if you will pay attention, I shall explain it for you."

"Not Iran," Hawthorn injected. "The Caribbean."

"The Caribbean, yes. All of it. The basin."

There was a long moment of silence. Drinkwater used it to search for his pipe. He leaned across his chair and found it in his attaché case, then spent the next half minute filling and lighting it. He blew smoke at the ceiling and began.

"Let us dispense with Iran and that business first. I know about the coup because I planned it. I, together with several of your countrymen. We seldom work in total isolation, you see."

"We. The Commission, I suppose."

"Exactly. Incidentally, what I have told you is most secret. That must be obvious, and what I shall say in the next few minutes is also privileged information. I hardly need remind you that any leakage would be unfortunate." He paused. "It's in frightfully bad taste, but I shall have to say that several times to insure your complete understanding."

This time Drinkwater snorted loudly, spat into his handkerchief, inspected it and looked up again at Hawthorn.

"Forgive me. Sinusitis. All Englishmen have it."

He pulled out a drawer, thrust the handkerchief inside, and slammed it shut.

"Now then, to continue. NATO was formed after Russia demonstrated that she was not to be trusted. We had the Truman Doctrine and the First Statute of the Council of Europe, then NATO. Within NATO there are several commissions. I was appointed to the Commission on Petroleum Economics, later to be renamed and called the Commission for Petro-Politics. In the course of events, we studied the supply and demand, the movement of petroleum throughout Europe. I was its chief analyst and I saw our role as that of a paper bulwark against the kind of ignorance that drove Hitler into his bunkers.

"But our role changed over the years. We became actively involved in formulating policy, in causing small but significant changes in the parade of history that were favorable to the West." He stopped, puffed on his pipe, lit a match and sucked on the stem until smoke appeared. He looked up.

"You're smiling, Mr. Hawthorn. Is this amusing?"

Hawthorn stood, went slowly to the window, paused there and then paced to the far side of the room. He faced the wall and spoke over his shoulder.

"No. I'm not amused." He turned to face Drinkwater. "I'm dumb-founded, sir. How can you expect to bring a man, a total stranger off the street, disclose enormously important secrets to him . . ." He leaned forward. "That much I do believe . . . and then proceed to recruit him and all his resources for some kind of clandestine war without so much as a polite word of apology?" He stepped toward the desk. "I'm not amused, sir. I'm beginning to feel offended, if that makes any difference."

Drinkwater was not looking at him. He placed his pipe on the desk and pushed the envelopes behind the lamp.

"I am often offended, sir. After which I begin to feel helpless, then angry. I understand, Mr. Hawthorn. I would beg your indulgence for a short time, please."

Hawthorn approached the desk and lowered his head to catch Drinkwater's absolute attention.

"I don't feel helpless very often, sir, and you'll know when I'm angry." He straightened, moved around to his side of the desk and sat down. He lit another cigarette.

"Let's hear the rest of it."

"Good, I'll be as brief as possible," Drinkwater said, posing himself for another start.

"The Commission is connected to NATO, as I said, fingers on the same hand, so to speak, grasping the problem with a common understanding. But we have little to do with those who serve on the regular body. We work closely with the formal intelligence community and we are extremely careful to avoid meddling, that is, mucking about in affairs that are outside our specific parameters. In the case of Dr. Mossadeq, I was called in by the Shah's ministry and I in turn made the necessary contacts with your people, the CIA. There were no budget problems, no particularly distasteful measures to be taken."

"Excuse me, sir. The CIA. You told them what to do?"

"I didn't say that, Mr. Hawthorn."

"Forgive me. I thought you did."

"Our objective, expressed in its broadest terms, is to hasten the inevitable end of communism. We do not favor violence nor do we . . ."

"War in the streets of Tehran, sir."

"Yes, that will be violent. I offer no apologies."

The room fell silent again. The sound of a siren, perhaps the same one, the sound of Drinkwater's nasal breathing. Hawthorn was not a pacifist. He thought absently about the Hamburg blitz, the burning waters of the Alster. It was a sine qua non decision then, to drop incendiaries on the city, to ignite the canals and the buildings, to suck the people and the dogs and the children up into the ensuing fire storm. Did a man like Alan Drinkwater make the decision, without apologies?

"As to the present, we are faced with a number of circumstances that speak in warning against a Russian assault on the Caribbean basin. We see a strong leftist influence in Trinidad, in Jamaica, in British Guiana. We also call to our own attention the fact that the British islands, the Commonwealth possessions, are scheduled to become independent in the coming years. The Dutch islands have already begun to swing away from their parent Holland. Only the French will be wise enough to keep their fences intact. As for the Latin countries, Cuba and the Dominican Republic and those in Central America, the revolution is practically underway.

"Russia will not mount a frontal attack in the region. The Soviets will find a little fire here, ignite another one there, fan the flames and feed the skirmishes until there is a call for help, and then they will descend on the scene with their solution, and we all know what that will be."

Hawthorn inhaled, puffed, recrossed his leg.

"I'm sure there's a point to all of this, sir."

"A point? But the point is, surely, very evident! There is no reasonable way to stop them. Shall we barricade the region? Give cannon to the pro-West leaders, give them bullets, have them shoot the leftists? Give them books and pamphlets about Thomas Jefferson and the like? Send them food and money and missionaries? What would you suggest, sir, an approach that will convince the people themselves regarding the stupidity of a decision in favor of the Soviet Union?"

Hawthorn remained silent.

"In a moment I will show you something, Gregory Hawthorn. It will demonstrate quite clearly the double effect you will be able to create with the plan we have in mind."

"The 'double effect.' "

"The immediate and the long range, yes. The double effect. You will at one and the same time hand the Russians a false solution to a most aggravating problem, and dissuade them from concentrating on a truly viable solution to a much greater problem."

Damn riddles. The man was talking in riddles!

"The Caribbean business requires that we give the people a proof, show them how untrustworthy the Russians are by teaching them a lesson."

Drinkwater sat back, began a rocking motion in the old wooden chair. He put his finger to the spectacles, shoved them firmly onto his nose, wiggled his lips. Professorial theatrics.

"We are considering the probability of a revolution, fostered by the Communists. It is unlikely that any of the small countries in the target region will be prepared to go it alone, carry out a successful coup without help from the outside. They have no weapons, they have no money, and they have no oil. True enough, they can survive for a time if they find a bit of money to buy the weapons. They don't need unlimited quantities of it, just enough. One can buy guns as easily as popcorn, but who will sell them the oil?"

He stopped rocking, looking directly at Hawthorn.

"Who will sell them petroleum? Think of it, Hawthorn! There is only one self-sufficient state in the Caribbean capable of sustaining its own energy supply, and that is Trinidad. All the rest depend on the outside for oil, and oil is their only energy source. Imagine New York without oil, for a week. Imagine Havana without oil! How would they operate their trucks, their generators, their ships, their planes? How would they survive?"

"Petroleum. Supplied by American or British corporations."

"In this hemisphere, yes. Yes indeed. The commodity they need the most is under the control of those against whom they intend to do battle. Do you agree, Gregory, that a revolution is impossible without petroleum these days?"

Hawthorn noted the first name confidence.

"Over the longer term, yes. Almost certainly."

"And the potential revolutionaries are hopelessly dependent on others for that."

Hawthorn nodded his head. Overseas exploration . . . international shipping . . . a gamble . . . the nation's interest. There it was. His connection. A completely irrational idea began to float around in his brain. He was on the verge of becoming the biggest con artist in history. It was only a question of how and when, and where.

"And that's where I come in," he said.

The expression on Drinkwater's face changed, became that of a mischievous prankster.

"Go on, Gregory. Give it a shot."

"You want me to take over an oil field and deliberately foul up their refineries. Supply them with sugar water."

17

"Ha! No! Incorrect, sir." If anything, Drinkwater's grin became broader, his eyes brightened even more.

"We want you to *invent* an oil field, sir, the biggest, most prolific petroleum reservoir in the western hemisphere! Then we want you to make a deal with the Russians to supply their bloody satellites." He sat straight in his chair, placed his fists on the desk top, beat them up and down softly.

"Why?" Hawthorn said finally.

"Promises they cannot keep, miles to go before they sleep."

"To embarrass them? For six months?"

"Oh, my good fellow, there's more to it than that. You may be sure, sir. A good deal more."

Hawthorn felt the muscles in his face relaxing and sensed the beginning of a grin. He couldn't allow that. Not now. Not with this nut. Postpone it, yes, check on the man, yes. Laugh at him . . . no.

"I'll have to think about that, Dr. Drinkwater. I'll let you know what I decide."

"Decide? Oh, but, dear fellow, I think the decision has already been made!" Drinkwater looked genuinely surprised. "Here," he said, reaching for the envelopes. He pushed them to the center of the desk. "See for yourself, Gregory." He stopped, then added, "There is your decision."

Hawthorn was caught somewhere between disbelief and anger. *No one* made decisions for him. He made his own decisions. Who could presume to run his life all of a sudden?

"Am I to read these?"

"By all means, sir. Read them."

Hawthorn tore open the first envelope and read the single page of correspondence. He read it again, then looked across at the Englishman.

"Are they all like this?"

"They all say very much the same thing, yes."

He opened the second, read it carefully, then the third and the fourth. When he placed the last letter back on Drinkwater's desk he sat back and smiled. "Well, I'll be damned!" he said to himself.

"I saved the best for last, Gregory." He opened the desk drawer and removed the fifth envelope, held it in his hand and flapped it against his cheek. "This says it better than the others. It is more concise, more clearly defined, and is stronger in its guarantees." He tossed it on the desk. "Leave it to the British, of course."

The letter had no corporate identification. It was typed, single-spaced. A scrawl under the name at the bottom indicated that someone had been willing to put his reputation, his career, his corporation's assets on the line.

"Dear Mr. Prime Minister:

You will understand, most assuredly, when I inform you that I am unable to assist directly in the magnificent carnival you are planning. There is simply no way for me to involve the corporation of which I am an officer in a project of this kind.

I have suggested the name of several splendid alternates, however, and reiterate that my choice would be Mr. Gregory Hawthorn of the Globe Corporation. Our experience with him suggests his as being the most flexible and certainly the most likely enterprise to serve your purposes.

We are prepared to support the project in whatever other way we can, and will find it appropriate to establish a trust to cover possible contingencies at a level of BCL RVN LpT.

I have delivered a copy of this memorandum to Doloros and have trusted him to communicate directly with you."

Hawthorn tabled the letter and sat back, frowning.

"Shall I try to decipher them?"

Drinkwater was patiently, noisily drawing on his dead pipe. "No, let me do it for you. The letters are from the chief executive officers of Texaco, Getty, Standard Oil Company of New Jersey, British Petroleum, and, of course, the last from Shell, UK Shell. Each of them was approached with the problem, and they all agreed that what we have in mind is feasible if somewhat outlandish. They all demurred for a time, then gave us the answers you see here. Doloros is your State Department. We don't always speak directly, you understand. And there was no way to gain a written commitment regarding their financial support without actually putting it on paper. That would be the series of letters appearing in each of the documents. You would like to know what they mean."

"Yes."

"Gregory, what is your company worth today? What do you think it would bring, in cash, if you put it on the market?"

Hawthorn thought briefly. "Something over ninety million, I would guess."

"We guessed about a hundred million. And after you paid your creditors and assembled your remaining fluid assets, what would be left of that ninety million—for you, I mean?"

"I don't know. The bank owns most of it."

"Well, then, you will be delighted to know that each of these people"—he patted the letters—"has guaranteed an amount of two hundred million dollars in support of our little adventure, one half of that to go directly into its operating budget and the other half into the coffers of the corporation that does the job."

Hawthorn was suddenly aware of his own breathing.

"Where we are short on the operating end, the Commission will provide. In other words, Gregory, you will continue to operate your corporation as before, and you will carry on this project with the sure guarantee that no matter what happens, you will have five hundred million dollars in your business account when the last card has been played, having ventured no private capital of your own to accomplish that rather exceptional feat."

The room was silent again. Hawthorn gathered his feet underneath his chair, pressed on the armrests, and stood up. He walked to the window again and looked out over the dark, doppled Alster.

"Good Lord," he said quietly.

"The risk is considerable, Gregory."

Hawthorn circled the room, stood before the closed entry door, walked to the old sofa and sat down in the shadows.

Drinkwater folded his hands on the desk and closed his eyes, then began a recitation.

"It was the year of 1932, the darkest days of the depression. There was an enormous glut in the market, a superabundance of petroleum with practically no buyers. A small exploration company in Venezuela, Creole by name, had discovered a major pocket of crude petroleum, billions of barrels, they guessed. A pocket indeed! But they had no customers. Creole belonged to Standard Oil of Indiana at the time and they were short of money. What happened, do you suppose? I'll tell you: The president of another company, Standard Oil of New Jersey, bought the Creole company for one hundred and forty million dollars and became at once the world's largest oil producer, surpassing Shell and taking over nearly twelve percent of the world's total petroleum production. An incredible business!"

Drinkwater reached into the drawer and withdrew his handkerchief again, snorted into it, and went on.

"Shell is at this very moment drilling for oil in British Guiana, did you know that? Punching holes in some rancher's sod."

"I heard they were there," Hawthorn replied. "But they won't find oil."

"How do you know? How does anyone know?"

"It's a poor gamble."

"So it might be, Gregory, but the stakes are very big. I seem to recall that your first spuds or digs or whatever they're called were a bit on the risky side, or am I mistaken?"

"All right. Shell is digging holes in British Guiana."

"You will buy them out. It's all arranged. Then you will purchase a small fleet of tankers from a broker who happens to have excess capacity at the moment, and you will strike a number of supply agreements with islands and countries in the region. Whilst you are building that distribution system in the Caribbean, we think it a good idea to stir up as much exploration fuss as you can in British Guiana. We want to gain the attention of the Soviets as quickly as possible."

Drinkwater stopped for a moment to gauge the reaction of his American operative. He was already beginning to think of him as that. Hawthorn was gazing at him from the darkness of the sofa, listening patiently.

"And what will the Russians be doing all the while? I'll tell you, sir. They will be investing as much time and as much talent as they can afford in British Guiana because they want a base of operations in the Caribbean and because they are ten thousand miles away from the Caribbean and their nearest energy port is the Black Sea. They will want the base and the oil in order to have a bargaining instrument with which to gain the minds and the economies of the countries that surround the Caribbean Basin. And it is from British Guiana that they will mount their assault! That, sir, is the way it will happen."

"This is insane," Hawthorn said.

"No. No, sir. It is not insane. You will see. Allow me to continue. Let us take Cuba. She will be the first target to my thinking. On the day of reckoning, when the Americans have left the country, who will operate the refineries there? The Russians will offer to help, of course. And where will they get their crude oil from? Certainly not from Venezuela, you may be sure of that! No, they will take it from your wells in BG. And why? Because British Guiana is already in the hands of a Communist sympathizer!"

"Oh my God," Hawthorn sighed. "Cheddi Jagan."

Now Drinkwater stood up and walked slowly to place himself in front of Hawthorn, hands behind his back, bending back and forth.

"Yes. Cheddi Jagan. You will be partners with the Communist leader of a British colony."

"And when Cuba asks for oil . . ."

"Go on."

"I load my ships with aviation gasoline. They anchor at the refinery docks and at the given signal they blow sky high, obliterating everything within ten miles and blocking the only energy line available to the country."

"Marvelous!" Drinkwater clapped his hands. "And who is it that made promises to the Cubans? Who would 'bail them out' of their energy crisis?"

"Russian cargo, ships leased by Russia, sent by Jagan . . ."

"Exactly so, Gregory. However, you may have jumped ahead too quickly. What you have described is not exactly what we have planned. It is far more delicate than that, you see, and far more damaging to the

Soviets than a mere incident that could be explained or excused or soon forgotten. Nonetheless I see that you are able to join in the spirit of the thing."

He strode to his desk and reached for his attaché case. He sat down and pulled himself closer to the cubbyhole.

"Please come, Gregory. Have a chair for a moment longer, and then we shall enjoy a brandy."

Hawthorn crossed the room and stood behind the chair. He looked down at the green lamp, the torn envelopes, and the letters.

"No," he said softly.

Drinkwater didn't look up. He was unfolding a document, pressing it on the desk top with his hand to make it stay flat.

"The double effect, sir. The larger objective."

"I said no, Dr. Drinkwater. I understand your enthusiasm, because I've been there, I've felt it, but I can't share it with you now, not for this assignment. You've got the wrong man."

"No. I think we have the right man. Have a look here, Gregory." Drinkwater turned the document around, faced it toward Hawthorn. "The second objective. The Middle East, do you see? Give the Russians a sufficiently attractive alternate source for crude oil and they will leave the Middle East alone."

Hawthorn leaned across, brought the single sheet of paper to his chest and examined it.

"Read it very carefully, Hawthorn. The objectives are two-fold, as you will notice. One is very broad, to confuse their planning and eventually their petroleum distribution system; the other refers to our discussion this evening, to present them with an opportunity to make asses of themselves. You will accomplish both with your program."

It was a memorandum from the CIA. Very neat, very bureaucratic, very thrifty in its language.

CENTRAL INTELLIGENCE AGENCY
WASHINGTON, D.C. 20505

4497-33-PLT   Anr665 + 2L
PROP.
eer/tht/sva/wcc/sor/tjk/br

OBJECTIVE

Long Range: Disrupt (probable planned) Soviet petroleum distribution system in the western hemisphere.

Short Range: Discredit Russia in the Caribbean B.

STRATEGY
> Divert attention and resources from Middle East reserves.
> Offer (make available) unlimited access to "vast Caribbean reserves."
>
> Create a vehicle to foster dependency.
>
> Encourage (unachievable) Soviet commitments to the region; ensure maximum shortfall.

TACTIC
> A. Establish, in five years or less, an independent, self-suffi-cient, horizontally structured corporation capable of pro-ducing, transporting, and distributing petroleum pro-ducts throughout the Caribbean Basin. Controlled from well-head to final consumer.
>
> B. Arrange through clandestine means to supply all Soviet needs in the region.
>
> C. Secure and stabilize instant exit contingency.

Hawthorn read it a final time and placed it back on the desk.

"What do they mean by 'instant exit'?"

"Something to do with getting out alive, I should think."

CHAPTER 3

The Korean conflict was winding down, but men were still dying of wounds they suffered in combat, men were still flying regular sorties, and the ships of war were still on station. It was July 27, 1953; the U.S.S. *Ticonderoga* was steaming north in the waters of the Yellow Sea, ninety miles off the coast of Korea, preparing for yet another launch against the stubborn enemy.

Lieutenant Stephen Jonathan Moffit would fly this morning's mission. He made his way to the ready room, dressed in his G-suit and short-topped leather flying boots, tasting bacon and tomato juice in his mouth, wondering if he would get sick again today. He was tired of it, tired of stitching the backroads and the villages with .20mm cannon shot, hurling bombs and rockets at hilltops and trees.

There were twenty-four one-armed school chairs in the green-lit room, most of them already filled as he made his way to the second row and found an empty place on the aisle. There would be eleven pilots today, not twelve. Of the original eighteen Panthers that were loaded aboard there were only thirteen in operation and two of those were down for damage repair.

The morning sickness had begun three days ago, moments after he narrowly missed losing his head to a propellor. He had decided to watch the ADs take off, found a spot on the port catwalk just below the flight deck. The second plane got its tail wheel hung up in a deck wire, broke loose behind the sheer power of its huge engine and leaped forward, then sideways, careening out of control straight for his position. Moffit ducked, heard and felt the howling monster crash against the ship's steel as the Marine attack bomber hit the catwalk rail. He looked up in time to see it strike the water nose first, saw the slashing white water pick the plane up and hurl it against the ship's hull, saw it flip on one wing and and land on its back. The pilot had no chance. None at all.

That's when Stephen Moffit got sick the first time. He made his way to the head and controlled his stomach long enough to reach the stool before it all gushed out, stinging his sinuses and lodging bits of ham and potato behind his cheeks.

The day after his scrape with the AD Moffit took ground fire that ripped twenty-nine holes in his wings and fuselage. On the way back home, Percival ejected from his smoking plane. Moffit was having trouble controlling his own situation, but saw him pop up out of the cockpit like a piece of toast, then disappear behind as they flew on at four hundred knots. Moffit got aboard, but had to use a straight-in approach that denied him the comfort of the smooth, turning descent from a reliable path that Navy pilots perfect in their first hours of training. He came in high and fast, cut his power just in time, and caught the last wire, thrusting his nose into the nylon barricade that would have stopped him had he caught no wire at all.

That time he made it as far as the island and had to hurry around the superstructure to find a rail.

Yesterday was the worst, the most horrible. Dick Racer, flying number 306 and on his thirty-third mission, had the port side of his canopy blown away and caught Plexiglas in his face. He made it back to the ship, but instead of ordering him to ditch alongside the escort destroyer, they tried to bring him aboard. He flew his plane into the stern of the carrier, just below the flight deck. Moffit was still circling, waiting. He saw the angry red and black explosion, saw the parts fall into the ship's wake. Racer had violated the rule leaned by every Navy pilot from the day they entered preflight: *The ship's wake is an extension of the flight deck centerline. If you cross it on your low and slow approach to a carrier landing, you will never make it back. You will in all likelihood die.*

24

Racer had crossed the ship's wake, and he had disintegrated.

Moffit made his turns into the ship automatically, answered the landing signal officer's flags with expert corrections, felt himself thrown against the harness as his hook caught a wire. That safe feeling, the reassuring kind of tough love that welcomed the prodigal back home. He kept his vomit until he made his stateroom, then let it gush into the sink.

"Good morning, gentlemen. Sector forty-four."

Moffit pressed his lips together. Low and fast, kill and go, hit a fuckin' mountain, press the red button and pull hard, get the hell outta the way! Black balls, red tracers, do it again, shake the plane apart with cannon shots, bang rock your fuckin' head against the canopy, chase your buddy's red-hot ass home. Oh, Jesus, Donna, not again.

Moffit was hearing the information, making brief notes on his knee board. He was thinking of his wife, Donna, beautiful, long-legged Donna, her sweet, coiled, baby powder hairs, the goose bumps on her delicious breasts.

"The column will be heading south, driving toward sector forty-one. We think it may be a move to consolidate their position, to influence the negotiations . . ."

Moffit didn't care. They would aim their iron at his face and he would feel it explode in his chest. They would send a thousand white hot bits of steel in his path. Stephen Moffit was sure, as the voice droned on, he was sure he would never lie with his beloved Donna again.

CHAPTER 4

The skipper was wrapping up the preflight. Harding stood in front facing the pilots, holding a pointer between his legs tip down, like a burlesque dancer with his cane. The large-scale map behind him showed a north-south coastline, and to the east of that a seven-sector area dominated by hilly, rugged terrain. Dead in the center was the target, sector 44, crisscrossed by a spiderweb road network with a broad ribbon winding south, out of 44 and down through 41.

The squadron was to attack from the south with strafing runs along the road first. They were to wheel then and return from the north with cannon and rockets aimed at the mechanized pieces they were able to spot on the first run. If there was the opportunity, they would pull hard to the left after that run, stay low and fast and come in from the east for a last shot at the main junction. That would have them heading back toward the coast, well below the squadron of ADs that were to follow the smoke and unload their bombs on the main highway. The Panthers would be on target for a total of less than eight minutes. Their evacuation route would take them over relatively safe territory. They should expect heavy ground fire, but the attack was not expected to meet with MIG air opposition.

"I'll take Green flight. Jack, you've got Red and Steve, you're Blue. Steve, you'll be short a finger, so take your team in as a unit, a good, tight unit."

Each attack unit was to approach the sector in a "hand" formation resembling the staggering of four fingers. Moffit was leading the third unit, Blue, and would be short his "little finger." The others would split into pairs and make their runs on target two abreast, the leader just ahead of his wingman. Moffit would take his planes in three abreast, he slightly in front of the other two. He glanced over at Poor and Baker. They nodded.

Moffit checked his watch with the chronometer mounted on the front bulkhead, then adjusted the new goggles he had requisitioned after fighting too many hours behind his old, badly scratched pair.

The room was suddenly filled with an awful, squawking sound, then a commanding voice. "General quarters, general quarters! Ready the flight deck! Ready all stations for launch! Pilots, man your planes!"

Every time he heard that command, Moffit thought of the very first Navy pilot who heard it, how terrified he probably felt. He must have gotten excited and bolted for the exit, hurried up the ladder, rushed across the deck to his tiny Stearman or whatever it was and literally scrambled into the cockpit. Now it was a tradition. Nobody walked to the hatch or merely stood on the escalator or ambled out to kick his tires to see if they were still there. Hell, no! Harding led the way.

"OK, let's scramble!"

And everybody scrambled.

Moffit reached the flight deck hatch and patted the sign that hung above the exit as he dove through: THINK OR THWIM. He jogged to his own plane, number 309, saw that it had a tail and two wings, reached the port side and handed his helmet to the crew chief. He climbed up the side, dropped into the cockpit, and wiggled his fanny once to get position on the parachute. By that time the crew chief was on top of him, holding the shoulder straps at exactly the right spot for Moffit to reach up with both hands, grab them, and pull them down to his seat belt connection. He yanked the belts tight, leaned back hard against the seat and yanked them tight again. The chief handed him his helmet, open end front. Moffit strapped it on and plugged the radio leads into the jacks. In a second more he had connected his bail-out bottle to his face mask, hooked the G-suit connection to the plane's service system and was flicking the radio switches on. He felt the chief pat him on the helmet, looked left to catch the wink, then sat back to pull the yellow leather gloves tighter onto his hands.

The call came from the bridge, over the speakers and through the pilots' headphones. "All personnel stand clear of jet tailpipes, stand clear of propellors! Pilots, start your engines!"

Moffit brought his throttle up and around the horn, pressed the ignite contact and switched on. His taxi director stood to his right, at two o'clock, giving him a slow one-finger winding motion. Moffit glanced to his right, saw Baker minding his own duties, then turned back to his instruments. The plane was ready, its jet engine singing, hot, throwing burned kero fumes back. Moffit looked up again, saw the director watching him. He gave a thumbs up and the man half-turned to face the bridge.

"Aoooooga! Aoooooga!" The great bulk of the giant carrier began to lean right as the ship started into its port turn. The wind swung across the deck, past Moffit's face, the sharp list began to ease; the green shirts of the launch gang up forward were snapping smartly, their pant legs flattened against their skin. Moffit's director was leaning against the wind now, and the pennants that fell so prettily in the light breeze of a few moments ago were quivering, starched, all in a row, at brisk attention for the launch.

Moffit was third in line, still cocked to starboard with the wind on his left arm. Baker pulled ahead, roaring in front of Moffit's plane, heading for the twin catapults. His director leaned toward the prow of the ship, then threw one arm forward to turn Baker over to the catapult officer. The exhaust shield snapped up behind his tail and Baker was hidden from view.

Within seconds the already loud roar of Baker's engine became a horrendous howling scream as he added full power. His exhaust gasses whipped back, over the shield, and streamed down the deck to hover above the carrier's wake. Then Baker was gone, sinking a foot as he left the ship, thundering across the water in a slow, banking turn to port. Barely three seconds later, the plane on the other catapult was launched. That would have been Ensign Poor.

Now Moffit was in position, straddling the port catapult, his eyes on the catapult officer. He got the signal to add full power, a fast wind-up motion with one finger, then with two fingers. Catman leaned under to check his cable, kept the fingers spinning over his head. Moffit had a second to glance at his TOT gauge, then he pressed himself against the seat back, drove his palm hard against the throttle, locking it full forward. He dropped his heels to the floor, off the brakes, took his hand off the stick and, eyes directed straight ahead through the Plexiglas in front of him, he gave his salute. The deafening sound of his own engine ricocheted off the blast deflector behind into his own ears, his nose pressed down to the stops of the wheel shocks, and then he was thrown with incredible force against the seat. The ship became a blur out of the sides of his eyes, the stick came to life, the sound was gone.

He mushed for the first thousand yards, gaining speed and altitude, the powerful jet thrusting his heavy plane ahead against the air. Wheels up, canopy closed, pressurization on, radio-to-squadron frequency, easing to port, a smooth, winding turn, climbing at three hundred knots . . . so quiet now.

His squadron was at eleven o'clock, 30 degrees high. His rendezvous would be beautiful. To the east the sun was just over the horizon. In a few minutes they would be flying directly toward it, heading for sector 44. In less than two hours he would be back aboard the carrier, drinking cocoa. Nothing kills a pilot when he's strapped down, tight and secure, sitting on his gun platform with solid steel under his butt.

They formed up and passed through nine thousand feet in their climbing turn, then leveled off and continued the climb heading 096 degrees. They would reach the coast in thirty minutes, begin their descent, reach sector 44's first marker at nine thousand feet and five hundred knots. They would spot the column off to their left, and commence the attack with their noses pointed down, heading for the trees.

Between now and then there was nothing to do but fly the airplane and stay in formation. Moffit flew with his fingers lightly touching the stick, as though he were holding a martini, his toes gently tapping the rudder pedals to make small corrections.

He, along with everyone else, had been hoping, praying for the truce that was so slow in coming. If it came soon, he would be home in a few days, a few weeks at most. Moffit had pictured himself a hundred times standing in the doorway of a MATS Constellation, dressed in his whites with his ribbons, a damn hero standing there, saluting his family from the doorway. He could see himself going down the steps, Donna breaking away from the crowd to run into his arms, his dad and mom staying back with tears in their eyes.

Below, ahead of them, the clouds were heavier than the misty stuff farther out to sea. Their tops were peaked with red, taking on the sun's soft, pastel colors. Moffit was thinking about Donna's body, the way she walked, how tempting she was, how seductive a beauty for the men to desire, the men at home—the men who had managed to stay away from the fighting to look out for themselves and their women and their cars.

Moffit was a jealous man. He knew that about himself. He was a good engineer, a beginner maybe, but good at what he did. His job with the state of Illinois paid enough, just enough to maintain the little house in Aurora, the house they had bought after graduation with a loan from her parents. But he had no expense account, no fine automobile, no stature in the community. He was a river engineer and he wore brown boots and denim pants, not the clothes his civilian lawyer friends were wearing on Lake Shore Drive. He was a handsome man, if well-built, brown-haired men with good, clear features are handsome, but he was not gifted with striking looks or with unusual talents. He had a job, and he had Donna, and he had a little house in Aurora that was just adequate. He was twenty-five years old, on the way up. But up to where?

For the past two and a half years he had felt better about himself. He was on the front line, in a glamorous role, roaring into the sky with a fire at his back and power at his fingertips they could barely imagine, those lawyers, those wags in their gentlemen's suits. But it had gone sour, the glory and the honor. There was no applause, no sound of approval when he came back with holes in his plane, when he fought the controls to keep it in the air, when he squeezed his red trigger and felt the shudder of cannon fire.

When he got back, Moffit was going to quit his engineering job with the state and become somebody. He would finish his business degree, then offer himself to one of the big corporations. He wanted the fast track, the overseas assignment that paid good money, where reputations are built overnight. He could branch off into exploration, mineral exploration, sell his services to governments or to private developers. Then he might get someplace, out of the cold and away from the terrible boredom of being a clod on the state payroll.

"Buster Eight, this is Cocksure. We are Cocksure. Out."

The squadron was over the coast. Moffit eased back on the throttle and dropped off a hundred yards, then maintained that position. He raised his right hand in a fist and showed it to Baker on his right, Poor on his left. He reached across the cockpit, flicked the toggle guards up on his weapons panel and rocked the switches. Three lights glowed red, confirming combat readiness.

Below and ahead were green hills, not quite mountains, three thousand feet at best, with narrow, grassy areas, a house here and there, dirt paths leading to bigger paths. They were passing through eight thousand feet. He could see animals, cows maybe. Harding was up

29

front, Jack Carlson was to the right and below Harding. Moffit, taking up the rear, kept his Blue flight of three planes a step above.

"Cocksure, this is Green One. We're alive and on the air. Red Leader, do you have the highway?"

"Roger, Green One. Ten o'clock."

"Blue Leader, you got it?"

Moffit fingered the button on his throttle. "Affirmative, Green One." He was looking out the left side of his canopy, saw the wider ribbon of highway off his nose. He could see the dust cloud, the column. They had come in right on the money.

Harding came up again.

"OK, Jack, when I break, you hold for three seconds, then break and follow. Blue Leader, you hold after Jack and follow him. Confirm that."

Jack Carlson clicked his button three times, and Moffit clicked his three times.

"Roger. I'm going in. Pair up, Gooseball! Get behind me, Richie, stick on my wing. Let's go!"

Harding broke hard left and his wingman stuck like glue. Then the second pair fell in line, by now a mile behind Harding. Jack Carlson waited his three seconds, then cranked his flight down and to the left. Moffit waited, then executed, dropping his left wing and swinging the nose through the horizon toward the highway. His unit was tight, an arrowhead screaming down, bending straight, then easing back to the right to intersect the highway.

By now, Harding and his wingman were ripping into the column and his next two planes were close behind; Jack Carlson and his men followed seconds later with his split pair a half-mile back. With each attacking unit, the line of thundering fire rushed up the highway, the second wave beginning its assault where the first stopped, the third wave spitting its overlapping shells into the path the second wave had begun, until by the time Moffit's flight squeezed their triggers, they were halfway along the column and flying through smoke that exploded out of the destruction from the first eight Panther cannon.

Moffit held his nose down, keeping the angle steep enough to direct his guns on the highway until the last possible second, then he pulled hard to the left and up, resting his blazing weapons for the next sweep.

"Cocksure, Green One. Looks very good. I'm coming back and I want that intersection. Jack, you take the feeder on the left and Steve, you get the right feeder. Rockets now."

Moffit saw the other planes, above and to his right, making a wide banking sweep back toward the column, like a line of twin birds chasing the leader through the sky toward the prey. He soared up, bringing his flight into the line, following the path of attack that would carry his planes to the right of the main highway. They would spray the trees before the intersection, fire rockets at the feeder road, spray the side of the highway beyond that and get out.

He bent his flight the last few degrees, dropped his nose again, and started the run. There was static on the radio, a harsh, urgent, piercing noise that screamed in his ears. He set his angle, felt the nose begin to tuck as the speed shot up to five hundred fifty knots in the steep dive. He pressed the red button on his stick, felt the plane chug, saw his rockets streaking toward the column, saw them heading for heavy machinery to the right of the line. At fourteen hundred feet he squeezed the cannon trigger again, felt the plane vibrate as its guns spewed out a thousand shells. He saw tracers, black balls of smoke. He pulled hard on the stick and stood on the right rudder, urging his plane out of the path of enemy fire, putting distance between his flight and the highway. He twisted his head around as he streaked up, thought he saw his wingman behind, Baker or Poor. Suddenly the stick jumped from his hand, his plane lurched sideways, and he was thrown hard against the right console. He was spinning up, climbing and spinning, now tumbling up, out of control. His plane stopped and began to fall, a winding, slow autumn leaf.

He sat bolt upright in his seat, placed his feet in the stirrups below his body, grasped both armrests with his gloved hands, found the ejection trigger, and clenched his teeth. He squeezed, and the world exploded. He was hit by a force of air that threw him out of any dimension a living man can understand, and then he was tumbling head over heels. He brought his arms in to his chest, felt down to his lap and touched the seat belt. He shouted into his mask, *"The belt first!"* He yanked at the quick release and forced himself to a standing position. The seat flew away and he was free, falling in a flat spin, face up, spread-eagled, the wind howling through his helmet. He cranked his head around and saw the ground below, spinning as he fell. He shouted again, *"Not yet! Not now!"* He waited, the spin slowed, the ground was closing. *Now!* He pulled his right hand to his chest and tucked his head to see. He grasped the rip cord handle and threw his arm away from his body, he heard the flutter, the snap, felt a jolt in his groin, felt the chest straps tighten. Then he was swinging, softly, silently, floating down, a huge white canopy over his head.

He closed his eyes for a moment, then opened them in time to see his seat fall past, fifty feet from his face. He leaned over in his cradle and watched as it got smaller, saw it disappear into a stand of trees. He looked up then, peering around the perimeter of his chute. He could hear explosions in the distance, saw smoke off to the east. Had he gotten that far away from the highway? It seemed like he was hit, like he

31

exploded directly over the fight, but there was no sign of life below, only green and brown, ugly green and brown. And he saw no planes. Where were the planes? Where was Harding? Poor?

The ground was closing too fast, he would hit damn hard! He concentrated on that now, tried to pull on the lines to face himself in the direction he seemed to be drifting but he could do nothing about it. His feet struck and he fell over backward, rolling a few feet before he stopped on his hands and knees, the chute cords tangled around his body.

He kneeled there for what seemed a long time, staring at a rock, a hard, gray rock. On the ground he saw ants hurrying along in a line, tiny soldiers on their tiny highway, doing their work.

A truck . . . did he hear a truck? Quickly now, he pulled at the cords, stood up and gathered the parachute into his arms and looked around. There, beyond the knoll, the small woods where his seat had landed, he should get to those woods. He hurried, ran as fast as he could and entered the edge of the thicket, kept on going for a dozen yards before he stopped. He crouched down and listened. There was no sound now, no danger sound.

He squatted on the white nylon and began to pull leaves and small sticks over it, then began frantically dragging dirt to his legs to cover them up, pulling twigs and stones to his terribly exposed body. Hurry! Oh, God, hurry!

Now Stephen Moffit knew what Racer had felt in that terrible instant before he hit the ship. He felt the mushing, the hopelessness, the awful despair. He stopped clawing at the ground then, brought his hands to his face, and covering his eyes, sat back on his haunches and began to sigh.

When he stopped, lowered his hands and opened his eyes, he saw two men. They were twenty feet away, dressed in brown quilted uniforms and they were both holding rifles. They stood silently, quite still. Then, very slowly, one soldier raised his rifle and aimed it at Stephen Moffit's heart.

CHAPTER 5

Slowly Moffit began to rise. He felt as though he were levitating, weightless as he came to his feet. His eyes were fixed to the black hole in the end of the soldier's rifle and he expected to see the puff of spark, see the rifle jump as it went off. He reached his hands to his head and began to remove his helmet, still watching as the other soldier now, a smaller man, raised his rifle. He eased the helmet off, then held it in one hand and stood facing the executioners.

Now he heard a voice, a command, and saw a third soldier coming. This one was holding a pistol as he stepped between the soldiers and waved their rifles down with his free hand. He came closer, then gave a circular motion to Moffit, screwed his finger around. Moffit obeyed the obvious command and turned his back to them. Now? Would they shoot him in the back?

He heard footsteps crunching on the dry twigs and leaves, coming quickly toward him. Two hands grabbed his wrists and they were twisted, roughly pressed and twisted together. He felt twine binding them. Then an oil-gritty cloth came around his face, he felt them knotting it at the back of his head, and he could no longer see. His helmet was snatched away and he was turned, with unexpected gentleness, then pushed ahead. He walked, stumbled once, walked, tentatively placing his feet. A soldier was at his side, holding one arm and guiding him.

Moffit was listening for planes, cannon, explosions, but he heard nothing, only the sounds of shuffling feet and voices of men. They stopped; Moffit smelled fuel, diesel, a truck of some kind. He was helped up to the bed of the vehicle, one pushing from behind and the other pulling his arms from above, until they had him sitting against steel siding. Now someone was tying his ankles while someone else passed a length of twine under his chin, cinched it too tight.

They drove for what seemed about twenty minutes. When the truck stopped he heard men scurrying about, heard a command. Somebody was cutting his bonds; his feet, neck, and wrists were free. He was helped to the tailgate, eased to the ground and led to a place perhaps fifty feet away. Rough hands worked at the knot and removed his blindfold.

Dizzy and frightened, he saw he was standing before a big wooden crate. Someone roughly pushed his head down, and he was shoved into the crate. He struck something sharp inside and tried to back out, but hands pushed him from behind and he was forced to squat, his head pressing the top of the box, his shoulder forced against the sharp barbs inside. Barbed wire. It was barbed wire, coiled loosely against the far side of the box. There was just space enough for him to find a fetal position. A door was nailed over the opening.

It was hot inside the crate, had to be well over one hundred degrees. Moffit felt nauseated, weak. He tried to hold it down, but just as he swallowed an earsplitting blow crashed against the wooden boards next to his face. Again! Again! It didn't stop. Someone was banging on the crate with a club. Moffit let his head fall below his knees, and he vomited.

It was late in the afternoon when they let him out. He fell through the opening onto the ground and was helped to his feet. Now he could see where he was. It looked like a boy scout camp. There were a few soldiers, perhaps twenty, three or four small tents, a battered truck, some oil drums. It was a clearing in the woods, nothing more, with a trail that led through from one side to the other.

He was helped, partly dragged to a tent on one perimeter of the clearing, then left to stand in front of the green canvas tent flap. Now they came with the cord again, bound his wrists roughly behind his back, tighter than before. The flap parted and an officer stood there, looking at him, smiling. He held the flap open and ushered him inside. As Moffit was helped to a stool near a small field desk, he kept his eyes on the officer. He was short, well built, handsome, but he was not a Korean. Moffit had the feeling that the man was Chinese. The officer took a chair behind his desk and gazed at Moffit's face.

"Stephen Jonathan Moffit, four-three-seven, oh-three, three-five, USNR, A.P. Tell me, Jonathan, what does the 'P' stand for?"

Moffit's throat was dry, his mouth tasted the foulness of his vomit. He forced his answer.

"I'm a Protestant."

"A Protestant! Do you protest?"

It was a good voice, almost without accent, friendly.

"No, that's my religion. I'm a Protestant." He coughed.

"And the 'A' is your blood type. Is that correct?"

"Yes. Please, is there some water?"

"Certainly. In a moment, Jonathan." He gave an order and it was answered outside the tent.

"You have good names; from the Bible, are they not? Stephen was a martyr."

34

Moffit said nothing. He remembered the many times his mother had reminded him about his name: Stephen, the first martyr, stoned to death.

"Did your father want you to be a martyr, what do you think?"

He would be able to talk if he had some water. It was foolish to stick with the name and rank and serial number business. He knew that, but he was damned if the man would make him talk about his plane or his squadron or his ship without inflicting pain. He would cross that bridge . . .

"Did your mother want you to be a martyr, Jonathan?"

"I'm called Moffit, or Stephen. Don't call me Jonathan."

"Why not?"

Why not? Why the hell not?

"Call me what you like."

The tent flap opened and a soldier came in carrying a tin cup. He handed it to the officer, who gave another command. The soldier kneeled down behind Moffit's stool and cut the twine, then left.

Moffit massaged his wrists, examined them, then reached across to take the cup that was being held out. He drank, swished the water around, swallowed and felt better.

"Jonathan was an interesting boy, did you know that? Tell me, Lieutenant, was there a reason for naming you Jonathan?"

"I don't know."

"Did your mother and father want you to be faithful and loyal, as Jonathan was to David?"

"I don't know about Jonathan."

"That is shameful, sir. You should know about your names." The officer sat back and fell silent for nearly a minute. When he continued, his tone was more aggressive, it had more business in it.

"Get used to the idea, Mr. Moffit. Your name is totally unimportant to me. You are not a pilot, you have no home, you have no friends, you have no ship." He smiled slightly and went on. "The box was unpleasant. We use it for our own disciplinary purposes. It helps to remind one that humility is sometimes a painful lesson. Perhaps I said that incorrectly. It is often painful, the state of humility. You shall have to learn from the beginning that you are a very unimportant person.

"You came from the Ticonderoga this morning. You have been on station for nearly five months, you fly the F9F-5 Panther jet and you are attached to Squadron VF-81. Your commanding officer is named Harding."

"I would like a cigarette," Moffit said.

"Certainly. Here." He passed Moffit's own cigarettes and lighter across and Moffit flipped one out, lit it, and coughed.

"My name is Chou. I am a captain in the army of the People's Republic of China, temporarily assigned to the army of the Korean People's Republic. I was educated at the University of Southern California. I am telling you this because I think it is important for you to know that I am not a fool. I do not waste my time doing a fool's work."

Captain Chou watched Moffit's face carefully.

"We will feed you and we will keep you, in spite of your crime."

Moffit looked up, exhaled. "What crime?"

"You have violated the truce, Mr. Moffit."

This was a trick. He dragged on the cigarette and defiantly blew the smoke toward the officer.

"What truce?"

" 'Pretty Lady' was transmitted from your ship, from Buster at seven-oh-nine this morning. You attacked us at seven-fourteen."

Suddenly dizzy, Moffit felt himself slumping.

"That's a lie," he said.

"No, Mr. Moffit. That is not a lie. You murdered over a hundred men this morning, you butchered them during a period of truce. That is a crime and there is a punishment to suit the act." He paused. "You will say you did not know and we will say you did know. It really makes no difference. Because it happened."

Under his breath, Moffit swore. He tried to stay impassive, but he could feel shaking in his hands.

"I will be seeing more of you as time goes on, Jonathan. We will talk and perhaps we will come to know one another. I hope you will learn to trust that I do not want any harm for you. But I am afraid much of that will be out of my hands. For now, then, you had better try to make the best of it. You will not go home for a very long time."

The officer stood and gave another order. A soldier came in and took Moffit by the arm, stepped on the cigarette as it fell to the dirt and led him outside. They walked toward a tree that stood in the middle of the campground.

Moffit could almost feel tears in his eyes. He was no criminal, he had done nothing wrong. He remembered his father slapping him once for getting shoe polish on the carpet, when it was his sister who had done it. She had said nothing. They reached the tree and he was forced to sit on the ground, facing the trunk with his legs wrapped around it. They tied his wrists again, tied his ankles on the other side of the tree, and then they left him there.

Suddenly, as though it had been a forgotten thing, Moffit had to urinate. He thought of the many times on long missions, at high altitudes, after many cups of coffee in the ready room, when he was hit the same way with the need to urinate. He would drop back, unzip his

36

fly and find the relief tube, then fit himself into the funnel that was supposed to receive his fluid. How often had he gotten a tube that was crimped? He might just as well have peed in his pants.

He let it go and the urine puddled down his legs, his buttocks, turning the G-suit a dark green. It was warm; he leaned his head against the tree and let it all drain out.

He should try to escape. Get loose, then run like hell for the woods, go for the coast. But not now. He shuddered, squirmed on the ground, and tried to think about Donna. But his mind was soggy; all he could think of were the words of the Chinese captain.

"You will not go home for a very long time."

CHAPTER 6

They left Hamburg on the same aircraft, but traveled separately, Alan Drinkwater finding himself a place near the lavatories in the rear, Gregory Hawthorn in row number three, window seat. When they arrived in Amsterdam, separate taxicabs took them to different addresses, two blocks apart. They met again in the elevator of a commercial office building, strangers to all outward appearances, and rode up together, each holding firmly onto a brief case, each ignoring the other in polite silence. Twelve hours earlier, it would have seemed a foolish bit of melodrama to Hawthorn. Now it was expected, the *modus vivendi* of conspirators.

As they emerged on the fifth floor Drinkwater paused, pressed the button for number seven, and then took Hawthorn's arm, guiding him down the hall toward the offices of the British-American Tobacco Company, a suite that appeared to occupy the larger part of the etage.

"Bloody nuisance, isn't it?" He spoke cheerfully, openly, as though they had arrived home from a funeral and were now permitted to express their honest feelings about the departed. Hawthorn would have agreed, but there was no opportunity to ratify the other man's opinion. They reached the end of the corridor, a glass door opened and they entered the outer lobby of what appeared to be an administrative office.

The reception desk was manned by a neatly dressed gentleman, possibly in his twenties, whose obvious duty was to direct traffic from the door to the appropriate inner office. He smiled, extended his hand, and spoke to them in German.

"Ihren Ausweis, bitte."

Drinkwater handed him his passport. The young man examined it, smiled again, and looked at Hawthorn.

"You're with Mr. Drinkwater, I suppose. You would be Mr. Hawthorn."

"That's correct. You need my passport . . ."

"No need, sir." He stood up. "Follow me, please."

He handed the document back, then led the way down a narrow hallway, past several closed doors, through a fire door at the end of the passage. They were in a large corner office, well appointed, with tinted glass windows from floor to ceiling on two sides, sectional furniture against another wall, a large desk and several host chairs commanding the center of the room. If it was arranged for his benefit, the final touch was not lost on the American visitor: the fourth wall was dominated by a map of the Caribbean Sea, the northeast shoulder of South America in the bottom right-hand corner, the Central American peninsula slicing down on the left edge, and the familiar Gulf Coast bordering the top. Hawthorn knew the geography, could have spotted the islands within a few degrees either way on a blank chart. Dead in the center was Cuba, and there, falling off the map, sandwiched between Venezuela and Suriname, was British Guiana.

"Bitte, warten Sie. Mr. Kiley kommt gleich."

Drinkwater nodded, his eyes on Hawthorn. He lowered his briefcase to the floor and stepped in front of the map, clasped his hands behind his back and rocked slowly on his heels.

"Water, rum, sugar, bauxite, and poverty."

Hawthorn nodded. "And swarming with Communists."

"Oh, come now, Gregory."

They turned as a door behind them opened and closed. John Kiley stood there for a moment, his hand on the knob, then crossed the room to greet his guests. He offered his hand to Alan Drinkwater first.

"Alan, good to see you again."

He was a square man with short red hair, a ruddy complexion, big eyes, of medium build, fiftyish. There were freckles and a deep scar from thumb to wrist on the hand he held out to Hawthorn.

"Kiley, sir. John Kiley."

"Office of Naval Intelligence, Gregory," said Drinkwater.

"Pleasure, Mr. Kiley. Greg Hawthorn."

Kiley glanced at Drinkwater. "Former ONI, Alan." He walked to the desk, sat on a corner, and folded his arms. "He knows that," he said, motioning with his head at Drinkwater. "Special Services now. I scared the hell outta the brass."

"Yes, well. Same bloody thing, isn't it!"

Hawthorn moved a few feet to his left, set his briefcase on the sofa, and took his time lighting a cigarette. He blew the first drag toward the ceiling.

"I understand you've been in this business quite a while, Mr. Kiley. Long enough to be convincing."

Drinkwater was searching for his pipe. "Mr. Hawthorn seems to think the whole idea is bonkers. I told him you were an authority on bonkers."

" 'Preposterous,' Alan. I never said 'bonkers.' "

"Bonkers, preposterous. Same difference." Kiley was swinging a leg, thumping his shoe against the desk. He stopped. "Much of what I do, damn near everything I do fits that description. That's what they pay me for. The Commission doesn't screw around with a lotta predictable shit."

"Mind if I sit down?" Hawthorn pulled a chair away from its arrangement. Drinkwater moved to the windows, suddenly losing his identity, becoming a shape against the lighter background.

"He needs to be convinced," Drinkwater said. "That we're serious, I mean. He says we've got the wrong man for the job."

Kiley found an ashtray on the desk, brought it across the room, and handed it to Hawthorn. He planted himself there, in front of the chair, too close for eye contact, his knees an inch from Hawthorn's, intimidating, hands in his pockets.

"Get off it, Kiley." Hawthorn inhaled and blew smoke at the floor, then looked up at the agent. "I'm not one of your damn sailors."

Kiley smiled at that, walked back to the desk, and sat down. He drummed his fingers softly on a writing pad.

"I don't blame you," Kiley said. He seemed to be talking to himself. "No, sir. It's a real ball cracker, this job." He looked across at Hawthorn. "But lemme tell you somethin', mister." His fingers stopped their tattoo. "I've been on the payroll a long time, and I've taken a lot of crap from a lot of people, and I've slept in some gory damn beds. For thirty grand a year, my friend . . . thirty grand a year."

Hawthorn waited, the cigarette dangling in his fingers.

"OK, dammit! I'll tell you how it is."

Marching to the map, Kiley snatched a long pointer from a corner and whacked the length of it across the middle of the Caribbean Sea.

"Russia wants this territory, mister. She wants it bad, and she wants it now. What the hell makes you think we own this damn bathtub? We *don't* own it. It belongs to anybody who wants it bad enough to beg, bribe, break, or butcher the half-ass politicians who get elected to office in some of those tourist traps. This man"—he pointed the stick at Drinkwater's silhouette—"he spent some time with you on that point, so don't let's club it to death. But I'm gonna show you somethin' I'll bet he didn't cover."

Kiley moved several feet to his left and pulled a string. A map of the world dropped from the ceiling, covering what was left of the blank wall.

"You know this chart, Hawthorn. These red shapes here, and here, and over here, that's where all the oil is. Not some of it, I mean all of it." He moved his pointer to rest on the Persian Gulf States. "Right here, there's a damn ocean of oil we haven't even found yet. Ten, twenty, fifty million barrels a day, Hawthorn, right there." The rubber tip of his stick went *tap-tap-tap* against the map fabric. "Damn! The whole world can't use but maybe twenty million barrels a day, you know that!"

Hawthorn rested his elbow on the arm of his chair. He knew the chart. He knew where the world's petroleum reserves were, what the distribution system looked like. Sweeping red arrows curved across the map, starting with thick shafts at the producing countries, then boldly piercing the middle of Europe and North America. Smaller flow arrows indicated smaller amounts to the few other industrial nations, the consuming powers that thrived on the energy made possible by oil. He let the demonstration go on.

"Russia can't have the Middle East, Mr. Hawthorn. We're makin' damn sure of that in Iran, and we'll make damn sure of that in these other sandtraps."

Iran. Mossadeq. War.

Hawthorn fingered his chin. Two objectives, both designed to disrupt Russia's forecasting, to close off their alternatives. Embarrass them, sabotage their planning, confuse and finally defeat them.

"Look, Kiley." Hawthorn got up and crossed to the agent's side of the room. "Let's cut out the bullroar here. Even if the Soviets did buy this sham, even if they did invest manpower and money in a wild goose chase, where's the long-term gain? That's my first objection. The second is more practical; I don't think it can be done."

Kiley started to reply, but Hawthorn wasn't finished. A sharp look at his eyes told Kiley to hold off.

"And there's another side to this thing you people have failed to consider. I own and operate a very profitable business, but it's been a tough road getting to the place where I'm at right now. You seem to think I can hand it over to some second-string manager and spend all my time for the next five or six years building a trap for Moscow. Even if I did have that capability, what would I have when it's all over? The Soviets won't be likely to pat me on the back and congratulate me on the clever way I screwed the hell out of them. My business will fold, *that's* what will happen, and their spies will chase my backside from one country to another until they cut my throat! *That's* what will happen, Kiley! There won't be a cave dark enough or a hole deep enough for me to hide with my five hundred million dollars. If the thing works, everybody wins except Russia and Hawthorn. That's why I think the idea is—bonkers!"

Kiley backed away, folding his arms across his broad chest.

"All right, now. Let's start with your first problem. Long-term gain, you say. How about twenty years? That's long term in my book. You divert their interest from the Middle East oil, we'll lock it up so tight they can't get in there. That's twenty years. You make asses outta them suckers in the Caribbean, they won't get back in there for twenty years. That's long-term gain.

"Can't be done, you said. Not with unlimited cash, not with tough people." Kiley squinted his eyes shut and opened them again. "I'm here to tell you it *can* be done. We're talkin' about a war, Hawthorn, and there's no limit to what we can do when our back's to the wall."

The agent faced the map, stood looking at it for a moment, then turned to confront Hawthorn again.

"How many Germans did you kill, Hawthorn . . . *after* they shot you down?"

"That was a long time ago, Kiley."

The agent dropped his hands. "Twenty-seven. To reach the coast you strangled a man, stole his command car, drove through a barricade, put a knife in a guard's back, blew up a sentry station, stole another car, and jumped off a damn cliff to make the three A.M. rubber boat. Is that right? You missed the boat and swam back to shore and shot up a few more guys to get to a plane. Is that right? You flew the damn Fokker back to the damn White Cliffs of Dover and landed on some damn farmer's damn milk cow. It that right? Well? I mean, did you do all that shit or is that some story you cocked up to get a fuckin' medal?"

Alan Drinkwater emerged from the background and stood at the map, between them. Hawthorn was looking at the war, at the coastline of France, lost in the black and white memory of a cold night in 1944.

"The difference between Mr. Kiley and me," Drinkwater said, "is the irrefutable fact that I have brains and he has clout." He folded his small body into an overstuffed chair. "I wanted you to meet with him because he has been one of the chief executors of the Commission's work. He knows, as I do, that sufficient funds and competent planning will accomplish astonishing results."

Hawthorn was listening, understanding, but at a distance. He looked at his hands, saw them clean, but felt the warm blood between his cold fingers, slippery. He reached in his hip pocket for a handkerchief and wiped his palms.

"As for the aftermath, yes. You are quite right about that. The Globe Corporation, the business you have managed to build so successfully, will no doubt be lost in the battle, and you will perhaps be the object of some vigorous search and reprisal effort; but with the kind of bank account you will command, good heavens, man. You can surely think of something."

Drinkwater was watching Hawthorn. There was no longer any doubt in his mind. They had selected the right man, the only man for this dangerous, ambitious venture.

"Thank you, Mr. Kiley," Drinkwater said. "We have a rather tight schedule from now on, so I'm afraid we can't stay any longer." He looked again at Hawthorn. "If you have no more questions, Gregory, we must be getting along for your next appointment." He stood up.

Hawthorn caught himself staring again at the map, at British Guiana now. He glanced at Drinkwater.

"My next appointment?"

"Yes. The prime minister at his home in the country, the undersecretary for Colonial Affairs at a pub in Chelsea, and then off to Washington for a conference. I believe it is to be chaired by one of your own fellows, a man named Dulles."

Gregory Hawthorn returned to Baton Rouge on August first, 1953. His first stratagem was to invite Henri Amont to his penthouse apartment, where he served the man several drinks and a hearty dinner. He then handed his new vice president the domestic operation and the keys to his very big car.

On the nineteenth of August, a sudden and unexpected rebellion erupted in the streets of Tehran. Soldiers armed with automatic weapons stormed the residence of the self-proclaimed leader of the Iranian people and dragged him off to his own jail, leaving behind a trail of blood and destruction. The short-lived rule of Dr. Mossadeq was over, the Shah returned, and the oil that was frozen in the ground flowed once again to the West.

John Kiley was killed in the brief skirmish and lay where he fell, dressed in his sandals, his gunnysack shirt, and his bloomer pants, until they stacked him on a cart and carried him off to a hole in the ground, and covered him up with sand.

CHAPTER 7

Yu Hsin Chou was born on the side of a road near Sinyangchow on February 20, 1926. The heads of his father and brother lay not fifteen feet from the gully where his mother had fallen under the attack of provincial soldiers. They had been hurrying to the mission hospital when the marauders came, struck the men down, and threw her into the ditch to die. She lasted long enough to force the baby out, pull it to her breast, and cover it with her ragged coat. An hour later, an American minister who was hurrying by to assist in the administration of the sacrament to the dying and aid to the living heard the baby's cries and carried it through the rain to a nurse, who helped it survive the night.

Seven days later, the hospital staff and all of the mission workers loaded their wooden carts high with human and material salvage and pushed as fast as they could manage toward a railroad siding ten miles away. The soldiers nearly overtook them, but they made it to a waiting train and scrambled aboard as the engineer threw his throttle forward and set the old machine in motion.

The last to climb aboard was Pastor Sigmund Anderson, running behind the final car with the little baby tucked under his arm like a watermelon. A shot caught him in the left shoulder but he barely faltered. Another shot jolted his right side but he ran ahead, gaining on the train until he finally managed to grasp a side rail. Waiting hands pulled him aboard and he was safe.

He fell to the floor of the wood carrier with blood gushing from his wounds. A nurse took the baby and discovered that the second shot, grazing Anderson's rib, had passed through the infant's right foot.

Little Yu Chou was kept alive through a series of frantic miracles until the train reached the outskirts of Peking. There, two nights after the flight began, he was handed over to Pastor Anderson and the American Board of Missions, an orphaned Chinese baby with a ragged foot and a bloated stomach, barely a week old.

The foot had been restored through operations and bone grafts, but he would walk all of his life without a right heel, with a limp that was occasionally noticeable, depending on the temperature and the shoes he wore.

Pastor Anderson had insisted that he keep his name, the name he was given the night he was found on his dead mother's breast. Yu Hsin Chou. Yu Hsin was a good name, an honorable name in the province where he had been conceived. Chou was taken from the name of the hospital, Sinyangchow. The pastor wanted the boy to grow up and perhaps return to his home one day, to tell the story of Christian love and kindness.

He had been sent to good schools in the United States while the pastor, his father, carried the mission work to South America and to Cuba, to Africa and finally to India, where he had been lost in a flood.

When Chou graduated in 1946 he was two years younger than his classmates and was considered a master linguist, a superb logician, and a candidate for honorary placement in the school's department of psychology. Instead, standing alone as he received his degree, Yu Hsin Chou decided that he would return to China to help rebuild the nation he never knew.

When he applied for his visa, he was ushered into a private room and questioned rather thoroughly by a senior officer of the consulate. Two days later, under the watchful eye of that same man, he was delivered to Georgetown University in Washington, D.C. After a week of counseling and interrogation there he was again accompanied by a man, this time an agent of the United States Intelligence Service, to a small town in Virginia.

Chou arrived in Peking on his birthday, February 20, 1949. He had with him a suitcase full of clothes, a journalist's visa, his diploma from the University of Southern California, his birth certificate, an American passport duly amended to allow travel in China, and one additional certificate from Harvard University, a master's degree in abnormal psychology. His application for Chinese citizenship was held for continuing review while he attended the University in Peking.

In the spring of 1951, Chou was accepted as a citizen and a member of the Chinese Communist party. He was commissioned a second lieutenant and ordered to serve with the intelligence unit at Shenyang, near the Korean border.

Over a period of nearly three years, Chou had interrogated more than three hundred American prisoners, most of them officers, many of them pilots.

If Moffit was different from the rest it was only because he was an obvious political vehicle, a victim of circumstance who could be used as barter, or for propaganda. He had committed a war crime.

Chou's interviews with Stephen Moffit were enough to satisfy him that there was no diamond in the rough here, no gleaming pearl to be polished and displayed. This was a mediocre man, a frustrated man, a lonely man who had been caught at playing war and who wanted to go home to his warm nooky. Within hours of his capture, Chou knew all he wanted to know about Stephen Moffit.

After those interviews, he had filled out his report, sent it on to his superiors for their information, and then gone on to more important matters. He had in fact returned to Shenyang and was getting ready to leave for Peking when he received a call from his commanding officer at that station. It was in connection with the prisoner, Moffit.

Chou's report had been reviewed by a panel of psychologists, one of whom was attached to the KGB as a liaison-without-portfolio to provide continuity under their joint agreement, Chapter Ninety-Five, Intelligence Development. The panel had noted Moffit's profile with interest, particularly the segment that described him as a man with rich fantasy modes, exceptionally creative yet intolerant of unorthodox behavior in others. They also underlined the notation that alluded to an unusually wide divergence between his self-image and his own elevated self-ideal. They combined these with a later reference to a strong need for gratification, and therewith placed his file on top of two hundred thirteen others who would serve as candidates for their Chapter Ninety-Five program.

Would Captain Chou please consider these matters in the Moffit case and return to them with a recommendation at the earliest possible opportunity?

"Intolerant of unorthodox behavior in others." A policeman, a strong father. "Self-gratification . . . low esteem . . . rich fantasy . . . creative . . ." Was that material for an agent?

For several hours, Captain Yu Hsin Chou turned that information over in his mind, remembered the interviews he had conducted with the prisoner, rearranged the flaws, the weaknesses, the strengths, the peaks and valleys of Moffit's profile. He did fit one mold: A person with an unusual combination of traits could be bent more easily than one whose simplistic view of duty and self shut out other growth possibilities. Chou considered Moffit's religious background. Yes, they had been successful in bending a man's faith, breaking it, redirecting his faith in a higher power to suit other purposes. That was a more difficult assignment, but such a candidate, once bound over, was unlikely to come undone.

Stephen Moffit was listed on no official ledger. He was neither dead nor alive as far as the Red Cross or the Americans were concerned. He was one of the thousands who would remain on the rolls of war as MIA. He could be used.

It was not a game of ideologies they were pursuing. It was more a game of chance. Of the thousands who were available for this concentrated experimentation process, they could expect to succeed in several hundred to a greater or lesser degree. They might win a sympathetic supporter, an important decision-maker. And in some cases, they might gain a valuable agent who would work for the money, or the ideology.

The next day Captain Chou called Peking with his answer. Stephen Moffit could be reduced through the usual processes; he could be educated and possibly converted. Yes, Captain Chou could work with him, but as usual, he could make no promises. Moffit was not brilliant but he had certain valuable skills, and he could no doubt learn others. Moscow would be required to pay certain fees and accept responsibility if they chose to recruit the man after his initial work in China.

That night, as Stephen Moffit huddled against a plaster wall in his second camp, Captain Chou sat at his desk and wrote a short letter to his friend in Peking, Professor David Chung. He hoped they would see each other again soon. He was eager to read the professor's latest paper on the abuse of stimulants by the elderly.

The letter was only four paragraphs long, but it took most of the evening to select the right words. He did not want the message to be misunderstood in Washington.

CHAPTER 8

Five months of solitary confinement had taught Stephen Moffit the important lesson that, without some kind of intellectual stimulation from outside one's own mind, it actually works harder to compensate. Without willing it to do so, his mind formulated graceful, ingenious plots, with characters that, could he have described them on paper, would have been companions to those of Dickens or, in a different mood, Agatha Christie. The endless hours of slumping against a wall and looking at the ceiling set for him a theaterlike atmosphere. He could parade his people from one side of the tiny room to the other, giving them words and actions that were often delightfully amusing, sometimes very frightening.

The fascinating part about it all was that he was not in control. He could almost anticipate the time when he was ready, and he would assume the position, his legs spread out in front and his arms loose at his side, his head resting against the stones at his back, and let go. Sometimes it would start right away, but often he would have to consciously give it a nudge, and form a picture of something or somebody. From there on, when everything was right, he was a passive observer.

Quite often the sequence was absurd. The little people (they were not little; in fact, they had no size at all) would do or say things that had nothing to do with anything remotely connected with what was going on. At first he tried to control that, as one does in a dream, but he found after a while that he was much more satisfied if he just let things go along on their own.

His favorite character was a man he decided to call Ding How. This man was old and bent over and had a long, drooping mustache and he carried a crooked wooden stick and wore silk pajamas. Ding How would scold the guard who brought food and emptied the slop bucket, and point to Moffit and talk about him. Once the guard answered back, snapping at Ding How, (what was he saying . . . ?) and the old man hit the guard with his stick. Moffit had smiled at that and the séance ended quickly.

He tried to bring Donna into the dream-state, but he was only able to get her shadow and no words at all. His mind would not allow her in; nor would it allow his father. The people he wanted to see were excluded, except in misty forms he could hardly identify.

If a person really does live in three different worlds, as Doc Jensen had theorized in one of Moffit's psychology classes, Moffit was very definitely in the third one. His own first world had been filled with Donna, his home, his family, his hobbies. There, Jensen had postulated, one found passion and gave love, shared oneself. Moffit was not in that world, even found it hard to remember what it was like being there.

Nor was he in his second world, the place where he got up in the morning, shaved, ate breakfast, went to the job, used his professional talents, and then returned home. He wasn't even in the extension of that place, where he used his flying skills, applying himself to a task with certain demands, certain assurance.

He was, instead, firmly and irremovably entrenched in the third world, that place where men retreat to be alone, where fantasies become real, where a man can create things as he wants them to be. Only in this case he had not wanted to retreat to the harmless and often rehabilitating haven of make-believe; he was not there by choice. He was just there. That's all his mind had to work with.

He fancied himself digging his way out of the hut in the darkness of night, stealthily garroting a soldier and easing him noiselessly to the ground, making his way to the tree line, leaping easily over river beds and fallen trees, running to freedom. Then, in another mood, he conjured up the notion that he was an important scientist with American secrets that the Chinese wanted badly to learn. They would ply him with food and Black Label Scotch, give him a woman . . . a beautiful Chinese woman who knew wonderful positions. They would open his door and she would come in. "We know who you are. We need you."

Donna seemed very far away. He remembered how they had experimented, how she had surprised him with new positions, new adventures, doing things he had always considered indecent. He pleaded with God to let him think about other things when a vision of her with someone else broke into his dreaming. He could hear her panting, "My darling . . . Tommy . . . Ohhh, ohhh, yes . . ."

He never pictured Donna alone, sitting in their living room, reading a magazine or making coffee in the kitchen. There was always someone else with her.

But he was alone. It seemed, as he thought more about it, it seemed as if he had always been alone.

Things never worked out for him the way they did for others. God knows he had tried to please his parents and his instructors, he had taken a job in Civil Service to make sure his future was secure, he had married a decent girl, he had stayed close to home to look after his family. Not like some of the men he knew who had graduated and gone off to New York, or gone on to get higher degrees, or like James Wensman, who inherited his family's money and blew it in Europe while he, Stephen J. Moffit, was busting his ass in the Mississippi ditches for three hundred dollars a month.

Where the hell was Wensman when they called his name for the draft? Where was Berger, where was Finnegan? Home in their beds, or at the Stevens Hotel bar, sucking up to some twenty-year-old secretary while he fought their war for them.

So he was getting paid in full now, paid for the sacrifice and the honest work and the loyalty, getting paid for the faith and the dedication and the bravery, paid in the coin of cold rice and maggots and foul water. His reward was a stone cell, a rotten tick mattress, and the bitter loneliness of solitary confinement a million miles from civilization.

Did his father know where he was? There was a man to pity, his father. A harder-working guy never lived, a more decent man never lived nor struggled the way his father had done, and his reward was a job that barely paid the mortgage and a closet full of Goodwill clothes. His reward was a crappy house and lungs full of Chicago smoke. He deserved better. They both deserved better, he and his father. Things never worked out.

In his dreaming he often sought elevation. He wanted elevation, to be up high, above others and looking down at the tops of their heads. Poor people down there, wrapped in their robes and wandering aimlessly about while he floated above, light and serene.

Moffit found sleep his best escape from depression, and it came to him easily, often without his awareness. He simply eased himself down, pulled his knees to his chest, and drifted off into darkness. He imagined in those moments of vacancy before sleep that he would spend the days of his captivity as the dead spend their years, alone and afraid, waiting for the resurrection.

Moffit was in his fifth camp, somewhere near or maybe in China. Escape was out of the question now. He was too weak. He had spoken to no one for five long months—or was it longer?

It was cold, near Christmas, Moffit calculated. He had been given a padded cotton coat and a pair of cotton leggings that helped during the night. The food was poor, barely adequate. But it was the total aloneness that was so terribly painful, and the uncertainty too. What would happen? When would he be tried? Or set free? Was the war over?

When the guards came for him this time they fixed his wrists in handcuffs instead of ropes, and bound his feet in steel shackles with a chain between them. This at least was new. They loaded him into the back of a truck and pulled a tarp over the top to keep out the cold wind. A guard sat on the last bench and the truck lurched forward onto a road that soon began a slow descending turn. The truck bumped and bounced along for several hours.

When they finally stopped it was getting dark. A gentle snow had begun to fall, causing the ground to appear misty and light. Moffit got down with help from the guard and followed two soldiers to a wooden barrackslike building. They led him up two steps and, opening the door, motioned for him to go in. He heard the door close behind him, then the sound of boots clomping down the stairs outside. It was warm, almost friendly, very nearly a familiar setting. It could have been the superintendent's quarters at a building site, with a desk and several chairs, a drawing board on a tripod in one corner. There was a filing cabinet and a table, both painted green, both with stacks of documents on them.

Moffit hunched his shoulders. His face was wet from the snow and he felt sore, slightly feverish, not unusual now. He also felt excitement. And he was afraid again.

The side door opened and Captain Chou stood in the frame, smiling. He looked familiar. Moffit lowered his head, suddenly and inexplicably ashamed of the way he was dressed.

"Well! Lieutenant Stephen Jonathan Moffit. United States Navy pilot breaker of truces. My friend from the *Ticonderoga*. Welcome to China. Here," he said, moving forward and showing a set of keys, "allow me to remove your handcuffs."

Chou took the steel bracelets and tossed them on his desk. "It's been a tiresome journey, Jonathan. Do you want to go to the bathroom?"

"God, yes. Yes, sir," said Moffit.

"In there," said Chou, showing him a small door to one side. "Kindly leave the door open, please."

It was the gesture, the human kindness, that caused tears to fill his eyes as he turned toward the bathroom. He unzipped, wiped his eyes with his sleeve, and took a long time relieving himself, feeling the tension lift away, sensing the pleasure of having someone say his name. There was no washbowl, but a clean cloth hung on a rack. Moffit used it to wipe his face and his hands, then shuffled back into the office, the chains on his ankles clanking and rattling as he dragged them across the floor. He stopped, tried to think, and looked at Chou, who was still standing with his hands clasped in front of his belt.

"Where am I?"

"In China, Jonathan. A safe place, a good place for the time being."

Moffit wondered what to ask next.

"Go ahead, Lieutenant. Ask me questions. I will give you honest answers if I can."

"The war is over?"

"The truce remains in effect, yes."

Moffit was silent, looking first at the small, trim, polished officer, then at the wall, then at his feet.

"Am I a prisoner of war?"

"In a manner of speaking, yes," said Captain Chou.

"Are there other Americans here?"

"None at the moment, Jonathan. You are the only one."

Moffit fell silent again. Why the hell couldn't he think of questions? For a thousand hours he had asked questions, addressed the stone walls with his questions, cried his questions to himself. Now he was blank.

"It is quite late, Jonathan Moffit. I have had a long day and you are very tired. I am going to show you to your room now. It has a bed and a good toilet. In about an hour someone will bring you a hot meal. There is a light in your room and you may read until you wish to go to sleep. I have marked the pages for you."

Pages in what? What was happening?

Chou took Moffit's elbow and faced him around, then led him into a small corridor. At the end of the hall was a young Chinese soldier, unarmed, standing at rest before another door. Moffit walked carefully, trying not to scrape his ankles as the manacles chafed against his skin.

Inside his room he sat heavily on the edge of the bed and turned to see Captain Chou give quiet instructions to the soldier. Then the door was shut and locked, bolted on the outside, and Moffit was alone.

The room was small, perhaps eight feet by ten, and had a bed with a mattress, pillow, and a white cover. There was a night table and overhead, recessed in the ceiling, a light, but there was no window. On the table was an ashtray and a book.

He leaned forward to reach for the book. It was a Bible. Suddenly he remembered the officer's name, the Jonathan business. He remembered the second session, and the third, the questions about his family. Had he been drugged? Why had he forgotten the captain's persistent exploration into the earliest days of his youth, his courtship, his job, his faith in God? Even now, as he closed his eyes and remembered, it was as though he recalled it from a dark room, a slow, heavy, cumbrous fog.

Moffit replaced the Bible and fell back onto the bed. He wanted to stay awake, to ponder this change, to remember more, but he was asleep in a matter of moments, dreaming of blackness.

He opened his eyes slowly, fearing that awful sense of disorientation that comes to a man who has been in a blackout, wondering suddenly what he has done, where he has been, where he is now. It was a smell that had reached his mind, the smell of cooked meat, an odor from long ago. It was a smell from the cabin up north. His dad was making hamburgers.

Moffit sat on the edge of the bed, reached greedily for the tray of food that had been placed on his bedside table. He ate the meat and the rice together. Beef, with stew gravy, and white rice. It tasted better than anything he had ever eaten in his life. When the food was gone, he wiped the plate clean with a crust of fresh rice bread. *God!* he thought to himself. "Goddamn food!" he said aloud. Then he belched and wiped his mouth with his sleeve.

He fell back on the bed once more and the light went out. Moffit slept without moving for twelve hours.

When he awoke his leg chains were gone and there was another tray of food on the table. He rolled his legs to the floor, rubbed his ankles, and looked around the room again. There, in the corner, was a curtain. A toilet, probably. He went as quickly as he could to the corner, drew back the curtain, and found a one-holer with a lid on it, the pit dug under the building's floor. A roll of hard paper was next to the lid.

Moffit undid his trousers and sat down. When he was finished he wiped his hands and his face on clean paper and threw it down into the hole. He very nearly smiled as he closed the lid. His escape route. Tunnel out through the shit.

51

He sat down on the bed and attacked the tray of food. Pork? Yes, it was pork, and fried vegetables.

The Bible was a small Gideon edition. Moffit hefted it in his hands before turning the pages, wiping his fingers on his trousers several times to keep the new pages clean. Chou had indeed marked the passages by folding down corners and underlining the pieces he was meant to read. The first was in the Book of Matthew, chapter 21. Moffit read it carefully, slowly.

"And when he saw a fig tree in the way, he came to it, and found nothing thereon, but leaves only, and he said unto it, Let no fruit grow on thee henceforward forever. And presently the fig tree withered away."

Moffit read the verse again. The next dog-ear was at chapter 25.

"And unto one servant he gave five talents, to another two, and to another one; to every man according to his several ability; Then he that had received the five talents went and traded with the same, and made them other five talents. And likewise he that had received two, he also gained other two. But he that had received one went and digged in the earth, and hid his lord's money."

Moffit closed the Bible. He stared at the wall for several minutes. What was it supposed to mean? Why had Chou selected those verses for him to read? He opened the book again and found the next verse, in the Book of Acts.

"And Stephen, full of faith and power, did great wonders and miracles among the people."

That was all he could find. Chou had selected only those verses, verses dealing with fruitless trees, buried gold, and his namesake, Stephen. What could those possibly have to do with him, as a prisoner? He wanted to talk to Chou.

There was no answer when he knocked at the door to his room, no guard, no sign that he had been heard at all. Moffit sat on the edge of the bed again and saw for the first time that they had brought him cigarettes, Old Golds. They were on the table in plain view, but he had not noticed them. He opened the pack, put one between his lips, and reached for the book of matches. He opened the cover, tore a match out, closed the cover again and looked in astonishment at the advertising. "Jason's Restaurant." He took the cigarette from his mouth and held it, unlit, reading the ad for Jason's. Jason's . . . the restaurant in Aurora, the place he had taken Donna so often. His imagination was racing now. He looked up, stared at the wall. What were they trying to do? Was this brainwashing?

He tapped the cigarette firmly on the table, then lit it and inhaled deeply, allowing himself to get dizzy with the first smoke he had tasted in over five months. It felt like the first gulp of a cold martini, overpowering, heady. He rested his head on the pillow and smoked, thinking about the matchbook, about Jason's.

An hour passed before the door bolt slid open and the door latch turned. The young guard came into the room with a brown envelope in his hand, approached Moffit and handed it to him, then left and locked the door.

Moffit stubbed out his cigarette, the third since he found the pack, and sat up, crossing his legs on the bed. He opened the envelope and, feeling inside, he withdrew a glossy photograph and focused for a brief second on the scene. He let out a sharp gasp and threw the picture to the floor, saw it land face up. It was a head-on shot of two people at a restaurant table. There was a bottle of wine, a rose in a delicate vase. The man was dark haired, handsome. The woman was his wife, Donna.

Moffit's gaze was fixed to the awful glossy, lying there, mocking . . . they were *looking* at him! He slid to the floor, snatched up the photograph, and ripped it into small pieces, then crossed to the latrine, stopping abruptly as he was about to throw the fragments into the hole. He squatted down instead, over the hole, and tried to fit her face together again. Tears flooded his eyes. He squeezed them shut and felt the warm drops slide down his face. Clenching his fists, he crushed the pieces in his fingers.

At noon the guard came again and brought rolls and a hard cheese loaf with cold tea. There was another pack of Old Golds on the tray.

"I want to see Captain Chou," Moffit said softly.

The guard nodded and backed out of the room, locking the door.

It was an obvious assault on his balance, a transparent attempt by Chou to weaken his survival instincts. But why go at it this way? What did they want? A confession to war crimes, perhaps. In exchange for a lighter sentence, or maybe repatriation. "Dammit! Sure I did it! What the hell, it was a mistake! I'm sorry the fucking war turned out this way!" Why not let him say that and be done with it? They would know, at home, that he said it under threat of punishment.

Over and over he played the role, knowing he was letting his mind speed along on the track they had provided, yet unable to stop it.

Late in the afternoon he tried to get Ding How into the room. He relaxed and invited his fantasy to wander, but all that came into his mind was the photograph. Who was he? Why? *Why?*

He finally reached for the Bible and began to read:

"In the beginning, God created the Heaven and the earth."

53

CHAPTER 9

"What figure did you have in mind, Mr. Hawthorn?"

"Twelve million, Mr. Hornby."

"Pounds or dollars, Mr. Hawthorn?"

"Dollars, Mr. Hornby."

"And with that you want our findings to date, of course."

"Yes."

"I was instructed to make it difficult, sir."

"Thirteen million."

"Pounds or dollars, Mr. Hawthorn?"

"Dollars."

"Done."

The entire business was concluded well before teatime.

Gregory Hawthorn had purchased the British Guiana oil concession from Shell UK for the sum of thirteen million dollars. Roger Hornby had no idea whatsoever how much it was worth, nor did he care. The transaction had been arranged weeks before by other parties. Their little office exchange was merely a preliminary to signature.

The government in British Guiana would be due another million for tax stamps, documentation transfer, and the like. They had agreed to the transfer of ownership when the United Kingdom herself issued an opinion regarding Shell's sincerity in the project.

In any event it was all over in a trice, as predicted, and the cash was paid one hour after Gregory Hawthorn emerged from the building on Picadilly Square. He strolled down the gaudy avenue toward the Circus, and eventually came to his next objective. Mister Hornby had mentioned a fine deli there, known for its hard salami on rye.

He spent Christmas with Alan Drinkwater at his country estate, Quaile Manor. Drinkwater lived alone there, near the sea, a comfortable distance from the confusion of London.

It was built in the fashion of a cottage, but its size and setting qualified the old home as a manor indeed. It was surrounded by huge oak trees, whose ancient branches swept across the yard like protective arms, nearly hiding two brick chimneys and casting soft shadows along the stucco, wood-trimmed exterior of the home. The foyer floor was gray tile, polished to a stain finish; a stairway wound gracefully to the balcony above; a burnished brass chandelier hung from the vaulted ceiling by a chain. The library was an elegant room graced with velvet furniture, cushioned carpeting, a large, mahogany desk, and a world globe mounted on its cherry wood base. The walls were paneled with fine oak, the ceiling was crossed with heavy cedar beams, the fireplace was a country hearth.

After they had eaten their Christmas dinner, the two men went into the library for their coffee and brandy. The Christmas tree sat decently out of the way, in a corner of the room. The fire in the hearth snapped, coughing its oak and chestnut smoke up through the one chimney that had been cleaned for the winter.

"Yes. Historical expectation. Businessmen use it all the time."

Drinkwater had assumed his professorial chair, a high-backed rocker close to the warmth of the fire. A brandy glass rolled in his palms. Hawthorn was smoking and drinking coffee.

"Businessmen, like yourself, they chart a course that is along a straight line, usually up if it's a sales course and down if it represents costs, and then they observe their actual performance against those lines. When they see a sudden change, they call a meeting of their department heads to examine the reasons for the deviation." Drinkwater raised the glass, held it to the firelight to examine the color of his brandy, and sipped, smacking his lips.

"If the change portends trouble, they correct the problem. If the deviation is an unexpected boon, they exploit it. You do see what I mean, of course. You do it all the time, I should think."

He didn't expect an answer. He was hardly aware that Hawthorn was in the room. His fingers dropped to a lap robe and fitted it more snugly around his knees.

"It is my task, on the other hand, to look along those lines of expectation and to *cause* a deviation, to inject into the vein of a living project some irregular substance that causes the project to change its character. Mind, when I say 'project,' I might as well have said, 'forecast,' or 'strategem,' or some such. It doesn't have to be a program in its operational stages."

This time he looked over at Hawthorn to see if he had the man's attention. Satisfied, he continued.

"Because I deal with highly intelligent adversaries, I hardly ever expect to destroy the opposition's project altogether, but I do expect to alter the outcome in one way or another, possibly to delay or to minimize its implementation and final effect. In some cases, I must admit, they have given it up completely and gone on to other matters that are less tedious. Finland, for example."

Hawthorn stared at him.

55

"Finland?"

"I merely said that to see if you were listening, Gregory." Drinkwater found a handkerchief and touched his nose with it. "I say, I do hope you will be able to use the sweater. My dear wife made it for me. Far too big. But I told you that."

They spent three days at the manor discussing the project. On the morning of his last day, sitting at their coffee in the large, old-fashioned kitchen, Hawthorn consulted his *Caribbean Gazette* for the last time.

In it were recorded the names of the governors, the prime ministers, their advisors, the chief cabinet officers, and their sundry responsibilities for every country and island in the Caribbean.

On his notepad, he had listed those names he would contact in the order of their importance to the project. One by one, island by island, he would engage their attention, enlist their support, win their confidence.

His tool was money. Most of the smaller islands were little more than eruptions in the sea, a few hundred square miles in size, with shallow waters and sandy beaches that denied them a deep harbor shipping capability. Their fuel came in drums on schooners, and it was expensive.

Hawthorn would offer them fuel in bulk. A few large tanks on shore would satisfy most of them. To supply those tanks, he would introduce a floating hose operation; his own handy-size tankers would park offshore, run a floating hose to the bulk installation with a motor boat, hook up, and fill up. He would install the tankage at his expense in exchange for a long-term supply contract. He would supply them with finished petroleum products refined from his own crude oil, oil taken from the bosom of their neighbor to the south, British Guiana.

Hawthorn's plan to create and foster a dependency would take several years, and he would need the cooperation of Shell, Texaco, and Esso. There was never a question in his mind that his allies, indeed, his sponsors, would agree to meet his sundry needs, regardless of the cries he might hear from their middle management.

Drinkwater stood in the kitchen doorway, going over the final items before driving Hawthorn back to Heathrow.

"I've never been to Greece, Alan."

"One day will do it, I should think. The funds have already been deposited. You need only attend a meeting at Pondopolous's home near Athens. He has the papers. Eighteen small tankers and one larger vessel, average one hundred thousand barrels or something. You will add to your fleet as the situation demands."

"And the crew. Greeks and Panamanians."

"For now, yes. They have a good reputation. You will replace them with our own people as time goes along."

"Shipping department . . ." Hawthorn ticked it off on his list. "Personnel . . . disbursement . . . legal . . . tax . . . I feel like a damn clerk here."

"Good God, Hawthorn. That *is* a clerk's affair. Surely you can manage the simple business of shuttling eighteen tankers about the Caribbean! You don't have to show a bloody profit, you know."

Hawthorn stopped, looked at Drinkwater, sipped his coffee, and set his cup down.

"I'll make a profit, Alan. I always make a profit, even when I'm playing a risky game with somebody else's money."

"Yes. I daresay. I should have expected nothing less." Drinkwater stepped to the wood-burning stove, lifted a teapot from the iron plate, and poured into his cup. "The engineer . . . you mentioned his name."

"Dreier. Sandy Dreier. I've had him on the payroll for several years."

"I believe he should be an engineer and nothing more for the time being. Tell him nothing about the Globe project, about the Commission. Nothing about the hoax. A need-to-know precaution, you see."

"That might be tough, Alan. He knows this business. He knows about first-things-first. Hell, it won't take a month for him to see that I'm building a damn network before I have any product. He'll see that."

"Does he trust you?"

"Of course. And I trust him. I can tell him what he needs to know. Let the CIA do a check on him."

"He needs to be an engineer. It will have to be managed somehow. Please, Gregory, the time will come when you can take him aside. But don't give the man more than he needs for now."

Hawthorn looked out the large kitchen window at fog-shrouded trees. He leaned across from his chair and reached the coffeepot, refilled his cup.

"All right, Alan. We'll keep him in the dark for a while. You might be right. Now then." He sipped the hot coffee. "The political situation in British Guiana."

"Yes. Things have changed somewhat since Britain suspended the new constitution. Cheddi Jagan is on the streets again. But I can't say as I blame them. They . . . we were afraid of a Communist dictatorship."

"The man was only in office a few months. That would have been a ripe situation for us, Alan. It was the situation you wanted."

"And so it will be again, Gregory, but for the time being you will deal with an interim government in British Guiana, a caretaker government."

Hawthorn pursed his lips, thinking. "All right. I suppose that might be in our favor too. Give us some breathing space."

"That is essentially correct. They will hold new elections in 1957 and Cheddi Jagan will win again. England is sure of that."

Hawthorn nodded his agreement. He would have about thirty months, perhaps as long as three years to get his organization in place, to establish his position as the new gun in the petroleum industry. He would send a team down to assume the property, start some improvements, assign them to work on the river, bring in some equipment, spend a few million on barges and collateral trappings. He had a good second man for that job, Dutch Schultz, who could start it rolling.

In the meanwhile he himself would be working the Caribbean market, playing up to the politicians and installing his new delivery system. With any luck, he would make an early connection with the Russians, unless they decided to keep a low profile until they actually smelled the beautiful naphthanic odor of crude petroleum.

Gregory Hawthorn had already figured out a way to invent an oil field. That was a mechanical operation with some very unordinary logistical maneuvers. That part would come, but in the interim he had to do a puppet show clever enough to fool a lot of people for a very long time, and create a distribution system that was not only believable but enviable.

And after he had done the impossible, after he had built that distribution system and invented the oil field, after he had the Russians solidly locked in to his enormous charade, then what? If Cuba became the first satellite, as Drinkwater was predicting, would the Commission actually get license from the United States to blow their harbor to smithereens? They had talked about that, he and Drinkwater. And they had discussed the other tactical possibilities: blockading the harbor with his fleet of ships, sinking them in the narrows, or a simple disappearing act that would leave Russia and Cuba high and dry for many weeks, perhaps months. The American refineries were engineered to handle South American crude oil, with its own peculiar chemical and physical characteristics. It would take a very long time to convert the stills and the cracking towers and all the rest of the refinery hardware to handle Russian crude.

They had covered those questions, and arrived at no answers. But the significance of Alan Drinkwater's "line of expectation" theory was not to be dismissed. Hawthorn would give the Russians a convincing, extremely attractive line of expectation, and then he would shatter it without warning. In the final analysis, what would actually happen to his fleet, to the satellite's energy-producing capability, and to the physical plant in British Guiana would be less important than the unheaval that would occur when Russia discovered that they were short

58

a hundred billion barrels of oil, their plans for Western domination floating on sand, their shunning of Middle East opportunities a disastrous blunder.

As they rode to the airport together, Drinkwater sat in silence and stared out the window, his lap robe tucked nicely under his legs. Gregory Hawthorn passed that hour thinking about the events that had brought him to this journey and wondering where he would be when it was over. They hadn't crossed that bridge yet, either.

But when they stopped before the terminal building he smiled to himself. Today he would spend one hundred million dollars. Even for a man who played with millions as a child plays with wooden blocks, that was a lot of money. He was beginning to enjoy the game.

CHAPTER 10

During the Korean War, seven thousand Americans were captured and held in prison camps. Approximately three thousand of them died in those camps, or in the death marches.

After the war was over, toward the end of 1953, a neutral zone was established by the United Nations in a province of North Korea for the purpose of convincing prisoners who were unsure of their loyalties that they would be better off in their home countries.

Three hundred and fifty-nine men chose to remain in China; among them were twenty-one Americans. On January 23, 1954, those twenty-one were dishonorably discharged.

Stephen J. Moffit was not among this number, nor was he among those who had been given the opportunity to make a choice. He was one of hundreds who were neither alive nor dead on any official listing.

In early January 1954, he had been given a note by Yu Hsin Chou that informed him of his father's death. Lung cancer was given as the cause, but Moffit chose to believe it was more than that. After the years of struggling and stoic enduring, his father had finally managed to escape, to get away from it, all of it.

Moffit spent the following days in sullen, withdrawn silence, trying to bring his father into the tiny room, to visit with him and Ding How, to tell him that everything was all right. But the vision wouldn't come. Chou, fully aware of the pain Moffit was suffering, worked on his student and expertly moved him through the shock, denial, guilt, and depression stages to the stage where anger rules. And then he cut off the normal process before Moffit could himself work up to the level of acceptance. When he was finished, Chou had yet another tool in his repertoire of psychological devices: Moffit had been abandoned by his own father.

In addition, Chou had the photograph to work with. He saved his explanations for that until later, until mid-February, when Moffit had done as much internal damage to himself as could be hoped for. Donna Moffit was lonely. His name was Richard. He was a former Marine, a combat veteran. That was all the information he had. It was all he needed. By the end of April 1954, Stephen Moffit had undergone a radical change in his emotional disposition.

By July he had been subjected to nearly one thousand hours of tutorial instruction in the mythology of American freedom, the inhumanity of the industrial revolution, the abhorrent manipulations of capitalism, and the foul treachery of Western diplomacy.

In October he was sent to the University of Peking to study the science and tools of industrial espionage, using textbooks and manuals and models and equipment supplied by but without the knowledge of the American intelligence community. While he was there he occupied much of his spare time in the code library and on the firing range, adding tools to his growing repertoire in preparation for a task that was as obscure to him as it was to his instructors.

In January 1956 Stephen Moffit was sent to Moscow under an exchange agreement between China and Russia that proceeded under the direction of the KGB, most probably without the blessing of the Politburo but most certainly with their financial cooperation.

Moffit remained in Russia for thirteen months before returning to China on February 11, 1957. His first stop was in the city of Shenyang. A taxi took him to the comfortable hillside apartment of Captain Yu Hsin Chou. Moffit was dressed in a business suit and had grown his hair quite long. He looked fit, perhaps a little on the thin side and very pale, but that was now in accordance with the schedule.

Chou met him at the front door and showed him through the dusky foyer, across a wide terrace and onto a heated balcony. They took places in wicker chairs, a bamboo coffee table between them. On the hill below and stretching for several miles were the galvanized steel rooftops of houses belonging to families who were not as well off as Chou. Their corrugated metal and scrap lumber shelters served the single purpose of providing shelter from the cold rain and the snow.

Chou's balcony faced the west; they held fragile cups and sipped tea as the sun dropped quickly below the hills of Liaoning Province.

Chou set his teacup on a tray and looked at Moffit.

"I assume there is nothing for me to add," he said. "They have explained everything to you?"

"Yes," replied Moffit. "When will I go into hospital?"

"Into 'the' hospital, Stephen. You have begun to reflect a foreign influence."

Chou had never clarified the biblical interpretation of his middle name and Moffit had never found a satisfactory explanation for the captain's earlier preoccupation with it. He had dropped the "Jonathan" business in their second week at Liaoyang, though several letters from Chou had arrived in Russia with that name on the envelope.

But he had explained the parables, the biblical verses he had given Moffit to read on his first night at the barracks. The barren fig tree was stricken down because it was a worthless ornament. It was, quite simply put, not doing its job. The servant who buried his master's talents—the bags of gold he was entrusted to manage—was punished because he did not put them to good use. He allowed them to be idle.

"*How about you, Stephen,*" Chou had said. "*What are the fruits of your life? Or are you a tree that stands naked and bears no fruit? And what of your talents? You have been given certain treasures, certain skills, certain responsibilities. Have you used them wisely? Have you been allowed to use them productively? Or have you buried them in the ground?*" Chou had been patient, clinically perfect in his instruction. "*I can help you, Stephen. I can help you to become the man you were destined to be, a worker of miracles among the people, a man of power and influence. Are you willing to let me help you?*"

"Tomorrow morning, to answer your question," Chou said. "They were expecting you tonight but I got them to postpone for a day."

"I understand there will be some pain."

"Very little, I think," said Chou. "Pain is quickly forgotten and is most difficult to describe to others. There is no long-term benefit in causing you to experience pain."

"Afterward, then."

"Does it matter?"

"I suppose it doesn't. I guess it's necessary."

Chou got up and went into his small kitchen. After a few minutes Moffit followed him. Chou was stirring something on the stove.

"You know about your wife, of course," said Chou.

"Yes, I know about her. I was told in Orekhovo. She's had a baby with him."

"What do you intend to do?"

61

"Nothing," said Moffit. "Divorce, I expect. Nothing more."

"I see," said Chou. "That's good."

"Yes. I suppose it is. I really don't care."

"I believe you're ready, Stephen."

The next morning Chou accompanied Moffit to the military hospital and walked with him to the front desk. There, he said his farewell and turned to go, but as he was walking away, he stopped and faced the American.

"Stephen," he said. Moffit was looking at him. "Have you read the book of First Samuel?"

"No," replied the American.

"Perhaps you will some day. Good-bye." With that, Yu Hsin Chou hunched his shoulders and left the hospital.

On the operating table at a quarter past twelve the doctors broke all of the fingers in his left hand and set them slightly crooked. One doctor examined his mouth and expertly broke several teeth with a hammer and chisel. They pierced his left cheek with a sharp, sterilized rod and passed it through his mouth to the other cheek, then pierced that as well, fixing the rod in place with bandages. Another doctor arrived at three o'clock and removed Moffit's appendix, cutting the skin badly and stitching the wound closed with heavy thread.

Two days later, with Moffit still under heavy sedation, they broke and reset his nose and removed the steel shaft, then badly scarred his right ear. They created and then bandaged welt marks on his back and on his lower legs, inflicted deep lash cuts on the bottoms of his feet, and wrapped them in heavy gauze.

On February 25, Moffit was taken to a common prison camp forty miles north of the Korean border and placed in a cell, dressed in filthy, padded clothes. He waited there for three weeks. On the evening of the twenty-first day, a truck pulled up at the shoddy front gate, was allowed to pass through, and stopped in front of his compound. Several neatly dressed men stepped down from the truck and were led to his cell by the camp commander, who opened up the barred door. An officer wearing the uniform of the Indian army stepped forward and addressed Moffit in crisp, military language.

"You are Lieutenant Stephen Jonathan Moffit? United States Navy? Serial number four-three-nine oh-three three-five?"

To each part of the question Moffit nodded a sick affirmative.

"You are liberated, sir. Please follow me."

Two of the civilians helped Moffit to the truck and laid him in a stretcher in the back. The truck ground to a start and turned in the small clearing to pass back out the gate. An hour later they stopped and Moffit was helped into a waiting DC-3, marked with the insignia of the United Nations.

Stephen Moffit awoke the next morning in a hospital bed at the Osaka Naval Base in Japan. He had been a prisoner for nearly forty-five months and he was on his way home to the United States, a free man. The date was March 17, 1957.

Part Two

CHAPTER 1

The years following the Korean War were bonanza times for small, independent oil companies like Tidewater, Atlantic, Signal, and a host of others. The Iranian Consortium of 1954, resulting from the ouster of Mossadeq and the return of the Shah, opened up the vast reserves of that country for the independents, giving them access to Iranian oil without the enormous risk of exploration. In 1955 the Libyan government, determined to avoid the dangers and the strangling monopolies imposed on other Arabian countries by giant corporations, passed its own petroleum law, inviting those outside the sacred circle of the "Big Seven" to join them in production agreements.

By the time Libyan oil was flowing in quantity, half of it was coming out of wells owned and operated by independent oil companies. The glut of crude oil that Hawthorn had anticipated, following the brief but lucrative Mossadeq shortage, forced prices down and gave rise to the introduction of new and innovative marketing techniques in the United States and in Europe. New names appeared on service stations, entire new networks of retail outlets were built, gas wars became common.

And, as Hawthorn had predicted, tanker rates in the western hemisphere were rising sharply. The new demand had outgrown the antiquated distribution capacity, and Hawthorn's shipping profits rose to handsome levels. Japan's shipbuilders were signing contracts for huge supertankers, but few were building the smaller vessels that were ideally suited to Caribbean operations. Hawthorn had a lock on his part of the market.

By 1956 he had closed eleven contracts and his man, Sandy Dreier, had constructed eight ocean terminals to receive Globe's floating hose deliveries. The major corporations appeared to be content for the time being to lose some of their volume in the smaller islands, to concentrate their attention on Central America and Puerto Rico, Cuba, Jamaica,

Barbados, where deep water was not a consideration, and a profit was still to be made on the marketing end of the business.

Hawthorn had made several trips to British Guiana, had met with the governor, Sir Hillman Gomes, and had shared his optimistic view regarding the country's hidden wealth at every opportunity. The government politicians who managed to corner him on his visits were quick to point out to him that Shell, certainly no youngster in the business, had failed to come up with anything that even resembled a positive sign. Hawthorn's answer to that was a secretive smile, a wink, and a single word. Glut.

The governor extended every courtesy to the American oilman, appeared in public with him, and invited guests to his home to dine with him. He was hopeful, he admitted, that the country would indeed prosper with the advent of its own oil age, and he encouraged all political leaders to work toward the common cause. Sir Hillman Gomes, a close friend and confidant to Alan Drinkwater, was behind the venture all the way.

Sandy Dreier was a big man, a strapping man, an Oklahoma native whose most exciting trips prior to 1938 had been the bus ride to Norman, Oklahoma, and his flights down the football field with nine men on his back. He was caught in the war draft and served his time aboard three of the Navy's biggest ships, seeing two of them go down before his discharge in 1945. He finished his engineering degree at Oklahoma and was immediately hired by the young upstart, Greg Hawthorn, to help build an oil company.

When Hawthorn called him to work in the Caribbean, Dreier brought his wife along. She managed to endure the carnival for two years before she packed it up and went back home to Tulsa. She would wait it out there.

Dreier had raised questions about the operation, but when he saw the profitability picture and the growth of volume generated by his labor, he let the British Guiana thing drop. That was management, a bigger picture, and he trusted the judgment of his boss.

Now it was time to move down, to get some holes in the ground. He could build tankage, he could do a dock on a beach, but his first love was drilling for oil and all of the engineering challenges that went with it.

The flight from Baton Rouge took them over fourteen hours. Hawthorn and Dreier rode the sluggish Viscount with a joint determination that the corporation would invest in its own jet as soon as time allowed, as soon as Lockheed came up with something that was suitable.

It was dark by the time they cleared customs, endured the terrible taxi into Georgetown, and checked into the Tower Hotel. At the bar Dreier drank his bottle of warm Banks Beer and Hawthorn smoked his cigarette. They were unwinding, feeling the night humidity, the heat of March at the equator.

Hawthorn had already changed into a light bush jacket and denim pants. Hunched over the bar, he looked more like a commando than a millionaire.

"I'll be with the minister all morning, Sandy," he was saying. "I haven't met the man, but I hear tell he's a little on the peculiar side. He hasn't been on the job very long."

"Good," Dreier said. "That's what we need down here. Peculiar." He tipped the bottle back and finished it, set it on the bar and pushed it away. "I'll get down to the docks and have a look at that warehouse. I guess Schultzie's gonna be there."

"I cabled this morning. Make it about nine o'clock. You might want to check on space for the gear we've got coming in."

Dreier stared at the mirror across the bar and passed his fingers through the shock of hair that tumbled down his forehead.

"I sure hope there's oil in that swamp," he said.

"Look, my friend." Hawthorn turned in his bucket chair and faced the big man. "I'd like to tell you how important this job is."

"I know it's important. Don't worry about it."

"You only know half of it, Sandy."

Dreier returned Hawthorn's serious look.

"I never heard you talk like that before, boss. It was always a kind of a checkers game, but this here . . ."

"More like a war?"

Dreier thought a moment.

"Yessir. A damn war."

Hawthorn was quiet now. That's what was going on. A war. But he couldn't tell his artillery what the target was.

Hawthorn had been warned about Jeffry Burrowes.

Jeffry Burrowes occupied the position of minister of Petroleum, Lands, and Mines because someone thought he had a degree from Oxford. He was fat, black, balding, and forty-two years old. He had been appointed by the governor as a surrogate until new and hopefully honest elections could be held. He was blessed at birth with a magnificent black wart that rode above his eyes in the middle of his forehead like a mighty badge of honor.

In many ways, then, a rather unimpressive man. But now, if one were to hear him tell it, *now*, with exploration once again in progress and with the probable discovery of the earth's richest petroleum reservoir only weeks away, he was becoming one of the most important men in the country. They were saying he was more important than the governor himself. His name appeared in the local press, he spoke on the radio, and he was invited to speak at weddings and banquets across the country. He had even been invited to speak in Trinidad, but there were no funds available for the trip.

Hawthorn had never met the man face to face. Now, at ten o'clock in the morning, as the sun began to bake the street, he mounted the steps to the country's Victorian government house and structured his presentation again in his mind. Inside he asked directions at the entrance desk and was shown the way to Burrowes's office. He knocked and went directly in.

It was a shoddy room very much like the old postmaster's office in Tulsa, with dirty yellow walls and a high ceiling where a fan turned slowly. The minister's desk was broad and wide, and very old. His leather chair was torn at the seams, where his fingers played on the armrests. There were three windows in wooden casements veiled by English curtains that had tassels hanging from them where they were fastened to the sides.

Minister Burrowes introduced himself, the large, black wart going up and down as he exercised a common nervous twitch. Then he introduced the two men at his side, Mr. Thomas Knight and Mr. Cobley Driver. They were his aides, he said.

He invited Hawthorn to sit in a comfortable chair opposite the desk while he seated himself in his leather executive chair, one aide on either side, armed with pencils and folders.

"Your trip was satisfactory, Mr. Hawthorn. I can see that. You look rested, sir. Allow me to extend my personal welcome to our country, on behalf of my colleagues and on the behalf of my government, sir."

"Thank you, sir."

"Ah, you have been to the site, I understand. The well sites, I mean."

"Yes. I've been there several times. I like what I saw. We expect to begin with the actual drilling soon. I believe you know that we've probed the area quite carefully. We're only waiting for the heavy equipment now, and the well caps."

"The well caps, you say. Oh good Lord, yes! The well caps," Burrowes sputtered. "We don't want the stuff spilling all over the ground then, do we? And the other things?"

"All aboard the *Tengen Maru*, sir, due in the morning I believe. Your customs people could be helpful there, might help us to expedite transfer to our warehouse. It's all duty free of course."

70

"Good heavens, yes. Duty free, by all means, sir. Everything is duty free." He turned to his aide. "Mr. Knight, make a note. Be there yourself, you see? Be there personally. Make certain the caps are freed up *immejutleh!*" He said the word like an English parliamentarian.

"Also," he added quickly, "contact the harbor master to get the exact arrival time. Yes, yes, sonny, do it now. Go on!"

Knight jumped out of the chair and disappeared.

"Anything else, then? Anything at all? Perhaps you have some other needs?" He looked at the other young man.

"All right, Driver, go on! Go on!"

Cobley Driver, too, left the room.

"Yes. Other needs," he said again. "You have fuel and lubricating oil? From Esso, I think? Arrangements have been made for that, have they not?"

Lord! Hawthorn thought. *This man can easily be managed, but Lord!*

"That's correct, sir. We've had a man here for almost two years, Mr. Minister. But there is the question of personnel training I would like to discuss."

"Training, you say. Good heavens, I am for that, you see."

In the next half hour they concluded an arrangement that covered job interviews, a training location, union regulations and policies, transportation of workers, and pay-for-learning wages. The minister was delighted with the prospect of employing upward of eighty people in his very poor country.

"Now then. The establishment of controls. How does that look, Mr. Hawthorn?"

Hawthorn explained in some detail how the system of volume monitoring would work, finding it difficult to keep his eyes away from the mammoth wart bobbing up and down as Burrowes nodded continuously.

When he was satisfied that he had covered the most important points, Hawthorn stopped, but the minister continued nodding. Hawthorn was sure Burrowes had understood little or nothing of his simple explanation.

"Well, now then. Yes. I shall inspect it, you see. Good heavens, man! We don't want to lose any, do we? We don't want to misplace any, do we?" He paused a moment.

"How could we lose any? A few hundred barrels a day? That would add up, wouldn't it?"

Hawthorn wasn't sure if Burrowes was verifying the system's integrity, or if he was asking for a private little pipeline with his name on it.

"Your own men will walk the line with our men, day and night,"

Hawthorn said. "There will be a constant check on the flow with special equipment. We may lose a little, maybe one-fiftieth of one percent from wellhead to barge. But with temperature conversions back to sixty degrees, it all comes out in the wash."

"An error of, say, *half* a percent? Could we lose that much, do you think?"

"Doubtful, sir." *Balls!* The man was talking about four million bucks a year!

"Well, now. That seems to be in excellent condition, Mr. Hawthorn. We shall see as we move along. I will want to inspect it personally, you see. That must be clearly understood, sir." Burrowes patted the top of his head to straighten a hair.

"Now then, I am aware that the campsite is not exactly downtown Port of Spain. I am aware of that. You and your people will want to stay here in Georgetown from time to time. I have made arrangements for you to stay at a very nice place on Victoria way, a flat that will accommodate three . . . or six." He said it seriously, then he grinned, showing large white teeth. "I think you will find it quite comfortable, Mr. Hawthorn."

"That's very thoughtful, sir."

"And a maid. I have arranged for a maid. Those extra touches, sir." He slapped the desk with an open palm. "Who knows, I may bring a lady one evening for drinks. We shall see." He giggled. "Yes. We shall see."

Dreier was at the hotel when Hawthorn finally finished with his morning chore. The engineer gave him a report on the situation at the warehouse, suggested they plan on dinner with Schultz later on.

It was after noon by the time they checked out of the Tower and found a taxi. Hawthorn gave the driver the address Burrowes had given him, and they moved into small-town congestion.

The streets were broad, well maintained, a center strip planted with trees serving the pedestrian traffic. Their route turned and meandered through the city, taking them past old English and Dutch houses graced with frilled woodwork.

Everywhere they looked there were people walking, talking, women with baskets on their heads, children in blue school uniforms, taxis and lorries, and donkey-pulled carts plodding down the middle of the road, ignoring the honking and the shouts of motorists.

The city of Georgetown was below sea level, protected from tidal inundation by a system of dikes and seawalls that had been built by the

Dutch two centuries before. At that elevation, and with no breeze whatsoever, it was miserably warm.

Globe's flat was a spacious apartment with three bedrooms, kitchen and bath, and a wooden porch that looked out over the sea wall onto the chocolate waters of the Atlantic. Here, a delightful breeze rippled the white curtains and flowed through the huge living room that was furnished comfortably, English-style.

They found cold drinks in the refrigerator, settled themselves on the balcony, and watched the afternoon come on.

"Well? How about this, Sandy? Want your wife to come back down and try it again?" Hawthorn waved his hand around. "Not all that bad."

"No, sir. I don't much like the politics. Thanks anyway. I'll spend my time down in the camp, sir. I guess if the ground's got any oil I can most likely find it."

Hawthorn wanted to tell him now, let his man know what he was in for. But that was against the rules, rules he had doubted at first but agreed with now.

"You think there's oil down there?"

"Now that you ask, no. Shell would have hung on tighter."

"They had reasons to get out, Sandy. I'll explain it to you some time."

They spent the afternoon going over charts and budget figures. Hawthorn gave Sandy a list of telephone numbers to use for emergencies, and set up an appointment for a day later in the week when Dreier could check in with the embassy, a courtesy Hawthorn had learned not to ignore. He also outlined the main points of the morning's discussion with Burrowes.

"Get to know that man, Sandy. He's odd, he's pompous, he's an honest pain in the ass. But get to know him. We're going to wrap that guy up in a neat little package and use the hell out of him. He's not as slow as people might think."

The sun was almost down when the telephone rang. Hawthorn answered it.

"Mr. Hawthorn, my name is Carlysle Ramprashad. I wonder if you might kindly have an hour or so to share with me this evening, sir?"

"In what connection, Mr. Ramprashad?"

"The oil, sir. In connection with the oil. Prime Minister Jagan would like you to know his position, to understand his position regarding the petroleum, sir."

Jagan. He wanted to get his oar in. The alleged Communist was three years out on his duff, and he still thought of himself as the head man. He wanted to let the Americans know that he still considered himself the people's choice.

"Can we discuss this on the phone, sir?"

"I think not, Mr. Hawthorn. It is a delicate matter."

Hawthorn would be picked up at eight o'clock. There was plenty of time between now and then, between his three years of plotting and tonight's confrontation with the victim, to have a bite of dinner.

CHAPTER 2

They drove in Carlysle Ramprashad's white BMW to a small hotel on the East Bank Road. There was a minimum of polite conversation during the fifteen-minute ride. Ramprashad spent most of the time explaining the division of races that characterized British Guiana's politics and its social system.

"So you see, Mr. Hawthorn," he said as they parked, "the East Indians want only what is good for the country, since that is good for them as well. I cannot speak for the Chinese because they are such a small segment of the population, or for the Negroes, or for the few British, only for my comrades in the East Indian population."

Ramprashad continued his pitch as he turned the key, rolling the window up against thieves or vandals. "Mr. Jagan was never given a chance, then, in 1953. He led our party to a deserved victory based on his campaign to decolonize this poor country, to extend the vote to our people." He looked across at Hawthorn. "That doesn't seem much to ask for, sir. But the Crown would have none of it. The British stepped in and suspended our newly won constitution. We see that as an unfortunate postponement of our destiny, the destiny of a free and a democratic nation."

They got out and Hawthorn followed Ramprashad into the hotel and to a private dining room overlooking the seawall. Three men at a table rose and extended their hands as Ramprashad and Hawthorn approached. They introduced themselves, bowing slightly. Hawthorn would try, but he would not remember their names. They took chairs at the table and Hawthorn politely refused a drink. Ramprashad began.

"As we have been discussing, Mr. Hawthorn, the East Indian in British Guiana has been denied his rights for many years. We are hard workers and we deserve the opportunity to plant and to prosper along with everyone else. We will not, this evening, try to convince you of our political philosophy, but please do not believe those who will try to say that we are Communists. That is not true, sir. We are Socialists, and we will very soon have the opportunity we are seeking, the chance that was taken away by the British action shortly ago, the chance to achieve our own destinies."

Ramprashad spoke very well, carefully and softly, almost in a feminine voice. If there was hostility there, Hawthorn was unable to detect it. He listened, his hands folded on the table. The others were listening as well, nodding and agreeing with their spokesman.

"When the elections are held, sir, Mr. Jagan will win and I will become the minister of Petroleum, Lands, and Mines. That means the end of Mr. Burrowes, of course, but it does not mean the end of our relationship with you, sir, with the Globe Corporation. We want to work with you under the most advantageous conditions. We will honor your agreements and we will endeavor to strengthen our ties with the rest of the Caribbean as you have suggested on a number of occasions.

"Now, Mr. Hawthorn, I must ask you to clarify a few points; your response will determine our approach to several important policy matters. But first, do you have any questions about our sincerity, or our desire to work in close harmony with the company and the country you represent?"

Perfect! "The company and the country you represent." It was the opening Hawthorn wanted.

"Gentlemen," he said, pausing to light a cigarette. He blew on the match and placed it carefully in the ashtray. "I think I had better make my own position clear to you." He paused again, for effect this time, allowing his eyes to wander from face to face.

"I do not represent my country, or any country. Nor do I represent my company. I *am* my company. Let there be no doubt in your minds, *none*, that I run my business as I see fit."

He stopped again to let that point sink in. His eyes were hard now, a shaded overhead lamp casting the suggestion of a deep shadow across his brow, his voice fairly rumbling over the table.

"I am in the business of finding oil, my friends. And when I find it, I bring it to the market and I sell it to the man or to the country that will pay me the best price. I will stop short of that only when I have certain knowledge that a potential customer is a thief or a murderer or a war mongerer, and I can't be dead certain about the last one. That is my position, gentlemen. I am here for only a short time and I intend to make the best deal I can and live the best way I can. My record will suggest to you that I have done that very successfully up to now, and I don't feel like changing a helluva lot."

He paused, took a deep drag on his cigarette, and exhaled slowly, looking directly at each man again. Then he riveted his attention to the future minister of Petroleum, Lands, and Mines.

"Does that answer your question, Mr. Ramprashad?"

It took him several seconds. He swallowed.

"Yes. Yes! Most emphatically it does. It does, sir."

CHAPTER 3

The day after Easter Sunday, 1957, Gregory Hawthorn's secretary politely dropped a courier-delivered envelope on his desk as she was leaving for the afternoon. He thanked her, opened the envelope and read the few lines:

"Mr. Hawthorn:

I have been following your activities in the Caribbean region with considerable interest, noting with particular enthusiasm your work in British Guiana. Since these are the areas of my own concern, it would give me pleasure to meet with you in the hope that we might find it to our mutual advantage, engaging in a frank and open discussion of the opportunities that present themselves and the problems that confront us both. Please call me at your convenience to arrange such a friendly meeting."

It was signed by Josef Podgorsky, Russian Trade Office, Washington, D.C. Hawthorn let the note slip to his desktop and slowly turned in his swivel chair to look out the window. In the distance he could see smoke filtering skyward from stacks at the Humble refinery, seven miles away. He watched the smoke join the evening clouds and trail off to the east where the higher wind gained control.

"Bingo!" he said softly to himself.

They met in the Washington Hilton in a room maintained by the Russian Office under an American corporate name. Hawthorn had done his homework.

Josef Podgorsky was a man in his late forties, a Russian citizen and a member of Moscow's "quiet circle." He traveled with diplomatic immunity and was known in Washington for his influential role in

76

stabilizing east–west oil movements between Rumania and Germany. He was, in fact, the man responsible for the pipeline route that supplied much of Germany's heating oil from the Ploesti region. It was also surmised that he was involved in, if not the head of, a very complicated and very effective agency network in the southern Americas. His office was undoubtedly the switchboard and the clearing house for vital information that found its way back to Moscow through couriers and other less mundane carriers.

He was as tall as Hawthorn, with a receding blond hairline and a good slavic face. Hawthorn guessed he had been something of an athlete as a younger man.

They were alone in the room, but Hawthorn reminded himself that the room would be wired, almost certainly. Podgorsky offered to pour drinks, then made himself a light Scotch and soda when Hawthorn refused. They wasted little time in getting down to the business of "mutual advantage."

"It would be surprising to me, sir," Podgorsky began, "if you came here without researching me and the work I do. Please let me assure you, sir, I have nothing to hide; I am not a member of a secret bureau or anything like that. I am in the United States on a mission to develop ties with our Latin American friends and with other countries in the area, to assist them in their development if we can and to gain the trust and the trade—selfishly I might add—of those who feel inclined to be our allies."

He was watching Hawthorn closely, prepared to defend himself against the sundry challenges he was accustomed to receive as a spokesman for Soviet doctrine. His facial expression was friendly, a practiced countenance he had learned to develop in America.

"Should you have any reservations about our talking together, I beg you to dismiss them. I have conversations with many Americans in your position, and none of them have been branded as 'pinkos' to my knowledge." He smiled broadly, showing teeth that were brown and crooked.

"I have no such reservations, sir," Hawthorn answered, "and as you have guessed, I do know something about you and your office. You've done a great deal for your country in the interests of world cooperation. No, sir. I have no reservations about meeting with you and speaking freely. I am a businessman, sir."

"That being the case, Mr. Hawthorn, let us get directly to the matter. Would you lease your ships to my country, given the proper set of circumstances?"

"Lease them? No, I doubt it, Mr. Podgorsky, but I might charter them on contract, by voyage or on some time arrangement."

"You want to keep your flag and your own crews, then?"

"For now, yes. I think so, sir."

Podgorsky fell silent. He sipped his drink and lit a black cigarette. Then he cleared his throat. "You have, what is it now, eighteen vessels already? And they are fully occupied?"

"Nearly so, yes. I plan on buying three more this year."

"I would judge most of them 'handy-size' carriers."

"Now, Mr. Podgorsky, I'll wager you have the name and the gross tonnage of every ship in my little family."

The Russian smiled again. "Good! We shall come back to your fleet another time. Please believe me, sir, we might definitely be interested. I don't like dealing with that Greek."

"Niarchos?"

"Him. Perhaps when your ships are not so fully occupied." Podgorsky cleared his throat again. "Then tell me how it looks in British Guiana, Mr. Hawthorn. How do you see that poor country's future?"

"British Guiana." Hawthorn repeated. "All right, I suppose I see Cheddi Jagan winning the elections this year, in late summer I believe, and the People's Political Party will take control again. I would imagine a development along those lines might please you."

"Jagan? Oh, I'm not at all certain of that. I don't much like the man. His wife is a Communist, of course, from Chicago! Did you know that? She runs the show, not him." Podgorsky rubbed his chin. "That will be touch and go for us, I think. The British and the Canadians are too well entrenched there to give us much encouragement."

Hawthorn didn't believe any of it. He decided to turn the question on Podgorsky.

"And your view? I have a sizeable investment there, as you know. My men have started constructing a pipeline and a headwater harbor. Tank steel is on order. I expect to find oil down there pretty soon. I would value your opinion, Mr. Podgorsky. What will happen to me, to my investments in British Guiana, when Cheddi takes over?"

"Nothing. You are afraid of some act that may nationalize the industry, take your investments away. No, I don't think so. As I said, the British are there and they won't allow it."

"But the country will gain its independence."

"Or the people will revolt? Or both? Not for some time, sir. I think your investment is safe. But let us pursue that point for a moment." Podgorsky turned in his chair.

"What makes you think there might be petroleum in British Guiana? Shell was there for some time, and they sold it to you for a pittance."

Hawthorn was waiting for that. "Do you remember what happened in 1933, Mr. Podgorsky? When Jersey Standard bought the Creole field from Indiana?"

"A classic example of Western capitalism." Podgorsky smiled. "I never cease to be amused at how clumsy it is." He nodded at the American. "But Shell is not short of capital, Mr. Hawthorn. In fact, they sold you a . . . help me, please. . . ."

"Pig in a poke," Hawthorn offered.

"A pig in a poke. I learned that expression on a trip to Iowa, sir. No . . ." His smile disappeared. "The elements are not the same. They gave up for some reason."

"I'm afraid I can't disclose that reason, sir, but in fact, the elements are very much the same. I will help you out by suggesting that there's too much oil on the market now. Shell is up to its ass in petroleum in other places, and they have better uses for their money. Frankly, sir, they know damn well there's oil in that country, but they don't know how much, and they're not willing to gamble. I am."

Podgorsky was prepared to let it go at that for the moment.

"All right, let us suppose you do find oil in some worthwhile quantity. What do you intend to do with it?"

"I believe I would sell it, sir, to a buyer who has the cash to pay for it."

"In today's market? You just said it yourself, Mr. Hawthorn. There is a glut in the world market. Who wants your expensive oil when they can buy high-grade Libyan crude for a dollar a barrel?"

"That's today. Tomorrow there will be a shortage. That's one guarantee I'll make to you. Then there is the matter of proximity to the user. Western customers will always take oil from this hemisphere if it's low sulfur, low vanadium, low wax oil, because it's closer to home, cheaper and less vulnerable to the ups and downs of Arabian politics."

"You expect the Guianese oil to be low sulfur and low wax?"

"And low vanadium."

"Optimistic."

"Realistic."

Podgorsky stood now, walked to the kitchenette, and poured himself another Scotch.

"Would you sell your oil, your Guianese oil, to Russia?"

Hawthorn answered as rehearsed.

"If you pay me in dollars and give me the shipping contract, yes. Providing the State Department doesn't close me down." He paused. "But I can't imagine why you would want my oil, in this hemisphere. You have enough of your own." *It was worth a small risk.* "And you don't have any customers."

"Curiosity, sir. Idle curiosity."

Hawthorn had prepared himself for this meeting as carefully as a surgeon might prepare for the correction of an aneurysm. But he had expected a polite, nondefinitive give and take revolving around politics, economics, and the future outlook of the petroleum industry. What he was getting was a hard-core probe. Is that the way it was supposed to work? Did a foreign agent simply pop the question and ask for the secret microfilm just like that? What would he say to somebody in his business who was giving him a snow job?

"I don't believe that, sir." Hawthorn said. "I don't think you indulge in idle curiosity."

Podgorsky did not respond. Instead he approached Hawthorn, stopped beside his chair, and looked intently into his face.

"When, Mr. Hawthorn? When do you expect these wells of yours to be on stream?"

Podgorsky's slavic brow was furrowed. This was very definitely not idle.

"In less than a year. Make it the middle of 1958. I trust you can keep that information within your own community, Mr. Podgorsky. It's not the kind of data I share with my competitors in the free-enterprise system."

Podgorsky smiled.

"You could hardly resist that, could you?"

Hawthorn started to feel it as he drove off in the taxi, a feeling of excitement, of elation. On the plane, he thought back to their conversation, replayed it to himself, made hard mental notes of Podgorsky's questions and the answers he had supplied. They were taking the bait; the little tugs on his line were solid evidence that he had the right can of worms.

He arrived back at his apartment very late. Baton Rouge was a good place to live, but it was too damn hot. At least in his penthouse there was a breeze from the river side. But that was hardly enough to cool him off when he finished his telephone report to Alan Drinkwater.

Talking to London was tough enough. Talking in code about "grandmother's relationship with the county commissioner" and "Fred's reaction to the news concerning a possible gold mine in his own backyard" was damn near impossible. But it was the other part, the part that could be managed in plain English, that ruined his day.

"I'm afraid you have some bad news, Gregory. I received word this afternoon from Sir Hillman that the fellow in British Guiana, the rancher who owns the ground you're digging next to . . . what's his name . . . ?"

"Thaddeus Bishop. What about him, Alan?"

"He has filed an injunction against you. The bloody magistrate has posted no-trespassing signs from one end of his property to the other. You have no route to the river, Gregory."

Bishop's land, the four hundred square miles of hard ground that separated Globe from the river, was off limits. Hawthorn now had two choices: lay a pipeline in quicksand, or start to build an airport that could handle barges.

CHAPTER 4

These were not the best of times for Alan Drinkwater. He had survived the winter of '57 passing well, though the cold and the damp had permeated his London flat like a wet towel, and the little office on Water Street was hot and dry beyond reasonable endurance. His sinusitus was so severe his housekeeper had given up on the handkerchiefs and laid in a stock of tissues.

He was still angry with John Foster Dulles, though he had never met the man, for botching up the Guatemala affair with his United Fruit Company spy force. That, however, was a private feud between himself and his own ego. Alan Drinkwater believed he should have been consulted by the CIA and he had not been.

None of this, however, affected his business with the Commission or his on-going relationship with Gregory Hawthorn and the Globe Corporation. The Podgorsky connection had given him enormous pleasure, just as much as if he had personally confronted the Russian and managed the interview himself, according to his own script.

On this particular day in May he was going finally to lay down his professorial chalk and be finished with that duty. And later in the day he would do what he had wanted to do for several years, revisit the beautiful country of Haiti. It had been a long time since he was there. Hawthorn and the new fellow, Reinaldo Villar-Cruz, were already at the hotel, he would wager, basking in the sun and leaving the creative thinking, the really sticky thinking, up to him.

He was not happy with developments in British Guiana. He knew that if the British could have mustered up the courage they would have dumped the sad little colony long ago, and he was afraid that this time, after Cheddi Jagan and his band of rascals gained power, the British might do exactly that. Such a development could play into the

Commission's hands, of course, opening the way for the Russian show of strength they were counting on, but he had no faith in Jagan. The man was an enigma, worse by far than Fidel Castro. One could never guess what course he might take, and two of the three available to him would destroy the Globe project altogether.

Drinkwater was getting tired. He had not received the credit he thought he should for his work of the last few years. Not that a man must be given full marks when he hasn't earned them, but surely now and then, from time to time, when it was appropriate.

Of one thing he was very certain: this would be his last lecture series at the university. His views were neither popular nor were they even remotely believeable in 1956 and 1957; they would become even less important during the coming decade, he knew.

His continuing theme was the collision course of man with nature, his warnings were preachments against waste. His favorite lecture, his most dramatic of the series, fell on the ears of men and women who were not in the slightest concerned with the future of their environment.

On this day there were twenty-five or thirty students and a few outside visitors, but nearly two-thirds of the theater was empty. He had paraded up and down past the huge screen with its slides and charts, and had pointed with some enthusiasm at the posterboard presentation he had developed to demonstrate the growth of fossil fuel consumption since 1932. He was about to complete his time-line graphic, the zenith of all his stage appearances.

Walking around the periphery of the large room, he slowly unrolled a wide red ribbon, which an assistant, following close behind, pinned to the wall so that it completely encircled the audience. As he progressed, foot by foot, Drinkwater described the point in time where he was standing, beginning with a tremendous explosion that rocked the universe and sent a hot metallic ball hurtling into space. He passed the ice ages and the first generations of beasts, buried and resurrected a billion more generations of plant and animal life, and came finally back to the platform again.

"And here we are, my friends," he said, "at recorded history. Note that I shall allow the Chinese first place, here!" He stabbed at a spot on the ribbon to dramatize his questionable conclusion. He moved his finger an inch to the left.

"Here we have the Greeks." He moved one more inch. "Here the birth of Christ. Do you begin to see my point? Look around you, look at the passing of time. I have measured a billion years in a hundred feet, and now we are measuring a thousand years per inch!"

He paused to allow the students to turn their heads and look at the walls, but only a few did so.

"Now pay close attention to me!" he said. "I shall take this piece of thread and tape it across the ribbon here, at this point." He stretched a length of common black sewing thread across the red ribbon at right angles and taped it in place.

"If I set the tip of my pencil on the right side of this thread I shall be pointing at the year 1858, the year Colonel Drake produced oil out of the world's first well. For all of these millions of years"—he swung his arm slowly around the room, pointing at the ribbon—"the good earth was creating oil for your generation . . . an ounce per hour perhaps? A gallon a day? As much as that, do you think? And here! At this point in time"—he stopped and raised his arm high over his head and brought the pencil point down on the other edge of the thread line—"here is where the oil is all gone!"

He turned to face his small audience, surprised that they were beginning to applaud. He had surely given this performance his best effort, but only rarely did the students even nod their heads, to say nothing of clapping their hands.

"In two hundred years, my good friends—let us be overgenerous and credit the best of mankind with some conservation sense—say in three hundred years, but not a day more, *there will be no more oil!*"

He shouted the words and the audience stopped clapping. But he went on. The crucial point was yet to be made, the point that had driven him to a world of international espionage.

"Imagine it," he said, softly now. "Try to imagine the day when the world will have to accept the terrible truth, when the world's leaders will be forced to acknowledge the fact that there is oil enough to last five more years, no longer. Imagine the day, my friends, when crude oil is more precious than blood!"

He paused and found his handkerchief, mopped his forehead.

"Mankind has waged war for reasons that are far less compelling, my friends. We have seen nothing. We have seen nothing compared to the battle that will be waged to control the last remaining oil well. Nothing! *Nothing!*"

In the back of the room, a man dressed in a black suit and wearing a chauffeur's cap got up and quietly left the theater. He had heard the lecture as many as a dozen times before. He enjoyed this part, the theatrics of it, but he knew that Drinkwater would spend the next eight and one-half minutes describing how civilization would react when the crisis situation was fully understood. It was a powerful climax to his series, but the chauffeur didn't care to hear it again. He stood on the front steps until finally people started to come out. When he saw Drinkwater he met him halfway and took the small briefcase, led the way down the steps to a waiting Bentley, and opened the door.

"Well, Harris? What did you think?" Drinkwater sat back and waited as Harris started the car and made his way into the light traffic.

"A fitting performance as your finale, sir. I believe it might have been your best. Was it BOAC or Pan Am, sir?"

"Pan American, Harris. Yes, I think it was probably my best."

Drinkwater relaxed in the backseat and put his hands in his lap. In a few moments he was asleep. The driver woke him at the Pan Am loading area, helped him with the two small cases he was taking, then tipped his hat, got back in the car, and drove off.

An hour later the plane was crossing over the Bristol Channel, heading for New York City. Drinkwater sat in the rear and read a magazine, drank a small amount of sherry, ate one sandwich, and then settled back to sleep for the remainder of the flight.

In New York he asked for directions and walked briskly to a small bus that took him to the Air France ticket counter. He finished the check-in process and had time for a cup of coffee before departure. There would be two stops enroute and he would arrive well after dark.

He was carrying with him a number of weighty concerns. There was the Bishop affair. That a clod such as he should be allowed to interfere with the workings of the Commission was intolerable. That he should be doing it for personal gain—and what other reason could it be—was positively criminal.

There was the Podgorsky-Hawthorn meeting. They had two full days to discuss their response to Podgorsky's overture, but in view of some other disquieting news he was going to spring on Hawthorn, the discussion could take somewhat longer.

There was the question of Cheddi Jagan, and there was the matter of timing. Fidel Castro was making the headlines again. Soon, certainly within two years, he would be knocking at the gates of Havana, and he would be asking the Russians for oil. Hawthorn had to produce it for them, not too soon, not too late.

One matter he had already solved and solved well, he thought. For over two years he had kept his eye on a young man in Colombia, a man who had applied to his own country's secret service and been recommended to the Commission by a Drinkwater agent within the Colombian network.

His name was Reinaldo Villar-Cruz. His curriculum vitae qualified him for a position at the highest level of academia, but he had chosen the service. Magna cum laude from Stanford, four languages, cryptography, political science—the boy was a genius. A pity he was so diminutive in size, so plain in appearance. He would have made a marvelous politician.

And now he was on the Globe team. Drinkwater closed his eyes, hoping as he drifted off that Gregory Hawthorn would one day appreciate the Commission's good sense in its people recruitment practices.

It was nearly midnight when the Air France Viscount bounced to a landing in Haiti and rolled along the bumpy airstrip to park in front of the shabby little terminal building. Drinkwater was the only passenger to disembark, the others heading farther south to spend their tropic vacations in Trinidad, or in Martinique. The terminal was dark except for the yellow-lighted customs clearance counter. There Alan Drinkwater declared himself and was allowed to pass.

Had this been his first time in Haiti or his first visit to the hotel he would have wondered at its name. But he had stayed at the Olaffson several times, including once during the war when he was assigned to the Office of Naval Intelligence and was looking into the matter of German provisioning in French Antilles waters.

He did not expect to find anyone at the hotel up to greet him, but sitting in the quaint, dark lobby was Reinaldo Villar-Cruz, his bright and promising recruit. Drinkwater dropped his suitcases on the floor and stood to face him as the young man rose from his chair.

"Well," said Drinkwater. "Look who we have here!"

"Good morning, sir." Villar-Cruz smiled. "You've come in very late."

"Delayed, my boy. Fog and drizzle and bloody mechanics. The flipping pilot got lost, I believe."

Villar-Cruz was wearing horn-rimmed glasses. His jet black hair was combed neatly, with a sharp part down the right side.

"Here, let me get your bags, sir." Villar-Cruz stood only an inch or two taller than the Englishman, but his frame was neatly assembled, well balanced. "We checked you in already, room two-eleven. We can go right up."

"Where's Hawthorn? In his bed, I suppose." They were winding their way up the beautiful staircase that rose gracefully from the foyer to the balcony floor.

"No, sir. He's in the sitting room at the end of the hall. I expect he saw you arrive."

"Indeed I did," Hawthorn said. He was standing at the railing looking down on them as they ascended.

"Clever of you to find a taxi this late."

"Taxi, my giddy aunt!" countered the older man. "More a bloody rickshaw!"

Drinkwater stopped at the landing, puffed, finished the climb, and shook Hawthorn's hand.

"All right," he said abruptly. "Let's get on with it."

"It's one in the morning, Alan."

"Come on." He gave the American a nudge, then followed him down the hall to a common sitting room with a balcony that looked out over the garden. The atmosphere was very French, with wrought iron furnishings and a delicate fleur-de-lis valance skirting the portico.

Drinkwater stopped, bent toward Hawthorn.

"Safe, I suppose. We can talk?"

"Reinaldo checked it, Alan. It's safe."

Drinkwater cocked his head in the direction of their bedrooms where Villar-Cruz had gone with his suitcase.

"Well? What do you think?"

"Think? About what, Alan?"

"Him."

"Reinaldo? I think he's fine. He's a good man." Hawthorn wondered for a moment if he was supposed to think something else.

"Fine. Very good." Drinkwater paused, looked about for a place to sit. "Then let's hear about this Bishop business." He lowered himself into a wicker chair.

Hawthorn described the problem. The Globe concession began eighteen miles east of the Demerara River and stretched for over fifty miles on relatively hard ground. To the south was a mud dish that ran from the river, bordering the concession. The only route from the camp to the river that was suitable for a pipeline crossed directly over the eighteen-mile-wide piece of land that was owned by the Canadian playboy Thaddeus T. Bishop.

"I can't go around him, Alan. It would be like laying a pipeline over quicksand."

"Buy the bugger out."

"He won't sell. He won't even talk to us. He wants his land and he doesn't care about the country or the oil."

"How about the courts, national interest, that sort of thing."

"We've already started that, but we're looking at a year, maybe longer to settle it that way."

"What if he dies?"

"He has no heirs. It reverts to the government."

Drinkwater wiped his forehead and his nose.

"Well, then?"

He tossed the handkerchief onto the small table at his side. Hawthorn was looking at his bulbous nose.

"Well, then, what?" he asked.

Reinaldo Villar-Cruz came into the room and found a chair, adjusted his horn-rimmed spectacles. Drinkwater concentrated on him for a second.

"Reinaldo shall we allow this Bishop to destroy our project?"

"No, sir."

"Shall we shoot him, then?"

"Alan, for God's sake. You can't be serious." Hawthorn lit a cigarette. "Listen, it's the middle of May and Castro is nowhere near Havana." He blew smoke into the garden air. "If I go full steam ahead, I'll finish my tanks and my pipeline and the harbor and the whole project way ahead of schedule. One thing I don't want to do is discover oil a year ahead of your damn timetable and then have to sit on it while your Caribbean kettle comes to a good boil."

"Quite right, Gregory. That would be awkward. The timing of this affair is a matter we must discuss at some length. I had it on my agenda. Speaking of which, I suspect you've come up with some clever way to make crude oil appear where there is none."

"Of course. That was the easy part. But we're talking about Bishop now. I'm going to suggest that we *use* his injunction. Hell, we're stuck with it anyway. We can do some construction, finish the river harbor, finish the field tanks, go about our business, but hold off on the drilling until the court case is settled. Oh, we can drill a few holes, test wells."

"Delay. I should think the people at the site would start asking questions, Gregory. How long has that fellow Schultz been there?"

"A couple years, Alan. But that's no big thing. Tidewater had a team over there in Libya for nearly seven years. BP was in Iran for over twelve years before they smelled a drop of oil."

"Yes, I understand that. I assure you I do. All right then. Use the Bishop injunction is what you suggest. Use it to buy time."

"More than that. Control the timing. It's a blessing in disguise."

"Possibly, yes." Drinkwater was stuffing his pipe. "But how do you 'control the timing,' then? You can't very well tell the courts when to grant a release and discharge the case."

"In a roundabout way I can. In order to settle this matter, it may be necessary to go to the courts in England. There are a hundred ways to slow things down and speed them up under any system."

"Not bloody likely, sir. Not under British law, sir."

"I've spoken to the governor," Hawthorn said. "In this case, with the blessing of the crown, it can be done."

"You've spoken to Sir Hillman, you say." Drinkwater massaged his chin. "Yes, well, under the circumstances, if it can be managed with Her Majesty's permission . . ."

Hawthorn tossed his cigarette over the rail into the garden below. It sailed, tracing a pretty arc as it fell. He was unaccustomed to the feeling of acting under supervision, of getting permission to handle what he considered minor matters. At the moment, he knew his decision was right; he was humoring an older citizen.

Drinkwater paused to light his pipe. "All right. Give it a go. I trust you know what you're doing." He blew a cloud of smoke into the darkness. "Just keep me posted, for heaven's sake."

"Now then," he continued. "Tell me about the oil. How will you do it?"

Hawthorn smiled. "No, Alan. That's all mine for the time being."

"Come now!" Drinkwater lowered his pipe.

"Sorry, old man."

"And you should be, sir! It is my show!"

"I'll tell you as soon as I have the details worked out."

"The details. I must wait for the bloody details." He glanced across at Villar-Cruz. "I must report to the Commission that I am not allowed to know how my operation is to be conducted. Then perhaps I should hold back on my pretty little piece of information as well." He was pouting now, playing with his pipe.

"Don't worry, Alan. I'll let you know some time next week. How about a brandy?"

"No, thank you. Do I judge correctly that my information is unimportant to you?"

Hawthorn was grinning. "No, certainly not. Go ahead."

"Yes. Ah, then, what if I were to tell you that the Russians are planning on depositing a spy in your camp?"

"A what? A spy?"

"An agent. How would that affect your plans?"

Hawthorn turned in his chair. He edged closer.

"You're joking, Alan."

"No. It is not a joke."

"A Russian spy? Affect my plans? You're damn right it would affect my plans! What are you talking about?"

Drinkwater had the upper hand now. He relaxed and struck a match, held it to his pipe, and sucked noisily.

"His name is Moffit, Stephen Moffit. He was released from a Korean prisoner of war camp last spring and is presently undergoing a debriefing and rehabilitation course in Virginia."

It took a moment for that to register.

"Wait a second. This guy's an American?" Hawthorn looked at Villar-Cruz, then back at Drinkwater again. "A Russian spy . . . an American." He paused. "That's crazy."

Drinkwater was silent, allowing Hawthorn to work on the idea.

"How do you know this, Alan? Who comes around and gives you that kind of information?"

"That will be my secret, Gregory. You have yours, I have mine." Drinkwater took a final puff and set his pipe on the balcony floor.

"See here," he said quietly. "I'm deadly serious, I'm afraid. I honestly cannot tell you my sources. The fact of the matter is, the man is a trained agent, and he has been assigned to you. He has been schooled in river engineering, demolition, geology, plumbing, electronics, communications, weaponry, and—bless us—and in petroleum exploration. He is also a pilot, a military pilot."

"Good Lord!" Hawthorn whispered. "Good Lord!"

"Can you deal with that?"

Hawthorn thought a brief moment.

"I can shoot the bastard," he said.

"You seem to be selective in whom you may and whom you may not execute, sir."

Hawthorn had no reply to that.

"Well, you can't shoot this one. Not possibly. They would send another and then another. You would have a full-time firing squad at work."

Hawthorn got up and stepped to the rail, leaned on it, swore softly to himself. There were no sounds in the night other than the night sounds of the insects, the breeze rustling the palm fronds. Hawthorn turned again, spoke deliberately.

"How much do you know about this guy? How smart is he?"

"Not very," Drinkwater replied. "His reputation is a bit on the shaky side. But we must be careful when we use the word 'smart' as ascribed to a person in the intelligence business, Gregory. He has definite skills. But in this case, the man is reportedly an average man rather than a super man."

"OK. You say this man is assigned to me. Say his name again."

"Moffit. Stephen Moffit."

"What does that mean? 'Assigned to me'? Does he sleep in my tent? Does he stand around with a damn camera hanging off his neck? Can I talk to him? Will he know I know?"

"I have no idea how he expects to gather his information, Gregory. He's assigned to British Guiana. His job is to verify whatever you do, keep his Russian employers informed. That's the best I can do for now."

Villar-Cruz had been sitting quietly in the corner. Now he came forward.

"There are several ways to deal with him, I would think. One way is to tell him we know who he is, and then go right ahead with the project. There's nothing for him to see except a gang of men building an oil production facility."

"Exactly right, Rei." Hawthorn looked at Drinkwater. "You said he's an engineer? Fine. That's fine. I'll put him to work on that miserable river. The thing's a bottomless mud bath."

"Sandy Dreier could use some help on the barge harbor," Villar-Cruz said. "But he can't be told about this agent. It would make an impossible working relationship."

"Excellent, my friends," Drinkwater said. "All except the part about telling Moffit that we know about him. We cannot do that."

"Why not?" said Villar-Cruz.

"That would prompt them to find out *how* we know. And that would prove fatal to our informant." Drinkwater joined Hawthorn at the balcony rail. "In addition, the Soviets would simply manage to send someone else. At least, in this case, we know who the emeny is." He thought for a moment. "It might be possible to use the man, as you intend to use Bishop. Feed him information we would like the other side to have."

Hawthorn drummed his fingers on the wooden balustrade.

"I still think we should shoot the son of a bitch," he said.

"You know, Gregory, sometimes you remind me of that Kiley fellow. Well, never mind." Drinkwater half-turned, saw Villar-Cruz standing at ease behind them.

"Come here, my boy. Stand at the balustrade with us and tell me what you know about Josef Podgorsky."

CHAPTER 5

The connection between the KGB, the Russian Trade Office, the People's Political Party of British Guiana, and Stephen Moffit was demonstrated, though its workings were not, when the American hero passed through Guianese customs as a Very Important Person on the first of June, 1957, was greeted by Carlysle Ramprashad, and escorted to temporary government quarters by a trio of PPP politicians. It must be assumed that his salary as an advisor to the minister of Public Works began the same day, though the conservative party still in power had no particular voice in the matter. One might also assume that Moffit's wage as a paid agent-in-place began the day he left China, those funds going regularly and automatically to an account in Geneva, or possibly Zurich.

His arrival in the country was reported by the local press as "an important event in the development of our country, for this man brings with him a wealth of expertise that will benefit the people and the building program we have undertaken for the future."

The impression a citizen must have gotten from that back-page news was that this visitor had arrived with no political ties, that he had come for the people, not for the good of one party or another. There was no way for them to know, from reading the article, that his "wealth of expertise" lay in areas other than public works. In fact, only a select few in the PPP heirarchy were aware that Stephen Moffit had been assigned to British Guiana, that they had neither asked for nor been consulted about his posting. Those same few were aware that he was to be Russia's eyes and ears at the Globe project, whether copies of his reports went to the locals or whether they did not. Moscow was calling the shots; Cheddi Jagan was a middleman who would be told what was necessary, no more.

In fact, there was very little to report from the Globe camp. The river harbor was in serious trouble, thanks to the bottomless mud that made construction a near impossibility, and the route between the harbor and the camp was all but closed to everything but light traffic, thanks to the Bishop interference. There were several drilling rigs on site, but there was no drilling going on. A few dozen men wandered about with charts and spades in their hands, and a few were moving some dirt, completing the short jet airstrip, but there was hardly a sign that could not have been interpreted by a schoolchild, much less a highly trained Soviet agent.

At that point in time, just two months before the elections would turn the pro-West politicians out and install the East Indian socialists, the Globe project was in a holding pattern.

The meeting in Haiti had concluded with the parties in agreement on all counts.

Stephen Moffit would be treated with courtesy, allowed general camp liberties, and assigned to work projects that were theoretically productive. They would keep their knowledge about his true status to themselves, although the governor was to be advised along with other need-to-know people as the situation dictated.

They would continue their work at the concession with all possible vigor under the circumstances, and allow the Bishop court action to proceed at its own regulated pace. Toward that end, the governor would permit certain platte documents to disappear. They would no doubt turn up in England.

In the matter of Josef Podgorsky, Drinkwater agreed that he would never have made the contact had he been only superficially interested in Globe's activities. That was not his pattern. As Hawthorn had correctly judged, the Russians did not make idle inquiries. But it was also agreed that he, Podgorsky, would most likely be working against his own timetable. For the moment, Russia's own national oil reserves were adequate, but it was only a matter of time before they would be eager to join the rest of the world in exploiting the Middle East, providing they had no other place to go.

In the very probable event that Podgorsky was in contact with the Cubans, Castro's future would also be on his mind. Russia would need oil for the new satellite, and then oil for the others that would be added to their list, oil from British Guiana to win the minds and the economies of the West. Hawthorn had already established the delivery system, and soon he would have the crude.

And if that were the case, Josef Podgorsky would be angry as hell about the appearance of Thaddeus Bishop.

Hawthorn had used his contacts in Canada to double-check on Bishop. The reports about him were true. He was a fat, rich playboy who flitted between his club on Yonge Street in Toronto, his villa on New Providence, and his ranch in British Guiana. His gin and tonic friends at the club were under constant threat of being bombarded with yet another tale about his South American safari expeditions, his hunting lodge, his bush ladies. He would give that up only when he was dead and in hell. He was, in fact, firmly ensconsed at his lodge now, determined to stay there in defense of his property.

Hawthorn hired an exceptionally clever local lawyer, who sought to have the injunction put aside. But there was very little he could do when the land records were found to be missing, sent to England for some unknown reason, hopelessly lost in a library of the Commonwealth Regency.

In Baton Rouge, Gregory Hawthorn interviewed and trained a new employee named Gene Tinker, a CIA operative whose specialty was flying and whose collateral skills and personal circumstances qualified him for the position. He was a bachelor, he was a big man, and he was an expert pistol marksman. It was Hawthorn's idea to buy a Lockheed Jetstar, to have it equipped with long-range radio and navigation gear and outfitted with extra wing and belly pods for long-range trips. It was Drinkwater's idea to hire a pilot from the ranks of the closemouthed CIA.

Hawthorn voiced no objection to the Tinker assignment, even though from the very beginning he had wanted as much distance between himself and the CIA as possible to guarantee his own independence in the formation of policy and procedures. His single stipulation was that Gene Tinker be informed that he was Globe property, was answerable to Globe management, and was to submit such reports as he must through the Globe system. And he, Hawthorn, was the system.

On a warm June morning shortly after Tinker's appointment, Hawthorn was in his Baton Rouge office, managing his paper war. He had completed an operations briefing with Henri Amont, keeping him posted on the general affairs of the Caribbean fleet, and had closed his office door. He would sign a few papers, then go home and pack his suitcase again. As he sat at his desk and turned the first page, the telephone rang.

"Good morning. Hawthorn speaking."

"Mr. Hawthorn. I'm glad to find you back in your office."

"Mr. Podgorsky?"

"Yes. I understand you have run into some difficulty."

"With the Bishop thing. Is that what you . . ."

"Yes. The Bishop injunction. What do you intend to do about it, Mr. Hawthorn?"

"We're doing all we can, Mr. Podgorsky."

"Are you? Doesn't it worry you that one man can cost so much time? So much money?"

"Of course it does. But the law is on his . . ."

"I understand, sir. And that is all you have to tell me? The law?"

"Yes, I think so."

"You are not as concerned as I, then."

The line went dead. Hawthorn replaced the phone, rocked slowly in his chair. A smile formed on his face and he put his feet up.

"Gottcha," he said softly.

CHAPTER 6

The trip down was by far the fastest, the smoothest, and most comfortable ride Hawthorn had ever taken. Tinker knew the plane inside out, had been taught by the Lockheed field representative, and was as sharp a pilot as he had ever known. Tinker gave him the controls on the last leg, turned the autopilot off, and let him fly it.

The yoke, rudder, and all the basic instruments seemed familiar, even after a fourteen-year furlough from the cockpit. But the maze of navigation aids and radio dials were useless to him.

Villar-Cruz rode in the cabin, studying his part. He would stay in

British Guiana as Globe's liaison for the last part of the exercise, keeping track of Moffit, watching the progress in the Bishop matter, and finally coordinating the piece that counted the most: getting the oil into the country.

When they settled on Dreier's balcony at the Victoria Way flat, the big engineer opened a can of beer and announced that the American, Stephen Moffit, was a snoop.

Hawthorn took a deep breath. Sandy Dreier had to be told. Soon! He had to be told what the hell he was doing.

"How do you mean, Sandy?"

"Came around the warehouse, asked a lot of questions, wanted to know if he could see the camp."

"He'll see the camp," Hawthorn said. "We might be asked to use him at the project. I thought he might help with the harbor."

"Sure. Under my supervision, though," said Dreier. "They say he's supposed to be working on bridges and like that, but I can use him down there."

Dreier was standing against the rail, sniffing the scent of curried goat that drifted across to them from a settlement farther up the coast.

"He was at the airport when you came in," Dreier added. "He's a Navy pilot, ya know."

The phone was ringing. Dreier went into the bedroom and came back a moment later.

"It's for you, boss."

Tinker held the screen door open, let Hawthorn pass through.

"Hello. Hawthorn speaking."

"Good afternoon, sir. Carlysle Ramprashad here. Welcome once again."

"Thanks. What can I do for you?" The PPP must have been at the airport as well. He couldn't make a move without their shadow.

"I only wanted to inform you that the minister of Public Works met with us today. We are staying in close contact, you see, with the elections so close at hand."

"Yes?"

"Yes. And the Bishop matter has us worried."

"Sorry, Mr. Ramprashad. That's out of my hands."

"I understand, sir, but have you spoken to him personally? Will he not consider a financial settlement of some kind?"

"I'm afraid not, sir."

"A pity. Something should be done. Well then, Mr. Hawthorn, in another question, sir, the minister approved the temporary posting of the American, Mr. Moffit. To work with your firm at the camp, in the exploration work, sir."

"I see."

Now what? He should be polite, of course. Perhaps a little surprised. "I thought you might have him building bridges or something."

"That may come later, Mr. Hawthorn. Can you make some provision for him, beginning tomorrow?"

"You mean a tent? An assignment?"

"Both, yes. It would be appreciated."

"Of course, Mr. Ramprashad. I'll take care of it."

"Thank you, sir. If you would be so kind, please call him directly to make the arrangements for a meeting. I'm sure it will be a good exchange. His number is four seven-seven-three-nine."

"I've got it, thank you. I'll try to see him this evening."

Hawthorn returned to the balcony.

"That was the future minister of Petroleum, Lands, and Mines, gentlemen. Mr. Moffit is assigned to us."

"Starting when?" Villar-Cruz asked from his place in the corner.

"Tomorrow. I'll call him in a few minutes. Maybe we can have a drink or something tonight. I'd like to see how a—." He almost said "spy."

". . . a former POW thinks." Hawthorn looked at Tinker. "Gene, I've got a meeting in the morning with Burrowes. You could keep Moffit occupied for me, get to know him. You might show him the plane. Meet him early, take him up for a ride."

"Sure, no problem, Greg. Maybe I could learn something."

No doubt. It was Hawthorn's guess that Tinker had been programmed by the CIA to listen and to learn. He stood in the doorway and beckoned with his finger at the big pilot. They stepped into the living room together and Hawthorn opened his briefcase, took out a notebook, and leafed through it. Drill-core analyses, temperature readings at thousand-foot intervals, site locations for test wells. Thirty pages of material borrowed from Creole a few hundred miles to the west, all on Globe paper. He handed the notebook to Tinker.

"You might forget this, leave it on the seat while you're checking the wheel rubber or something." He spoke softly.

"Sure. I do that sometimes," Tinker replied.

"Gene, about tonight . . ."

"Don't worry, sir. I can land that thing in the dark on a parking lot."

"I want Bishop to be kept out of sight. I don't care if you have to tie him up in a sack. I want that man out of the country."

At eight o'clock Hawthorn changed into his work clothes and got into the Jeep. His pet spy shouldn't be kept waiting.

CHAPTER 7

"You've been here for a few weeks, I understand."

"Since June first, yes, sir."

Moffit sat back, turned his drink glass in circles, and stared at Hawthorn. He was good at eye contact, sure of himself, obviously aware of the discomfort it caused others. His eyes were pale blue and placid, very unlike Hawthorn's. He seemed to be centering on a spot between Hawthorn's dark eyebrows, daring him to blink. A match flared, Hawthorn lit up, and swallowed the smoke, still making connection.

"Like it down here?"

"I don't know yet. It's too damn hot, I know that."

The old Palm Court restaurant was as good a place as any to meet for a drink on a balmy evening. It was downtown, if one could call the main street and the central market downtown, across from the Tower Hotel, not far from Moffit's quarters. The familiar overhead fan sluffed around, turning some air, the wooden chairs were clean, the table was private. A bar at the north end had seen better days and a smell of curried food lingered in spite of the fan.

"Have you ever eaten here?"

"I ordered a chicken sandwich yesterday." Moffit started a grin. "The waiter said they didn't have chicken sandwiches. I asked him if they had chicken and he said yes so I told him to bring me a piece of chicken and some bread."

Hawthorn exhaled and laughed at the same time. He coughed, Moffit dropped his eyes, and the contest was over. He looked up again.

"What's it like down in the bush?"

"Not bad. It's quiet," Hawthorn said. He had taken careful inventory of his spy. He had been surprised at first, wondering how a twenty-nine-year-old man could have gone through so much hell and come out looking like a slightly tarnished college student. Then he reminded himself that the newspaper accounts and the scars and most of the other trappings were probably installed by experts. How much he had actually gone through was anybody's guess. His body frame was a little thin, but well engineered; his face was stronger than a boy's, the jaw too large, cheeks too prominent, eyes too serious for a boy's face. It was the haircut that made him look so young—thick, brown, straight hair neatly parted with a shock falling down over his brow.

"Ramprashad wants me to take you on down there." Hawthorn paused, inhaled, puffed. "Do you know why?"

"I think so."

Hawthorn waited.

"I don't know what this will sound like, Mr. Hawthorn. I feel myself like it's a cop-out, but I couldn't take the crap I was gettin' back home." He stopped, looked at the wall to his right and was silent for a moment. "I came back and found my wife gone, mixed up with some gyrene captain from Chicago. She wasn't even there at the airport when I got home." His gaze was still on the wall. Now he dropped it, drank his beer, held his hand out. "Can I have one of those.?"

Hawthorn passed him a cigarette, struck a match. "I'm sorry about that."

Moffit blew a stream of blue smoke at the wall.

"Aw, hell, it wasn't that bad. But then they had the damn functions. Appearances. Job offers from crooked senators, all that medal crap." Hawthorn knew he was listening to a professional foreign agent do his act, and he caught himself believing it.

"I finally told the people at Great Lakes I wanted out. I mean, I was out of the service, but I asked them for some help to get me a job out of the country. Why, hell! They practically carried me to a psych ward right then and there."

Hawthorn nodded, smiled.

"So anyway, I had to go to Washington for one last debriefing and I ran into this guy Wiltrop or Welltrop, and he told me about a job overseas, engineering, some kind of a consulting job, and I went down to G Street and checked with the British Guiana Economic Development Office, and they gave me the forms. That's about it."

Moffit looked back at Hawthorn again. He seemed to be waiting for a response, an approval. Hawthorn leaned over the table, raised his lemonade just off the table and sipped it, eyes on Moffit's face.

"You a good engineer?"

"I think so, sure. I can manage a water job, dams, bridges."

"OK. But the government wants you down at the camp. Why?"

"Christ! That was your first question, wasn't it. I'm sorry. Yeah, I think I know why. You might not like it."

"Go ahead."

"Two reasons. They gave me two reasons, no, three. One, they haven't got the funds yet to start on the Corentyne River work. That's a big job, plans for a bridge between British Guiana and Suriname. I was supposed to help with that. Second, they got their belly full of Shell

97

down there, down in the oil concession. Ramprashad says all they did was shoot stray cows and make excuses for negative findings."

"Wait a second." Hawthorn held his hand up. "Shell was dragging their feet? Is that what Ramprashad says?"

"That's what he says."

"OK." Hawthorn smiled broadly. His white teeth showed and his tanned face broke wrinkles at his eyes. "I'll tell you about that in a minute. What's the third reason?"

Moffit hesitated. "They don't want to get screwed."

"Screwed how?"

"They've had Canada taking out their bauxite, Great Britain taking out their sugar, all the capital in the country comes from offshore. Come on, it's a typical Socialist point of view, Mr. Hawthorn. They don't want any more exploitation."

Hawthorn sat still. His cigarette was burning short.

"That's what they say, Mr. Hawthorn. They want me to keep an eye on material imports, manpower treatment, living conditions, that kind of thing. Then, when the oil comes up, if the oil comes up, I'm supposed to help them monitor the export."

"To make sure they don't get screwed."

Moffit nodded. He hunched his shoulders and clasped his hands. "Not my idea of engineering either, but I figure they'll have me on the Corentyne job in six months anyway."

For the past minute, Hawthorn had been listening to his voice, paying attention to it. Now it struck him. His enunciation was letter perfect, except where he wanted to slur. His diction, his tone, his delivery—the bastard had been standing in front of a mirror practicing this whole spiel.

"He wants you in charge of imports and working conditions. OK. In my company, those are collateral duties. Starting tomorrow morning you'll be in charge of imports and labor management. Sandy Dreier will be glad to hear that." Hawthorn forced his cigarette into the little glass ashtray and tapped it dead with his finger.

"I'll be happy to take you on, Steve. You're on the government payroll, so let's not have any confusion about that, but you'll do more than import toilet paper and wipe the workers' noses, my friend. I've got a problem with that river down there."

"I heard that, sir."

"You'll spend your productive time finishing the harbor and cleaning out the channel. Because when we find oil, and we will find oil, I'll be damned if I'll build a pipeline from there to the ocean to get it out."

"Yes, sir."

"Dreier will show you what the problem is. In a word, it's mud. A hundred feet of slime. You want another beer?"

"No, sir. Thanks."

"As for the Corentyne job, sure. They can have you back when they're ready. I don't have much to say about that."

Hawthorn was wearing green bush pants and rigger's boots, heavy in the heel and sole, strapped with leather thongs. He hooked a chair with his toe and dropped one foot on its seat.

"Now, about Shell. Those people have the best exploration teams in the business. They quit down there for two very good reasons and I'll tell you what they are." Hawthorn leaned back and folded his hands in his lap.

"They don't want a war with our neighbor to the west . . ."

"Venezuela . . ."

"Venezuela. Shell owns a lot of rights in that country, proven reserves. They've got a profit pot over there. So if they come up with a high-priced bonanza here, they'll have to sit on it for ten years. Any flooding of the market at this time will give Venezuela one more reason to nationalize the industry, and Shell doesn't want that."

It sounded good. Partly true, good enough for Ramprashad. Maybe good enough for Podgorsky. But he wasn't quite finished.

"That's one point, and the other is stronger yet. In about six months, there's going to be more damn oil in the world than it can consume. Shell's got too much crude now."

Hawthorn dropped his foot to the floor and leaned forward toward Moffit. He lowered his voice.

"But I don't."

It was time to plant, to sow the seeds.

"I'm a little guy, Steve. I've got the cash and I've got the organization, and I'm a hungry man." He looked around the room, then back to Moffit. "But I don't have enough crude to put a squeeze on. You understand? I want Guianese crude oil, and I don't care about a war with the major oil companies. They have a thousand white shirts to pay for, they're top heavy with office boys on big salaries. I've got one white shirt in my company, and she's got a perfect ass."

Moffit grinned at that, and Hawthorn waited a moment before going on.

"You'll have to send reports back to the government. Get yourself a typewriter from supply. Can you still fly a plane?"

"I got a few hops in, mostly light stuff."

"I'm going to buy a Cessna. You can use that to get back and forth. You can help some of the other men make trips."

"Fine. I'd enjoy that."

"Have you seen my jet?"

"No, sir."

Liar. "She's a beauty. I'll ask Tinker to give you a ride in the morning."

"Thank you, sir."

"One last thing, Steve." Hawthorn folded his hands on the table. Now he would start dealing hypocrisy from a brand-new deck. "I know you work for Ramprashad, but some of the equipment and some of the tricks we use in our work are corporate confidential. Some of Dreier's methods should have a patent, but they don't. Now, it won't do them any good to get all the details of what we do. All they want are the results. Right? So do me a favor. Separate the results from the methods and processes. Give them the results. OK?"

The spy was fatigued. The small white scars in his cheek holes had reddened with the conversation; his hand and his bent fingers appeared to be swollen. Pressure. He had performed under pressure. But his eyes were clear. He leveled them at Hawthorn.

"You're sure you'll find oil."

"I'm sure."

"You've already spent . . ."

"Several hundred million dollars."

"Jesus . . ." Moffit repositioned himself on the chair.

"When?" he asked softly.

Not a chance, Mr. Spy. Not a chance.

Hawthorn stopped the Jeep along the seawall road and got out. He walked for a short distance and found a place to sit. He listened to the ocean, felt the warm breeze on his face.

He believed some of Moffit's story, the part about his wife. A little investigation had confirmed that he was divorced, that his wife had been unfaithful.

A long time ago, before the war, before the killing, before the oil, so long ago it was hardly real anymore, he had loved a woman. She had been faithful until the end, when her legs had wasted away and her face was ash white. He had been with her for many hours, hearing the iron lung do its automatic work, his hand on her hair, his fingers touching her lips. He hardly knew when the final breath came.

Far down the coast, a little out to sea, there was a light, a beacon of some kind. Hawthorn watched it turn slowly across the distant horizon, come back, swing quickly past his face and continue in its circle of warning.

CHAPTER 8

If Alan Drinkwater was right, if the Commission's intelligence sources had sorted out their facts correctly, the Globe project had a little over eighteen months to live. With luck, six or more of those months would be eaten up by the Bishop delay, another eleven could be used to finish the trappings of an oil field and they would have the rest of the time, as little as possible, to squat on a million acres of dry sand.

Whatever happened, come the revolution and the urgent call for oil, the Kremlin would fall on its face as the Globe carpet was pulled out from under its boots.

One of the dangers Hawthorn could foresee in the whole complicated mess was the possibility, the probability of a national takeover. It had happened before; Mexico, Africa, the Persian Gulf, Indonesia, a sudden and unexpected rush of soldiers, a bewildered American manager, five hundred technicians and their families scooting for the nearest boat.

If that happened, if the Guianese sent their little army of soldiers with their toy guns down to the Globe project, it would be all over.

Now, before the elections, was the time to prepare for that contingency, and Jeffry Burrowes was to be the bastion. He would make a marvelous commandant.

They met in the Tower Hotel breakfast room: Hawthorn, Villar-Cruz, and Tom Fitzsimmons, the local lawyer who had passed inspection. They saw no way to get things done without his assistance, and that meant drawing him into their confidence. That part of it was accomplished in the governor's home, with Sir Hillman Gomes lending his authority and his position to the Globe cause. When that meeting was over, and the contract was in his pocket, Fitzsimmons would have prosecuted the case of Saint Joan. For the sake of his democratic ideals, he would have done it for nothing.

When they finished their coffee, Fitzsimmons brought the car around to drive them to the picturesque old Parliament Building for their nine o'clock appointment with the soon-to-be-removed minister of Petroleum, Lands, and Mines, Jeffry Burrowes.

"I never knew a man who was so glued to his office," Hawthorn said as he got seated. "I wanted to have this meeting someplace else, but he's fixed to that damn throne of his." He sat back. "Are you ready with your gear, Rei?"

"Yes. Of course. I'll know if there's a bug in there."

It was a short drive. The streets were already hot, the people were busy, the donkey carts were plodding as Fitzsimmons rolled into the driveway before the main steps. The lawyer led the way to a disinterested security guard on the main floor, where they were directed down the hall, under the turning fans, through the yellow plaster tunnel to Burrowes's office.

The minister was dressed in a blue suit with a red tie and had a white flower in his lapel. His wart bobbed between the brow lines as he rose from his desk and came around, holding out his hand to greet his visitors.

"Aha! Fitzsimmons, isn't it? I have the briefs on my desk, you see. And Mr. Hawthorn. How good to see you, sir. And you would be . . ."

"Villar-Cruz, sir. Mr. Hawthorn's assistant."

"Aha. Well, then. Good for you. Good." He clapped his fat little hands, waved his arms to invite them to chairs. He sat gracefully in his own leather antique, rubbed at the arms with his fingers, then made a little fist with both hands on the desk top.

"And how is it, then? The flat is satisfactory? The weather is treating you well?"

"Thank you, Mr. Minister," Hawthorn said, quickly. Knowing he wouldn't be able to handle much of that, he got right to the point. "I've seen no signs of trouble, sir."

"Trouble? Oh, the elections, you mean. I expect you mean the elections, the thuggery and so on. No. It has been decently quiet for the past few days. Riffraff, you see. Unemployed people."

"Speaking of which . . ." Hawthorn stopped abruptly, deliberately, concentrating his attention on the minister's lapel flower.

"Yes?"

"Mr. Burrowes," said Fitzsimmons, interrupting, "what we have to discuss this morning is frightfully important, sir. As you know, I am representing the Globe Corporation in the Bishop matter, and I have come to know these gentlemen and their enterprise most intimately. They are here, *we* are here, to invite your cooperation in a business that is vital to our country, indeed vital to the free world, sir. They are here to ask for your help, Mr. Burrowes."

"Indeed? Is that so? I'm afraid I do not follow that, Mr. Fitzsimmons." Burrowes sat back, dropped his hands to his lap. "As Mr. Hawthorn was about to suggest, I will be out of office soon. I know that and you know that."

Hawthorn looked across at Villar-Cruz, nodded.

"Sir," Villar-Cruz began, "forgive me." He brought his briefcase to his lap. "Is there the remotest possibility that we could be overheard in this room?"

"Overheard?" Burrowes sat straight. "Overheard? Do you mean listened in on? Eavesdroppers? That sort of thing?"

"Yes, sir. Or possible . . ."

"Please! Please explain yourself, Mr. . . ."

"Villar-Cruz, sir. Electronic devices perhaps."

"I beg your pardon." Burrowes started to get up. "This is my office, gentlemen. I assure you what I say in this room is confidential, most confidential."

Villar-Cruz had his hand inside the briefcase. He opened the lid an inch wider, looked inside, saw his dials on the zero mark, and nodded at Hawthorn.

"In that case, I would like to ask a simple question, Mr. Burrowes."

"Please do so, Mr. Hawthorn."

"Are you a Communist?"

The startled look on the minister's face was almost comical. It was far too real to be a show.

"Good. Then you will help us." Hawthorn stood up and circled to the back of his chair, Burrowes following him inch by inch. "Please say nothing for the next few minutes, sir. Mr. Villar-Cruz is going to give you a folder. Inside the folder are several pages of typewritten information. I would like you to read that material. Read it twice if you like. Study it as long as you wish. Then I would ask that you hand it back to him without any comment. Will you do that for me, Mr. Burrowes?"

The fragile lace curtains moved softly in the air, the fan whirred quietly overhead. Burrowes opened his desk drawer, found an ivory cigarette holder, and fitted an English Player into it. He flicked a butane lighter several times until Hawthorn reached across with his Zippo. Burrowes sucked without inhaling, blew a thin stream of smoke toward the ceiling, saw it disperse with the fan's breeze. Only then did he hold his hand out and accept the folder that Villar-Cruz passed to him.

He read it all in less than five minutes, finishing a page, turning it over, starting another, referring back to the first briefly, then going on to the next. Hawthorn was gripping the back of his chair. Villar-Cruz's hand was resting on his briefcase handle, ready if necessary to fire the dart that would strike Burrowes in the neck. When he was finished he glanced up at them. He had not blinked an eye, moved a facial wrinkle, or showed a single reaction. But his cigarette had burned itself out in the ashtray.

"Extraordinary," he finally said. He handed the papers back to Villar-

Cruz, folded his hands on the desk top, and looked from one man to the other.

"Now? May I say something now?"

"Quietly, please," replied Hawthorn.

"Very well." He spoke in a whisper. "What do we do next?"

They arrived at the airport terminal shortly before noon. Fitzsimmons parked the car, then turned in his seat to face Hawthorn and Villar-Cruz.

"It will go all right, won't it? I mean, you fellows are the professionals in this caper."

Hawthorn smiled and reached for the door handle. "Don't worry, Tom," he said. "You just look after the Bishop case. Keep it going until I give you the word. If Burrowes starts to act strange, call Reinaldo. He can handle it."

They left Fitzsimmons in the coffee shop, then headed for the passenger apron in front of the terminal building. Outside, Hawthorn stood quietly and watched the heat waves shimmering above the hot asphalt.

"It went well, sir." Villar-Cruz was still holding onto his briefcase, now full of shredded paper.

"Very well. Better that I had hoped."

"And how about the last part, sir. After we left you alone?"

"As we expected, Rei. He's a shareholder."

Villar-Cruz nodded. Across the field, the Jetstar was taxiing in, heading toward the apron. The shrieking noise was deafening as it got closer, until it swung its tail and stopped a hundred feet away. Two men got down and started toward the shade of the passenger canopy, then changed direction when Villar-Cruz waved and caught Tinker's attention.

Even at a distance, Hawthorn could see the scars on Moffit's cheeks. He wondered, suddenly, how they got there, and then he found himself wondering again what they had promised him in exchange for his services. What would cause a man to desert his country, his loyalties? What had the Russians done, what had they said to convince him that he was better off on their side?

He might never know the answer to that question, and in the final analysis, it didn't matter. That was somebody else's problem.

CHAPTER 9

There were a dozen people in the airport café, counting Hawthorn and his group. They found places near a window and ordered cold drinks.

"Helluva plane, Greg. She's full of tricks." Tinker was sitting next to Moffit. "But the U.S. Navy here says she's too sluggish with full tanks." He glanced at Moffit.

"I didn't say 'too' sluggish, Gene. It's like everything else, you give up something to gain something." He looked at Hawthorn. "She must have very good range with those extra tanks."

"About a thousand miles, Steve. We can make Puerto Rico no sweat if we get some altitude."

Hawthorn, observing their interaction, was looking forward to the CIA agent's report when they were airborne. They would be leaving soon, heading back to Miami, then to New York, and finally, maybe for the weekend, back to Baton Rouge.

"You'll be riding into town with Reinaldo and Ftizsimmons, Steve. I think Sandy Dreier is supposed to meet you at Ogle right after lunch."

Tinker looked across the table at Moffit. "Ogle's that little strip just outside of Georgetown, Steve. We use a Cessna 182 for our trips down to the camp." He paused as the drinks came, waited until the waiter had gone. "You have any time in a 182? You ever flown one of those birds?"

"A few times. Not much to them, is there?"

"You'll like Sandy," Hawthorn said. "He's a very capable engineer, but you'll find him a little frustrated these days. The Bishop tangle has got his hands tied."

"I guess we can work on the harbor, sir."

"Don't let the legal problem get you down," Hawthorn said. "We'll be loading crude through those lines soon enough. I'm content to see the foundation work get finished."

"You sound pretty confident, sir," Moffit said.

Hawthorn let his eyes make their penetrating contact, dug into his shirt and found a cigarette, lit it and blew smoke across the table.

"I am," he said. His eyes had never left the spy's face.

Moffit said very little on the drive back into town, commenting only rarely as Fitzsimmons pointed out the depressingly uninteresting sights along the way. When they arrived at the square he got out, thanked them, and promised to see Villar-Cruz later in the week at the camp.

Moffit's first stop was at the Cable and Wireless office, the country's telegraph link to the world. He went inside and asked at the counter for Jennifer Moengo. She came around from a side office, a lovely girl, perhaps twenty-five years old, blond, slim.

"Yes?"

"Miss Moengo?"

"Yes?"

"My name is Stephen Moffit." He hesitated. "I have a message from Able."

"Do you?" She smiled, only faintly, with her eyes. "Able Queen?"

"Able King."

"Just a moment, please."

She disappeared and returned a moment later with her handbag, walked behind the counter, and came out to the front, heading for the door. Moffit followed. They strolled a short distance and stopped at a café, near the Barkleys Bank. She led him to a corner table, sat on a booth bench with Moffit seated opposite.

"Have you been doing this for a long time?" Moffit asked.

"Not really." She lowered her eyes. "You're the first."

Moffit frowned perceptibly.

"I have something for you already, Mr, Moffit. Would you like to have it now?"

He glanced around, noted the few remaining luncheon guests.

"Sure. I guess so," he said.

She took a paper napkin from a holder and found a pen in her purse. Moffit watched her draw the characters, tear the napkin with the tip, start over. A very short message. She pushed it across the table.

MOTHER XCLTH RODSS GLRIA IMMEDIATELY.

"It looks garbled to me," he said.

"Our machines are outdated, Mr. Moffit," she replied.

"Copies?"

"We don't keep spoiled messages."

Moffit saw a waiter coming in their direction. He picked up the napkin and tucked it in his shirt pocket. They ordered coffee, drank it quietly, and then left the café. As she turned to make her way back to the cable office, Moffit took her arm.

"Are you married?" he asked.

"No, I'm not." She had a beautiful mouth, a delightful accent, and he saw that under her tight skirt she had a soft, warm body. It excited him.

"I guess we'll be in touch quite often."

She smiled. "That may depend on the message traffic."

106

"Not necessarily." He took her hand, then turned and headed toward the taxi stand. She reached into her purse for a pair of sunglasses, put them on, and watched him disappear around the corner, then stood for a moment before a store window, looking at her reflection in the glass.

Steve Moffit's total flying time in a Cessna 182 was something less than two hours, half of that practicing touch and go landings and the other half doing basic flying maneuvers at altitude to get a feel for the plane. He had never flown a high-wing aircraft before, but it made little difference.

His takeoff was smooth, even on the bumpy little private strip. They took a wide swing over the city, then put the big river on their right wing and headed south.

"The river flows north, obviously," said Dreier. "It's fed by small streams we can't see, only where they go into the river. Then it looks like somebody pouring Coke into a stream of chocolate milk."

"Is that a bauxite ship?" Moffit asked. A long, narrow vessel loaded with cream-white rock looked as though it might be standing still, except for the shallow wake behind its dark stern.

"Right. Headed for Trinidad to load into ocean-going carriers. Globe barges will be smaller. They'll ply back and forth a lot faster and a lot deeper, keep the river bottom from filling in. Lots of width here," said Dreier.

Moffit nodded again. He had faced the Mississippi years ago in floods and in ice, had learned to respect the slow-moving power of giants that inch along the ground like enormous worms, cutting their own way, moving at their own pace.

He flew easily, ignoring the minor turbulence that rose up from the forest below. The cockpit was noisy, they spoke little, and Moffit let his mind wander.

He had never felt uncomfortable about doing this job. He had felt some letdown when they told him it would be industrial and not political or military. He would have preferred an assignment in Europe, but he had no language skills, and most of those went to nationals anyway. So, for the most part, he accepted this as a first lesson, a short-term job with potentially important contributions to the bigger cause.

Chou had painted a picture for him, one that had him emerging from this assignment with important credentials that would give him entree to any number of positions. That was the word he had chosen to remember: "position." This job would give him "position."

He was beginning to feel an urgency about his immediate assignment. For an instant he saw the Luger, wrapped in a towel, tucked into his briefcase in the back of the plane. He forced his mind to let the image go.

One by one he checked his mental catalog of Globe people. Dreier, the loyal company engineer; Villar-Cruz, the smart-ass junior assistant; Schultz: He had seen Schultz, but he had no slot for that man yet. Tinker—what about Tinker? He could drive an airplane, he had a string of foul words, he seemed bright enough. But he was careless. A man who was careless with corporate-confidential information might be careless about other things, other kinds of data that could either validate or mitigate Podgorsky's concerns. Moffit took his hand off the yoke and felt his jacket pocket. It was zipped shut. The Minolta was still there.

Ahead now, clouds with anvil tops and gray, billowing centers. Cumulonimbus thunderheads. Gregory Hawthorn. His mind had gone to find him, to place him in a category, and it had found Gregory Hawthorn in a dangerous thunderstorm. "Go around them, or go over them. Do not try to go through them." They had not taught him that in China or Russia. He had learned that lesson in Pensacola.

On the horizon they saw the white hills and craters, the railroad tracks, the red roofs of the dusty mining town, the giant excavators and the trucks hurrying down the road loaded with aluminum ore; like ants on their way—like ants, Moffit thought. Long ago he had seen trucks on the road, moving slowly on the highway, like ants. He had dropped his wing and pressed down, forward and down, gaining speed, his nose tucking as he worked the trim forward. The red button under his thumb, the red trigger under his finger . . . Carlson . . . "Sheeeit!"

Dreier's voice brought him back to the cockpit.

"Third biggest mine in the world."

They were at thirty-five hundred feet, above the smoke that left the stacks and bent to the east. Like the stack gasses from a carrier. Moffit raised his hand to his face, adjusted the dark sunglasses, and brushed the hair back from his forehead.

He bent the plane right and pulled the throttle back, starting a steep descent in a narrow turn to starboard. The right wing appeared to be pivoting on a clearing in the jungle as they dropped nine hundred feet per minute in the swift, smoothly controlled turn, until they were again parallel with the river, heading south at one hundred feet, the sound of the engine bouncing back at them as they flew through the canyon of trees.

Huge monsters on both sides rose above them, giants reaching from their shallow hills to heights two hundred feet above the river level. The smooth carpet they had seen from above was in fact a timberstand of a million trees, mammoth fibers trapped in tangled matting, a web that had snared many pilots and consumed their bones, one Moffit would avoid.

108

Twenty minutes south of the bauxite mine and the smoke, the river began to widen, then squeeze together, then widen again, as though God had shaped an hourglass there to mark the passage of time. And a few minutes ahead, they saw the Globe basin.

Moffit added power; they climbed to eight hundred feet and began a slow turn as the basin came under their wing.

The work under construction resembled a huge horseshoe, the open end being the downstream outlet. At several points along the closed end were gates that could be opened or shut, depending on the season and the amount of water in the tributaries that joined to form the big river.

"Those two corners," said Dreier, "over there, see? Southwest and northwest. They're pure mud down to eighty, ninety feet. You drive piles down along the bank and the damn mud squirts up in the middle. It's like sittin' on a fat lady. Hold it down one place and it bulges up someplace else. We tried concrete but the damn forms won't hold long enough to let it set up."

"I see it," said Moffit. "Looks like the photos. Where's the Bishop place?" He had straightened the Cessna and was flying now to the east, away from the basin.

"We're over his land now."

"Where's his house?"

"There! We just passed it, to your left now. It's under a stand of trees, a pretty place. Go around, Steve, I'll show you."

Moffit turned and maintained his eight hundred feet, looking out the side window and feeling the nose of the plane with his fingertips. He had lost none of his precision, his sense for razor-sharp adjustments to make the machine perform his way.

Below them now and under the left wing Moffit saw the Bishop lodge. It looked from the air like a great white Iowa farmhouse. It was square, with a screened veranda on three sides of both the upper and the lower levels. There were gables in the top level, and wide, tall windows with small hexagons of glass in them on what looked like the back of the house. A small shed, maybe a garage, was set apart from the house about fifty feet, and another house, a much smaller building, squatted on the north edge of the clearing, the servants' quarters, Moffit guessed. They could see a path that led from the house to a road that disappeared in the trees, and another path that looked as though it might find its way eventually to the river. Moffit continued the turn and banked sharply as they crossed the river's edge. There was a wooden dock. And a boat.

Suddenly he thought of his first long-distance night trip. He was alone, flying at forty thousand feet. The night was clear, the sky was black. Norfolk to Rhode Island. He had crossed over New York City. He remembered it vividly. He had turned the radio off, turned his cockpit lights off, and looked down. The lights of New York stretched halfway to the horizon . . . and there was Philadelphia. *And he was God*. Poor people down there, wandering aimlessly on your dirty streets, hot in your small beds, crushed against each other, clutching each other. I can see you, but you can't see me—you don't even know I'm here.

"That's Bishop's boat. I guess he's still there, waitin' for us to quit screwin' around with his property."

They covered the last eighteen miles in minutes, staying low over the thick forest, the dense tree growth that was the pipeline route.

"Ground's pretty hard along here," said Dreier. "All Bishop land from the river to the camp. You get a few miles south, you're in mud again."

As they neared the field the trees began to thin out. Ahead was flat land, spotted with thickets and a few low hills. It looked like western grazing acreage.

There were no signs of active drilling below, none of the typical indicators of an oil field apart from the camp itself. Now, as the plane crossed over the threshhold on the long, easy approach, Moffit pulled the throttle back and eased the yoke toward his belly, holding the nose just high enough to keep the front wheel off the ground. The main gear touched lightly, skipping dust into the air behind them, and Moffit worked the rudder pedals to keep the plane running straight down the center line. The nose wheel touched and they rolled to a slow taxiing turn to the left.

"We're puttin' the big tanks right along here," Dreier was saying. He pointed to a position along the right wing. "That'll make the takeoff pretty dicey for a big plane if there's any fog, or if it's at night. I wanted to stick the tanks down by the river end of the camp, but it's too soft."

When he was on the small packed apron in front of the hangar Moffit gunned the engine, swung the plane around to face the wind, and cut the ignition.

Waiting for them in a pickup truck was a husky young man dressed in khaki browns, wearing a Yankee baseball cap.

"Hello, Dutch. Here, meet Steve Moffit. Steve"—he turned to Moffit—"This is Dutch Schultz. Jack of all trades."

They shook hands. Dutch Schultz was from Pennsylvania, a Korean War veteran himself.

"I read about you, sir," he said. Moffit was holding his briefcase, while Schultz was unloading the other baggage. "Glad to have you here."

"Thanks, Dutch. Glad to be here."

"Well, let's go." He got behind the wheel with Moffit next to him, Dreier in the backseat. They turned away from the landing strip and sped off down the dusty road. Moffit saw the markers where the big tanks would go, iron stakes in the ground twenty feet off to the side of the runway. They drove past a garage, and a toolshed, then a fuel dock for the trucks, an equipment depot, another shed. Then they were in the camp, two rows of tents with a road down the middle, twenty or more tents of all kinds. A few workers were sitting outside, gathering in the afternoon sun, waiting for their shift to begin. But there weren't enough men to work an oil field full time. The Bishop problem.

Schultz pulled to a stop in front of Dreier's tent and the engineer got out.

"Thanks, Steve. Nice flight. Dutch is gonna show you your place and I'll send Shawhan over to get you started at the basin. You got any questions, just holler."

They went on and stopped before Moffit's new home. Schultz helped him carry his few things into the spacious, comfortable tent, and showed him his locker, the desk, the drawing board and file boxes, the night table and the propane lamp. A cozy arrangement.

It was cool there on the savanna. A constant breeze stirred the warm air and there was little to hold the sticky heat. The grassland seemed to absorb it, or to counter it with some chemistry of its own. Moffit was settled in by the time Dan Shawhan pulled up and called him out.

"Let's go, pardner. Day's about gone!"

Moffit ducked out through the tent flap and climbed into the Jeep, shaking hands with the older roughneck as they tore dust off the road.

It took less than ten minutes to reach the working site, sitting on top of a low hill overlooking the camp. Shawhan pulled a chart from the backseat and unfolded it for Moffit to read.

"The one in the middle, there at the bottom of the triangle, is called Winkin', and the one to the right is Nod. There's no Blinkin' anymore. It was a dry hole."

They climbed down and walked ten feet to stand next to a pipe that had been driven into the ground. A bright red handkerchief dangled from its top, waving limply in the soft breeze.

"If you've never stood on top of it before, you can't know how it feels. We might be standing on top of enough oil to run New York State for a hundred years!"

"You believe the charts?" Moffit asked.

"Maybe. The charts and the cores. But I've seen some losers too."

"Could this be a loser?"

"No way. Mr. Hawthorn doesn't screw with losers. In six months we could have rigs from here to the damn horizon. Two thousand barrels each. More. That's what the charts say."

The forest road was as rough as it looked from the air, winding around gullies and across rocky falls, cutting through the jungle where

111

enormous Purple Heart trees rose to an incredible height above the forest floor. Here the ground cover was thinner, starved of sunlight by the lofty branches, but smaller trees only two feet in diameter were still fierce competition for those who would lay a straight, wide line to the river. Moffit was at the wheel now. They drove for forty minutes until they came to a split in the track, the main road continuing straight ahead, the fork going off to the right. They slowed to a crawl.

"Bishop's place is up there a few miles," Shawhan said. He spat a stream of tobacco juice onto the dirt.

"I haven't seen many signs, Dan. The trespass warnings. Where are they?"

"Fell down, a lot of 'em. We don't pay much attention anyhow. Thing is, we start carrying any heavy equipment along here and that fart Bishop, he'll get the damn army down here."

They drove on. The tree line began to thin out now, as they were nearing the river, and soon they were driving through the edges of heavy brush. Ahead was the fence, and beyond that, Globe land and the muddy harbor.

Shawhan directed him to the concrete bib that circled around to the south of the basin, holding the softer ground away from the main channel. They stopped and got out. To their right the concrete became a solid platform, with muddy water lying ten feet below, dead water that was part of the river but not in the stream. At regular intervals mooring cleats had been imbedded in the concrete, ready to accept the lines of barges when the river was ready to carry its traffic. Ladders ran down to the water, protected by bumpers made of old tires, hung there with thick ropes.

Completed pipeline segments ran along the dock area, turning gently at obtuse angles to face the dockside, each twelve-inch pipe section capped off at the end, ready to be connected to a heavy-duty hose for crude-oil loading. At the junction of the pipelines, near the base of the tank farm, they joined to enter the pump and meter station, a small, white building Moffit had seen from the air.

At the south end of the horseshoe, the closed end, they stood above the main gate and looked down. Water was flowing freely through the open gate beneath their concrete walkway. It was a full ninety feet wide, twenty feet deep.

They walked farther along the concrete until they came to an abrupt end, where the work had stopped and the muddy shore of the basin rode thickly down to the waterline. Shawhan looked around and found a large chuck of reinforced concrete, a relic from one of the failed pilings they had driven and lost. He walked to the edge and threw it with both hands down onto the mud.

They heard it splat as it hit, sending a little shower of wet slime to the sides. Then it settled half of its thickness into the brown ooze.

"I've walked in that crap," Shawhan said. "You can if you're ready to lose your boots and maybe your pants. It goes down like that forever."

They finished their inspection of the basin at seven o'clock and headed back to the camp, arriving as the last of the day's light was turning to shadow.

The gruff, burley-mouthed old veteran of a hundred worse jobs took a liking to Moffit, introduced him to the mess hall and to a few of the men, then made plans for their morning labor. But by ten o'clock Moffit could no longer concentrate on Shawhan's friendly chatter. It was his first day, and he was very tired.

Shawhan headed down the road to his bunk and Moffit, yawning broadly, sauntered off in the other direction, closed the flap of his tent, and sat down at the desk.

He read for a few minutes, then turned out the light. There had been no rain that day, though they had seen and heard thunderstorms. That was good. Moffit had no desire to drive through the mud that night.

CHAPTER 10

He lay on his bunk bed for over an hour, picturing the road to the basin. They had gone very slowly, stopping several times. It had taken them three-quarters of an hour to reach Bishop's road; it was certainly too far to walk.

The Jeep was at the vehicle pool, an open area at his end of the camp, separated from fire hazards by a distance of several hundred feet.

At 2:00 A.M. he put his feet on the canvas floor and pulled on his boots. He listened for sounds but heard none. He kneeled on the floor and reached under his bed, pulled out the briefcase he had shoved underneath, and placed it on his bed. He took a key from his pants pocket, opened the case and withdrew the Luger, wrapped in its yellow towel. He carefully unwrapped it, replaced the towel, and closed the briefcase, snapping the two locks shut. Then he unscrewed the silencer, placed that in his left pants pocket, and put the gun in his jacket pocket. It was too big; the handle stuck out three inches. He tried to tuck it into his belt, but when he leaned over to shove the briefcase back under the bed the gun jabbed him uncomfortably between the ribs. He pulled the the briefcase back out and opened it again, placed the gun inside and locked it shut. Then Moffit sat down on the bed and listened.

He waited fifteen minutes and heard nothing but his own breathing. He went to the tent flap, opened it, and slipped outside.

A generator in the distance rumbled, an electric lamp on a pole cast a dim light at one end of the tent row. Moffit walked slowly, casually toward the west, toward the river side of the camp where Shawhan had parked the Jeep. He passed the last tent, heard a snoring inside, and went on. At the Jeep he stooped down, as though to tie his shoe, looking back to see if he had been noticed. The camp was asleep.

He turned the ignition and rolled slowly ahead, lights off, driving onto the road he and Shawhan had covered that afternoon. When he was out of sight, around the first turning, he switched the lights on.

He arrived at the Bishop trail sooner than he expected to, slowed, stopped to make sure it was the right place, then headed off onto the rougher, darker ground. Now the trees were thicker, the brush more sparse. The ground under his wheels was softer than before, built up over the centuries from forest debris. The trail was barely wide enough for the Jeep to pass, tree branches swept past his face, and he slowed to a crawl.

The headlights pierced the darkness, casting shadows to the sides, creating images of nightmarish beasts among the tangled branches of the low brush. How far had he gone? Less than ten minutes from the main road. Ten minutes. Moffit tried to visualize it from the air, decided to be safe, slowed and turned the Jeep onto a hard widening and cut the engine.

Without lights he was now totally blind. He sat there with his hands on the wheel and waited for night vision to come. Five minutes would be enough, then he would walk for another ten minutes and be fully acclimated by the time he reached the house. He could hear the night sounds now, the crickets and the other insects. He reached behind and got the briefcase, took out the Luger, and closed the case again. He got out of the Jeep and leaned against its bumper, reached into his pocket for the silencer, screwed it on, and dropped the gun to his side.

The school at Orekhovo: Absently he thought of the school, the bitter-cold night, waiting in the snow for his target, the sounds of crunching ice under the man's boots, the shot, a good score. He remembered how still it had been then, until the dead man rolled over, got to his knees, and brushed the snow from his coat.

He started to walk, conscious now of the sound his feet made as they touched the dirt. He could see patches of dark sky through the high branches above, and he could see ahead for some distance, well enough to set a brisk pace.

Suddenly he stopped in his tracks. Directly ahead was the small shed, the garage. He leaned against a tree, hefted the Luger in his hand, then crept slowly to the edge of the clearing. Beyond the shed, he saw the white house. He stayed in the deep shadow, focused his eyes on the entire scene, followed the layout from left to right, looking for movement, listening for sounds. Then he took a deep breath and ran to the shed, stopped, flattened himself against the wooden boards and looked around the corner. He was already breathing hard. He waited, let his pulse slow down, allowed the breathing to stabilize. Again he waited, leaning against the house, his shoulder blades pressed against the chalk-white boarding. Cautiously, carefully, he lowered himself to the ground, edged to the corner, and looked along the front of the house. There, not ten feet away, were four wooden steps leading up to the porch. He moved slowly, half bent, made the wooden staircase, and placed his feet carefully along the step ends as he took them one at a time, avoiding the middle where the boards might groan under his weight. The screen door had a spring on the inside.

He pulled and the door swung open, a small whisper in the spring, an almost noiseless sighing in the hinges. He stepped through and approached the heavy front door from the left side, away from the glass window in the door's center. He listened at every move he made, listened for sounds, for foreign noises. The white porcelain doorknob turned easily and the old door cracked open, wood parting reluctantly from mate wood. It was darker inside and Moffit leaned against the door frame for a moment to adjust his eyes once again to the change. Immediately ahead was a staircase.

He crossed the wooden plank floorboards and found them solid, no betraying noise in them. One by one he ascended the steps, turned on the landing, and made the second floor. At the top railing he saw doors to his left and right, guarding the dark corridor. He went to the end first, the door on his left. It opened with a gentle push and Moffit looked inside. The room was empty. There were curtains against the far wall, and a door that led to the veranda. It was a corner room, big enough to be the master room, but it was empty, no furniture. He slipped out and crossed to the room opposite. That door was already ajar; he peered through into the shadows. A large poster bed occupied the far center of the room. There was a mosquito netting over the bed, hung from a hook in the ceiling. Moffit could see perfectly now, light from the moon entering through the screened veranda. He held his breath and glided across the space. He would shoot Bishop in the head as he slept. Then again. There would be no great gushing blood, no convulsing, no

115

drama. Breathing, then not breathing; dreaming, then not dreaming. He stood at the end of the bed and looked through the netting. The bed was neatly made, the single pillow puffed and waiting. But the bed was empty.

He walked slowly to the door, into the hallway, and down to the next room. It, too, was empty. The room across the way was empty. He turned abruptly, then headed quickly back to the first room, looked again, went out onto the veranda and walked around the perimeter of the upstairs, looking again into each room, checking behind the doors.

He went down the stairs and searched the ground floor. As he entered the huge kitchen, he froze. On the counter was a candle, burning dim yellow, and standing at the sink, an old woman, facing him, staring at him. She was dressed in a long white nightgown, her silver hair was hanging in strings to her shoulders. Her mouth was open; she had no teeth. Moffit swung around and ran through the hallway to the front of the house, pushed the doors open, vaulted down the steps and across the lawn. He ran as fast as he could, through the garden and onto the road, gulping in air, his hands striking out in front as he threw them up with every stride of his legs. He nearly fell, slowed to a fast walk until he reached the Jeep. He dropped the gun on the backseat and leaned against the fender, breathing heavily, his heart pounding under the sweat-drenched shirt.

She had seen him! His mind was racing. Should he have killed her? Why? No, she was too old. It was too dark. She would never know who it was in her kitchen. *Where the hell was Bishop?*

Moffit stood straight and took a dozen deep breaths, then he leaned forward and put his hands on his knees. *Where was Bishop?* Should he go back? The easy kill was out of the question now. He would have to chase him out of the garage, run him down in the other house. *Oh, shit! Damn!*

He got into the Jeep and jammed it off the road, then backed and got straight. He gunned the engine, scattering stones as he spun his wheels, and jumped ahead onto the dark track. He switched on the lights and drove as fast as he dared until he reached the fork, then turned the wheel hard and gunned it again, driving fast toward the basin. He would sit on the concrete and observe the fucking mud. Let Bishop scream about intruders, assassins. He was at the basin.

The moonlight was fading in its part of the sky, washing away with light of a different color in the east, a grayish-blue tone. It was several hours before daybreak, but it wasn't night either. Moffit drove slowly now, carefully, sensing the air and feeling the breeze on his face. When he arrived at the head of the basin he stopped and got out, looking down into the shallow valley that cradled the horseshoe harbor, the turning pond for Globe's barges.

The brown water was barely discernible from the dark shoreline, but he could relate river sounds to the direction he was looking and he could see movement there, a sparkle or a sheen as the river moved through the basin and on toward the deeper trench to the sea. He leaned against the fender and lit a cigarette. Far away he heard a bird caw.

The old woman was still in his mind, the frightening old hag he had seen for that fleeting second in Bishop's kitchen, like an apparition, a ghost in the moonlight. She was a servant, probably, an Amerindian woman, he guessed. There was nothing he could do about her, nothing he thought he should do.

He blew smoke out and watched it disappear into the darkness, moving slowly with the slight breeze. He thought of the cable, the message Jennifer Moengo had given him:

"Washington Authorizes Execute Bishop Immediately."

He thought for a fragmented moment of a night trip to Baltimore, a meeting with some Latin, his feeling of naive dishonesty as he left a dirty saloon booth with the gun in a brown sack under his arm, the foolish melodrama of it all—the sensation he had then of being watched.

He stood by the Jeep, smoking, looking down into the semidarkness. He wondered how he would be feeling if he had killed Bishop, seen the black holes jump onto his forehead, seen the mound jerk under the sheets and quiver, the eyes pop open and turn glass-opaque, lifeless. He tried to picture himself standing over the bed, tucking the gun into his belt and walking away, out of the house. But he couldn't get past the twin black holes and the staring eyes.

Moffit was trying to think clearly but his thoughts were coming in short, jerky spasms, none of them formed into useful ideas. He turned and leaned over the steel side of the Jeep to get his gun. It had become lodged between the back and the seat cushion. He wiggled it free and held it in his hand, thumbing the safety on; he unscrewed the silencer, pushed the gun into his belt, and dropped the silencer in the briefcase, shutting it.

Then he turned and started to walk down the slope toward the concrete damwork, feeling the stones under his boots, seeing very well by the light of the eastern sky.

The river was flowing as before, as it had done since the gate had misdirected its own natural flow, gurgling and perhaps even protesting at the intrusion into its centuries-old privacy. Moffit walked to the gate and looked down toward the water, imagining the mud and the swirling debris that was flowing with the stream as it headed through this basin enroute to the ocean. He heard the bird caw again, and wondered if it was the same bird. Then he heard another, from the other side of the basin, and presently another. He walked farther, and had it been very

117

dark he would have stepped off the concrete and fallen into the water below. But he stopped, turned, and looked in the direction of the pump house, then let his gaze wander around the chocolate waters of the harbor.

He tried to imagine the width of the basin in terms of a barge, then in terms of a long golf shot. He had once set a golf ball on the front end of the port catapult aboard the *Ticonderoga*. It was a late watch and they were anchored in the Philippines. The ball was teed-up on a matchbox. Moffit had taken a well-balanced, hefty swing and struck the ball squarely, sending it directly down the centerline of the big carrier, a two-hundred-yard shot. He remembered seeing it streak into the darkness, then hearing it hit the steel plates near the stern of the ship. Was the basin that wide?

Moffit looked to his left, to the south, toward the undisturbed river, and tried to distinguish the form he thought he saw in the water; a turtle crossing the river at its broadest point, heading for a small island that had managed to hold on for the years it took the river to go around. The turtle left a V, a ripple in the water, as it swam across the smooth surface. Then, as he watched more closely, he saw that it wasn't a turtle, but the snout of an animal. He could see the ears, and the eyes peering above the water line. The ripple became a wake as the animal reached shallower water. Suddenly it broke the surface, plunged out of the water, and stood on the shore, shaking itself. It was a cat, a jaguar. It looked slowly around, saw the concrete dam and the end of its world, then sauntered off into the island thicket.

How long had it been since he had been so silent, since he had been alone in the forest? He tried to remember: He was tied to a tree, locked against hard bark; he had suffered the dawn through the ammoniac stench of his wet flight suit. The hut and the image of Ding How flashed across his mind. *How now, Ding How? Give me an illusion.*

The pain in his legs, the pain in his back. Strange that he couldn't remember pain, the pain in his face when he woke up after surgery in China. He had told them in the Philippines, and again in Hawaii, and again in San Diego. He had told them in Washington, at the recovery center, how he had been wounded in the face.

"There were four soldiers, sir. At my fifth camp. They tied me to a tree and strapped my head against the trunk. One of them made me open my mouth and he put an egg between my teeth. A raw egg, sir. Yes, sir, a chicken egg. Between my teeth, sir. Then one of the other soldiers got back twenty yards and shot at the egg with a target pistol. He missed it the first time and the bullet went through my cheeks. But I didn't move, sir. He hit it the second time."

* * *

118

What about Bishop? *Sheeit!* Get 'em, Jack! Zoom, the red trail of a rocket-pack screaming down on a truck, a silent burst of red and black as they hit, the immediate execution of war, body pieces flying up to meet the plane as it thundered past.

Moffit sat down on the concrete and dangled his feet over the side. Would Podgorsky want him to do it now? Some other way, then. Not the gun. Moffit had never liked the idea of a gun, the idea of sneaking it into the country. He pulled it out of his pants and held it in his palm, feeling how warm it had gotten against his belly. It was heavy, a good weapon. He put it on the concrete next to his leg, then pushed it back so it wouldn't fall over into the mud.

It had been a long time since he had thought about Donna. Donna. Oh, God, Donna. Moffit knew after he was shown the picture that they were working on the enormous power of rejection.

"Your flight mates have rejected you. They never searched for you. Your father has abandoned you. Your country has rejected you. Your faith has rejected you! Your woman has rejected you! Look at her, look at her face, how content she is, how happy she is with another man. You weren't good enough, never good enough. How many others were there? Fool! How many others?"

They had worked on that and on his own ambition to become bigger than, better than, stronger than, higher than. They had not humbled him, they had given him power to *become*. The words were so easy to say, to repeat after Chou's interminable lessons:

"I am a cut above! Money? How much will it take to make me into the man who is a cut above? Position, perhaps. Achievement, public acclaim. What is 'a cut above'? To float higher! To know that I am a man who has done, can do, and will do things beyond the range of others. Secret things; others will believe I am doing mundane, normal work when in fact my secret things are being done without their knowledge, things that will alter their lives. Secret things. Secret, important things that only I can do, because they have made me a cut above, because I have become a man who is a cut above."

Donna was standing alone at the rail, on the observation deck. Everybody else was down below, the cameramen and the reporters and his mother and friends. They were all down below as he stood in the doorway of the big Pan Am plane, dressed in his Navy blues and his polished black shoes. With his ribbons and his cane. Donna stood there apart in her raincoat and watched him with her hands in her pockets. Before he started down the steps she turned and walked away. He had never seen her again.

119

* * *

The trees along the shoreline were turning from black and gray to a dark green now, and the sky was a misty blue in the west, a pinkish aqua color in the east. A light fog, more a haze than a mist, was lying near the treetop level. Moffit stood up, took the gun in his hand. He had never fired it; now he stood and held it with both hands, aiming at a leaf that had fallen into the stream. He followed the leaf in the gun sight, one eye squinting nearly shut. Then he made a little sound with his mouth: "Pfff . . . pff."

Moffit could not have known that his intended victim, Mr. Thaddeus Bishop, had been sitting in the airport VIP lounge that morning, drinking rum and smoking a cigar, or that while he was riding back to town in the Jeep, the fat Canadian was slumped comfortably asleep in the executive cabin of a bright new Jetstar and was even at that moment riding atop the brown belly of a Nassau teenager.

Moffit shoved the Luger into his belt, turned on his heel, and marched smartly across the dam toward his Jeep.

CHAPTER 11

Josef Podgorsky was not amused when his secretary presented him with a birthday cake on the fifteenth of August. It was a Thursday, and he hated Thursdays more than any other day of the week because it was too late to start anything constructive and too early to consolidate the business he had begun. It was always Friday in Moscow when it was Thursday in Washington. His weekends were boring because he had no one to share them with or they were tiring because he was on an airplane to or from some city or country that bored him even more than Washington.

Still, he should have at least smiled when she placed the cake on his table. It was shaped in the form of the country he had been watching with considerable interest lately, and the woman had gone to considerable trouble to find fourteen miniature chairs to set in the creamy pink frosting. Thirteen of them were painted white and the fourteenth was black to honor the PPP's victory the day before when it had won thirteen of the fourteen elective seats in Parliament, an election he himself had influenced to some degree.

His mood was not to be blamed on the fact that it was Thursday, or that he had turned fifty during the night. Podgorsky considered himself to be a man whose years were an advantage rather than a liability.

There were three reasons for his irritation, all related to his present status as file coordinator for the British Guiana-Cuba interface.

One primary provocation came from Fidel Castro, the revolutionary who demanded and fought for change but who was afraid to give it a proper name. He wanted his cake and he wanted to eat it as well; he wanted to be the author of a Cuban democracy built on a foundation of social and economic equality for all. He wanted a capitalist state with the benefits of a Socialist state. He wanted American aid and American support without the interference of the Mafia, and he wanted assurances from the Soviet Union that were equally preposterous, including guarantees of economic and trade alliances, arms and defense grants, endorsements from the Soviets in the chambers of the United Nations.

Podgorsky's last meeting in Moscow with Malenkov and the Caribbean desk people had ended in a statement of ultimatum that was to guide Podgorsky's course for the next months. It was an either/or proposition: either Castro decides for us or he decides against us. If he decides against us, the Caribbean picture will change, the target will become the British Islands and Nicaragua. If he decides for us, that decision will have to be made soon, before he moves into Havana.

Podgorsky had never met Castro. He had met Che Gueverra in Guatemala years ago, but only briefly, and only socially. Apart from the reports he read and the information he received from his agents in Havana, he was in no better position to predict what Fidel Castro was going to do than the boy who shined his shoes. He wondered if Fidel himself knew, beyond the next hour, what he was going to do.

His second problem, one that gnawed at his belly lining like a peptic ulcer, was the status of his network in the West, or in the South, to be more accurate, because he had little or nothing to do with North America except for the use he made from time to time of couriers, communications runners, and industrial agents who supplied him with production and shipping information.

He dealt very rarely with the diplomatic corps; they were shoddy little people with shoddy little jobs, administrators whose imaginations led them no further than the nearest toilet in time of crisis.

He and his little Caribbean staff had concentrated their recruiting efforts on local nationals and American businessmen, both reliable sources of information and both easy to persuade. Across his desk flowed a constant stream of documents, borrowed or stolen or photographed. The physical capital budget plan for any given multinational corporation for any given Caribbean country was his, practically speaking, hours after he asked for it. The estimated cash flow for any project, the building program for any city, the competitive bidding for a refinery, the so-called secret formation of the Federation of Caribbean Nations—Podgorsky was privy to it all, and to matters far more intimate.

He gave himself some credit for the development of the Oil Workers' Union in Trinidad, though he probably had less influence on that development than he thought. But his network was weak in the area of productive, energetic, action-oriented people who could initiate a program and see it through to some kind of a conclusion. He had been given Pamela in the American Embassy in Honduras, and she had failed. They had given him Rodney in Dominica and he had become a drunk, then was shot in a parade. Sidney had done well, organizing the dock and hotel workers. But that was long range, below the level of government infiltration that he wanted to establish. Now they had given him Moffit, the American who was to be his eyes and ears inside the Globe Corporation, who was unable to carry out a simple order.

But the most troublesome thorn in his side was Globe itself, Globe and Gregory Hawthorn, one and the same. Podgorsky had thus far made no commitment, offered no incentive, but he had asked questions and Hawthorn, Podgorsky knew, was not an idiot. He must have realized immediately what the Russians wanted. If he were a man whose wits were intact, he would also have realized why.

Podgorsky would have to take a risk very soon. He would have to develop an avenue that would tie the fortunes of Globe to his own, generate a mutuality of some sort. For hours at a time he tilted the matter back and forth in his brain, ruling out the idea of a threat, considering and then ruling out, too, a large sum of money, considering an appeal to Hawthorn's greed, or his ambition. With the correct backing and the proper support from his government, Podgorsky could help Hawthorn become as big as the majors. Would that be enough to gain his willing cooperation?

Locked in his safe was a folder that Podgorsky had prepared for his superior in Moscow. On the cover was a typed label, "The Communist Federation of Caribbean States." Inside was his plan for the achievement of that federation, a major consideration—indeed a pivotal consideration—being a secure source of petroleum in the region.

Podgorsky was convinced that Gregory Hawthorn was acting in good faith. A thorough study of his background and record showed him to be a practical man, one who dealt with realities and gave second rank to ideologies, a businessman first and foremost, answerable only to himself. He claimed, interestingly, to be apolitical.

Podgorsky had also seen the geological surveys provided by Moffit, and the core sample analyses received in July. His people had researched them and had come to the conclusion that the BG concession was only months away from fruition.

The Bishop business had infuriated him. The obstacle appeared to be a legitimate one, but his senses told him it was contrived. Josef Podgorsky despised the idea of being cheated. To him it was like standing helplessly by while punks were stealing his hubcaps. The order to Moffit, his first assignment, should have disposed of the problem. It had not.

Podgorsky's "first aide," an appellation that he hated, was Lieutenant Ivan Rasmonovich, a bright and energetic young man from Kiev who had joined the diplomatic service to avoid being drafted into the military, then found himself going through the same harsh basic training as any foot soldier before earning the lowly rank of lieutenant. It was a commission he didn't want but couldn't refuse if he wanted to work in the United States.

"Congratulations, sir." Rasmonovich stood behind the secretary as she set the cake on the side table. "You have won two victories today. You celebrate your defeat of the forties and your success in British Guiana. They both deserve a small celebration."

"You think so?" Podgorsky got up and left his desk, stood with his hands on his hips looking at the cake, frowning. After a moment he smacked his lips and clenched his hands together, then acquiesced. "Very well. You might be right." He held his hand out as the secretary served a piece of the cake onto a small plate and passed it to him.

"I shall take credit for bridging the middle years, but none for the events in British Guiana. That was bound to happen in any case."

"I nevertheless congratulate you, sir."

"And I as well," the secretary added.

"Thank you both." Podgorsky took a bite, then set his plate on the table and crossed the fork over it. "You have made the arrangements for my trip next week, Ursula?"

"Yes, sir," she said. "Your messages are in cryptography now, sir. I expect them back this morning."

"That's fine, Ursula. Thank you. Just put the tickets on my desk. And Ivan," he said, turning to the young man, "I want you to handle a rather special matter for me."

Ursula collected the plates and placed them on a tray, then excused herself.

Podgorsky stood in front of a Socialist-realist painting, rooftops in a small Russian town, rich fields and green hills in the background. Fecund Mother Russia.

The room was very quiet. Podgorsky looked at Rasmonovich, and studied him. He was rather on the handsome side, if somewhat too proper, too well polished. There was never a hair out of place, his clothing was always fresh from the laundry.

Podgorsky pointed to a chair opposite the desk and, walking slowly around to his own side, sat himself in the fine, leather chair he had selected when they opened the office in 1953. He glanced again at the painting. That scene, so familiar to him, was in another lifetime. He had often walked across the high bridge and looked out over the rooftops of his hometown, wondering as a boy does what might lie beyond those hills, what adventures he might one day find there. The war and the realities of the world were unimaginable then.

Rasmonovich was sitting very still, his legs firmly under his knees, like a schoolboy sitting at class.

"You've been here less than a year, Ivan. You have learned the routines very well. I commend you for that."

"Thank you, sir."

"Still, there are lessons I've kept from you. It is time, I think, to assign you a passing mark and graduate you to the next level."

The young lieutenant was obviously pleased.

"So! We begin with information and apply that information to a practical problem. Then we shall see how to go about executing a correction." Podgorsky took pride in developing his people. This one, his aide, had excellent potential.

"I will give you four names, two of which you already know, and I will expect you to remember them all. I will then tell you how these names relate to one another. The names are Howard Barry, Stephen Moffit, Gregory Hawthorn, and Yu Hsin Chou."

"I'm sorry, sir . . . Yu . . ."

"Yu-sin-chow."

"Thank you sir, Yu Hsin Chou."

"Now, then. The relationship: Hawthorn is an American oilman with an incredible ambition. He wants to become a giant in his industry, but he's restrained by the Atlantean elephants, the Seven Sisters—Standard and Texaco and the rest. He knows Stephen Moffit, but he does not know the other two.

"Stephen Moffit is an agent for our side. He was recruited by the Chinese at our request and was given instruction by Yu Hsin Chou. In addition, of course, we had him in our schools for a period of time. He was sent to British Guiana by us—not by the Chinese—by us, to keep an eye on the Globe project. We paid for him, we maintain him. He is ours.

124

"Yu Hsin Chou is no longer connected with Stephen Moffit and it is not reasonable to assume he knows the others, except in the case of Hawthorn perhaps, by reputation."

"Yes, sir. I understand."

Podgorsky turned in his chair and concentrated on a treetop in the park across the street.

"How is it, then, I wonder . . ." He stopped. "No, let us finish with the fourth man. Howard Barry." He turned to face Rasmonovich.

"As you know, we have a small network of people in this hemisphere who work for us, many of them Americans. The information they give is often interesting. At times it is crucial, often quite vital. When the communications system was established in 1951, my predecessor thought it wise to route all incoming traffic away from Washington, traffic from the agents-in-place.

"He had a fellow on the string, a biology professor in Williamsburg, Virginia, who lived alone. He was a bona fide party member, and he was poor. An ideal communications drop. That man was, of course, Howard Barry. He's still in that position. The agents write him a personal letter and fix their microfilm to a corner or transmit their information in a simple code and he passes it to our courier on a set cycle."

"Understood, sir."

"Good. That being the case, let me ask my question."

Podgorsky faced the window again. "How is it, do you suppose, that I have in my desk the contents of a letter written by Stephen Moffit to the Chinaman, Yu Hsin Chou?"

He turned very slowly, allowing his gaze to slip past the painting and come to rest on Ivan Rasmonovich's eyes.

"Stephen Moffit is a Russian agent, Ivan, not an agent for the damned Chinese. He has no reason to communicate with the Chinese. None whatsoever!"

"How did you come by the letter, sir?"

"Not the letter, comrade. The contents of the letter. The answer is simple. Moffit is sleeping with a communications clerk in British Guiana. One of our people. She read it and conveyed the contents to her connection."

"Howard Barry."

"Exactly."

"What does his letter say, Comrade Podgorsky?"

"See for yourself. You may read her memo, received in this office last evening." Podgorsky opened his desk drawer and passed an envelope to his aide.

With difficulty, Rasmonovich managed to unravel Jennifer Moengo's handwritten sentences. He held the memo in his lap and looked up. Podgorsky waited a moment, then repeated the key lines from memory. "'Mother is fine. I am bored. The heat is terrific. Work is stalled. Hawthorn is a phony.'" Podgorsky clasped his hands on the desk top.

"And tell me, if you can, what the last line is supposed to mean?"

Rasmonovich read the last sentence again and shook his head. "'The closets are full of Philistines.'" He paused and looked at Podgorsky. "I don't know, sir."

"Nor do I. The Philistines are a tribe in the Bible. A tribe in the Bible." Podgorsky massaged his jaw. "But what is the reference? And what do you think of the other lines? *Hawthorn's a phony . . . Heat . . . mother . . . bored . . .*"

"Comrade Podgorsky . . ." Rasmonovich placed the memo and the envelope on Podgorsky's desk. "I believe I would be most concerned with the part about Hawthorn. If he's a phony . . ."

"It would appear so on the surface, Ivan, but American slang is often deceiving. Consider the possibility that this is nothing more than a friendly letter to a friend. In that case, we have only to reprimand Mr. Moffit, remind him of his protocol. In the same sense, he may consider Gregory Hawthorn something of a boorish snob, an ungenuine human being. Such a person could be called 'phony.' Yet, he uses the word 'mother.' That is our code quantum word for Washington."

"Did you ask cryptography, sir?"

"No. I did not. I will not." He sat back and cracked his knuckles one at a time. "You have the information and you have the problem. The next step . . ."

". . . is the execution of a correction, sir."

"Precisely so. Have you read yesterday's embassy summary?"

"I glanced at it this morning, sir."

"Page two." Podgorsky leaned forward, flipped a page on his summary papers. "We are required to attend a reception to be given in honor of Comrade Malenkov's fifty-first birthday." He smiled. "The chairman is only a year older than I. Well, in any case, we shall both go."

He straightened and stood, walked around his desk, and placed himself behind Rasmonovich's chair.

"I will take the opportunity to speak with Comrad Bochev. He has the authority to go through his offices in Moscow, the KGB, and I believe will be able to arrange for us to meet with the Chinaman."

"Yu Hsin Chou here, sir? In this country?"

"Here on the coast, somewhere on the coast. I will make the arrangements when I know his arrival schedule. It may take several weeks. However, when he comes, you will meet him and escort him

126

with all good courtesy to the meeting place that I will determine. Do you understand?"

"Yes, of course I understand, sir. And we shall find out what interest the Chinese might have in British Guiana."

"We shall find that out, and perhaps a good deal more. Now then, I shall thank you once again for the birthday remembrance. You were kind to think of me. I am going to go for a walk now. Please take my messages."

Podgorsky went to the coat tree. Rasmonovich helped him with the light plastic slicker he wore on rainy days.

He left the building and headed toward the bus depot. There he waited inside for several minutes at the magazine stand, then walked casually across the street to a park and sat down on a bench.

There was nothing he could do about Fidel Castro. The reports he received placed the guerrilla band in the Sierra Maestra, near Santiago de Cuba, almost as far from Havana as the geography would allow. The papers were full of reports dealing with barracks shoot-outs, executions, and village plundering.

As for the network, he would simply have to continue working on that one piece at a time. He had inherited a mess, a shambles since the Korean conflict, and it had gotten worse with the McCarthy hearings. Even the nationals were frightened.

Globe, too, was out of his control for the moment. He could only assume that Hawthorn would continue to work on his harbor problem until that was finished, lay the pipe and install his pumps where the trespass order allowed and bring his derricks and tank steel into the site as best he could. He would do these things because he could ill afford to waste time, when time was money under his rules. His objectives were the same as Podgorsky's: to get the oil out of the ground and into the refineries.

But they shared a common problem—Thaddeus Bishop—and Hawthorn was not the kind to deal with it forcefully.

At noon he was joined on the park bench by another man who sat down and began to read a newspaper. A few minutes later, Podgorsky stood, pulled the slicker straight, and went to lunch.

That would do it for Bishop. A man to do a man's work. Now, as that thought entered his mind, he wondered again about Moffit. He did not come with strong credentials. They had examined his profile carefully, studied his training record with concern. When he was passed on to Podgorsky, they had suggested a minor posting with growth potential, and then proposed British Guiana. Did they consider that a "minor" assignment?

Where had the information originated, the data that suggested a less-than-brilliant operative with limited horizons? Some from his time in Russia, to be sure, but mostly from the Chinaman. Who else had the Chinaman given them? Maurer was dead. Dalante was missing. Ballentine, active and under surveillance; Brandt, imprisoned for tax fraud.

Was Chou being honest when he downgraded Moffit? Or was he using Moffit in some way?

It was a matter that had to be straightened out, and he had ways of doing exactly that.

CHAPTER 12

Between Stephen Moffit's arrival in June and the elections in August, he and Dan Shawhan solved the mud problem. They sacrificed a barge at the troublesome corner, anchored a massive net to that and to solid positions around the perimeter of the basin, and filled the net with stones. The rest was easy.

As far as the harbor and the river were concerned, Globe was ready to begin operations on a full scale.

With enormous difficulty, they had been able to bring some of the heavy equipment from the harbor to the camp, but it was a winch and dragline nightmare. Guards had been posted along the harder road, instructed to allow small vehicles and men through as a concession to the government, to permit "reasonable and necessary maintenance of the exploration facility," but anything larger than a small truck was routed to the south, over the marsh and soft mud, a route that looped under Bishop's land and then back to the north for a total one-way distance of over fifty soggy miles.

There was one derrick at the camp and sufficient pipe and drilling gear to permit Dreier and his men to spud, go down a few thousand feet and bring up cores. What he was getting was not what the charts said he was supposed to get, but he wasn't new to the business; these things happened sometimes.

On the last day of August, Gene Tinker arrived at the camp in the corporation's Jetstar. His passengers were representatives from the Chicago Bridge Company, contracted to do much of the heavy tank construction as soon as conditions—Thaddeus Bishop conditions—permitted. Tinker deposited the men in their business suits at Dreier's tent, and went in search of Stephen Moffit.

It had never been explained to him why he had been selected for CIA recruitment. Tinker had asked, several times, but they had never given him an answer. As a kid growing up in New York, he had always wanted to be a G-man. He used to listen to *Gang Busters*, pictured himself riding in a car with Colonel Schwartzkopf, shooting out of a side window.

When the war came he enlisted in the Air Corps and they put him in a fighter group, but just barely. He was an inch over the height limitation and had to hunch his back as he stood at the tape.

He guessed, later on, that they had their eye on him after he applied for G-2 when the war was over. He had married an English girl, brought her to his home in Yonkers, and discovered too late that he didn't love her enough to live with her.

It was when he went back to school and graduated from the college of liberal arts with a degree in political science that they nailed him. He was interviewing for a job, looking for a position that might get him close to some international excitement. That's what he told the counselors. A lady had invited him for drinks at a lounge, he had accepted, she had taken him for a ride along the river, and by the time he got out of the car he was employed by the CIA.

It was not what he thought it should be. They assigned him to an office and gave him several books to read, not to be removed from that room, and there he sat for over a month. He was assigned to live in a sheltered apartment with a dozen men who were unfriendly, he rode to work in a 1947 Ford, he was given no secret code words, and he was given no gun. In the second month they moved him to a new office and he was allowed to look at movies of men and women entering and leaving a pawnshop.

But in the third month he accompanied a man named Peter to the firing range, and they gave him twenty-four bullets to shoot at a target. Peter became his sponsor, and his partner, and his friend.

In the fifth month, Peter called him on the telephone at his sterile apartment and asked him if he could fly a T-6. Of course. Children could fly a T-6. Peter arrived one hour later and they drove to a secluded airport near Washington. There they boarded a DC-6 and when they were airborne, Peter gave him a .45 pistol. The next night, Peter rode in the back and Tinker flew in the front as they crossed over the border into Mexico in an unmarked T-6. They refueled and continued on through the night until they reached San Felipe, a small town near Honduras Bay in Guatemala.

They climbed down, Peter said thank you, told him to go back home, and then he disappeared. It was three o'clock in the morning, he was several thousand miles away from what he called home, and he had no idea what Peter's assignment was.

On his next office day a new man approached his desk and asked where he had been. He responded that he hadn't been feeling well and had gone to stay with friends at the lake. It was strange the man hadn't been informed because he certainly had left a message. The man then told him that Peter had been stabbed to death in a street fight somewhere near Detroit. Tinker reacted correctly, and the man gave him a job as his personal pilot, a job that lasted until the man became too big for his britches and was kicked upstairs. That was in June 1957. A week later he was working for Gregory Hawthorn.

"See if he has anything to say, Gene. See if you can find out what he feels about this operation."

Tinker found his man at the harbor, checking on a generator wiring problem that had confused Shawhan. He invited Moffit to go for a ride in the jet, see some of the country to the south.

It was a beautiful trip. They flew nearly to the border of Brazil and returned by way of Kaiteur Fall, cutting low over the ledge, then dropping fast and hard right to swing through the gorge, then up the river and back to camp.

They took turns at the controls, showing off. Tinker showed Moffit a maneuver that had saved his life in a dogfight over Holland, a simple negative-G pushover that resembled an inside loop, down and through an anvilhead cloud that left the attacker several miles ahead and out of sight. The Jetstar responded decently to that abuse, but was hardly able to match the performance of Tinker's wartime Lightning.

When they landed, Moffit demonstrated his carrier technique. Tinker, who had always wondered at the mentality of fools who flew from ships, was impressed. He sat rigid in his right-hand seat as Moffit brought the plane in, low and slow, nose too high, gear down, flaps fully extended, grinding through the heavy air at just above the stall point, hanging it over the "deck," and then . . . *plop!* When they stopped and started their turn toward the hangar, Tinker was sweating and Moffit was laughing. Tinker had never seen the man laugh. No one had seen Moffit laugh for a very long time.

That evening they ate no dinner. They sat in Moffit's tent and drank Scotch without ice cubes. At nine o'clock they drove the Jeep to the Cessna. Moffit flew and Tinker held the bottle. At Ogle, the tiny strip north of Georgetown, they landed and wired a van, then drove into town and drank until morning at a whorehouse. Tinker flew back and they slept till noon.

Tinker was up first, growling and forcing coffee into his belly. When Moffit came into the mess hall, he leaned over and spoke softly into Tinker's ear.

Together they drove again to the airstrip. Together they inspected the Cessna. A tree branch, not a large piece, but part of a tree nonetheless, was sticking through the left wing. Neither of them could remember how it got there.

For a long minute or two, Tinker and Moffit stood under the wing, staring at the branch. Then, without a word, they walked away, stopped fifty feet from the Cessna, and looked again. Moffit started to laugh, Tinker snorted, and they trudged off in the direction of a scrub tree that sat in the middle of the field tank site, cussing at the limb that got in their way.

They sat for a while, Tinker chewing on a weed, Moffit with his legs stretched out in front, his back against the rough bark.

"I did a lot of sitting like this, Gene."

Tinker squinted, spat a seed out, brought his knees to his chest, and leaned back.

"Yeah. I'll bet you did. Over there, with those chinks, huh?"

"Not 'chinks.'"

"How did you get those scars on your face?"

Moffit didn't answer.

"Sorry. That was a bad question."

"No, that's all right. I'm stuck with the scars, on my face and other places. I can live with it."

"You mean rough treatment? Torture? Did they do that shit on you, Steve?"

Moffit was staring at the sky. He picked up a stone and tossed it aside, then stood up, took hold of a tree limb, and looked straight at Tinker.

"Let me tell you something, Gene," he said. There was no anger in his voice; his expression was passive. "I had a pretty rough time over there." His brow darkened then, his eyes seemed to harden.

"I would just as soon forget it, and I'd like you and your people to forget it. You understand? I've been had by experts, my friend. You're short about a quarter."

He turned and headed for the Jeep.

Tinker's objective had been to learn what he could about Moffit's attitude, his impression of the project, his reporting channels if possible. He came away with very little.

Yes, the man made regular reports to the government. He thought the project was being handled recklessly. He thought Gregory Hawthorn was a playboy who let his thugs do the dirty work while he pranced around the Caribbean sticking his face close to the backsides of the politicians.

But Tinker's bigger impression was a more personal one. He came away with the distinct feeling that Stephen Moffit was a very unhappy young man with no friends on the block his own age. He had no one to play with. He interpreted the reference to "experts" to mean his treatment by American psychologists who had been involved in his rehabilitation program. Since there was no evidence that Moffit might believe he was under suspicion, that interpretation was reasonable. Someone suggested the possibility of a moderate paranoia, or an oversensitive defense mechanism at work, and that, too, was reasonable.

But Tinker's final conclusion regarding the Soviet plant came down to the simple observation that Stephen Moffit was, at worst, bored to death.

At four o'clock the next afternoon, as Tinker was getting ready to fly the contractors back home, Reinaldo Villar-Cruz told him about Thaddeus T. Bishop.

The news of his death had come across the camp radio-telephone via Globe's Georgetown office. Bishop and three others were killed when his boat, traveling at high speed, exploded in the channel between New Providence and Hogg Island. There were no details.

When the news reached Gregory Hawthorn, he turned in his chair and faced the window, thinking of Alan Drinkwater's words: "Shall we shoot him, then?"

When Josef Podgorsky heard it in Washington, it wasn't news. He grunted in satisfaction and reached for the last stale piece of his birthday cake.

Part 3

CHAPTER 1

The Miami sky was redder than normal, sunset and Everglades fires casting a glow against some low clouding. Hawthorn stood at the hotel bay window and watched it turning to purple.

If he had been even the slightest apprehensive about his ability to carry off this incredible charade in the beginning, he was more so now. Consciously, he was running the show as it had been programmed, using innovations and inventing explanations for those innovations to keep his reputation clean in the industry.

In St. Vincent, in Grenada and Dominica, in St. Kitts, his terminals were applauded by politicians and consumers alike. In St. Lucia and in Montserrat they were saving money hand over fist thanks to his bulk delivery system, and Globe's shipping department was running out of space to store the profits.

But some of his customers and many of his competitors were expressing distrust of this man who appeared to be doing things backward in British Guiana. It was incomprehensible that a man who had shown such skill in building his business in the past would now be constructing a delivery system before he had the product. Each time he heard such an expression of distrust, Hawthorn unconsciously wished something would happen to stop the project altogether. Bishop's death was not the answer.

Nowhere was it written that the passing of Thaddeus T. Bishop should spell disaster for the Globe project. He had been a gift to Alan Drinkwater and Gregory Hawthorn, and they had used him, and now the gift had been taken away. Bishop had given them three months to drag their feet, to keep their eyes on Cuba, to establish a more accurate critical path toward a successful and a timely conclusion to the Globe project.

Hawthorn had never planned on him. There was nothing in the

original outline that suggested they had to have, or even *should* have a Thaddeus T. Bishop. It was so damn convenient! That was the nut of it. It was like winning a big pot with a dollar bet and then losing it all again. Nothing lost. But tell the player that.

Upon hearing of Bishop's death, he had spent the better part of that same afternoon considering his position, his involvement in the conspiracy. His reputation was in jeopardy, and his future was uncertain. Yet, he would "find" oil and he would be vindicated, but only for a short time. Under the rules, he would not be permitted to explain his actions, and he would be forced to bear the ridicule of others in his industry, most of whom used judicious care in their dealings with questionable allies and host countries. When the hoax was finally revealed, he would be forced to admit that he had in fact discovered a remote pocket of crude oil and spent hundreds of millions in borrowed capital to exploit it.

He would then be a very rich man, given the Commission's terms of agreement, but in all probability he would also be a hunted man. Why, then? Why had he agreed to do the job? Perhaps Kiley had been right. His escape during the war had been more than a simple, impulsive act of survival. There had been, in retrospect, a *need* for him to escape, to get back into the battle, to fight the enemy.

He remembered his first experience on a ski jump. He was too slow and too awkward to make the slalom team, so he had climbed to the top of "Big Chester" in Duluth and had strapped on jumping skies. He had stood at the top for a full minute, looking out toward the distant horizon, then down at the tiny people, the cars parked a mile away, the chalet rooftops in the valley. When he had tipped the long skis over the brink and started down, nothing short of a suicide stop on the scaffolding could have prevented him from going off the end and flying through the ice cold air.

He remembered the elation he had felt then, standing at the bottom of the hill, on his feet, looking back up—the thrill, the satisfaction, the sense of accomplishment. Maybe he was trying to recapture those feelings. But whatever it was that had convinced him to join the Commission's carnival, it was too late to turn back now.

The lights in Baton Rouge had been on a long time when he finally put his yellow pad aside and fed the top three sheets into the shredder. With them went his notes: "Must control pace." "Barge . . . sink in river." "Dynamite something and blame somebody. Who?" "State Dept. calls and demands stop. Why? Think reason why." And similar.

None of those ideas had seemed very logical. It would be very logical for him to go and dance on the man's grave, and then hurry on down to rip his signs off the trees and send a telegram to Chicago Bridge to demand immediate action on their contract. That would be very logical, and Gregory Hawthorn was a man who thought logically. It was a sure bet that Josef Podgorsky, the man who without a doubt had arranged Bishop's accident, would have expected him to be just that: logical.

It would seem, then, that he had been given no choice. All through this affair, he had been faced with no-choice decisions. This had been another one. So the last thing he did before turning off his own office light that eventful evening was to write a cable, addressed to Sandy Dreier, short and to the point. Hawthorn hoped it would be intercepted and read by the other side. How and by whom were items beyond his ken or caring.

"Sorry for Bishop good for us. Stop. Go like hell."

Hawthorn checked his watch again. He knew it would be a typical September night in Miami, better than July and August but still too warm for his comfort. He was beginning to despise the heat. He carried his light suitcase to the elevator, rode down, and hailed a taxi.

In keeping with his cable directive, he had ordered Tinker to stay with the Chicago Bridge people, provide them transportation, make every effort to get the tank construction underway as soon as possible. Consequently the Jetstar was in Chicago, loading passengers for a quick trip to Pittsburgh. It was one of the penalties one accepts in ownership. The expensive airplane is never available when the boss needs it.

Hawthorn was scheduled to be in British Guiana for a tape-cutting ceremony. Bishop or no Bishop, the harbor work had gone ahead and the damn thing was finally completed. The prime minister and his new minister of Petroleum, Lands, and Mines, Carlysle Ramprashad, were to be on hand, together with the governor, several of the Globe people including Sandy Dreier, and the government advisor, Stephen Moffit. They would watch and clap as Hawthorn cut the ribbon that would allow the first oil transport barge to pass into the harbor.

It was about dinner time when he arrived at Miami International. Hawthorn checked in, left his single bag at the counter to be sent along, and went to the coffee shop to wait the half hour he had allowed before flight time.

He ordered coffee and toast and was reading the evening paper when he was joined by a stranger wearing a light raincoat and a summer fedora. The man sat down opposite him and smiled.

"You would have the courtesy to come with me, please. It is Mr. Podgorsky would like to see you. Thank you."

The man then got up and left the shop, turning to the right as he entered the wide airport lobby. Hawthorn sipped his coffee, folded the newspaper, and took out his billfold, finding a dollar and leaving it on the table. He followed the man to the taxi stand out front, and when a black Citroen stopped he got into the backseat next to the stranger.

The lock buttons snapped down and the car pulled away before Hawthorn saw that Podgorsky was not in the car.

"Where's Podgorsky?"

The Citroen was in traffic, turning onto the ramp to exit the airport. Hawthorn tested the door handle, found it solidly locked from the inside. He looked to his left and saw the man's hand tucked inside his coat, between the lapels, a bulge near his right chest.

"Where's Podgorsky?" he demanded.

"We are going to meet him," the man said.

"Who are you?"

The man was looking out the window and did not reply until they had crossed 36th Street.

"I am Lieutenant Rasmonovich. I work for Mr. Podgorsky. In this instance I am only meant to deliver you to him. I know nothing about it more than that."

Hawthorn waited a minute. "Can you tell me how far? Where it is we're going? I have a plane to catch."

The man looked across at him. "I am sorry, sir," he said. "We are going to downtown, on the bay. It won't be long."

They drove quickly through the Friday evening traffic, turning right on 79th Street toward the ocean, then left on U.S. 1. When they passed 163rd Street, Hawthorn knew he would spend the night in Miami, or somewhere near Miami. If they had uncovered the hoax, he might well spend the night at the bottom of the bay. He cursed himself for being so unsuspecting. He had reacted as naively as a schoolchild being kidnapped.

It was after six o'clock when the driver finally pulled to a stop near a fishing dock. A seafood restaurant nearby had already turned its lights on, and when they opened the car door Hawthorn smelled fish and oily matter, cooking scents he associated with rotten lobster.

The driver stayed in the car as the young Russian got out and motioned for Hawthorn to go ahead. They walked past the restaurant to the back, where a short dock jutted out from the seawall. Hawthorn stepped onto the wooden boards, turning left as the dock became much longer, running parallel to the shoreline for a hundred yards or more. When they had gone half the length, passing small dinghies and fishing boats, stepping over sundry kinds of debris left there by the daylight people, Rasmonovich told him to stop.

"Wait here. Someone will come in a few minutes."

Hawthorn watched his back as he disappeared down the smelly dock, certain now that he would live awhile longer. If they had meant to kill him, they would not have left him alone.

He smoked a cigarette and was ready to light another when he saw and heard a rowboat approaching the dock from his left, from the north. It bumped against a ladder at his feet and the oarsman waved him down. Hawthorn used the ladder, took a seat in the bow, and pushed them off.

The oarsman said nothing; he was dressed in a dark blue sweater and he wore a seaman's pea cap. He pulled at the oars silently, moving them slowly through the water. Hawthorn had seen a small fishing schooner tied to a buoy perhaps two hundred yards from the dock where he was standing, but he had not considered it as a possible meeting place. They were heading straight for it.

Hawthorn climbed aboard as the sailor held the boat close to the scow, then hoisted himself up, brushed his pants, and pointed to a hatchway.

Hawthorn crossed to the hatch and opened it, then felt carefully for the narrow ladder that led below. The light was poor and the smell was nauseous. He stood at the base of the ladder on wooden deck boards and allowed his eyes to become accustomed to the dim interior glow, an orange light given off by a single kerosene lamp, turned down to its minimum brightness.

"Good evening, Mr. Hawthorn." It was Josef Podgorsky. He sounded congenial, friendly. Hawthorn remained standing, looking toward the sound of his voice.

"Podgorsky," he said. "I can't see very well."

"Come in, please. I'm here, in the pantry."

Now he could see a curtain drawn across a part of the room, and behind it he could make out a small kitchen. He parted the drape and saw Podgorsky sitting at a table, a bottle and a glass in front of him. At the same time he saw the other man, the Chinese man. He was sitting on a chair against the bulkhead.

Hawthorn stopped just inside the curtain and stared at the Chinese.

"Jesus!" he whispered.

"Yes," said Podgorsky. "I don't like this very much. We have had to do this in the past, but I thought I was finished with it."

Hawthorn looked at Podgorsky and then back at the man. He was gagged, with a huge wad of cloth in his mouth and a piece of rope tied tightly across his open lips and in back of his head. His eyes were nearly shut from a beating, his face was torn open, blood had dried and caked on his cheeks and forehead. He was bound, his arms pulled tightly around the back of the chair. The chair itself was tied to an upright pole.

139

They had clubbed his legs until they were broken. He was wearing only his underpants. Burn marks on his chest—Hawthorn could only guess they were burn marks—looked as though someone had used several cigarettes, pressing the hot tips against his skin in a hundred different places. The man was conscious, breathing heavily in short gasps through his nose. They had broken that as well.

"God!"

"Let us go up and talk."

Hawthorn looked at Podgorsky, felt rage, a terrible rage rushing to his head. He turned quickly and climbed the ladder.

Topside, he placed his hands against the rails and looked down, seeing the dark, dirty water a few feet below, slopping against the wooden side planks. Podgorsky stood next to him and lit a cigarette, held it out as an offering. Hawthorn's head turned slowly, saw the glowing cigarette in Podgorsky's fingers. He turned until he was looking at the Russian's face.

His pulse was racing, his veins bulging at the temples. His jaw was clenched, his knuckles white as he gripped the rough wood. He took a deep breath and looked down again, concentrated on the black water.

"His name is Chou. I don't think you know him. He has been an American agent in China for several years," Podgorsky said, "passing intelligence to the British and to the Americans through former prisoners of war, training double agents for industrial work. He has caused considerable confusion for our side."

Hawthorn's mind was spinning. Revulsion, confusion, a sense of chaos, were tangled together.

"But you know Stephen Moffit."

Stephen Moffit . . . Chou. Hawthorn felt a tightness in his chest, a pressure at the back of his neck. He backed away from the rail. Drinkwater's contact, the Commission's intelligence source. Hawthorn stopped five feet away, turned, and stared at the Russian.

"What the hell is this, Podgorsky? What kind of animal are you?" He felt the rage boiling, trying to escape. "You aren't in Russia now; you can't torture a man in this country! You can't grab a man off the street at the point of a gun!"

Podgorsky met Hawthorn's stare without answering, then turned to look at the dark horizon. He was facing the water, the ocean side of the boat. He spoke to Hawthorn from a profile.

"I would ask you to try to forget the poor man below. I will say again, though, that I am not in favor of these things." He paused and flicked an ash. "No matter. We shall finish about him in a moment. Let us first do some business." Podgorsky puffed and then crushed the black cigarette under his heel.

"I think it is possible that Moffit was trained by the Chinaman to be a double agent. Mr. Moffit is possibly an agent for the United States government, acting on orders from the man below, the Chinaman. It is also possible that he is working for the Chinese. It is a riddle."

"I don't know what you're talking about."

Logic. Hawthorn was trying to fit the pieces together, but his brain was at dead slow. Chou trained Moffit. Chou works for the Commission. Logic.

"This is difficult, you know? If he is working for the United States, how do I know who Moffit's target is? The government of British Guiana, or you? Do you see the ambiguity? And if it is you, then I am also under observation."

"Yes. I see the ambiguity." Hawthorn closed his eyes. "And what if he's working for you?"

It was still for just a second, then Podgorsky slapped the rail. "Ha!" he shouted. "Then we are both victims of a comedy. It is an ingenious scramble. It cannot be both ways, sir."

The boat groaned, boards clamped in iron softly protesting as the old schooner rolled on a swell.

"No, Hawthorn, he is not working for me. You have no choice but to accept that as the truth." He paused. "In point of fact, you have few alternatives open to you regardless of what you choose to believe. Never mind the question of Stephen Moffit; your situation is precarious enough without his presence, threatening or otherwise. You have spent millions upon millions of dollars already. I happen to know that you have antagonized the major oil companies to such a degree that they are considering a boycott against your domestic operation. It is possible they will cancel their supply arrangement with you in the Caribbean, and you will be left with nothing to sell through your elaborate distribution system."

Hawthorn looked at the Russian.

"Where the hell did you hear that?"

"We have sources, Mr. Hawthorn. Now, then, given your situation, I am not reluctant to let you know mine. I am faced with this problem, sir: Let us assume that a country in the Caribbean region, wherever it may be in the general region, let us assume that country calls on us for assistance in some way. Please, sir." He held up his hand. "I am not suggesting that this will happen, but you are not a naive man. Should this happen, I would like to be able to help them. This may be in the way of economic assistance or technical advice, in trade, in any number of ways."

Hawthorn was standing against the rail a few feet away. Now he leaned over, squaring his face with Podgorsky's.

"That's a pile of shit!" He stood erect again. If this was going to be business, it would be business the Hawthorn way.

"I know what you want, Podgorsky. You want British Guiana, and you want Cuba. But more than that, mister"—he pointed his finger in the Russian's face—"you want my damn oil!"

"All right. All right, then. Let us be frank!" Podgorsky slapped the rail softly. "It is not an accident that a Socialist party is in power in British Guiana. Such developments take a very long time in their making. But it is done. It is a first step toward a greater change, a change that may benefit you greatly. I want you to understand that my government is prepared to assist those who seek change and it makes little difference to me whether you agree with that or not, or whether you endorse the change or not. You are in a position to take advantage of what is going to happen in the Caribbean. Yes, in Cuba and in the Dominican Republic and in Central America. Throughout the Caribbean, Hawthorn! I can help you to become one of the giants in your industry, and you will find that we understand the profit motive. We understand it very well, and we are fully prepared to pay the price in exchange for your cooperation."

Hawthorn thought of the battered body below, the blue and purple skin, the mangled, crushed human being tied like a animal to a pole, worthless debris. He was trying to think with the Russian's mind. *What if this American should decide against a cooperative effort? What if he should go to the CIA with the information I have given him regarding our ambitions? I will show him something to dissuade him from that course. I will show him what horrible pain looks like.*

"Go on. I'm listening."

"One of the difficulties we face is that of petroleum. Should we become interested in a country, and they in us, we are certain the Americans and the British will use petroleum, use a threat of its withholding, as a device to dissuade that country from its course. We naturally have our own oil, Mr. Hawthorn. Do not be fooled into thinking that our success or failure in the Caribbean hangs on the question of petroleum, for it does not."

"You go one step forward and you back up two, Podgorsky. That's a lousy way to get to the point."

"I was about to say," continued the Russian, "that our supply of petroleum is practically unlimited, but it is in the wrong hemisphere. Its transport would be less convenient than would be the case if we had a supply source in the region. No, I stand on what I said, sir. Petroleum is important, but it is not so important that we face defeat without its local availability. That is my point, Mr. Hawthorn."

142

"The point is, you want to make a deal with me."

"Is that how you negotiate, Mr. Hawthorn?"

"It saves a helluva lot of time."

"All right. I would like to make a deal. And if that's how you negotiate, I shall be blunt." He left the rail and walked a short way toward the bow of the boat. He stopped, clasped his hands behind him, then turned and started back.

Hawthorn was watching him.

This is it. This is the big bite. Let's go, Podgorsky. I'll be greedy enough to make you believe it and I'll be impressed with that tortured body, but don't expect me to fall apart. Come on with your deal, Mr. Russian. Podgorsky was standing two feet away, his legs spread apart, his shoulders squared for the confrontation. *Forget the dying Chinaman, forget Moffit, forget the inevitable aftermath, when they come into my cave and blow my brains out.*

"I will make this agreement with you, Mr. Hawthorn. I will agree to purchase your oil at the market level plus a charge of some kind—I hope at least that can be negotiated—and we will pay the extra charge in some unofficial way, into an account of your choosing. I will agree to use your fleet under the same arrangements, paying the standard rate plus the other charge in the same fashion."

Hawthorn showed no reaction, but his breath started to come easier. *Not yet. Let him get it on the table. Eat a little more celery.*

"And what if I say no?"

Podgorsky bent his head forward and whispered his answer.

"Then you will lose it. It will be taken away from you."

"Who will take it away?"

"You have two enemies, Hawthorn. They would both be glad to have you dismissed. Your own industry friends would be happy to shut you down, and the people of British Guiana would gladly take one hundred percent instead of the fifty percent you have offered them."

"Horseshit." Hawthorn stuck his nose close to the Russian's face. "Nobody shuts me down, Podgorsky, not you or Jagan or Esso or Texaco . . . nobody. I've got a lock on that crude oil. I'll find it and I'll ship it anywhere I damn well please." He paused, gauged the reaction, and finished quickly. "If you want that oil, you'll have to buy it from me on my terms, because I'm your only hope for a peaceful entry to the Caribbean. I can make you a hero without dropping the British Crown on your foot!"

Podgorsky backed off, turned to face the water again.

"You will ship it to my customers, Mr. Hawthorn. You will forfeit your political allegiances and you will become enormously wealthy. Globe's volume will surpass that of any European marketer, and soon those countries will be yours."

Good. Now he could dictate terms.

"Forget the superpower crap, Podgorsky. I'll get volume my way, and I'll get the European market and the South American market with or without your help."

"We will make it easier for you."

"Never mind that. I move one step at a time. For right now, I want your assurance that Jagan and his Communist buddies in British Guiana won't start a takeover. If they do, Mr. Podgorsky, I can guarantee you the British and the Americans will be swarming all over that field and you won't have a prayer of smelling one drop of my oil."

"I have given you a Communist country and I have given you assurances that we will purchase your oil, not steal it from you. Now you want me to guarantee the policies and the activities of a man like Cheddi Jagan!"

"That's what I want."

"How would you suggest I do that, sir. Shall I send the Russian army down to your camp?"

"Don't take me for an ass, Podgorsky. You have ways of keeping people in line. You do whatever it is that you do to keep Jagan off my back. I'll produce oil, and I'll sell it to you." Hawthorn stopped, let his deep-blue eyes land squarely on the Russian's face. "You stay out of my way, and keep that guy out of my way, and we can do business."

"All right, Hawthorn. I will keep Mr. Jagan away from you."

Podgorsky was standing like a statue, facing the bow of the schooner. He had listened very carefully, and he had extracted his deal. He would have his oil without a show of force, without the risk of war.

"Let us forget Stephen Moffit," Podgorsky said. "You have nothing to hide. If the man is in fact working for the Chinese government, his information will be useless. If he is working for the Americans, he will report that you are an inefficient exploration manager, nothing more."

Hawthorn waited, chilled. "Explain that," he said.

"You have been wasting time there, Mr. Hawthorn. You know full well you control an important resource, and you are stalling. You are afraid of the glut and you are afraid of the politics."

By God! The man was hooked clear down to his gonads! He trusted the hardware more than he trusted his own spy. It was an impulsive thing Hawthorn did then, something he couldn't resist.

"Podgorsky, have you ever considered the possibility that I'm a secret agent trying to sucker you into a mud hole?"

"Yes. I have."

The sailor drew his oars smoothly through the slick water. A humid fog curled above the swells, causing the yellow restaurant lights on shore to glow like distant Christmas tree ornaments. Halfway in, Hawthorn began to sense the putrid smell of rotten fish again. His eyes were on the lights and his hands in his lap as he rocked gently with the oarsman's easy stroke. He barely flinched when he heard a muffled shot. For the compromised Chinese soldier, the agony was over.

Podgorsky's message was crystal clear. The moment of quiet jubilation for Gregory Hawthorn, that moment of doubt-erasing elation, quickly melted, as though the slug had passed through his own heart, deflating it and laying bare his fears. For the first time, Gregory Hawthorn began to sense how dangerous the game had become.

CHAPTER 2

During the early part of 1958, amidst reports of rape, torture, upheaval, and misdirection among the guerrillas, the Cuban revolution was making troubled headway and modest headlines in its march to dethrone Batista. But the battle was still far from Havana, where life went on as usual and where the schism between the haves and the have-nots continued to grow wider.

But at least there was some evidence of action in that country, unlike the climate in Jamaica and in the Dominican Republic, where politics went on as usual with minor bumps and scrapes being taken and administered by opposing forces. Guatemala and Costa Rica, even Mexico and Nicaragua, were better candidates for Russia's ambitious assault on the Caribbean than those two.

Several of the Antilles islands were leaning to the left, but to hear the politicians in Grenada or in Dominica chant their somniferous incantations was about as inspirational as watching a floor dry.

Gregory Hawthorn, sitting in a comfortable Toronto hotel room, had come to the conclusion that Alan Drinkwater, like it or not, had called the shot accurately. He had said back in 1953 that Cuba was his choice for a Russian satellite, had even predicted the approximate year, 1959. That was still twelve months away. Today was January 20, 1958.

Hawthorn had arranged a meeting to prepare the semifinal act in the charade they were conducting for the benefit of Josef Podgorsky and company. His dinner tray and the dirty dishes had been set in the kitchenette; several chairs were placed around a coffee table in the suite's sitting room.

At a quarter to six there was a knock on the door. He opened it and Alan Drinkwater stepped in, took off his topcoat, and threw it on a chair.

When Hawthorn had reported the episode involving Yu Hsin Chou, Drinkwater was furious. His anger seemed to override any compassion he might have felt for the man. The mere idea that Chou might be working for the Chinese was preposterous, and the idea that Stephen Moffit could possibly be engaged in some kind of intelligence work for the Americans was absurd. Indeed, Podgorsky's suspicions might have seemed funny if the matter were not so serious.

The unsettling part about the episode, apart from Chou's terrible agony and dying, was the possibility that they had broken his spirit and compromised the Commission's information system. Still, Chou's knowledge of the network was limited; he could not have given them very much, apart from the names of some who knew even less than he did about the workings of the CIA or the secret Commission.

Drinkwater was careful in his sharing of the detailed information concerning Chou's activities. He admitted that Chou had been their informant, that he had been a valuable agent, but he would not go much beyond that with Hawthorn.

As for Podgorsky's assertion that Globe was in danger of being boycotted by the majors, Hawthorn had confirmed that Russia's industrial agents were reporting rumors in the field, spread by low-level territorial managers who were hardly privy to the high-level agreement that remained in effect.

What, then, was behind Podgorsky's actions? Why had he inter-rogated Yu Hsin Chou? Why did he mistrust Moffit? Or did he? Moffit's post-Bishop behavior had not changed, his attitude appeared to be the same as far as they were able to determine. True, they had pulled him off the job as a full-time site worker, but that was probably because his reports were so boring that nobody cared to read them.

Of one thing they could be sure. Never mind the side issues; Josef Podgorsky was hungry for Guianese oil and he would commit murder to get it. More: Podgorsky wanted that oil soon, suggesting that he was indeed following a timetable that jibed with the Cuban operation.

There was a second element that now loomed from their meeting on the scow. Podgorsky had not invited Hawthorn aboard to discuss the Moffit case. He would have guessed that Hawthorn could shed no light on that business. He had summoned Hawthorn to establish the ground rules. In effect, he was saying, "Here's what I want you to do and here's what will happen to you if you don't."

Drinkwater knew the substance of the meeting that was now to take place between them, but he did not know precisely what Hawthorn was going to propose. Tonight he would be hearing the long-awaited secret so closely guarded by Gregory Hawthorn, who had not kept his promise, who had not shared his plan with the Commission. For once, Drinkwater was to be the listener.

Reinaldo Villar-Cruz and Gene Tinker arrived at six-thirty and deposited their coats in the bedroom. Five minutes later Henri Amont was admitted. Hawthorn's senior vice president in charge of domestic operations looked younger than his fifty years, attributable perhaps to a vigorous exercise program he maintained in Hawthorn's private gymnasium.

At six-forty-five Hawthorn went to the door again and opened it for a very thin gentleman dressed in a business suit and a felt hat, wearing a light tan camel's hair coat. He could have been a model for middle-aged men's clothing, with graying sideburns, a handsome, suntanned face, and a trim, salt and pepper mustache.

"Gentlemen," announced Hawthorn as he presented the newcomer, "I would like to introduce a friend whom I have known a long time: Edmond Jones Brookings."

Brookings greeted them one by one, shaking hands with a firm grip and a secure, broad smile.

"Mr. Brookings is president and chief executive officer of the Brookings Aluminum Corporation, our neighbor to the north in British Guiana. He served during the war on the President's advisory staff as the Canadian expert in the area of critical materials procurement. I suppose I could also tell you that he holds a bona fide clearance from every important agency in both Canada and the United States, and"— Hawthorn nodded at Drinkwater—"in Great Britain. I've briefed him on the Guiana project and was only mildly surprised that he knows about our work there."

"Might I ask," Drinkwater interrupted, "where you heard these, ahh, these stories?"

Brookings looked carefully at Drinkwater. "You are Alan Drinkwater. Did I get that correctly?"

"You did, sir."

"From the President, sir."

"Of . . ."

"The United States, Mr. Drinkwater."

"Thank you, Mr. Brookings." Drinkwater managed a wan smile for the Canadian.

"All right," Hawthorn said, "if you'll all be seated we can get started."

They found places as Hawthorn sat down and pulled his chair closer to the table.

"Gentlemen, I have invited Mr. Amont to join us this evening because he's been in on the plan from the beginning. He has played no significant role, nor do I expect him to. It's purely a selfish move on my part to ensure some continuity for the business should I suddenly and unexpectedly expire." He glanced at Amont. "Thanks for coming, Henri. I hope you don't mind being the silent partner tonight."

Amont scanned the group, smiled, and relaxed as Hawthorn began.

"Let's keep our main objectives in mind here. First, we want to discover oil where none exists. That's a mechanical trick that will be disclosed to you tonight. To accomplish that, I've called on Ed Brookings. Second, we want to convince Russia that we can supply their western satellites without starting a war. That has been largely accomplished through the creation of a large and a very flexible distribution system, via my fleet of tankers and our terminal construction in the islands."

Hawthorn was addressing the small group without notes. His faithful yellow pad lay unmarked on the table in front of him.

"Third, and in concert with the first two, we want the Russians to be locked in to our oil as firmly as America is locked in to Venezuela's oil. So far, they've stayed out of the Middle East and we have reason to believe they won't buy into those concessions as long as they have a shot at petroleum in this hemisphere."

Hawthorn shoved his coffee cup out of the way, dropped a pencil on the note pad, and sat back.

"Josef Podgorsky wants our oil soon. He's got his eye on Cuba and a lot more. He's got his foot in the door in British Guiana and he's made me an offer that's acceptable. I deal with him or I get my throat cut.

"In essence, then, we've fooled them thus far, and we intend to fool them all the way home, to the point where they'll have all their eggs in one basket with no clue that the eggs are rotten.

"Now we're going to show them an oil field. Here's the timetable. Today is January the twentieth. The harbor is finished, ready to take barges. By April first, the pipeline will be completed, all the way from the field holding tanks to the basin, over Bishop's property. The pumping stations are ready, have been for several weeks.

"My plan is to fill everything up on or about July twelfth. That means the shore tanks, the pipeline, the field tanks and the lines, all the way to the wells and into the ground to a depth of about one thousand feet. That entire inventory will consist of Venezuelan crude oil, delivered in my ships from Lake Maracaibo to Brookings's Bunker-C fuel oil tanks in Trinidad, and from there to our barges in the river by way of his ore carriers. I'll let him tell you about that."

Edmond Jones Brookings cleared his throat.

"In the normal course of business, gentlemen, our operation at the bauxite mine uses roughly one million barrels of Bunker-C fuel oil per year to feed our furnaces. We dry the ore, run it through a number of processes that require a large amount of heat.

"For many years now, we have taken that fuel from Trinidad to our docks on the river in our own ore carriers. They have what we call 'double bottoms,' meaning space between the bottom of each hold and the actual outer steel of the ship's hull. We fill our own tanks that way and we save on freight as well as some other fees. I guess you know that our carriers are too small to make the trip all the way to Jamaica or Canada a worthwhile venture, so we take the ore to Trinidad and stockpile it there, where it's reloaded onto ocean-going carriers for the trip north. That's what makes the return trip so logical for us."

He paused a moment. "Shall I go on, Gregory? Does anybody have any questions about that?"

"Yes, sir," said Villar-Cruz. "The capacity of each ship. What would that be?"

"I was coming to that, Reinaldo. Thank you. We normally carry about thirty thousand barrels when we haul back. We don't always need to, of course. We have on the average four ships a day going out and maybe one will be used for hauling fuel. That's all we need. But we could, and I guess that's what we're discussing here, we could haul up to thirty-five thousand barrels in each ship, six trips per day, bringing in over two hundred thousand barrels in one day. I don't mind telling you, that's a lot of oil."

"We need four or five days' worth of that kind of tonnage, sir," Villar-Cruz said, "if we are to fill everything Mr. Hawthorn says we have to fill. I haven't made the calculation, but . . ."

"I have," Hawthorn said. "Eighteen barge loads. Work your pencil on that and you'll see that Edmond has a little excess capacity over the four-day time frame."

"Yes. We can manage that, all right."

"Forgive me, Gregory." Drinkwater leaned in. "The four-day time frame. Would you expand on that just a bit?"

"Right. We have to perform this operation at night, under a dark sky, a moonless sky, and we want to do it over a dead weekend, when the river is empty, without commercial traffic. It's not exactly a river for water sports or relaxation, so all we have to worry about is the commerical traffic. We've selected a long weekend when there's no moon, and that's the four-day period we're talking about."

"I see. Extraordinary," Drinkwater said.

"Anything else?" Hawthorn waited a moment. "Thanks, Ed. Now

there are some problems here, obviously, but we think they can be handled. Mostly, the problems have to do with people. For example, what will the captains of the ore carriers think? How about the crews? The men who handle the barges and the people at the Trinidad terminal? And what do we do with the harbor master in British Guiana, and the dozens of other people who get involved in transfers of this kind?

"Mostly, gentlemen, those people don't really know or care what's going on. They write out their little tickets and they handle their hoses and they stop for lunch and put in their eight hours and then they go home. In the case of the Brookings ships, Ed has a select crew that has managed other kinds of transfers not unlike this one, with similar demands for security. He'll use those people with the proper briefing. There are a few other sensitive positions involved as well, but we've already established the ground rules for these people and we've made our personnel selection accordingly."

If they had been transferring a few hundred thousand automobiles or pianos, or a million tires, the problem would have been insurmountable. Those could be seen, counted, and weighed. But liquids are virtually invisible; they move through lines and are measured for volume through meters that could be bypassed or fiddled with. Even the ore carriers, the largest ships in the connection, had a crew of only five men. Hawthorn estimated that he would have, all told, fewer than one hundred positions to manage.

"The sequence is this: I'll have four of my big ships haul the crude oil from Venezuela. That will be a cash purchase to avoid any questions from their end. Each ship will deliver its cargo to the Brookings tanks and take off for another assignment. Business as usual so far, except for my captains and the Brookings's terminal personnel."

"No problem there, Gregory. We've handled storage and transfer for a dozen outside projects."

"Right. The Brookings ships will dump their cargo of bauxite ore and simultaneously take on thirty-five thousand barrels of my crude oil. That's about a four-hour operation. Four hours, Ed." Hawthorn glanced at Brookings. "That's going to be critical. Our plan demands the four-day package, not a day longer."

"We can manage it, Gregory."

"We can't have equipment failure, Ed."

"My ships aren't in question, friend."

"No," Hawthorn replied. "They wouldn't be."

"Of course, you will be limited to a maximum of six loads on any given night, Gregory."

"Tell them why."

Brookings eased himself back against the stiff hotel chair and crossed one ankle over the other.

"Two reasons, actually, the first being that I only have nine ships and three of them will be somewhere between British Guiana and Trinidad, unless you can think of some way to fly them back and forth. The truth is, they will all be steaming at full bore the entire time to make your schedule. I can only guarantee six at the estuary during any one night."

"And the second reason?"

"The channel. It's too narrow and too shallow for my ships to pass one another, except at the broadening—what we call the broadening. Effectively, it means we can have one ship in that rather wide and deepish river bulge, another on the way to it from the estuary and another on the way back from your harbor. More than three ships in the river at once would create a traffic jam, an impossible or at the least a dangerous situation."

Hawthorn was watching their faces. That rule was apparently heard and digested. Five ships per night, OK; six, barely possible.

"It seems to me," Brookings said, "the bigger problem will be at your end of the river, at the harbor. Here, look at it this way."

He leaned forward, hands on his knees.

"Where the river meets the ocean, you have that damned harbor master's tower. But that's all you have. Two miles inland the shoreline is as inhospitable as the Amazon. I doubt you'll have any eyes there, except far into the river, opposite the Shell and Esso terminals, and by that time the barges will be hooked up and hidden behind my ships as they pass. So, then, if we start after dark, say at ten o'clock, and if your barges are on time, we should have our estuary perfectly clear well before daybreak. But you have a slightly different problem at your end."

"I've considered that, Ed. After my barges disconnect from your ships, we have another two hours to go before we reach the harbor. Give us ninety minutes to pump out, using all of the barge pumps and the onshore pumps and every connection we can make, and we still won't finish before ten in the morning. I don't mind that, providing we don't have any sightseeing airplanes or unwelcome prowlers, but we have a camouflage plan worked out if that happens. We've gone over it a dozen times. It's the only way.

"If we're clear on that?" Hawthorn looked up, made a note on his pad, a scratch. "Good. As Brookings's ships reach that secluded point in the river a few miles south of the estuary, our barges will hook up and take on the oil as they proceed deeper into the country. The exchange will be finished before they reach Brookings's terminal. They disconnect, our barges continue on, and his ships duck into their own berths.

"We'll need to repeat that maneuver eighteen times to get six hundred

151

and thirty thousand barrels ashore, and that's what I want—six hundred and thirty thousand barrels' worth of field production."

"You'd better explain that, Gregory," said Drinkwater.

"We can't invite Mr. Podgorsky down there to show him one well or two or twelve, Alan. I've got to show him lots of wells, all capable of producing at least a thousand barrels a day. I've got to show him that my tanks and lines are full to the brim, that I can't pump any more oil out of the ground until I start shipping. The valves will be closed, the pumps will be stopped—and the capacity of my entire installation is exactly six hundred and thirty thousand barrels."

"Excellent! Yes, I quite see the idea." Drinkwater was beaming. Suddenly he dropped the corners of his mouth and frowned. "But you will tell us before too long how you intend to manage our Russian spy and the harbor master and Sandy Dreier. I assume you'll cover that matter before the night is gone."

"In a minute, Alan." Hawthorn met the Englishman's look. "But I trust you understand that this is going to cost us some money. Crude oil and those Brookings ships aren't exactly free of charge."

"How much?"

"One and a half million, maybe two."

"Yes," Drinkwater said, fingering his lip. "Well, let's see how we get on with the rest of it. In for a penny, in for a pound, I say."

Hawthorn grinned at that and went on.

"When the transfer is completed we'll announce the discovery. I'll word the release in such a way as to avoid a big stir in the industry, using words like 'cautious predictions' and 'evidence of possible commercial potential,' phrases like that. Our announcement will be conservative enough to keep the uproar to a minimum, and at the same time we'll be able to confide to the Russians that we have found exactly what we thought we would, a field with something in the neighborhood of a hundred billion barrels under the ground."

"One hundred billion? With a 'B'?" Amont had been listening patiently, but that figure overloaded his quietude.

"Divided by twenty million equals something like thirteen years' worth of oil, Henri. Pretty far out for one field, but what the hell."

"Yes, I guess it is," Amont replied. "What if the Russians want to start buying it right then and there? What if British Guiana demands that oil for their own consumption? What happens to your stockpile then?"

"Russia doesn't want it yet. They have enough of their own for the time being, but we'll ship a few thousand barrels in a small parcel carrier for their inspection, for lab analysis. As far as British Guiana is concerned, sure. They can have as much as they want. It's their oil, after all, half of it anyway." He looked at Drinkwater.

"More cash, Alan? Because we may have to quote ship unquote that oil out and bring it back as finished product for their own consumption, as Henri says. That's easy enough. I just turn on the pumps and cycle the oil around from one tank to another and let the barges take on river water and sink to the right Plimsoll mark. They head out to the mother tanker, which is mine, and I take their river water and give them diesel fuel, or gasoline, whatever they want. I rig up some exchange documents with my refinery friends and that's done with. But over a period of time, that will cost us some money, because the refiners will want cash for their good oil. Alan's got that tucked away someplace, right?"

"Dear mother!" Drinkwater sighed. "I rather expect we're in for a beating if this thing drags on too long."

"A billion-dollar hoax, Alan. That's the budget. You said so yourself."

"Yes. I believe we did say something like that."

"Which brings us to the production people in British Guiana. We'll start some serious drilling in late April and drill as we do in a normal operation for three months. We'll stop at six thousand feet and start over in several different sections until we've punched a few dozen holes. That will bring us to June, at which time we'll send the old crew home and take on the special assignment men"—he glanced at Drinkwater—"the people from your force, Alan"—he addressed the group again—"highly paid mercenaries who have been screened and cleared for this kind of work. They will be our operational unit for the duration of the job."

Hawthorn clipped off the categories, identified the men, provided the solutions and the cover for each situation.

"And now for the key people, Dreier and Moffit and the harbor master." Hawthorn leaned forward. "Dreier's OK. I'll bring him into the picture very soon. I think those of you who know him will agree that he can handle the role without any problems. Reinaldo, you work with him, rehearse for a few days. He's got to be familiar with every possible slip, every government contact that could cause trouble. He's got to know as much as you and I know."

Villar-Cruz nodded.

"The tougher problem is with Moffit. You're all aware of the problem there, but actually, we're faced with only two danger points. The first occurs with the false discovery, that is, with the Brookings transfer. Moffit's got to be away from the camp, preferably out of the country during that period of time. The second danger period will run much longer, assuming he stays on. From the day the tanks are filled until the day we close up shop, we'll have Moffit on site, looking over our shoulders.

"The truth of it is, however, that second part doesn't bother me very much, and I'll tell you why. After the so-called producing wells are on stream, we aren't going to drill anymore."

Hawthorn stopped, sensed the mild reaction.

"There's a glut, my friends. There's too much oil in the marketplace already. As a businessman, I don't want to spend any more money than I already have until the price starts to go up. I'd be crazy to sell oil for less than two dollars a barrel when I can get three a year from now. That's the logic, anyway. We'll have enough to satisfy the local government, but they won't want to give the stuff away either, and we can do some shipping, using the river-water gimmick.

"So, no more drilling. That eliminates the need to hit with a few more holes while Moffit stands around and wonders where the geysers are. All we've got now is an oil field that's waiting for the glut to go away." He paused. "Have you ever seen a producing oil field?"

Hawthorn looked at the faces of the men. "A producing field looks to be—and is—deserted. The pumps nod their heads all day and all night and the oil just keeps passing through the lines and that's all there is to see. It's as boring as hell."

His reaction came now, smiles and bobbing heads. The records would be manipulated, the logs and the charts could easily be managed. The rest was duck soup.

"By George, Gregory!" exclaimed Drinkwater. "I think you've got this thing licked!"

"I think so, Alan. I think we've got our oil field."

Brookings had been listening carefully. "It's none of my business, perhaps," he said, "but what happens when Fidel Castro rings you on the phone and places his order for a few hundred thousand barrels of diesel fuel, for his hotel generators and his electric plants?"

"We are not at liberty to discuss that yet, Mr. Brookings," answered Drinkwater.

"It's safe to say, however, that he won't get what he wants," added Hawthorn. "Now, then, the business of Stephen Moffit. What do we do with him during the period of discovery?"

"Now might be the time to call on your shooters," said Drinkwater.

Hawthorn looked at him. "I don't have any shooters, and if I did, I can't think of a worse time to use them." He stood and went to the kitchenette, poured coffee into his cup, and returned.

"Let me ask you something, Alan," he said. "At the risk of being naive in front of these people, it's my observation that Stephen Moffit doesn't seem to be a very satisfied man. He's not exactly my idea of a dedicated Russian agent. Is there any chance, in your opinion, to win him over to our side?"

"How shall I say this?" Drinkwater closed his eyes. "I might dictatorily say 'no.' But it would be better if I could place you in the hands of the KGB for a time, have you undergo the brainwashing he underwent. He is not with us in any sense whatsoever. His mind, his spirit, his entire philosophy is against the West. Even to suggest that we know he is an agent for them would set the project off balance. I trust you can see that. You must be thought of as an ally to the Russians, at war with the major oil corporations. I believe we must leave it at that and deal with Moffit in some other way."

"I suppose I have to agree," Hawthorn said.

Edmond Brookings straightened in his chair. "I very often send one of my people off to Canada or to the States on a training program, something that will improve their productivity to my plant."

"Not bad, Ed. A business trip of some kind. But he's on the government payroll. How would you get Ramprashad to agree to that?"

"Surely there's some service, some kind of skill you might need, something out of the ordinary that might call for special instruction."

"Reinaldo," Hawthorn glanced across at his aide. "Do you think Ramprashad would let him go to the States for a week or two on some kind of Globe business?"

"I think so, or he might go up to visit Chicago Bridge on that Corentyne project, but that's out of our control. I can check on it."

"Right. Please do that. Let me know what you come up with." Hawthorn thought again, picked up his pencil and toyed with it.

"How about the harbor master? He's a key block, he's the man who sits at the river entrance and spies on everything that moves in his dirty water. What do we do with him?"

"A hunting party, sir." This time, Villar-Cruz sounded very sure of himself. "He's an avid hunter, goes out every chance he can get, way down in the deep bush. Maybe we can organize a big safari for him, with all the trimmings."

There was a sudden, quiet knocking at the door. All faces turned, voices stopped; Gregory Hawthorn got up slowly and crossed the room.

"Yes?" he said through the door.

"It is I, Mr. Hawthorn. Am I late?"

Hawthorn turned back to the group and smiled, then opened the door.

"Good evening, Mr. Burrowes," he said, taking the stubby little fingers in his hand, leading him into the room.

"My friends, please welcome the commandant of the British Guiana Defense Force, Mr. Jeffry Burrowes."

Burrowes was fairly beaming, his round, puffed face filling the room with a new, innocent freshness. The wart on his forehead was tucked neatly between two lines that crossed his brow. Hawthorn held the commandant by his elbow as the assemblage rose to greet him.

"Jeffry," he said, "do you ever go hunting?"

CHAPTER 3

It is so often the case: The really important event, the dramatic, highly visible event, is left for last. With Globe's project in British Guiana, the dirty work had been completed in August. The harbor was finished. Before Thaddeus Bishop was cold in his grave, Dreier had begun the tedious clearing and the road building that would link the harbor with the camp, but it was slow going.

Even after they had laid a decent track, wide enough to move heavy equipment, it was too narrow to accommodate both the road and the pipeline. They needed room for the slings and the trencher and a shipload of specialized equipment to complete the job. Hawthorn wanted drilling to begin in April, and it was already late in January.

But eighteen miles of road through timber and dense jungle land was a job most engineers would study very carefully; it was a job that might be given six months under good conditions, with the best assortment of earth-moving equipment. Globe didn't have six months. Sandy Dreier was under orders to get the oil up and "flowing" before the end of July. Those were orders he intended to carry out.

A man doesn't need a bulldozer to clear land. Wire explosive looks, feels, and handles exactly like fourteen-gauge electrical wire, the kind one might use on a lamp, except that it's a single wire. There's no need for the power to proceed along one line, do its work, and then return whence it came along another line. One might mistake it for an electrical connection, but only once.

A man could, for example, purchase a roll of this wire as one buys a roll of thin rope, wrap it around a tree, and then run it to the next tree, and the next, and the next. Then, with a single impulse from the proper source, all the trees and much of everything in between would disappear.

Dangerous stuff, this wire explosive. In the wrong hands, it could become an enormously destructive device, but Globe's field demolitions man, a character named Blumber, had used it on a dozen occasions to clear unmanagable terrain for other jobs. He knew how to rig it and he knew how to protect against its misuse.

On the ninth of February Blumber arrived in British Guiana with one hundred thousand meters' worth of the wire, wrapped on wooden spools.

On the fourteenth of February, Valentine's Day, eighteen miles of forest measuring twenty feet across disappeared, roots and all, leaving a swath that needed only leveling, debris clearing, and rolling.

Stephen Moffit watched the operation with interest. Peking had not only introduced him to the wire but had made him an expert in its use.

In a locked shed, three hundred feet from the field tank location, fifty thousand meters of surplus explosive wire waited, wound on its wooden spool.

CHAPTER 4

The little war in Cuba prattled on and on, with little to show for it. Of considerably more importance to Gregory Hawthorn and his Globe organization, and to Alan Drinkwater's commissioners, was the other war, the continuing battle between the huge oil corporations, the producing countries, the independent producers, and the world market provocateurs, those who for one reason or another were contributing to the imbalance between world demand and world supply.

In a report submitted to the Commission, and thence to the heads of every European country, Drinkwater warned of the consequences of the glut they were enjoying: He predicted increased downward pressure on prices stemming from Occidental's entry into the Libyan fields, a systemic attack on the Western economy through Russia's extraordinary exports to the West (particularly, he suggested, to Italy), and a surge in Japan's economy based on cheap oil imports. All of these were either taking place, or were visible on the horizon in his view, and he urged a slowing down of imports to discourage what was becoming a stampede for cheap oil by everyone who had an interest in the business.

Oil was pouring out of Middle East holes at the incredible rate of four thousand barrels per day in some cases, compared to fifty, one hundred, and, on the better sites, two hundred barrels per day from wells in the United States.

This circumstance was quite agreeable to the Globe Corporation, and to Alan Drinkwater's Commission. It lent credibility to their planned argument that enough was enough, that the addition of more wells after the first few were producing would only create more havoc in the 1958 marketplace.

On the tenth of June Gregory Hawthorn met again with Alan Drinkwater to set the last brick in their foundation. Sandy Dreier had stopped drilling on 5, 6, 9, 13, and 22 and had begun in sections that were selected as first alternatives.

He was already down to five thousand feet on the first three when he was called by Hawthorn to Trinidad. He was to bring his personnel files, was given an address in Maraval, where new housing was going up faster than owners could be found. Many of the handsome little middle-class homes were still empty, nestling below the hills that surround Port of Spain, their tiny gardens still black with newly turned earth.

Hawthorn had spent the day in Trinidad inspecting the Brookings facility, the terminal they planned to use for their transfer of oil to British Guiana. The plant superintendent was courteous, understood he would be helping to supply crude "to one of the islands." If he suspected the Mobil refinery on Barbados, he would have found the manager there closemouthed on the subject.

They were sitting, Hawthorn, Drinkwater, and Dreier, on the enclosed outdoor veranda discussing the project, Hawthorn's words bouncing off the concrete patio wall.

"Sandy, I asked you to come here for a special reason. I want you to settle back and just listen."

Obediently Dreier set his glass of beer on the terrazzo by his feet and crossed an ankle over his knee. He was wearing khaki trousers but had bought a new pair of cordovan military shoes that were shined to a high mirror gloss. He concentrated his attention on Hawthorn's face.

First Hawthorn told him about Alan Drinkwater, but did not elaborate on his connection with an international commission. That was information his man didn't need to know. Then he dealt with the Russians, the current situation, the estimated strength of the Soviet threat in the Caribbean and their suspected involvement in the Cuban revolution.

Dreier was an intelligent human being. Much of what he was hearing was public knowledge. Even locked away in the deep bush, they had the BBC. He nodded his understanding, not finding it necessary to interrupt for questions. But he knew something was coming.

When Hawthorn stopped, got up from his chair, and circled the patio, Dreier stood and went into the kitchen. He came back with a glass in either hand.

"Mr. Drinkwater, I don't know what you drink, sir. That's a whiskey on the rocks. Me, I've got a double whiskey on the rocks. The boss here knows what he wants." He raised the glass and took half of the drink in one swallow.

"OK, boss." Dreier sat down again. "Now you're gonna tell me what I'm doin' in a place that hasn't got enough oil in it to fill your goddamn Zippo."

Hawthorn looked directly at Drinkwater.

"I wonder if I mentioned it to you, Alan. About the people on my team."

"That they are a select group? Yes. You did mention that at one time or another."

"Who else thinks that, Sandy?"

"Just me. I don't think it, I know it. But I've been tellin' the men we're stoppin' twenty-one hundred feet short. There's a crust down there, a dome, and we're not deep enough to penetrate that dome. That's what the other guys think."

"How come you never said anything to me?"

"I did. Four or five times. You just said to follow the charts, and that's what I did." Dreier took another swallow. "But I *know* you, boss. I don't exactly know what you're doin' now, but I know it can't be wrong. So I told the guys to keep sluggin' away."

The rest was easy. Dreier sipped his drink, wagged his head several times and said, "Well I'll be damned" once or twice, absorbing the information Hawthorn told him about the hoax.

"It's perfect. Just perfect." The big engineer plopped his feet onto the deck and set his glass on a table. "I'm kind of glad I didn't know about it. Sure as hell I would have let somethin' slip."

"Perfect? How do you mean that, Sandy?" Drinkwater was leaning forward, waiting for his answer.

"I mean what we got there is a better oil field than anything I ever seen in Texas or Oklahoma or Louisiana. It's a classic, sir. I built a damn classic down there."

"Aha! Yes. Well, I'm glad to know that."

They were quiet for a few moments. Drinkwater went into the kitchen and refilled his glass, Hawthorn opened a can of peaches, and Dreier nursed his third drink. The frogs in the garden sounded like an army of burping, obscene old trolls; the smell of summer flowers hung in the air.

159

Hawthorn had decided the best way to manage the next part was a flat statement of fact. He waited until they were ready, then stood against the patio wall and made his announcement.

"Steve Moffit is a Russian spy."

"Oh, my God!"

Dreier's earlier casual attitude was suddenly demolished.

Hawthorn told him the rest, about Podgorsky and what they knew of Russia's plans. He gave Dreier his view of the relationship between Podgorsky, the PPP, and Stephen Moffit.

"We'll be playing a game of poker here, Sandy. We hold the good cards and they hold the gun; we have the chips and they control the clock. It's a tight-wire act, my friend. Now, I want you to get out your list of personnel, every man including the cooks and the local bookkeeper and the damn Amerindian scout you keep around there. Go ahead, get it now."

Dreier went into the living room and brought his briefcase out to the patio. He set it down and opened it, pulling out a file stuffed with personnel records. As he sat down again, placing the file on the table between them, he looked quickly at Hawthorn, then at Drinkwater.

"Did you know he's got a German Luger in his tent?"

"No," said Hawthorn. "But it doesn't surprise me."

"Yeah. He was layin' on his cot one night, early, before dinner. He was sleeping with his gun on his chest, like it was some kind of teddy bear. I never said anything about it."

"I'll try to get him out of there. I think I know how. But there's nothing you can do about the gun. He won't use it unless he has to. Sandy, is there any chance he might be as smart as you are? Could he know about the field? I mean really be sure about the fact that it's a phony?"

"You mean that it's dry? No. Not a chance. He hasn't been around as many fields as I have. Matter of fact, I think this is his first real experience on a drilling site. He's seen the charts like everybody else. He's heard me talk about the dome and all that crap. I mean, even if he's got petroleum engineer training, I don't think he can tell much from what he can see."

"You did."

"Only in the last couple months, though. I suspected it, but I wasn't a hundred percent sure. And I'm smellin' those cores a couple times a day. He's not. He's been up in Georgetown most of the time."

That answer would never be improved by speculating about it. So they went on. For the next three hours they went over the files, deciding who could stay and who had to go. The vacancies would be filled by the men from Drinkwater's mercenary team, men drawn from squads he had used in other work across the world.

When they were finished Dreier rehearsed the schedule again, studied his role with Hawthorn to be sure he understood the timing and the tricks of clandestine behavior. Villar-Cruz would work with him for several more days to solidify the process.

Satisfied that every angle was covered, that the plan was foolproof and the foundation laid for a long cover-up, Hawthorn clarified the positions of Jeffry Burrowes and Governor Hillman Gomes.

"Sure, Burrowes is a comical, pompous ass, but he drinks gin and tonic with the insiders; he belongs to the damn East Indian Yachting Club!" Hawthorn glanced at Drinkwater. "Did you know that, Alan? The guy's a chameleon! He's been helpful, Sandy," Hawthorn said. "And it was the governor who organized the transfer of Bishop's land records, kept us up to date on personnel moves and so on."

Hawthorn tossed his cigarette butt into the yard. "Now the governor has made Burrowes commandant of the Defense Force. The way we see it, that puts him in a position to blow the whistle if the army starts a rumble."

"And what about Moffit, boss? What do I do with him?"

"Good question." Hawthorn thought for a moment. "You know how the field will be filled and you know what's going to happen after the transfer is completed."

"Yes, I do."

"You agree that a casual inspection, even a deep inspection by an expert, will show him nothing out of the ordinary."

"I think that's prob'ly right."

"As Mr. Drinkwater so clearly pointed out to me, we can't just get rid of him, physically, I mean, permanently. Hell, Podgorsky would have another man down there in a flash. But we can get rid of him during the transfer."

"I've been waiting for this, Gregory," Drinkwater said from the corner. "How do you propose to manage that?"

"Sandy, how about that cathodic protection? Do we need it or don't we?"

"I think we do. I mean, we would need it if we were a genuine operator. That steel's gonna rust real fast down there."

"Could Moffit install it?"

"Sure, if he got a little basic information. He could do it."

"Let's have him go up to Miami and spend a week with Shorty Green. He's the man who invented the process."

"Catholic protection, you say?"

"Cathodic, Alan. An electrolic process that keeps steel from rusting."

"Yes, well I should think a week in Miami would do the bugger some good. Lots of Catholics up there!"

Dreier looked at Drinkwater and made a sound through his teeth. "What do you think, Sandy?"

"Sounds good to me, boss. I'd like to be sure he's up there and not in Georgetown someplace, or even in the country."

"Alan, if I sent him up there with the government's permission, I mean Ramprashad and all the rest, if I sent him up there during that week, could you get your friends in the FBI or the CIA to keep an eye on him?"

"Shouldn't be any trouble, Gregory. Yes. Sounds like an excellent idea."

"And when he comes back, we'll delight him with the good news that we've been digging too shallow. Two thousand feet deeper and voilà! We strike oil."

It was late when Sandy Dreier left to go for sandwiches and chips. Alan Drinkwater took Hawthorn by the arm and led him outside, through the small garden. There were only a few lights up in the hills now; the grass was wet with dew.

"A good fellow, your Dreier," Drinkwater said. They stood by the fence. The Englishman knocked his pipe bowl on the post and started the tedious business of filling it.

"Gregory, do you feel as I do that the project has gone well?"

"Yes. So far." Hawthorn was in fact constantly suspicious of their success. "I would never have believed they could be brought into it so easily."

"It hasn't been that easy, my boy. But the Russians are like children sometimes, allowing their dreams to run away with their sense of reality. That's what makes them such magnificent composers."

"Like children, you think? Maybe."

"And how about the Cubans? What do you feel will really happen when Fidel takes over?"

"Well, I'll tell you, Alan, unless the Americans poke him in the eye with a sharp stick, he'll play it safe. I think you and I are in the process of commiting the perfect crime," Hawthorn said, turning to look at the Englishman, "but Uncle Sam doesn't trust us with a loaded gun." He folded his hands on the fence rail.

"Furthermore, Alan, I think the American corporations in Cuba will hang on for dear life, and to hell with our CIA directive."

"Yes, well, I was coming to that. They plan on letting their tanks run dry, of course, have a few ships offshore in case it does go peacefully. But they'll be ready to fly off and leave, immediately they sense danger to themselves and their families."

"And if that happens, we step in with Russian flags unfurled, ready to save the revolution."

"At Mr. Podgorsky's frantic summons, Gregory."

"With his summons. That can be arranged."

Hawthorn thought of the spectacle. Eighteen tankers standing offshore, ready to save Castro's revolution. And then what?

It was a question that could only be answered by those who were placed in positions of very high authority. Sink them, blow them up, or make them disappear: Those were the options, and somebody in Washington would have to bite the bullet soon.

CHAPTER 5

High tide in Georgetown. The crushing rains of the late afternoon that had pounded the galvanized iron rooftops until nearly midnight had no exit to the sea. The ditches were full to overflowing, the dikes were closed, the gates locked tight against the brown ocean. The streets were empty; naked lamps hanging from wooden poles with halos over their heads looked down on barren gray pools of mud and ass dung that waited patiently for the ocean to ebb away.

Where the *Sanibel Voyager* was berthed, a guard lay slumped under his cover, a half-full bottle of rum near his hand. A dozen meters away the gangplank rolled back and forth on its ancient wheels, moving in an almost ghostlike way as the ugly freighter rose and fell in the uneasy harbor.

A man stood at the foot of the ship's ladder, pulling his hat closer onto his head and snugging the collar on his coat to the back of his neck, looking from right to left. He stuffed his hands in his pockets and bent his head down, then started off at a slow walk in the direction of the street, away from the sound of the slopping water.

The rain had stopped, but the man's face was already dripping from the heavy dew as he closed on the back alley, turned into it and slowed, then shuffled to a halt. His hand raised the coat flap, found a handkerchief, and brought it to his face. He wiped, blew softly into it, and returned it to his back pocket. He leaned against a boarded door, looked back, then peered ahead through the heavy night, as if he might be unsure. Then he set off again, continuing down the alley, heading for the next open street. At the sidewalk, as he was about to cross the dead, wide road, he stopped once more, looked to the right, then to the left. There, across the street, a sign. *Roti.* White on red.

He carefully stepped over a deep pool of standing water, made his way to the other side of the road, and huddled under the sign, his back against the old stone wall, his wet shoes standing on soft gravel. A wind was coming now, soft, a murmur in the boulevard trees a distance away. He waited, looking toward the boulevard.

At one o'clock a car drove by, slowed, then continued on. Minutes later it came again, from the other direction, slowing again as it passed his position. As he watched, the car turned from the boulevard, very slowly this time, and rolled to a stop across the street. The man brought his hand out of a pocket, flicked a penlight three times. He waited, saw an answering light from the closed car window.

Again the car drove off, returning this time on his side of the street. It slowed, the rear door opened, and he hurried inside, closed the door again and sat back. The driver eased again onto the road.

They drove more quickly now, along the side streets, onto the seawall road, then across railroad tracks to a wider road, a highway. Three minutes, four. The drive-in theater was closed, dark and empty. There were no houses, no buildings, only the rows of parking stalls, the giant screen, the projection booth, all deserted. They drove into the darkest shadow near the tree-lined southern boundary of the huge lot, and the car crawled to a stop without lights, none since turning into the lot.

The rear door opened, the passenger moved into the front seat, and shut the door quietly. The dome light came on, illuminating the face of the driver, a young face with a shock of brown hair.

One hour passed. The side windows were fogged over; one of them opened and a cigarette was thrown out.

Far from them, a ship's horn sounded. The car engine turned over and they drove back to the city. Under the *Roti* sign, the passenger got out, leaned toward the car, nodded, and closed the door, nodding again as the car disappeared into the fog.

By morning, the *Sanibel* was at sea, steaming toward Trinidad with a cargo of shrimp, jute, charcoal, rice, brown sugar, unfinished lumber, and one passenger.

Soon that passenger would board a schooner to Tobago. Then a flight to Miami. And then, Williamsburg.

CHAPTER 6

Did he have to believe Howard Barry?

He said it had been an unfortunate mistake, her memo to Josef Podgorsky, but it had not been the cause of Yu Hsin Chou's execution. For many months, perhaps years, Chou had been suspected of treasonous conduct. Unfounded suspicions, perhaps. But Josef Podgorsky was unwilling to take chances. Barry's words.

Did he have to believe that?

Moffit was not to blame Jennifer Moengo. She was doing her duty, nothing less and nothing more than was expected of her. If it played any role at all, her note was a mere catalyst, inciting an investigation that had indeed revealed some flaws in the system.

Six months ago, longer, Moffit had received his reprimand. It was in the form of a letter delivered to him personally by a diplomatic courier working for the German government, carefully sealed. It referred only to his contacts with persons outside his own system, a reminder that he must observe communications protocol. There had been no reference to China, no allusion to Chou or to Jennifer.

Now he knew why his recent letters had not been answered. The Russians had slaughtered him.

He could scarcely control his rage, his fury, his *loathing* for Josef Podgorsky. But he had to work with the man, at least for now.

How would he manage his new role? How would he manage to contain his hatred for Jennifer, his anger? Now—especially now—he would have to accept the facts and deal with them. Barry's bargaining on her behalf, his plea for restraint vis-à-vis Josef Podgorsky, emerged from a selfish motivation. The new plan—their final statement—would tolerate no righteous revenge.

In fact, he had no choice. If she were to die now, Josef Podgorsky would surely suspect bad manners again, and possibly remove him from the country.

His relationship with her would change. It had been warm, now it would be mechanical. He would have to sublimate his anger, deal with his emotions somehow.

Jennifer had become his mistress, his lady. Before, when he was in town, he had stayed with her and told her about his dreams, his nightmares, his purpose. Her skin was fair and soft, her body was like warm silk next to his, and she had covered him with it, closed it around him, stroked him with her comforting flesh.

He had told her about Yu Hsin Chou, his friend, his teacher. He had told her about their meeting, when the captain had called him "Jonathan," how he had sometimes written to him in Russia, addressing the envelope with that name. He had told her about Chou's promise that he, Stephen Moffit, would soon become the power behind the power.

First would be the trial, the suffering, the agony, then the waiting and the watching, and finally he would become the secret generator, rising above the rest, riding on the victory. He had come to understand what Chou meant when, the day before he left for Orekhovo, he suggested that his middle name, Jonathan, was to be a sort of living cognomen for the execution of his career.

He had told her those things, and she had seen his letter and had found it suspicious. He could confide in her no more. He would use her for his purposes, if those purposes appeared to be legitimate, but he would not trust her with his personal feelings. He would not tell her about King David.

He had studied the section of Chou's Bible, underlined in red ink, the section commended to him by Chou as his mentor was leaving the hospital in Shenyang. It was in the First Book of Samuel.

Jonathan had betrayed his father, Saul, to save David, a friend who would one day be a great and a very powerful king. Moffit had read the lines over and over, Jonathan speaking to David: *"Do not be afraid; my father's hand shall not touch you. You will become king of Israel and I shall hold rank after you . . . and my father knows it."*

He, Stephen Moffit, would be the faithful friend of the Russians, would help them to gain the victory over the West, and then he would prosper as the faithful servant and be rewarded with gifts of power and rank and riches. That's what it said.

But in chapter 31 he found a passage that didn't make sense. The chapter described how Jonathan, fighting with his father against the Philistines, had been killed. Who were the Philistines?

Moffit was in town, spending a day at Public Works to order parts for a government project when Sandy Dreier stopped by, offered to buy him lunch, and escorted him down to the hotel.

"Got a job for you, Steve."

They had already ordered. Glasses of ice water were sweating on the Formica table top.

"At the camp?"

"Stateside first. Mr. Hawthorn wants you to install a rust-prevention system down there, cathodic protection."

"Sorry, Sandy. I don't know that much about it."

"That's why you're supposed to go up to the States, to Miami. There's a man up there who can show you."

"I'm assigned to another job right now. You know that."

"It's already cleared, Steve. Ramprashad cleared it this morning."

"I think I ought to talk with Ramprashad myself."

"OK." Dreier leaned back and allowed the waiter to set his sandwich down. "You could save yourself the trip, though. I told the minister we'll be moving some equipment around for the next few weeks. We're going to go deeper on some of those holes."

"It's not that, you know. It's that damn bridge."

"You talk to Ramprashad. It's all set."

"Have you had any good readings?"

"Not yet," Dreier said. "Too shallow. The cores are full of sand and crap that's supposed to be a thousand feet deeper."

Moffit bit into a raw carrot. "Your cores are terrible." He leaned across and pointed at his carrot.

"See that core?" he said. "That's better than what you guys bring up from your big oil field."

His meeting with Carlysle Ramprashad lasted only a few minutes. The minister was preparing an agenda for guests from abroad and could spend no time with the engineer.

He probably would have dismissed the man regardless of his schedule. Moffit's reports from the oil field were far too technical, and they were all the same. Ramprashad wondered why Moscow had assigned him to their payroll in the first place. He would discuss it with his guest. Perhaps that man would know someone who could relieve their payroll burden.

Yes, by all means. Go to Miami. Go to hell for all I care.

Stephen Moffit left the country on July 6 and arrived at the offices of the Berger Company in Coral Gables on the morning of July 7. Shorty Green was waiting for him.

Together they went over the oil field layout, traced the pipeline route to the basin, and located the holding tanks and the pumping station on site plans.

"Cathodic protection works best with saltwater, Steve, but I think you'll be all right with the hardware I've got in mind."

"I knew that much about it. Same with any electrolysis."

"Well, that's right. We use a big chunk of steel immersed in water, connected by electrical wire to each of the units to be protected. By

167

introducing a very small electrical current into the system, the steel in the water bath acts as a cathode and the steel on shore is the anode."

Green used diagrams and drew cartoons to demonstrate the process. "Electrons act to cause the rust to occur in the sacrificial piece and leave the shore tanks and lines sweet, clean."

The sacrificial piece of steel could be a mill roller from one of the sugar factories, ten tons of solid steel that had already outlived its usefulness and was rusting away in the backyard of nearly any given sugar factory in the country.

Moffit spent another day with the engineer working out the details, ordering the necessary parts and materials, trading ideas with the staff.

By the third day, Moffit knew all he wanted to, all he needed to know about cathodic protection. He returned to his hotel that evening, used a pay phone in the lobby and called a number in Williamsburg, let it ring, heard a voice answer, gave his own number and a code, then hung up and waited. Fifteen minutes later his phone rang and he answered.

"Yes, Howard. I think it's that time," he said. "The other party should be told as soon as possible." He listened, then added, "Of course. What was I thinking of."

He hung up, dialed a local number, and waited.

"I am very cold," he said.

"No. Twelve degrees centigrade."

He listened, hung up slowly. At eleven o'clock he left the hotel, walked half a mile. He stopped at a phone booth, made another call, walked across the street, and entered a rundown apartment building near the Orange Bowl. It was one A.M. when he appeared in the doorway again, lit a cigarette, and walked back to his hotel.

A woman, quite certainly a prostitute, followed him part way, disappeared behind a night bus, and was replaced by an old man carrying a sack. He vanished into an alley, and a taxi driver, cruising the street for a fare, took up the vigil. When Moffit finally rode the elevator up to his floor, the front desk clerk took over again.

If they didn't know what he said or who heard it, they were certain at least where he had been. That was all anyone could have expected under the circumstances.

The United flight arrived in Chicago at noon. Moffit rented a car and drove to Cicero. Across the street from Sportman's Park there was an electronics supply center, one of the biggest in the country. It handled everything from electronic hardware to light switches, from the new portable radios to sophisticated UHF transmitters and receivers.

He made a large purchase and paid for it in cash. Then he drove to his mother's house in Chicago.

That night, after she had gone to bed, he went out to the garage and opened the car trunk. He made three trips to his father's workshop, carrying the purchase in large boxes, setting them on the bench his father had used to fix the sled, the wagon, his mother's old ironing board.

At three A.M., a car stopped in front of his house. Moffit was waiting. There was an exchange, the driver helped carry the packages into the garage, held out his hand, and left.

He worked until nearly morning, and the next night, and the next. He fabricated wooden crates for the gadgetry and labeled it for his attention, to be sent as excess baggage on his own flight back to British Guiana.

Secret things. Important things. Things that will alter their lives. Because I am a cut above. They have made me a cut above.

CHAPTER 7

On Wednesday, July 9, Gregory Hawthorn flew to Curaçao, rode into the city of Willemstad in a taxicab, and stopped in front of the Royal Dutch Mercantile Bank. There, with the friendly assistance of one Dieter Rheinstadt, he deposited the sum of nine hundred eighty thousand dollars. An hour later he flew to Maracaibo and had dinner with Alexander Belway, the general manager of Antilles Petroleum, Ltd. and the coordinator of export activities for Petroleo del Carib. After dinner they stopped briefly at Belway's office and conducted a transaction that would later be reviewed under the title of "Crude Loans and Borrowings."

The next morning he stayed until his first ship was loaded at the Texaco terminal, confirming that three others were in line. Then he left the country and headed for Trinidad.

When he arrived at his hotel in Port of Spain he immediately placed a call to Georgetown, British Guiana. Reinaldo Villar-Cruz answered and reported that everything was ready.

Hawthorn hung up and sat on the edge of the bed.

"Everything is ready." That's all Villar-Cruz needed to say.

The seven barges that had been lying dead in the water like half-sunken bricks for so many months were primed. Their powerful engines and their new deck pumps were tuned to their peak operating efficiency. Dreier was ready, his tanks and lines checked, tight, his valves open. His men, the few he will need for this four-day marathon, were rehearsed experts, prepared for emergencies, trained to deal with trouble should it happen along or should it be brought to them with a purpose.

Stephen Moffit was in the States, far from the action. And the harbor master would be on the Corentyne near the Suriname border, heading downriver with his party of three, going for jaguar.

Hawthorn reviewed it again as he waited in the small room. Of all the possible sources of serious trouble, the one that posed the greatest threat was in the person of Neville Singh, the harbor master. He was a sea lawyer of the first order; he knew every law, every punishable infraction of the law, and he was the master of the waterways in British Guiana, his beloved country. His post at the tower overlooking the entry to the Demarara River was occupied twenty-four hours a day, at least twelve of those hours by himself.

Not a rowboat came or went without finding a place in his logbook. He could tell the cargo of a schooner by the way it rode in the water; he could spot a vessel riding below its approved Plimsoll mark, running too heavy and therefore running afoul of the law from a distance of two miles. And a phone call from him had the Guianese River Patrol or the Harbor Police alongside the questionable ship in minutes.

Neville Singh was a member of the People's Political Party, a staunch supporter of Cheddi Jagen, a protector of the people against deceit and treachery and thievery. Passing the Globe-Brookings parade before that man's castle would have been like cruising past Hitler's SS troops with an American flag.

It was thanks to Jeffry Burrowes that the man was out of the picture for a full four days and four nights. Burrowes knew him from school days, was a fellow cricket team member on the old West Indies Match Club, and had presented him with a new rifle as a gesture of thanks when Singh endorsed his posting to the Defense Force. He had insisted that they take these days, when Burrowes's wife was out of the country, to go hunting. He settled the matter by showing Singh a picture of their hunting companions, two Dutch nightclub entertainers from Paramaribo who had those days and none other for the adventure. They would leave on Friday, head into the bush, and be gone until Tuesday morning.

Hawthorn's tankers would offload in Trinidad on Thursday and the first Brookings ship would leave from that terminal the same day, arriving at the river just after dark Friday night. They would deliver five barge loads each night over the weekend, three on Monday night. That would make the eighteen. Each of the Brookings carriers had to make two trips, one hundred hours of nonstop running and loading and discharging. The schedule was tight, but with any luck they would make it before 6:00 A.M., Tuesday morning.

Hawthorn planned to stay in Trinidad until late Friday night, monitoring his tankers, the arrivals and departures of the ore boats. If something should go wrong at this end, he could still halt the operation, but once they had thirty-five thousand barrels on the river or in the system there was no turning back.

It was going to be a very long weekend.

CHAPTER 8

His first tanker eased up to the Brookings docks at precisely two o'clock Thursday afternoon. Hawthorn watched it hook up, discharge, and back out again five hours later. His vantage point across the road kept him away from the terminal, a consideration recognizing his reputation and the possibility of a chance connection between him and the location, but he was able to time the operation and satisfy himself that the ships were operating on schedule.

He and Gene Tinker alternated watches through the night, one of them staying close to the hotel phone while the other kept his stopwatch on the boats. At eleven o'clock Friday morning the fourth Brookings ship left the harbor, loaded with crude oil, and Hawthorn's second tanker came in, discharged, and made room for another ore carrier. It would go like that for another two days.

They stayed on, keeping score as the ships discharged their bauxite, white dust rising from the mountain they were building on shore as they loaded Venezuelan crude oil, riding low in the water, too low in the water for empty ships. Hawthorn thought of the harbor master with every departure.

Reinaldo Villar-Cruz was not an experienced agent, certainly not in this business, and he was worried as he sat in the back of the company's river launch that he might fail. If preparation was the key, he was ready; but if some kind of emergency came at him, an emergency demanding physical action, fast thinking, decisive control, he wasn't so sure. They were heading out toward the channel, leaving the tower and the city docks far behind. From corner to corner, the estuary measured well over eight miles, but the channel was on the tower side of the river, less than two miles from the harbor master's window.

He had made it a point to meet the youngster who was taking Singh's place, a horny kid who was unaccustomed to night work, unfamiliar with Brookings's ships, unmindful of their regular draft as they plowed into the river.

Villar-Cruz faced the bow, then turned his head again and saw the light from the tower. He put it out of his mind and concentrated on the tidal chop in front of them. His pilot was a recruit from Drinkwater's stock, reliable, trustworthy.

There! He saw the barge a hundred meters ahead, a dark, ugly beast riding the water like a battering ram, hulking there, waiting for the first ore boat. His man saw it too, slowing the launch to an idling glide as they pulled closer, drawing them to within a foot of the steel side. Villar-Cruz threw a line, saw a strong arm reach out and grab it. He took hold of the port ladder and climbed up, felt the sailor's hand on his wrist, and got his feet on the gunnel and swung aboard. He waved below, hearing the rumble as the launch backed away into the darkness.

The sailor was Big John, able seaman first class. He was wearing a hooded parka and dark gray coveralls. Rubber gloves were folded and tucked under a canvas belt around his waist. The rubber boots were heavy and well-heeled.

"The *Maria Baker* just called in. She's five miles out." He pointed to the wheelhouse near the stern of the barge, a dozen paces from where they stood. "There's hot coffee inside; the captain's about ready to pull up anchor. We got to be movin' at five knots when she comes in."

"Thanks, John," Villar-Cruz said. He looked forward to seeing the huge screw pumps and started in that direction. John followed behind, kicking a line aside as they went, stopping momentarily to check a hatch cover. Villar-Cruz stood beside the pumps, then walked around them, touching the new steel, seeing the "caution" and "use" plates riveted to their bodies.

"Big suckers, aren't they?" he said.

"Eighteen U-bolts holding 'em down, sir. We could push cold asphalt up Kaiteur with these buggers!"

The night stillness was broken only by the deep pulsing of the barge's diesel generator. Then a soft, airy horn, like an oboe's lowest note, floated forward. They heard the sound of an electric winch turning as the anchor chain started to come up, growling deeply as it crossed through the bow window and wound itself around a giant spindle.

172

Villar-Cruz turned and headed back toward the wheelhouse, feeling the barge moving now, rolling slightly as it came free in the tidal stream. He heard the engine rumble louder, knew they were making way slowly, heading into the river to time their rendezvous with the big ore ship, the crude carrier now. He opened the narrow cabin door and stepped inside.

The bridge was rigged only for its business purpose except for a small table, a chair, a counter cooler, and a heating element. There was a pot of coffee on that, steam rising from the spout. The captain was standing at the wheel, his instrument panel lighted in soft red color, the only other light a shrouded twenty-watt bulb aimed at the navigation board. He turned and nodded at Villar-Cruz, who was already pouring himself a cup of coffee.

"You're ready for a hard job," Villar-Cruz said.

"Nothin' new. I been working hard jobs all my life."

They were in a greenhouse with glass windows all around to give the captain full vision through 360 degrees. The panel to his left controlled the pumps, the winches, and the line hoists. A small transmitter-receiver was recessed above his head. Only a black dial with white letters and a crank showed, and the mike with its curled cord hanging down to his left. They were moving with some authority now; the shoreline on both sides appeared to be getting closer as the estuary narrowed into the river.

"Here she comes," said the captain. He was looking into a rearview mirror outside the cabin, on his left. Villar-Cruz turned and saw a vague shadow on the dark horizon. He watched the captain make his adjustments to the wheel, the throttles; there was little to do now but stay on the right side of the channel and keep the speed a constant five knots.

Now the big ship was directly astern, easing to its port for the midwater connection.

"Four-seven, do you read?"

The captain reached for his mike and pressed the side button.

"Roger, *Maria*, five by five."

"Roger, Four-seven. Two minutes. Watch my wake."

The big ship had to pull ahead of the barge at a speed of eight knots to make position: Her wake would cause a few bumps and maybe a wheel adjustment, but it would be minor.

She moved slowly up, her great bulk blocking out the sky on that side, darkening the deck, making it seem as though they were inside an enormous steel tank. They were cruising side by side now, less than five feet apart. Villar-Cruz stepped onto the deck, looked up, saw a crane lowering a fat rubberized hose toward John's station amidships. When the hose was at his waist level, John took it in both arms and led it into position against his receiving line valve face. With a swift pull he dropped the locking arm across the connection, then let the hose swing away. They could go ahead, in formation, moving up to ten knots.

The radio spoke again.

"Nice job, Four-seven. Who are you?"

"I'm Globe Four-seven."

"I know that. What's your name?"

"Globe Four-seven, *Maria.*"

Silence from the ore ship, then another voice.

"Open at 'mark.' Five . . . four . . . three . . . two . . . one . . . mark!"

The captain flicked a toggle switch on the left and turned his attention to the wheel. They saw the hose jump nervously in midair as it hung like a giant black snake, draped from a fallen tree. They were taking on crude oil, would soon be dropping lower in the water as they moved ahead. By the time they reached the bauxite mine, the bow would be awash.

Villar-Cruz stepped over the deck hatch covers and moved forward. He found a comfortable spot near the bow and eased himself down, crossing his legs under him. He pulled his coat higher around his neck and folded his arms against his chest. He smiled to himself. A piece of cake.

If it all went as easy as this, he had nothing to worry about. Except the harbor master, and maybe the Guianese Navy River Patrol. He smiled again. A twelve-foot duck boat with a Sears and Roebuck outboard motor and a boy dressed in a navy suit: That was the Guianese River Patrol.

As they passed Long Beach Island and a wider piece of river twenty miles inland, they saw another Globe barge waiting for them to go by. When they were through, that captain would head for the rendezvous point and repeat the maneuver, and then another, and another, until all eighteen ore carriers had made their crude transfers. The procession would stop at daybreak, begin again at night.

The hours passed, the shoreline drifted by. There was no sign of life, no sound but the rumble of the ships' engines. At twelve-forty Villar-Cruz was in the cabin. The radio crackled on.

"Four-seven, we're empty and you're full. You read?"

The barge captain pulled the mike to his mouth.

"Thank you, *Maria.* We'll disconnect."

He replaced the mike and pressed a red button on the console in front. The same small oboe sound floated out over the deck three times. Big John stood next to the coupling, pushed against the steel locking arm, and the hose fell away. A few drops of black oil on the deck would be washed away soon. They moved past the ore boat slowly, the radio came to life one more time.

"Good night."

Ahead, perhaps two miles upstream, they saw a lighter sky, a glow from the ground. Brookings mine and the never-sleeping furnaces, the ever-lighted offices of the aluminum plant. The timing had been perfect.

The Globe barge glided past and on up the river, leaving the ore carrier behind to turn into its own basin, load as much bauxite as possible, and head back to Trinidad for another cargo of crude.

At 2:00 A.M. they entered the Globe harbor, plowing at a crawl through the muddy water, small waves splashing up over the deck plates as the barge eased its bulk alongside the eastern dock. Sandy Dreier was waiting with two men.

In less than a minute they had tied her to the dock, swung a twelve-inch hose toward the junction, and Big John was completing the connection. He went around to the side of the pump control and pressed the auto start.

"Let 'er rip, John," Dreier shouted.

This was a different sound, a powerful, whining sound, like motors in a hydroelectric plant. John turned the knob on his pump control panel and saw the hose stiffen, find a comfortable position for itself, then begin to vibrate as it handled the heavy oil. He eased back on the pressure and whistled through his teeth.

"Jesus," he whispered to himself. He looked at Dreier.

"How fast can you take it, Sandy?"

"What do ya mean, how fast? How fast can you pump it? You've got ninety minutes, mate!"

He turned the dial knob slowly and the pumps wound up, sucking the oil out and pushing it ahead. The two men were scurrying along the line toward the pump house up the hill.

One disappeared inside, the other ran on ahead, stopping every few seconds to hunch over the pipeline, feel it, inspect seams. When he was out of sight, the first man returned from the pump house. Villar-Cruz heard his report to Dreier.

"Dry as a bone, Sandy. Runnin' backward and dry as a bone!"

"Damn! When we get the third barge, get the lines to the field wide open! Damn!" He slapped the man on the shoulders and stepped aboard the barge.

"You hear that, John? You hear that, Rei? Damn! We got ourselves a damn oil field here!"

He jumped off the barge, clapping John on the arm as he passed, and ran up the hill. Villar-Cruz heard a Jeep's motor crank up over the sound of the screw pumps. Dreier, satisfied that he and his men had passed a miracle, was going to the camp to check his field tanks.

Villar-Cruz stepped off the barge and walked a short way up the hill, then turned to his right and ambled along the concrete basin, stepping over the cement cracks, watching the river water pass through the gates.

Hawthorn slapped his briefcase shut, locked his door, knocked for Tinker in the next room.

They were on schedule. There was no reason to stay in Trinidad any longer than necessary when he could be standing at the mud hole in British Guiana, watching his cheese flow into the mouse trap.

At Piarco they left their rented car in the lot, passed a cursory customs inspection, and walked out to the Jetstar. The plane looked dark and sleek, its wing tanks hung like a pair of bombs, the auxiliary fuel pod sweeping the undercarriage.

Hawthorn strapped himself into the copilot's seat and watched Tinker go through the preflight, the start sequence. He could fly the damn airplane if he wanted to, probably.

"Piarco Tower, this is Globe four-niner-three-seven-seven, taxi please."

The tower directed them to the runway, then gave them the clearance for takeoff.

"Globe, the wind is oh eight six and your visibility is ten. You are off at two forty-five. Good morning."

They headed to the right after the wheels came up, eased into a climbing turn as Tinker pointed his nose into the darkness, heading out over Mayaro toward British Guiana.

Hawthorn tried to relax, but he could not. After twenty minutes, he reached across and turned off the automatic pilot and took the controls. He flew very badly at first, yawing because he treated the rudders with the same rough heel and toe crap he had used with the big prop planes, overhandling the yoke, losing his trim, dropping his nose.

It had been fourteen years since they came at him over the coast, came and shot his tail off.

CHAPTER 9

Tinker brought them in low over the coast without lights, cut across Guianese jungle, and cranked the Jetstar sharply to the east as they crossed over the dimly lit harbor. He stayed close to the treeline as they swept down the pipeline route at four hundred feet, hitting the final approach straight in. He rotated the landing lights to give them perception, slowed the silver jet to eighty knots, and brought her in nose high, dropping the main gear onto the hard sand with a whisper of dust in trail.

"Damn tanks should have been put someplace else, Greg," he said as they taxied back. The huge field units looked like monstrous black coffee cans squatting on the edge of the runway near their 090 touchdown point. "Dangerous as hell."

"Can't help that now, Gene. We didn't plan on coming in here like damn night commandos."

Dreier met them in the Jeep and waited while they climbed down the three forward steps. He let them get settled before starting back.

"Boss, I think we got an oil field here," Dreier said. His face was beaming in the five o'clock darkness. "It's beautiful."

"How about the tempo, Sandy? Every ninety minutes?" Hawthorn was slumped in the seat, one foot lodged against the dash.

"A little slower than that. The stuff's pretty cold, but we'll finish five barges by ten this morning. Even if a plane comes over, that's no sweat. He won't see a thing." He slowed as they entered the compound. "There was a call for you from Mr. Brookings, up at the bauxite mine. He said to call him right back."

They were a few yards from the radio shack. The engineer eased over, stopped.

"Wait for me," Hawthorn said. He climbed out, went inside, and connected with Brookings's private office.

"Brookings."

"Hawthorn. You're up late."

"Damn foreigners, Gregory, setting an impossible work schedule! Listen, I received a message from Guantanamo, Admiral Barnes. He used a hundred code words of course, took me an hour to figure out what he was talking about."

"You should have called Villar-Cruz, Ed. That's his department. What was the message?"

"It's your friend in America, Moffit. He's been strolling around Miami, visiting some of Fidel's comrades."

Hawthorn frowned. "Is this call safe, Ed?"

"Damned if I know. My end is, direct to yours. Unless somebody has climbed a pole or something."

"What else?"

"Whoever was tailing him lost track somehow. They picked him up again in Chicago."

"They did what? They lost him?"

"Found him again, Greg. In Chicago."

"Well, dammit, Ed! We thought he might go to Chicago. His mother lives there. But Alan was supposed to have somebody on his ass every minute."

"Don't get mad at me, Greg. I'm just the parrot around here."

"I'm sorry. No! I'm not sorry. What else?"

"That's all I know."

Hawthorn waited a moment, thinking. "Thanks, Ed. Are your ships OK? Is everything on schedule?"

"Perfect. Working like a Swiss clock. But the water is very low. Gregory. The narrows are very narrow."

"Thanks again. I'll talk to you later."

He hung up, searched in his pocket for a cigarette, and found an empty pack. He crushed it in his fist, threw it on the tent floor, and stepped outside.

"Let's get to the basin," he said.

Damn! What was Moffit doing in the company of Cubans? Did Podgorsky know about that? Of course Podgorsky knew about that! Was Moffit acting as a go-between? Not just Cubans, dammit! Castro Cubans. And the fancy-pants professionals lost him. How? Where? What did he say to those people? What did they tell him?

Hell with it. He would get on a scrambler in the morning and find Drinkwater. At the moment he had oil to unload.

Five barges came in on Friday night, nearly on schedule, the last disconnect coming at almost eleven o'clock in the morning. The basin was steaming by that time and sleep was impossible except near one of the mess hall fans. Hawthorn and Villar-Cruz walked the basin with Dreier, stopping to check seams and pipe joints, all dry and tight. There was no oil in the pipeline yet, the line that connected the basin to the field eighteen miles away. That would come later, with the seventh barge, when the head pressure at the basin tanks, combined with the land pumps, would force it through the line and into the field tanks. Then they would fill up, and the slightly higher lines that ran uphill to the wells would fill up and drop oil a thousand feet into the earth, into the special drilling pipe that was corked at the bottom. And then they would have an oil field.

Between now and then, all they had was a half-baked pie, solid and indisputable proof that the Globe Corporation was conducting a class in illusoriness deceit.

Shortly after lunch Hawthorn tried again and failed to reach the governor, Sir Hillman Gomes. His was the only telephone equipped with a scrambler, and he dared not communicate across three thousand miles or more on the public system. If all else failed, he would cable his questions to the admiral and have him work through the CIA to get answers. He had to know what Stephen Moffit was up to. At the very least he had to be assured that someone was sitting on his doorstep, listening on his party line, keeping track of the man.

He had given specific instructions. Drinkwater *knew* he was responsible for him. Dammit!

At four o'clock Hawthorn went to the radio shack and composed a cable. Then he called Tinker away from his card game and gave him the folded sheet of paper.

"Can you land the Jetstar at Ogle?"

"No, sir. But we got the Cessna. She's ready down there." He thumbed over his shoulder. "In that lean-to."

"Good, Gene. Take this up to Georgetown, over to the British military compound. Have them send it off from their station. And then take a ride over to that tower."

Hawthorn rubbed his eyes, scratching the corners with his knuckles. "Here." He reached for a detective paperback. "Take this up to the kid, tell him Villar-Cruz sent it over."

"What for?"

"I want you to see what he looks like, see what kind of job he's doing. Reinaldo says he's a carbon copy of Lou Costello."

Tinker grinned. "Sure, OK. I'll catch a look at his logs, maybe."

"If you can. Don't make a big deal out of it." He thought for a moment longer. "There's a coffee shop or something at the turnoff, where you start into the tower peninsula. Stick around there, keep your eye on the place, wait for the first two Brookings ships to pass, and see what it looks like. Our barges hook up way past his tower, but I want you to see what you can see."

On a clear night, with a big moon, a man might have seen the barges squatting near the bend, deep into the estuary. He had thought of posting a man there, but it was so damned black on the river.

Hawthorn's doubts, his feelings of nakedness, were starting to assail his firm conviction that it was a perfect gambit. He thought of Yu Hsin Chou.

At seven o'clock he ate a sandwich, forced it down between gulps of cold coffee. Then he went to his tent, cooler now, and slept for one hour.

At 2:00 A.M., they heard the rumble far down river, and twenty minutes later the black, ugly, misbegotten hulk of number six-one started to pump its cargo into the shore tanks. By the time the tenth barge drifted away from the mooring, oil was dripping from a seam weld at the bottom of one of the huge black tanks near the airfield, and everything was beautiful.

Tinker poured coffee into Hawthorn's tin cup as they sat on camp stools in front of the executive tent. It was Sunday noon, hot and humid, and they were more than half finished.

"Good thing it's dark out there," Tinker said. "I sat at the foot of the tower and watched three boats come in. Sure, I saw 'em, vague out there, and I looked down the river and saw our old barge too, but I was lookin' for it. I've got perfect night eyes. I could see it, like a helluva big log out there, no lights showing."

"The hookup. Did you see that?"

"No, because the big ship came along and blocked it out. When it passed, the river was empty. But I could barely see it. And that kid up in the tower, he was readin' his damn thriller. Buddy, I wouldn't have that kid on my side."

Hawthorn shrugged his shoulders, sipped his coffee, and tossed nearly a full cup onto the ground.

"How about the cable, the message?"

"It got off OK. Gomes is out of the country, up in Barbados. That's why you couldn't get through to him. And you won't get a reply on the cable until late tonight. Their receiver is fugged up."

Tinker paused, looked at Hawthorn, and saw the concern written on his face.

"Hell, Greg, for all we know, Moffit's eating jelly sandwiches with his mommy."

"Yeah. Maybe he is," Hawthorn replied softly.

Ten P.M.

The *Hanna Bee* moved slowly into the estuary, her captain peering through the darkness, searching for the Globe barge. It was supposed to be ahead, in line with the abandoned chimney stack on the west side. He saw nothing but empty water, darkness along the shoreline. He passed the harbor master's tower, saw a dim light glowing there, and now, far ahead, he thought he saw another light, deep into the river. He plowed ahead at eight knots, reached for his radio microphone, and called the Brookings office.

"Roger, *Hanna*, I copy. Try 117.6. See if you can raise Globe Five-five."

The captain switched over and made contact.

"Roger, *Hanna*. Globe Five-five. I've been workin' you on 109.3. Go home, *Hanna*. Watch your wake, watch your traffic, and go straight on home. Call your friends. Tell them to hold hands out there for a while."

The captain signaled off, hung his mike on the hook, and stared ahead. There wasn't just one light but many on the river, moving ahead of his bow, boats of some kind. A light appeared to swing around, then cut across the river, now another, and another. He eased back to five knots and continued into the river. The boats were moving ahead of him, more than a dozen of them.

As he approached the broadening, he understood what Five-five had been trying to say. Somebody was having a river picnic out there. He had seen them before, maybe twice in his life. Sixteen, maybe eighteen of the niftiest little rigs in the country, out on one of their twice-a-year river picnics. Lights were strung from their bows, across the mast poles back to the sterns of every friggin' boat. He could see them all now, lining up at one side of the broadening and racing through the dark for the other side.

As he watched, his hand on the wheel, one of the boats approached his port side, the skipper brightly illuminated by his own lights. A lady was filling his glass with good old West Indian rum.

"Ahoy, there, *Hanna Bee!*"

The captain leaned out his window and saw the sleek launch, saw the ladies lounging on the aft deck and men sitting on the roof, staring up at him. One of the men had a carbine resting across his legs.

"Ahhh. . . . Good evening," the captain said in a loud voice. "Out on the stream so late?"

"A frolic, captain; while you work, we frolic!"

"A long night of it? I wouldn't care for an accident with my vessel, Mr. . . ."

"Ramprashad, sir. Carlysle Ramprashad. Nor I. My guests would frown on that."

They were cruising side by side.

"Until very late, I think," the minister added. "Don't worry, we shall stay clear as you pass through. Good night, then, captain."

He hoisted a glass toward the bridge window and saluted as the *Hanna Bee* moved ahead, Ramprashad spinning the wheel to bring his own little toy out of the bigger ship's wake.

181

Aboard the yacht, they watched the Brookings ship disappear into the darkness. Ramprashad turned the wheel over to a younger man and stepped below, into the very fine cabin.

"The bauxite ships, gentlemen," he said to his guests. They were relaxed, sipping on dark drinks, smoking black cigarettes. "They work all hours, of course, carrying aluminum ore to Trinidad and bringing back some fuel oil for their furnaces. Soon that will be done with, I hope."

"Yes, one would hope so. You will have your own oil for their consumption."

"Well, yes, that too. But I meant the foreign ownership, sir. It is our resource, after all, the bauxite."

"Ahh, of course. But don't be in a hurry, Mr. Ramprashad. These things are better accomplished with a measure of patience."

"Of course. Everything in due time. Now, then, are you enjoying the evening?"

"Oh, yes. It's splendid. But I think the plan for tomorrow should change, sir."

"Oh? In what way?"

"Tuesday would be better. I'm afraid your hospitality tonight will have me in poor condition for a tour in the morning."

"Tuesday it shall be, then. I will make the arrangements tomorrow, first thing. We can have breakfast at the camp. That will give us the entire day to inspect the Globe facility."

"Don't you agree, Ivan? Wouldn't that be a better idea?"

"Yes, sir, Comrade Podgorsky. Tuesday morning would suit us much better. And I was wondering, Mr. Ramprashad, if it would be a good idea to visit with your harbor master. It didn't occur to me until just now. Your waterways are extremely vital, aren't they?"

In the dark river, the Globe barges rode silently, high, tucked near the shoreline, empty. And at sea, four Brookings tankers were joined by a fifth as the *Hanna Bee* chugged heavily into her own Brookings berth, loaded with Venezuelan crude oil. The five stayed in a circle, anchored in the shallow waters off the British Guiana coast, and waited.

CHAPTER 10

A yellow light burned in Hawthorn's tent. Villar-Cruz, Dreier, Gene Tinker, and Hawthorn hunched over a table.

"We can get a barge up and take that load from the *Hanna*," Villar-Cruz said quietly.

"And have the whole damn Guianese shore gang up there wonder what's going on? I don't think so, Rei," Tinker said.

"No. They'll have to burn that stuff, blend it, and burn it themselves," said Hawthorn.

"Eight ships in one night, sir. It can't be done."

"What if we got six?"

"Won't be enough, boss," Dreier said. "Those wells would be bone dry."

"We could wait, sir. Maybe we could finish a couple loads on Tuesday night." Villar-Cruz was out of ideas.

"Fill one of the tanks with river water." Tinker was no engineer, no strategist, but it wasn't a bad thought.

"And drain it off later, when we can top 'em off with real crude. Why not?" asked Dreier.

"How long will it take for the water to separate, Sandy, to settle out in the bottoms?"

"Couple days, maybe six days."

Hawthorn thought about that. "We'd have some pretty crappy-looking crude oil for those six days."

"Yes, sir. We sure would."

"OK, that's a last resort."

Dutch Schultz poked his head into the tent.

"Yeah, Dutch."

"Five-five just called in. Them little boats are still out there. Looks like they mean to stay all night."

Hawthorn looked down at the table. "That's it for now then."

Schultz backed out and it was silent for a minute. Hawthorn put his hands on the tabletop and rocked slowly back and forth.

"I'm dizzy as hell," he said. "We can't do anything more tonight. Let's hit the sack and work on this in the morning."

Hawthorn stared at the ceiling, at the canvas. Still no report on Moffit,

183

no word from Drinkwater, nothing from Admiral Barnes. But he had another problem now, a more pressing problem. Could they wait one more day? Two days? How urgent was it to fill the tanks now? It was the difference between a real oil field and a phony oil field.

That was the urgency. His entire argument hinged on a system that was overflowing, full to the brink.

Spots danced in his eyes, waves of sleep came and went, his body was soaked, the cot was black with his sweat. They were coming at him now, low over the coast, and he had two engines on fire. He was burning up, his body was melting.

"Telephone call just came in for Sandy, sir."

Hawthorn opened his eyes slowly, saw light through the tent flap. Villar-Cruz was there, holding a piece of paper in his hand.

"Telephone?" Hawthorn rubbed his face.

"I'm afraid we have some bad news, Mr. Hawthorn."

"Bad news." He urged himself to a sitting position, dropped his feet to the floor, and took the note.

"Singh? The harbor master?"

"Yes, sir. Government radio has been putting out a message for him all night to get back to town. You know the way they do: 'Your wife is ill, travel immediately.' That kind of message. Everybody in the bush listens to it. Sandy took the call from Mr. Brookings."

Hawthorn read the note, stared at it.

"Get Tinker," he finally said.

At that moment Dreier came into the tent and looked from one man to the other. His face was the color of potato soup. He gathered himself together and addressed both of them:

"I just got another call. From Georgetown." He swallowed. "Mr. Ramprashad's secretary." Dreier shuffled his feet. "She said not to fix anything fancy, just the usual fare."

Hawthorn sat quietly, waiting, watching the big man from Oklahoma stumble over the message.

"For breakfast. Tomorrow. For Mr. Ramprashad and his overseas guests."

Villar-Cruz sat down. "Go get Tinker," he said.

"That's right, Ed. Start your ships into the river at two P.M. this afternoon. I don't care what's on the river. I want eight loads tonight. If you have to run on a sandbar to make room, do it. But squeeze eight ships in!"

"Absolutely impossible, Gregory. The rip current won't allow it until at least four o'clock, not on my account, but due to the configuration of your barges and the maneuvers that must take place in midstream. The ships would blast holes in one another, man."

"Four o'clock. That puts my last barge into the harbor at nine in the morning. Damn!" Hawthorn thought for a moment.

"If you're absolutely positive, Ed."

"Absolutely. You would be courting a major disaster if we start any earlier."

"All right. Start the operation at four P.M. I'll handle the HM, I'll handle the river traffic and all the rest. Four P.M., Ed. My barges will be waiting at the chimney."

There would be waves on the river that night.

Hawthorn and Tinker arrived at the tiny airport outside Georgetown at two o'clock. A company car was there, a Rover. Tinker wore a light jacket to cover his shoulder holster.

They drove through town, past the Tower Hotel, past the riverfront docks, on toward the river. They drove past the yacht club, past their own warehouse and office, down the jetty trail, and onto the peninsula where the tower stood.

They stopped at the café, talked for a minute, then headed down the half mile of dirt road that led to the tower. They were still two hundred yards away when they saw it, the official government vehicle, parked in the space reserved for the harbor master. They parked next to it, got out, and saw two hunting jackets draped over the front seat.

Hawthorn leaned against the building next to the door. He glanced at his watch. Three o'clock. The first ship would be on the horizon by now.

"Maybe he isn't there, Greg."

"He's there."

"But Christ, man, one ship! They get one ship a week loaded like that, why not now?"

"We've got three like that coming in before seven o'clock. Brookings hasn't got room in his tanks for three loads. Singh knows that."

"Maybe he's not there."

Hawthorn looked at Tinker. "Did they teach you that in CIA school, Gene?"

"No. I was just . . ."

"He's there. And he'll be up there until midnight. I know about that man. He's like a McCarthy, looking for snakes on the front lawn." Hawthorn straightened, tucked his shirt into his pants, and stood against the wall, next to the door.

"Let's have it," he said.

Tinker hesitated, leaned against the wall next to Hawthorn.

"Negative," he said. "It's my job."

185

"Can it, Gene. Hand it over."

Tinker tightened his jaw and reached inside his jacket, slipped the .45 automatic from its bulky holster, and kneeled down, looking around as he jammed the barrel back, throwing a cartridge into the chamber. He released the safety and stood up.

"You ever fired one of these?" He handed it to his left, butt first, muzzle downrange.

Hawthorn didn't answer. He looked at Tinker and the answer was there. Twenty-seven men, one way or another. The piece had a bigger kick, a nastier bite. It was louder, but it accomplished the same thing.

He turned and found the doorknob with his left hand, holding the pistol in his right. Then he looked back at Tinker.

"Get the Rover." His voice was husky, clearly heard in the quiet afternoon. He listened to the sounds—the sound of the water slopping against the rocks twenty feet away, a sea gull, the breeze circling around the tower. "When I come down, we'll evacuate this area by the back door, down the river road. We'll cut back and get the main road up past the café."

Tinker nodded. Hawthorn turned again and went inside.

He closed the door behind, easing the knob to stop its click, saw the stairway a few feet ahead, a winding staircase heading to the top, three flights up. He counted them as he climbed, stopped at number 20, and listened to his own breathing. Up again, slowly, the steel-plated steps narrow, vertical, silent under his rubber soles. His left hand was on the winding iron rail; his right clutched the weapon, index finger tucked behind the trigger, squeezing the guard. He would have plenty of time.

He stood at the top, breathed deeply several times, his free hand floating to the door. Gently now, he turned the handle. The door swung silently open. He saw a man, dressed in a khaki uniform, wearing a khaki military cap, binoculars raised to his eyes, poised in front of the windows. He was looking out to sea. On the desk was a logbook, open, a pen resting across its face. Hawthorn raised the pistol to his belt and positioned his finger on the trigger. The cannon was aimed at the center of his spine. The slug would blow a hole in his stomach as it burst through, a fat lump of jagged lead flattened by bone impact. He readied himself, spread his feet, and spoke.

"Singh."

The man turned abruptly, lowered the glasses, and stared at Hawthorn. Then he faced the window again and brought the glasses back to his eyes.

"Heavens!" he said to the glass. "You startled me, sir."

Hawthorn blinked. "Burrowes?"

"Of course, Mr. Hawthorn. You were expecting to find the harbor master, I suppose."

Hawthorn was speechless. The fat little man lowered the binoculars and turned around, the brim of his commandant's cap covering his telltale growth.

"Poor chap is in hospital, you see. It seems I shot him in the fanny."

Hawthorn slumped in the right-hand seat, his legs extended into the rudder cavity. He could feel Tinker's corrections with his toes on the copilot's pedals. At cruising speed, the compact little 182 was quiet, cool, easy to take.

"You saw it out there."

"Yeah," Tinker replied. "I saw it."

"It's just after three o'clock," Hawthorn said. His eyes were wide open and his hands were resting on the control yoke, riding there with Tinker's touch.

"That ship is number eleven, my friend. They can hump like hell all the way down and never get there in time."

Tinker was CIA. He could handle many assignments with ease, but he was a B student in logistics. Now they were faced with a problem that spelled disaster, and he was poorly equipped to deal with it. Distance, speed, fluid bulk, viscosity, pumping rates, head pressures, channel currents, and time. Time.

"What time will it get down there? Number eighteen?"

"Eight in the morning," Hawthorn replied. "If they hurry like hell and don't hit any snags, the last barge can begin offloading at eight A.M.."

"And finish at ten. The field lines will be shaking like a leaf, all that high-pressure oil going to the wellheads, running backward."

Hawthorn glanced across the cockpit. "I know."

"There's Atkinson, under your wing," Tinker said.

"They'll be using a DC-3, out of that field."

"Forget it, Greg. It's a government plane, three soldiers on it all the time." He paused. "You're thinkin' . . ."

"Sabotage. That's out. They can get another plane."

"Why not call 'em, Greg. Just tell 'em to hold off for a few hours, like you've got a smallpox case down there or something?"

"Not a bad idea, Gene. But that would give us the added company of the national health department within sixty minutes. And if we asked for a postponement on some other grounds, Podgorsky would send his man down in a chopper to check on that. No good."

They fell silent, listened to the dull engine noise, felt the small air pockets, bumps,—windy objections to their passage. Hawthorn let his mind work through the next seventeen hours.

187

* * *

Barge number 18 ties up to the mooring cleats. Four men race into action, drag hoses, connect, the Sier-Bath pumps wind up, the howling begins . . . the oil rushes into the shore tanks, pressure builds, monster land pumps drive it into the pipeline and then across country; crude hits the bottom of number 2 field tank, forces its way into the fluid mass already there. Twenty minutes to make that trip. But the politicians and the Russian diplomats have already been on the ground for ten minutes and they'll have to wait nearly two hours before they can be told the happy news, before they can be taken to the producing wells.

Stall, show them the camp, the motor pool, the new electric generator, the fancy indoor toilet, the pet ocelot.

"Shall we forego the porridge? Take us to that famous harbor, show us the derricks and the prolific wells."

Stall for how long? What if they insist? What then? Tie them up and wait for a signal from Dreier?
"OK, fellas, the lines are full now. You can go on your tour."

Hawthorn caught himself frowning. He was projecting, and that was a bad policy in his business. Smallpox. Chicken pox. The black plague. He closed his eyes, his thoughts inexplicably going back to Podgorsky's curt remark on the scow: *"Shall I send the Russian army down to your camp to protect you from Jagan?"*

Then he remembered the last planning meeting with Alan Drinkwater, the meeting where he refused military protection during the operation.

"No soldiers, Alan. I don't want any British soldiers to spend their furlough talking about the way we fooled the Russians. I'll have sixteen trained experts on the site, my own people. That's enough risk in itself."

He opened his eyes again. Yes, his own men and their postoperational confidentiality were risky, but the immediate risk was suicidal.
"Turn this thing around, Gene. Head back to town."
Tinker nodded, glanced quickly to his right, saw Hawthorn sit up straight. He bent the little Cessna in a sharp turn to port, made his 180 and put the sun on their left side.

They used the same Rover, eased out of the little airport's deserted boundary, and sped back to town. Tinker had said not a word, asked no questions. This was Hawthorn's show.

The road was dusty, even on the asphalt section, but it was empty and quiet as they made the outskirts of Georgetown.

"Grace Street, Gene, down to your left. Stay off the main roads. When we get there, you wait."

Tinker eased into Grace, followed the boulevard for three blocks, and came to a stop at the entrance to a walled compound.

"Hupp!"

A British soldier blocked their way, quivering at attention, his rifle at the parade pressed against his nose. He slammed one foot down, drove his other heel to the smart arrest position, then unwound and came forward. He leaned over and stuck his red face close to Tinker's window.

"The governor, please. Mr. Gregory Hawthorn wants to see him. It's urgent."

"Suh! Wait, suh!"

He disappeared into a guard booth. They saw him use the phone, nod, and place the receiver on the table. He poked his head out.

"The name again, sir."

"Hawthorn. Gregory Hawthorn."

A moment later he hung up, looked through the glass window, and returned to his post at the drop gate. He leaned on his end, the gate rose, and they drove through.

It was a mansion, well protected from the road, with British soldiers at the security positions. Hawthorn got out, said a few words to Tinker through the window, and straightened his shirt. Then he mounted the steps and went inside. Tinker zipped his jacket shut, readjusted his pistol, and waited in the hot afternoon.

An overhead fan was moving some air in the foyer, over the duty sergeant's desk. Hawthorn stood for a moment, waiting for the young soldier to finish an entry in his journal. With deliberate care the man blotted his notation, opened his drawer, set the journal inside, closed and locked the drawer, replaced the pen in its holder, folded his hands, and looked up.

"The governor, please. My name is Gregory Hawthorn."

"Yes, Mr. Hawthorn. The perimeter guard just phoned in. I'm afraid the governor is away from office at the moment. Can someone else help you?"

"Where is he?"

"He's not available at the moment, Mr. Hawthorn."

"The regiment commander then. Is he available?"

"He is with the governor, sir."

Hawthorn clenched his fists, then unclenched them. He looked at the young man's ruddy face, his sharp English nose. His stripes.

"It's vital that I see one of them, Sergeant. My business is most urgent."

"I was given direct orders to set firm appointments, Mr. Hawthorn. Since you have no appointment, I would be happy to arrange a time that is suitable for you to meet with the governor. Failing that, you may take your chances and wait in the room across the hall."

"The governor, mister." Hawthorn leaned across the desk. "Now."

The sergeant reached for his phone.

"OK. Let's go." Hawthorn gave Tinker the command as he was halfway down the steps. He climbed in and they left the mansion behind, a puzzled-looking British officer standing on the steps, whacking a leather crop against his stiff breeches.

The Cessna behaved badly on the way back, buffeted by the hot late afternoon air. Tinker climbed higher to find smoother riding.

"It's going to be very close, Gene," Hawthorn said. "The men are on maneuvers and won't be back until morning. Gomes can reach them by radio and try to lift a contingent by helicopter, but it will be close."

"Where on maneuvers, Greg? Where are they?"

"Aboard a British frigate, off the coast of French Guiana."

Number one-seven was late. It arrived at six o'clock, meaning that number one-eight, if it came down as scheduled, would have to wait in line. The harbor crew wasted no time in cranking the pumps to full power, then threw fishing nets over her hose lines to cover the operation against airborne surveillance.

They would be lucky now to finish by eleven o'clock.

The frigate had responded, but it had taken over seven hours to obtain the regional commander's approval. The BG contingent was playing an important role in the Commonwealth exercise. They had left the area of Cayenne at 5:00 A.M.

To make it in time they needed to travel more than three hundred miles in two ancient helicopters. The weather over Suriname was rough, and the maximum flight time of the old choppers was three hours. If they made it by 7:55, Hawthorn would win. If they were five minutes late, he would lose.

After five years it was all boiling down to a spread of less than five minutes. He could have believed a calamity or a cancellation order, but to be so close and still so vulnerable was practically insane.

At 7:30 Hawthorn set his contingency plan into motion.

He was at the landing strip at 7:45, sitting in his Jeep, clean-shaven, washed, waiting. Behind him, standing in a ragged line like a squad of trench fighters, were his men, armed with carbines and submachine guns. "Orders from the governor," he would say. No visitors. A more transparent guise was hardly imaginable, but failing the royal dignity of an officially dispatched British military garrison, he had no choice.

At 7:50 he heard a sound in the distant north. He cocked his head, listened, and heard not the flupping sound of a chopper but the droning motors of a DC-3. Podgorsky and Ramprashad.

Hawthorn bowed his head and rested it against the Jeep steering wheel, trying not to think of the scene that was to follow, the scene he had so accurately pictured the afternoon before.

Now, from the other direction, he heard the choppers. His spine grew rigid, his blood started to race. He jumped down from the Jeep, shouting to his men, and waved them off. They scrambled into waiting trucks. In a minute they were gone, before the big machines touched down. Hawthorn ran to one of the wide chopper doors but had to leap out of the way as men dressed in green battle gear tumbled out and raced for the airport perimeter, the big field tanks, the campsite a mile away. Before he could get to the pilot's side to shout instructions, the blades began to beat louder and faster and both machines took off, staying low, heading south, away from the approaching DC-3, now only three miles away, coming in from the north.

It landed at 8:05 and rolled to a stop, then turned back to the boarding apron. Dutch Schultz was there with his squad of four polished Jeeps as the steps came down and the visitors disembarked. Hawthorn went forward to greet them, shaking Josef Podgorsky's hand, then Carlysle Ramprashad's, then the hand of the man who had met him at Miami International, the man who had escorted him to the dying of Yu Hsin Chou.

"You timed your visit perfectly," Hawthorn said. He turned Ramprashad over to another driver and steered the Russian visitor to his own vehicle. They sat side by side in the back, the young lieutenant in front.

"What the hell is this, Hawthorn?"

Along the airport perimeter, British soldiers. Guarding the field tanks, British soldiers, rifles at the ready. Beyond the field, flanking the camp, British soldiers.

Hawthorn looked across at the Russian, saw a grim face staring back.

"What I've got here is the biggest oil field in the western hemisphere, Podgorsky. We've driving right over what I'd guess to be about one hundred billion dollars' worth of crude oil, at a dollar a barrel."

"My God!"

Podgorsky's face was a picture of bewilderment. His mouth was working, his eyes were everywhere.

They hit a bump and Podgorsky's sunglasses fell down his nose. He shoved them back and got a tighter grip on the seat in front of him.

"The soldiers, Hawthorn, the soldiers."

"You look surprised, Podgorsky; what's so surprising, the soldiers? Or the oil?"

Podgorsky was staring at the huge black tank, turning his head as they passed it, seeing the collection of dark oil at its base. He looked at Hawthorn, his eyes hidden behind the glasses. "What are the soldiers doing here? You said . . ."

They were coming into the camp. Podgorsky's head turned every time he caught sight of another British military uniform.

"I'm afraid I can't do anything about that," Hawthorn replied. "I was under instructions by terms of the concession contract to inform Her Majesty's governor the minute I had a positive report. I did that several days ago. These folks are here to protect the field."

"From what? Tell me what they are here for!"

They rocked forward slightly as the Jeep came to a stop in front of the mess hall.

"We'll try to get a telephone connection with the governor after breakfast. I think you may get permission to go ahead and make the tour. I called him right away, of course, as soon as I heard you were coming, but he wasn't in. They said he was due back in his office around eleven this morning."

Hawthorn stuck a leg down and climbed out. He lit a cigarette and looked at Podgorsky.

"Are you coming? I think we got the cook to make us some waffles."

The tour was conducted as scheduled, albeit starting three hours late. It seemed the governor was unable to grant the necessary permissions without contacting his foreign office in London, though he himself thought it was an absurd and a completely unnecessary precaution.

A petroleum engineer, trained and experienced in field operations and equipped with several sophisticated pieces of hardware, might have detected a certain curious odor about the Globe discovery, given a week or two to study it very carefully.

But Josef Podgorsky and Carlysle Ramprashad and the rest of the company left Globe's basin that afternoon convinced beyond the slightest possible doubt that there, buried deep in the bosom of poor little British Guiana, was oil for the centuries.

CHAPTER 11

It was an exhausting day for the dignitaries and their wives and their secretaries. They looked haggard and wilted as they squeezed back into their DC-3 and went home. By the time the sound of the engines had faded beyond the tree line, tiny electric lights were blinking on in the camp tents, mute beacons to show bone-weary civilian soldiers their beds. They had fought a battle with tension and with time, and they had won. If there was to be a celebration, it would happen another day.

But for Gregory Hawthorn, the day wasn't quite over. At eight o'clock he gathered himself together and flew to Ogle airport with Gene Tinker. Once again they found Grace Street, confronted the brittle guard, and passed through to the governor's office. Sir Hillman Gomes was waiting for them.

"No need to give me a report, Gregory. I understand from my commander that it was a smashing good show."

He was a nice looking man with a pencil-thin mustache and dark hair slicked back to show his tanned brow. He stood straight and tall, slender and neat.

He had them take places in his studio, a sound-proofed room filled with his own assemblage of radio gear. Tinker sipped a neat Scotch whiskey, Hawthorn drank strong black coffee. The governor nibbled on pecans.

"Sir Hillman, I want your assurance that the officer in charge down there will remain totally ignorant of the truth. If one man, if just one man gets any kind of a suspicion . . ."

"You needn't worry, Gregory. The fellow I sent is cold military stuff. He neither knows nor cares what you chaps are doing there. His men are bivouacked near the airstrip, I believe, a good distance from the operation."

"That's where I put them, yes."

"No reporters, no visitors, and no mingling with your people. Those are his orders."

"And they go when I say so."

"Absolutely." Gomes waited a moment, then got on with it. "Now then, I understand you wanted to contact Alan Drinkwater. Was that correct?"

"That's right, sir. I must speak with him immediately if that's at all possible."

"Yes, well I have him on wait, of course. He's been on the alert since I reached him this afternoon."

"You have a scrambler here, I understand."

"Sometimes, yes. Fortunately, the damn thing is working tonight. Otherwise we would have to go through Barbados, and that is a bit of trouble." He stood and went to a console, picked up a phone, and pressed a button. He looked over his shoulder at them.

"In any event, the connection is already made. Scrambler on. Takes a moment, you understand." He waited, then spoke quietly into the mouthpiece. A few seconds more.

"Aha! Is that you, Alan? Say the words, then. Do it slowly, please." He smiled, cupped the mouthpiece and glanced over at Hawthorn, was about to say something when he got his authentication. "Oh, good, fine. Well then, here's Hawthorn." He held the phone out and Hawthorn strode across the room.

"Alan. It's all over, it's finished. The project is success fully in place. Now listen."

"You may have to speak a bit slower, Mr. Hawthorn. It's an echo thing, a recording trick of some kind."

Hawthorn nodded and spoke slowly.

"I want to know what instructions you gave to the Miami authorities regarding Stephen Moffit." He listened.

"I know he went to Chicago. We expected he might go there, but your people in Miami lost him! . . . Well, how the hell should I know that? . . . You did what? . . ."

Hawthorn listened for nearly a minute. He cradled the telephone on his shoulder and lit a cigarette, dropped the match in Sir Hillman's pecan dish, blew smoke furiously at the wall.

"I want to see you, Alan. As soon as possible. Toronto again. Fine. Sure, Julius is fine. Thursday at eight. Good-bye."

He hung up, stood still, poked a hand in his pocket, and stared at the telephone.

"Thank you, sir," he said. He came forward, nodded at Tinker. "We can't stay any longer, I'm afraid."

"I understand perfectly, Mr. Hawthorn. You must be exhausted. My congratulations, sir. If there's anything I can do."

This time, as Gene Tinker eased the Cessna off the ground and turned to the south, Gregory Hawthorn closed his eyes. He wanted to worry about Moffit. He wanted to worry about Alan Drinkwater's sloppy instructions to the CIA and their instructions to the local police. He wanted to zero in on the astonishment of Podgorsky, his own fears that there was something very curious about the whole thing.

But by the time they crossed the last rice field and hit the forest line, he was asleep.

They left the field on Thursday morning. Gene Tinker was at the controls and Reinaldo Villar-Cruz rode in the back, preparing the press releases for Globe. Hawthorn had no qualms about leaving Sandy Dreier alone at the field. The military cordon that surrounded his concession from the western harbor to the last well site in the east was strong medicine against unwanted invaders, sparsely planted though they were. He might have felt better had he stayed for another day, but once again he was faced with a no-choice decision. He had an appointment to meet with the Olympian Dr. Drinkwater in Canada.

It was warm in Toronto, sticky, only slightly more comfortable than the weather in British Guiana. They had registered as representatives of the Julius Foundation, a name Drinkwater came up with in honor of his dead uncle, Julius Drinkwater. At seven o'clock they finished their dinner and set the trays outside the door. At eight o'clock Alan Drinkwater was admitted, and the meeting began. Drinkwater was allowed to find a chair and get himself comfortable before Gregory Hawthorn let loose.

"Three points, Alan: What happened, that's first. What might be happening now, that's next, and what's going to happen. That's last. Let's start with your spy, Stephen Moffit."

Hawthorn was sitting opposite Drinkwater, facing him, two feet away. Their knees were almost touching; Hawthorn was leaning forward, crowding Drinkwater's space. It was an effective offense.

"I assure you, Gregory, this isn't in the least bit necessary." He was pressing away; he crossed a leg over his knee, tried to gain his space back by occupying it.

"It's necessary, Alan. Let me spell it out for you. I have taken on the Soviet Union. I've committed the single most outrageous sin in their screwed-up value system. I have trespassed on their intelligence and taken advantage of their trust. I could be shot for insulting them."

"But that was the idea, Gregory. Not to be shot, I didn't mean . . ."

"And I've done that with one of their supersecret agents waltzing around scot free! I entrusted you to handle that superspy, to keep him under surveillance while I pulled this thing off, and you let him slip away. He could have been suspicious, Alan, sneaked back dressed up like a friggin' wild turkey and watched the whole operation. Just what the hell went wrong?"

"Aren't you being overdramatic about . . ."

"No, I'm not. You told the CIA, some guy named Hulbert—you told him to make sure the police in Miami knew where Moffit was, where he went. They did that, all right. And when he went to the airport, they all went out for a sandwich! They had no idea who he saw, who he talked to . . ."

"Whom," said Drinkwater.

Hawthorn stopped, stared at the Englishman.

"You don't seem to care. You really don't seem very upset by any of this." He leaned back.

"I am. I assure you. Hulbert did not get the directive straight, sir. He was instructed to have a man in close proximity to Moffit the entire time he was in the United States. I'll speak with him about that. His superiors should know . . ."

"Too late, Alan. I've already called the CIA. Hulbert's on the job in Chicago right now. Personally. The Chicago police force is out of it. The FBI is working with him. I know that the apartment house he visited is a hangout for Castro Cubans, traders, informers. It was the site of at least two Mafia-related shootings that have something to do with Fidel. I know that much, but that's about all."

Drinkwater was toying with his pipe, head down, nodding.

"I am sorry, Gregory. You're quite right, of course. I should have followed through more vigorously."

Hawthorn stood and went to a window, parted the drapes, and looked down at the city of Toronto. Tinker was standing against a wall, back straight, hard-mouthed. Reinaldo removed his horn-rimmed glasses and wiped them clean, embarrassed for Drinkwater. He replaced his glasses and folded his hands. He wished he had chosen a more comfortable chair.

Hawthorn wiped his palms with a handkerchief. For a full two minutes deadly silence hung between the men. Then it was over.

"Next item." Hawthorn stood with his back to the window.

"When Podgorsky got off that plane and saw what he saw, I thought he was going to faint. I don't mean he was happily surprised, Alan," Hawthorn added, coming forward again. "He was in shock, he was flabbergasted!"

"Well, but what did you expect? Of course he was in shock. Put yourself in his position, Gregory."

"I did. I put myself in his place and I would have been jubilant! I saw myself grinning from ear to ear, shaking hands all around, congratulating the madman who said he would produce results and did just that. Sure, I would have been upset by the soldiers, and he was, but that's not what worries me."

"Nonsense, Gregory. You sound positively paranoid!

"Do I? Maybe so. Maybe so, but your whole hypothesis is based on the assumption that their ambitions in the Caribbean depend on oil, and all of a sudden I see a man whose behavior tells me otherwise."

Drinkwater thought a moment. "But if that were the case, why would they have expressed an interest in you at all? Good heavens, man! They dragged you off to see a brutally beaten man and they committed murder on poor Bishop! No, no. You are totally wrong about that." Drinkwater took out his handkerchief, mopped his hands. "No, I think Podgorsky was indeed flabbergasted because the previous reports had been so discouraging, but I am equally certain he is being considered for a medal of some kind at this very moment."

"Alan, if you're wrong, this whole project is a colossal waste of time and money."

"No. I am not wrong on that. The secondary objective, Gregory. You must not forget the Middle East. American and British and other foreign corporations are buying up oil leases and drilling for oil in the Middle East at a fantastic rate. But there are no Russians in view. Why not?"

"They're counting on British Guiana oil. I hope you're right."

"Leave that to me, sir. I know."

"Alan . . . we've come a long way together . . . a very long way since Hamburg." Hawthorn's sharp features, tanned face, and handsome smile covered an inner fatigue that he was fighting with every new parlay. "It's been a mechanical nightmare and a continuous game, a dangerous game of deceit." Hawthorn unbuttoned his shirt collar, loosened his tie.

"So far, it looks like we're ahead. We've given them an oil field, those 'vast Caribbean reserves' called for in the CIA directive. We've given them a reliable distribution network with entry to every port in the Caribbean basin."

Drinkwater remained very still, listening carefully, nodding, agreeing.

"I don't have any choice but to go along with you at this point. The Soviet Union seems to be convinced that their main obstacle to a successful, semipeaceful invasion of the Caribbean has been removed." He stared at the Englishman. "I hope you're right about the importance of that obstacle, Alan."

Drinkwater nodded more vigorously. "I am."

"Then we're ready for the last stage. I need to talk about that." Hawthorn pushed his notepad away, got comfortable in his chair, and concentrated on a spot on the wall, a target.

"We're at a position now where several things can happen. Let's look at them and our response to them. One, Fidel storms into Havana and shoots up the Americans and takes the refinery. What's our response?"

"You will send your ships in, I will give the command from Guantanamo, and your captains will either blow them to hell, or sink them. Eisenhower will have to decide that."

"Good. When will he decide? We can't keep putting this off, Alan. It takes time to organize a destructive course."

"Soon. I hope soon. But the President is influenced by your intelligence services, and they can't seem to come to terms with the fact that Castro is a scoundrel."

"Soon. All right, let's assume he isn't a scoundrel. Let's go to case two. Castro comes in like a pussycat and wants to be friends with the Americans, honor the agreements and all the rest. Let's have the response."

"But, my good man, what precisely do you think Stephen Moffit was doing in Miami? Do you think he was there on his own private initiative? May I suggest that he was there on instructions from Josef Podgorsky to confirm Russia's interest in their revolution? To promise them money and/or oil in exchange for their friendship? May I go so far as to suggest that Stephen Moffit made his contact to assure them that he, as an expert, was positive about the oil?"

"Unfortunately, we're guessing at that. We don't know. I've set a case for you. What's the response?"

"You wait, Gregory. You hold onto the field and you wait for the inevitable to happen. You wait for the Russians to take action in concert with Fidel Castro to complete the revolution by evicting the American capitalists."

"How long? How long do we wait?"

"As long as necessary. I will guess at a matter of days."

"Not months or years, Alan. Days. Because that brings up case three. While I'm sitting on that national resource, selfishly hoping for the world price of oil to go up, Cheddi Jagan is watching his people starve to death on their cassava and rice mush. How long do you think I can expect him to do that?"

"Quite right, Gregory. You are talking about an act of seizure, a nationalization of the industry. He may do just that. I think, however, with the threat of the British government hanging over his head, and British soldiers not too far away, he'll be wise to wait until he has the additional protection and support of his older brother to the north. Do you see how that ties in?"

Drinkwater sniffed. "But if I were allowed a chance guess at it, I would guess they might offer to buy it from you." He paused, wiped his brow with a handkerchief, and then removed his glasses, pinched his eyes. "That is the other possibility.

"But whatever you do, whatever happens in spite of our—my—confidence in the plan, you must not allow the field to fall into their hands before the Cuban incident is in place. Is that clear? If that means arming your men, so be it. If it means a battle, you shall have an outrageous act and wish you hadn't. But you *must* control the field until the very end." Drinkwater replaced his glasses and shoved them onto his nose.

"I want to avoid that battle," Hawthorn replied. "If there are no Podgorskies in sight, the world will see me as a shyster trying to pull the wool over the eyes of the poor folks. No, sir. No battle. I don't want a little war with Jeffry Burrowes and his band of boy scouts."

"God, man! A simple act of nationalization does not necessarily mean they must shoot everyone in sight! It does *not* mean they will assume physical control the moment they set foot on your concession, if ever they do."

Drinkwater stood now, assumed an arch-backed post with his jaw in the air.

"Gregory Hawthorn, allow me to allay your fears and relieve your anxiety regarding the final act. You have already won your decisive victory. Remember what Kiley said. Delay them, and you have achieved a magnificent advantage. You have already delayed them by many years. They have done no exploration work. They have not purchased leases in the Middle East. They have done no planning beyond what you have given them to count on." He looked squarely at Hawthorn.

"From now on, sir, anything more you are able to do will be frosting on the cake."

He stopped, played with his pipe, stuck his finger in the cold bowl.

"But it will happen the way I say. The Cubans may hold back for a day or two, but if we can get the American companies to turn off their supplies Castro will be forced to call on the Russians, and the Russians will call for you. Please trust my judgment on these matters. And then we shall do whatever it is we must do to invoke the most effective, reasonably provocative response."

Hawthorn had indeed managed to deceive the world. If he could buy the fact that the Russians were counting on western hemisphere crude oil to conquer the West, if he could believe that their absence in the Middle East was due to their hopes for British Guiana, if he could believe that Castro was a Communist and Globe could put a dent in his revolution, at least cost him a ton of money and *maybe* convince the rest of the Caribbean to take warning—if he could believe those things, then he could be proud of his cozenage. If not . . .

That night, try as he may, tired as he was, Hawthorn couldn't sleep. He had the very certain feeling that there was a fly in his bowl of buttermilk. And they still hadn't decided what to do with him and his five hundred million dollars when the fun was over. He drifted off as the sky was turning pink, his last thoughts returning time and time again to a deep black cave.

CHAPTER 12

The minister of Petroleum, Lands, and Mines, Carlysle Ramprashad, was unable to make a product exchange agreement with a single one of the major refiners in the Caribbean. Shell in Curaçao, Lago in Aruba, Texaco in Trinidad—even the tiny little Mobile teapot in Barbados turned him down when he offered them a throughput fee if they would refine his Guianese crude oil. They reminded him that there was a glut, that they had more oil coming out of their own wells than they could possibly use. Would he be kind enough to continue purchasing from them without an exchange agreement for the time being?

Gregory Hawthorn was able to intervene, and he did so under the condition that the government would use his ships and pay the standard rate for haulage. He would, in other words, haul the oil and earn his normal shipping profits, have it refined by a facility of his own choosing, haul it back again as fuel and earn a second shipping profit, then sell it to the government and thereby earn a profit on his share of the crude dollar. He did, after all, own fifty-two percent of the oil that came out of the Guianese wells.

Hawthorn had no difficulty making the arrangements since they were all a matter of paperwork.

The first shipment of Guianese crude oil went out on September 12. Ramprashad was there; several reporters and cameramen and a few ladies stood near the dock while the hose was disconnected and the engines growled to life. The minister broke a bottle of champagne across the bow and the big, ugly barge churned into the stream, faced the ocean, and plowed out of sight. In her holds, this time, was real crude oil.

A Globe tanker, one of the smaller ships, waited in the estuary as the barge snugged alongside ten hours later. It took two more hours to pump the crude into the tanker, switch valves, and then refill the barge with finished diesel fuel. The barge headed back into the river and stopped fourteen miles upstream, at Esso's Ramsburg terminal. That's the way it would go, until the country could justify its own refinery; for the moment, and as far into the future as anyone could see, that possiblity was very slim indeed.

Future deliveries, those made without an audience of interested observers, would vary only in that the barge would contain river water on the trip out, not crude oil.

In the field, there was virtually nothing happening. Dreier kept a few of the wells pumping for the sake of appearances, but the rest stood in the warm sun and the cool night, waiting, ostensibly, for the world glut to go away.

The British soldiers remained on station to protect the field from unwanted interference, and would stay until Hawthorn smelled or tasted or felt a revolution at his doorstep. Then he would check the status of Fidel, time his evacuation as precisely as possible, and make the field available for occupation when the circumstances were right. Come one, come all.

Dreier had kept a dozen of the Commission's people on site to maintain the equipment, fill the occasional orders that came in, and generally look busy. They kept their weapons under cover and oiled them at night.

Stephen Moffit was spending his time alternating between his Public Works assignment in Georgetown and his cathodic protection assignment at the field. He appeared to be in no hurry to fix his contact points or to install the cathode. The electrical wire arrived in mid-September on a great wooden spool, and Moffit was there to make sure it was the right kind, double-checking with Shawhan and Schultz to verify with them that it was the proper gauge. Then he had it set aside in a shed and found other work to do in town.

On October 14, Gregory Hawthorn left Baton Rouge and flew via commercial passage to Havana, Cuba. That evening he was joined in his hotel room by Josef Podgorsky.

"You have terrible taste in hotels, Mr. Podgorsky."

"It is not a popular place, and it is private."

"All right, let's get on with it." Hawthorn removed his jacket and threw it on the bed. Podgorsky sat in a chair by the corner.

"I believe it is your turn," Podgorsky began. "You suggested the meeting."

Hawthorn sat at a small desk, turned himself sideways to face the Russian.

"I did, and I believe you'll find what I have to say both interesting and valuable. I'm placing this information in your hands as a demonstration of faith." He leaned closer.

"You made me a promise, Podgorsky. You said, if I cooperate with you, Russia will buy my oil, the Guianese oil. What you said a while back is coming true. The word is out. I stand a good chance of being boycotted." He paused. "In the industry they're calling me a madman. I have enough oil to ruin the market a dozen times over, but I've spent my cash, I have no refining capacity, and I'm in bed with a Communist government."

Podgorsky lit a cigarette, blew the smoke politely away from Hawthorn's face.

"That's all right. I don't mind that. I'm successful because I'm not afraid to take chances, like the one I'm taking with you right now."

"Are you taking a chance when you discuss business with me, Hawthorn? Others don't think so."

He wanted to ask what Yu Hsin Chou thought about his business policies and negotiating tactics. He went on.

"When you hear what I have to say, you'll know what I mean about taking a chance."

"All right. Tell me and I will judge."

Hawthorn stood up and paced to the door. He opened it and looked into the hall, then shut it again.

"Never mind that, Mr. Hawthorn. I have taken the necessary precautions. Please go on."

Hawthorn sat down again and lit his own cigarette, thinking of the advice he got from Bill Koestner, a friend of long ago.

"The businessman's greatest asset, his cigarette. You're in a meeting, converging on the big decision. Blomworthy looks at you and says, 'Well, George, what do you think?' You sit back and you reach in your pocket for a fag. You look at it, dip into another pocket for a match, and you light it. You inhale, hold it a second, blow the match out with the first puff, and drop the match in an ashtray. You take another drag, puff the smoke out again, and look the guy straight in the eye and give him your answer. He thinks you're a goddamn genius."

"Do you know a man named Wade Humphry?" Hawthorn asked.

"Yes, I know of him. I don't know him."

"He speaks for the oil industry here in Cuba. He's tied in with the State Department, discusses politics and revolutions and oil with them, and passes their opinions on to the other oil people here. Do you understand? He acts on behalf of his company and he's responsible to his country. He is exactly what I am not, and he does exactly what I do not do. Understand?"

Podgorsky nodded imperceptibly.

"He and the rest of the refiners here are of the opinion that Castro will make his moves slowly once he's accomplished the coup. But they aren't certain of that. They'll be ready to pull out, shut down their plants, and pull out on a moment's notice if they see any guns at the gate. Maybe you know all this. Maybe you know exactly what Castro's plans are. I'm telling you this because it might help you decide what your action should be."

"Is that all?"

"No, there's more."

Hawthorn had lived in the sun for the past months; his face was as dark as tanned leather. When he set his teeth together and looked at the Russian, he appeared to be smiling. He was not.

"I've heard of a plan to place explosives at vital points in the refineries and at the dock facilities. That might interest you. That's unconfirmed, but I happen to think it's accurate."

He dropped his head for a moment, then brought it up again to catch Podgorsky's full attention.

"Now, this is not a rumor. This is a certainty: When Castro takes over, on that day, there will be no more than two days' inventory in the country. There will be a few barrels in the tanks and in the lines, there will be some gasoline in customers' storage and enough fuel oil to run the generating plants for a few days. But that's all."

Podgorsky sat back. "We have guessed at that," he said.

"There will be two tankers offshore, but they'll be anchored there, waiting to see what Castro does." Hawthorn pressed his cigarette into the ashtray.

"Now, Mr. Podgorsky, if you can be *sure*—if your people *know*—what that man is going to do, then my information may be superfluous. But if you have any doubt whatsoever, then I suggest you get your ass in gear and write me a check for a few million bucks to guarantee Cuba's energy supply."

The room was quiet for a minute. Podgorsky stood and walked slowly to the other side of the room, then turned and faced Hawthorn.

"You mean crude oil from British Guiana."

"I mean crude in four vessels and finished petroleum products in a dozen more. Crude if the refineries are intact, finished products if they aren't."

The Russian stared at Hawthorn's dark face. His eyelids fluttered as he thought, then they stilled.

"Where do you propose to buy the finished product, Hawthorn, for delivery to a so-called Communist country?"

"That's my problem. I can manage it for a short time by falsifying documents and paying my captains a fee for their confidence. But it won't last very long, Podgorsky. In a month, probably less, my ships will be recognized in Cuba's harbors and the State Department will pull my trading ticket. When that happens, I'm finished."

"No. No, when that happens, you are beginning. I would like to think of it as a beginning, Hawthorn." He grinned at the American. "I was not lying when I said we understand the profit motive. I was quite serious when I suggested that you would prosper, Mr. Hawthorn. It may take a while, but we have very interesting plans for the Globe Corporation. A private enterprise business with all of its efficiencies working independently for the Communist Federation of Caribbean States. How does that sound to you?"

"Not enough, Podgorsky. I need more volume than that. I need entry to bigger markets than this swimming pool down here. I need your assurance that if I agree to salvage the Cuban energy crisis, you will take a minimum of ninety-four million barrels a year out of my Guianese wells."

"My God, man! You've gotten very specific in your request."

"That's what I've done. My free-enterprise economics tell me that's what I need for a payout."

"And the price?"

"Ten cents over the low of Platt's, the posted Caribbean price, plus freight at two cents over Convention. That beats your price delivered from the Black Sea by about twenty cents a barrel."

"That would be an interesting piece of business. Is that all of it, then?"

"Yes. I want those guarantees in writing. If you're thinking of a stipulation placing the ships under your charter, forget it. I maintain them, I schedule them at the customer's demand. You're the customer."

"A very one-sided arrangement, sir. After all, you are the one who stands to lose everything if we don't agree, is that so?"

"Only maybe. But you stand to lose more."

"Yes. I see the point. The soldiers are still there?"

"You know they are. But not for long. The governor will be pulling them out very soon, probably before December."

"I see."

Time to think. Podgorsky was thinking, and Hawthorn was letting him. He stood, went to the window next to the Russian's shoulder, and parted the curtain. Bright sunlight shone outside while they were in a darkened room plotting the ouster of Shell, Texaco, Jersey Standard, Gulf, and a few others, the combined revenues of which could purchase the greater part of the British Commonwealth.

"There isn't much time, Podgorsky," Hawthorn said quietly. "Fidel will be closing on Batista's house very soon."

There was little real doubt in Hawthorn's mind that neither Josef Podgorsky nor Stephen Moffit nor anyone outside of Fidel Castro's own circle knew what would happen when Batista fled the country. But Hawthorn was sure, very sure of one thing: If there was any loss of American life or property during those first hours, the price to be paid would be very great.

Hawthorn circled around and faced him.

"Do me one other favor while you're getting my contract ready, Mr. Podgorsky." He stopped to make very certain the Russian was listening to every word.

"Tell your people, whoever they are, that Stephen Moffit is no spy for the damned Chinese. Tell them also that if he's a spy for the CIA, I'll eat your astrakhan."

CHAPTER 13

Carlysle Ramprashad and Josef Podgorsky had left the Globe oil field with the understanding that regardless of their own enthusiasm over the discovery and its obvious economic, political, and social implications, the official position was to be ultraconservative.

The world press would be notified via a joint communication, issued simultaneously by the government and the Globe Corporation, using terms that would raise no alarm in the world energy community. "Cautious predictions," "further testing," "encouraging indications," were among the disclaiming phrases found scattered throughout the releases.

For several weeks after the discovery the local press had bothered the offices of Carlysle Ramprashad begging for permission to visit the oil field. Unfortunately for them he was in no position to grant such permission; the entire concession was off limits to all but authorized personnel. The British military force would remain on site to guarantee its security.

Elsewhere the skeptics refused to be stilled. Petroleum journals and related publications called it a bathtub, a minor dome with limited commercial possibilities, drawing their expert opinions from quotes they were able to extract from spokesmen in the industry.

Votes of confidence from other countries in the Caribbean, however, poured into British Guiana. Old rivals were suddenly good friends, recent squabbles were forgotten, trade barriers were wondrously dropped. It made good sense to be friendly with Cheddi Jagan—and Gregory Hawthorn. Globe could anticipate, and was ready to consider, new proposals for supply agreements, shipping contracts, and harbor development schemes from every corner of the Caribbean basin. All of this in spite of the low profile their announcements had tried to project.

One country was not heard from. Cuba, it seemed, was totally uninterested in the happenings to their south. By December 3, 1958, Fulgencio Batista was far too busy with his own affairs to bother with what might happen after he was gone, though he continued to express a public opinion that the Castro movement would be put down long before it became a bloodbath in Havana.

At the oil field the status remained unchanged. A few shipments had gone out, but the amounts were too small to affect the inventory levels visibly.

Stephen Moffit had installed the cathodic protection system, but only up to a point. In the harbor, at one untrafficked end, he had submerged an enormous steel mill roller. It looked like a giant German hand grenade as it rolled off the barge into the muddy water. He had rigged the electric lines to a generator, welded one-hundred thirty-six anode connectors to the tanks and to the pipelines, and was only waiting for Dutch Schultz to repair the spooler truck. With that, he would be able to run the wire and make connections, thereby finishing the job. That would be a simple task, a few hours at most. But he had left the camp shortly before Thanksgiving and hadn't been around since.

Gregory Hawthorn arrived on December 4. Shortly before dark he assembled his foreman, Sandy Dreier, and his two work horses, Reinaldo Villar-Cruz and Gene Tinker. Together they drove to the harbor, climbed out of the Jeep, and found a place to sit on barge number 55.

"Next Tuesday. Start the pumps in the field, Sandy, make all nineteen of them go up and down, nonstop. While they're doing that, you load up your barges—river water—and send them out one at a time. My ships will be there to take it on. Four ships."

"Podgorsky?" Reinaldo was grinning.

"Podgorsky. He called last night. Here's the message." Hawthorn pulled a notepaper from his pocket.

" 'The contract is approved. Load and have ready six hundred thousand crude, one hundred thousand diesel, one hundred thousand fuel oil, one hundred thousand kerosene, four hundred thousand gasoline. Station off shore by December twentieth.' "

Dreier laughed and threw a stone into the water.

"That's it, then," he said. "We got 'em by the short hairs."

"There's one last item. Steve Moffit. On the day you ship your last barge load, I'm going to send the soldiers home. I'm also going to set up a block against our spy. He is not to show up down here. If he does,

206

send him back north. I'll clear that with Ramprashad on the way back out. Is that clear, Sandy? Rei?"

"Very clear, sir. Then what?"

"Then we wait. We wait and see what Fidel Castro does. If he waltzes into the city and has a rum swizzle party for the Yanks, we do one thing. If he comes in there and shoots up our installations, we do something else. If we're not sure, if it looks dicey, we wait. And we hold on down here until I give you the word.

"When it's time to go, you just get aboard the Jetstar and leave with Tinker. He'll have a location for you and enough cash to keep you happy for a while." Hawthorn gave Dreier a list.

"These are the men you keep on hand after the loading is finished. The rest can go up to Georgetown and catch a flight for Miami. Their separation briefing will take place at Homestead Air Force base. The details are all spelled out in that note."

"Tell them what we do if there's real trouble down here, shooting trouble," Tinker said.

"I don't think we'll have that kind of trouble. They won't shoot anybody. But if something like that happens, stay cool and we'll get the British down here to evacuate you. I hope it doesn't come to that. I want this operation to be deserted if and when they come calling."

"How about the inventory in the tanks?" Dreier asked.

Hawthorn smiled. "We're going to leave that for the Guianese. It's not enough to bail the Russians out, and it can't hurt to give the people down here a small consolation prize."

"The barges too?"

"Yes. Even if we're forced into the disappearing act, which is the most innocent option we'll have, I don't see any way of coming back down here after it's over to apologize for a gigantic miscalculation in the hopes of recovering some of the investment. The barges stay."

They sat quietly for several minutes, each with his own thoughts. Villar-Cruz would spend some time in Bogotá with his sister. Dreier would not go back to Tulsa. He had a year coming, a year to stay quiet, out of the way with his wife, in a new home with a new identification. Tinker didn't much care. He would be back on duty with the parent organization. He was hoping for some stateside duty for a change.

And Gregory Hawthorn. He would salvage what he could of his fleet, sell the domestic operation, take an enormous amount of money from the account that had already been placed in trust, and then he too would disappear for a while. Where? It didn't seem to matter very much.

The harbor was darkening; they would need lights as they drove back. Hawthorn remembered something that had been bothering him.

"Sandy, one last thing. That explosive wire you have spooled up there in the shed. Let's get rid of that stuff. Send it up tomorrow on one of the barges."

"Yes, sir."

"We should have done that a long time ago. We could have blown ourselves all to hell and gone."

CHAPTER 14

December 23.

The oil field was quiet again. All seven barges were tied to moorings in the horseshoe harbor, or just into the stream, their camouflage work completed: Four of the Globe tankers had been loaded with river water and sent on their way. The pumps, all except for three, were still again. Most of the men had been "sent home for the Christmas holidays." Only Sandy Dreier, Reinaldo Villar-Cruz, Dutch Schultz, and a handful of others were there to keep the camp running. Two barge captains stayed behind in case there was work to be done, but for now there was none. The Esso terminal at Ramsburg and the joint Shell-Texaco terminal had been topped off. They would need no supplies for another three weeks.

Stephen Moffit was in Georgetown on December 23, working on a project that would continue to consume much of his time, but a project that would be worth every minute he spent. Since the oil field was off limits to everyone except Globe personnel, including himself in spite of his protestations to the government, he had been obliged to manage his business, both official and private, from his small offices at Public Works. The items that occupied him on this day, however, were for his eyes only.

He worked at his apartment until very late that evening, applying the skills he had learned at Orekhovo.

At the basin, with little else to do, Sandy Dreier decided to finish the cathodic protection job himself.

He started at the harbor, connecting the leads to a forty-volt generator located near the pumping station. Then he ran the wire along the short pipeline to the big shore tanks, attaching it to the connectors with a simple clamp-down lever. Sharp teeth in the jaws of the lever pierced the wire, permitting a trickle of electricity to feed into the metal and do its work. From those tanks, he strung the wire along the pipeline, attaching as he went, the spooler unwinding its load as he and Dutch Schultz covered the eighteen-mile course. They finished at the camp end, having made their contacts at 136 seams on the most important steel segments from one end of the field to the other. They rested and drank cold tea in the mess hall.

"I feel better about that. Even if it's a small job, I like to see it done right."

"What does Green say about it? Would he do it on one of his own sites, this far inland?" Schultz was sweating.

"He's not sure. But with the kind of investment we've got, and for the small cost, he reckons it can't hurt." Dreier laughed. "This place needs long-term protection!"

At four o'clock Dreier drove back to the harbor and filled the generator tank with gasoline. He doubled-checked the battery cables and reached for the start button. He stopped, moved his hand to the oil dipstick, checked the level, and shoved the stick back in. Then he pressed the start button. The little machine snorted briefly, cleared its throat and settled in to a regular, quiet, efficient chugging.

Alan Drinkwater was in London, briefing the British members of the Commission on the status of the Caribbean project. He advised them that the tankers were in place, located between the Yucatan and Havana, ready to converge on the Cuban ports with a day's steaming.

He told them how the ships, before departing with their river-water cargoes, had been wired by a demolitions expert, waterproof explosives fixed to the forward and aft bulkheads near the keel, timers set in the stateroom of each captain.

He was able to report to them that the Russians were as much in the dark as everyone else about Fidel Castro's plans. He, Castro, either would not or could not tell them what he planned to do about or with the Americans and their refineries. But the Americans were sticking to their plan. They were allowing the inventories to dwindle.

He was certain, he told them, that New Year's Day was the target date. Everything pointed toward it. His own personal agents-in-place had informed him that Batista was packaging his records, sending friends and family out of the country and collecting his private treasures for shipment to Miami. Batista had made hotel reservations in New York and was ready to flee at a moment's notice.

He advised them that he would be spending his holidays at the Guantanamo Naval Air Station as a guest of Vice Admiral Duncan Barnes. He would coordinate the final stages of the project from there.

* * *

In Cuba the war was pressing nearer Havana. But those soldiers who had not already fled Batista's ranks were putting up a heartless defense in the face of Castro's advancing guerrillas, staging skirmish action where escape was virtually assured once their positions were threatened. In Havana itself one could scarcely tell there was a battle going on, except for sporadic bursts of gunfire and some action in the suburbs. Most of the shops were open, and the hotels, though not totally occupied, were nonetheless busy.

The refineries continued to operate on a reduced schedule, but with many nationals manning the positions usually held by Americans who had left the island for the holidays, trusting their homes and their possessions to the promises of Fidel Castro, whose pronunciations from the interior sounded more like Thomas Jefferson than Marx or Lenin.

In Baton Rouge, on December 23, Gregory Hawthorn was slowly beginning to show the signs of anxiety experienced by generals and Rose Bowl coaches and condemned prisoners. He was never more than a room away from a telephone, his cigarette consumption was way above his average, the coffeepot was in constant use.

Hawthorn's ship captains knew what to do: At the given signal from Guantanamo they were to up anchor, move as a squadron into their respective harbors, and dock as close as possible to the refineries and the other vital facilities. That signal would be given by Alan Drinkwater as soon as blood was spilled within the American community. The captains, when they were safely dockside or anchored in the harbor, were then to go to their cabins, unlock their safes, lift the red cover, and move the exposed switch from right to left. They were then to take all hands and leave the ship by the harborside ladder, and wait for a fast boat that would take them safely away from the area. Should there be shooting or action of any kind they were on their own. They had one hour to make good their exit from the harbor.

The options were down to three now. Disappear, blow the lid off the ships carrying fuel, and/or sink the ships carrying saltwater. It was a horror story made up of hypothetical contingencies. Hawthorn was weary of counting the possible chances for error.

At one o'clock in the afternoon Gene Tinker knocked on his door. Hawthorn opened it, suitcase in hand.

December 24.
Dreier and Villar-Cruz played cribbage until nearly midnight, monitoring the radio in the communications shack. Schultz and the barge captains celebrated Christmas Eve in the mess hall, their weapons

210

stacked against the front entry wall. The few other men stood guard in the field or were posted at the river.

In Georgetown Jeffry Burrowes opened his gift, smiled at his dear wife, Angela, and stood before the hall mirror, trying on his new cap. It bore the insignia of a commandant, and she was very proud of him. Burrowes smiled at himself, thinking in that moment of the wonderful surprise he would give Angela when this was all over, a new home in England. He could, after all, afford it now, when the sale of his ten thousand shares went through. And he was weary, God knows, of being Globe's puppet.

December 25.
Stephen Moffit slept until nearly noon. It had been a tiring week. But now it was over, the very long days in his office at Public Works, where he had assembled his collection of data relating to Globe's volumetric forecast and estimated long-term yield potential ex the BG reservoir. His conclusions left no doubt that British Guiana would outproduce Venezuela in less than three years. That package would be ready for Prime Minister Cheddi Jagan in time for his negotiations with Josef Podgorsky, scheduled to take place sometime in January.

Of equal priority was his own collection of data. Some of the sources were the same, but the conclusions he drew from those and from other less conventional sources told quite a different story.

Jagan's report would be left on his desk, no doubt to be read and studied in every detail when it was all over. As Moffit tucked the stack of papers into envelopes, marking each with its proper subject title, he couldn't help smiling. It would cause a helluva commotion for a helluva long time.

His private documents would travel with him. He would need them as proofs of his integrity.

December 26.
Sir Hillman Gomes, Her Majesty's appointed governor of the British Commonwealth Possession of British Guiana, was unable to reach Guantanamo from his office at home. From the military communications center, however, the British CIC were successful in patching him through their scrambler station in Barbados. He found Alan Drinkwater at the admiral's quarters at noon.

"Curious information, Alan," the governor began. "Cheddi Jagan has just left my office. He informed me, *informed* me, mind you, that he is going to nationalize the Globe interests straightaway."

"By God! What does he mean by 'straightaway'?"

"To coincide with the takeover in Cuba. So he said."

"Well!" There was a pause. "That's marvelous! I called it perfectly, didn't I? Who would have believed it."

"He wants the blessing of the Crown, Alan."

"What if he doesn't get it?"

"He says he'll take it away and argue the point later. There was some talk of a financial settlement, but he didn't say how much, or where he would get the money from. Not that these people care particularly about such details."

Gomes waited for several moments before Drinkwater spoke.

"See here, Hillman. I'll call you back. Let your man there give us the connection particulars. One hour, Hillman. Thank you."

Gomes spent his time waiting in the radio room. There was little news from Cuba, one hourly broadcast from the BBC. He was on his third cup of tea when he was recalled to the overseas radio telephone.

"Yes, Alan."

"Ask him if he will consider a management arrangement. Allow Globe to stay on and manage the field, the exports, that sort of thing."

"I asked him that and he seemed cool, cold in fact."

"Well, ask him again. And ask him what the terms might be for his nationalization action. Surely if he intends to offer the Globe Corporation some kind of compensation he must have a payment plan."

"I'll ask him that, Alan. He's expecting a reply from me this afternoon regarding a permission from Her Majesty."

"Yes. Well ask him those things, and ask him additionally if something can be firmed up, Hillman. Can Hawthorn come down there and sign something to that effect? Today or tomorrow. You do see what I'm driving at? We shall insist on a management contract and lock them into ownership. That way we will stay on until this Castro business goes one way or another and leave them holding the bag with blustering red faces, one and all!"

"I'll meet with him this afternoon, Alan. Can I call you this evening?"

"Eight o'clock, sir. I'll wait for your signal."

"Alan . . . it doesn't appear as though the Americans are in danger up there. Can you confirm that?"

"Not for the moment, Hillman. We shall have to wait the bloody thing out. That's why we want to hang on down there as long as possible."

"What about our British troops, then? Any changes in the tactic there?"

"None whatsoever. Keep them ready against a major disaster but allow the oil maneuver to proceed on the schedule. Remember, Hillman, we must hang on there. You must negotiate, but show no force, you must *negotiate* the management thing."

"All right, then, Alan. Until later."

Jagan was unavailable in the afternoon, but Carlysle Ramprashad was authorized to speak on his behalf. There was no need for Gomes to raise the questions of how and how much; Ramprashad laid it out for him in a neat package, on a take-it-or-leave-it basis. The government was indeed prepared to sign a transfer agreement with Hawthorn, but only on the basis of a cash purchase—a cash purchase, in the amount of one hundred million pounds payable on signature and another one hundred million pounds in two years, as long as Hawthorn would sign it personally before midnight, December 31. The cash had mysteriously been arranged during the day.

"Good Lord, Hillman. Cash! But of course. Moscow. Podgorsky!"

"He will be arriving Wednesday afternoon."

There was a moment of silence. Gomes could hear Drinkwater conferring with someone at the other end.

"Mission accomplished, Hillman. That does it, then. A cash deal it is, but have them include a ten-day transition period, a time for the check to clear or something. Do you understand?"

"Perfectly. But you may be sure it will be a cash bond, Alan, as good as bullion at any bank in the world. Still, he will agree to a few days, I think. I trust you know exactly what you're doing."

"We do. Right. Unless we hear differently, Sir Hillman, Gregory Hawthorn will arrive there in his own plane sometime before dark on New Year's Eve. He will be ready with his pen to sign the thing and take his draft or his bond or whatever it is."

Alan Drinkwater set the phone in its cradle and sat back. In a chair opposite was Gregory Hawthorn, in slacks and summer shirt for the warm Cuban evening.

Admiral Barnes was in another room with one of his aides, establishing his priorities in this state of emergency.

"You will arrive in the afternoon, collect a copy of the agreement, and then go directly to the camp. We shall sign it there." He paused to correct himself. "You shall sign it there."

"And that's the ball game," said Hawthorn. "We wait the damn thing out."

"Well, yes, but richer by one hundred million pounds, my friend. Ruddy close to the billion dollars we've spent on the flippin' project!"

"Castro won't spill Yankee blood, Alan. Let's take that draft and fly out of there, leave them with all that junk to play in."

Drinkwater sighed. "No, no. You must stay on. Even though the battle has already been won, there could be that last grand demonstration. If not, you have still set into concrete the most embarrassing, most devastating crisis the Soviets could possibly imagine as an adjunct to their Caribbean ambitions. I think it's absolutely marvelous!"

"No British troops."

"Good grief, man. And spoil their revolution?"

December 27.

Ivan Rasmonovich arrived in Moscow, was taken directly to the office of Georgi Malenkov, and, in the premier's outer office, was given a briefcase containing loan agreements, trade documents, and a certified government draft. He left in the company of a man who stayed very close to his side on the return trip to Washington.

In Williamsburg Howard Barry thanked his housekeeper, paid her a month's wages, and watched her walk to the corner where she would catch her bus downtown. Then he finished his packing.

December 28.

At 9:00 A.M. Carlysle Ramprashad motored to the ferry boat, crossed the Demerara River, then drove to a small town on the banks of the Essequibo River. He boarded a river launch and rode it for three hours, arriving at Bartica in the early afternoon. A Rover met him at the dock, drove him fifteen miles, and stopped at a wooden gate. He walked through, spent two hours with a captain in the British Guiana Defense Force, and casually inspected the camp.

As he was being escorted back to the gate he halted abruptly, faced the captain, and poked him on the chest.

"A show of strength. Nothing more. Can your children be restrained to that humble assignment?"

"Suh!"

December 29.

Josef Podgorsky sat facing the window, looking out over the bare treetops. Washington was a poor place to be during the winter. Ivan Rasmonovich was standing near the door.

"Did you say something, sir?"

Podgorsky maintained his gaze toward the gray sky.

"They are such fools. That's all I said." Now he turned and spoke to his aide.

"We will make it possible for them to take control of the oil field, an act that will anger the British most certainly, and they will turn around and tell us on what terms they will supply our friends in the Caribbean."

"They believe they can do it *without* angering the British."

"They are fools!"

In Geneva Howard Barry wrote a postcard to his sister and then read it back to himself. He looked up, tore it into small pieces, walked to the bathroom, and flushed it down the toilet.

December 30.

Henri Amont arrived in Cuba, landed at Guantanamo in a private airplane with special clearance, and went directly to the office of Admiral Barnes. With him he carried a small library of the Globe-British Guiana business, documents that would be needed for the purchase-sale agreement.

"As requested by Mr. Hawthorn, Admiral."

"Thank you, Mr. Amont. It seems we can neither screw nor get screwed without proper documentation these days." He signed the verification of receipt and handed it to Amont.

"Mr. Hawthorn will advise you regarding the details of your future modus operandi?"

"I assume so, yes, sir. Such as that may be."

In Havana, at the other end of the island, the stores were still open, the hotels were getting ready for their New Year's Eve functions, and the people were milling in the streets, wondering if the rumors were true. Their savior was coming to town.

December 31.

Reinaldo Villar-Cruz stood back, his hands on his hips, judging the appearance of the podium, the signing table, the guest seating arrangement. It was hot for this time of the year, humid. He turned and went into the mess hall, sat next to Sandy Dreier, and picked up his now warm glass of lemonade.

"Tonight, then. Five years for tonight," Dreier said.

Villar-Cruz was hunched over the table.

"That's right, amigo. Five long years. But it might not end tonight. I've got a feeling we'll be here for a few days more."

"When's the boss comin' down?"

"About eight, close to eight. Podgorsky should have been here already. He chartered his own plane this time. He wanted to get here before the others."

"How the hell do you know all that?"

"I'm a Latin smart-ass, Sandy. That's how."

It was dark by six o'clock. Dreier went out to the runway and switched the lights on, small silver bulbs that were mostly hidden by the grass. Good enough for this runway, for the bush pilots who used it.

At the edge of the camp he stopped and looked around. There were the big tanks, there were the well lines, and up above, a million stars. He glanced toward the north, saw clouds drifting over the horizon.

At the harbor, the gasoline generator chugged obediently on, its belly full of gasoline, sending forty low-voltage demons along the lines, through the connectors, trickling a tingle of electricity against the steel, keeping it sweet and clean.

Sandy Dreier, for once, had been completely outclassed.

CHAPTER 15

Whatever sins of commission or sins of omission may be laid at the feet of the British, the manner in which they handled the dissolution of their empire cannot be numbered among them. One by one, in the Far East, in Africa and in the Caribbean, they were determined to withdraw with grace and with dignity, leaving behind some semblance of stability and civil law. Some of those who are at all interested in the subject will argue that they gave up their colonies out of a sense of moral conscience and a respect for the legitimate claims of patriotism and nationalism. Others will show that those motives were forced upon them by external pressures, a tax levied on their values by the United Nations and by others after World War II ended. Another contention is that the British, finding their colonies to be expensive charges and no longer viable commercial investments, pulled out to salvage what was left of the royal treasury. There is probably some merit in all three arguments, but whatever the reasons may have been they proceeded cautiously and very correctly.

If the British failed in any one area of their responsibility, it might be argued that the military preparation of the national guard, or whatever it was called in the country, was that area. Such a suggestion, if it were put to a proper Englishman, would be thrown out of the conversation, and the person who suggested it would go as well.

Still, a brief look at the post-British years in many of their former colonies does seem to disclose a certain antiestablishment mentality among the military leaders and their soldiers after the superior authority of the British Crown had gone. In some cases, it was as though Mommy

216

and Daddy had left the candy store untended, opening the cabinet doors to their children who had never tasted sweets.

In British Guiana the soldiers with the guns were still from England and the ones with the just-pretend guns were the locals. That wasn't literally true in 1958, but it might as well have been true. The soldiers certainly felt that way, the local soldiers who had never, most of them, left the shores of their country, never been in a skirmish, never been wounded much less even shot at.

It was nevertheless the sworn duty of every soldier to defend his government against every foreign threat. Sadly, few of the rank and file would have been able to recognize a foreign threat if it carried a flag and sang its own national anthem. They were equally confused, many of them, about the threats and threats of threats in their own country.

By all accounts, Jeffry Burrowes had managed his job very well. He left the running of his troops to the officers who knew, or at least thought they knew, how to handle them. They paraded while he established the priorities and maintained a decent relationship with the government. If he did not command the all-out respect of his men, he did at least stay out of their way and let them do their work. So he was not prepared in any way for what happened on New Year's Eve.

At eight o'clock he had listened to the news from the BBC, was updated on the rapid advance of Castro's army toward Havana. He had been given no instructions, nor was he disposed himself to be on the alert for trouble. From his last conversation with Gregory Hawthorn and according to his understanding of the government's position, the transfer of ownership was to be accomplished peacefully and without the presence of armed forces. He assumed that it was a snub of sorts, offset by an assurance that his job was almost finished, his future secure.

He was locking his desk drawer and getting ready to go home, dress, and attend a gala New Year's Eve party at a friend's house when he stopped and listened. He stood, buttoned his coat, and went to the window that overlooked the parade grounds. A helicopter was landing. He cupped the sides of his face with his hands against the window to see better and observed a man getting down, several men. The chopper's blades continued to turn. The men were heading for his building.

He wondered whether or not he should call someone, his duty officer perhaps, or the captain of the guard, but he did nothing. Instead he went to a mirror on the wall and looked into it, placed his hat on his head, gave the visor a neat tug to set it just so. Then he faced the door. There was no doubt in his mind that these people, whoever they might be, were coming to see the head man. He heard the sound of boots on the stairs, several men in something of a hurry.

There was knock on the door and before he could work his mouth to invite the guests in, the door opened. Two men in the uniform of his own military police were there, flanking another man who was dressed in a captain's uniform, with epaulets on the shoulders of his raincoat. His shoes were stained with soil, wet from the march across the parade grounds. His hands were buried in the side pockets of his coat.

"Good evening, Mr. Burrowes," he said. He was wearing horn-rimmed glasses and looked to be a young person, unfamiliar to Burrowes who knew some, not all of his officers. Few of them addressed him by his correct military title.

"Good evening," replied Burrowes. "I trust your business here is legitimate." He was damned if he would be intimidated.

"Please sit down, over there." The captain pointed to an easy chair near the mirror, away from the desk. Burrowes stepped two paces to his left and stood before the chair, facing the visitor.

"Would you like to sit as well?" he said. "That chair is very nice." He waved his arm toward a host chair a few feet away.

"Please sit down!" the officer ordered. The two soldiers stepped into the hallway, the intruder closed the door and stood next to it. Burrowes sat down and started to remove his hat, then thought better of it and left it on his head.

"I am Captain Medas. I am here to help the government in the matter of security. I have taken the liberty of sending our guard force to the oil field."

Burrowes's eyes opened wide and his jowls were working. He raised one hand to his face and touched a cheek.

"But, good heavens, my dear fellow, by whose authority then? Who gave you the authority to do that? I am the . . ."

"By the authority of Mr. Ramprashad," he replied.

"Nonsense," said Burrowes. "That is nonsense, sir!"

Burrowes stood up and crossed to confront the man, the mutineer. His advance was halted by a stiff-arm to the chest that pushed him awkwardly back into the chair. Burrowes sat heavily, tried to catch himself with his hands on the armrests.

"Please don't waste the little time we have, Mr. Burrowes. It has been deemed a wiser course of action to enlist your cooperation rather than cause a disturbance among the soldiers. If you will permit me, I will explain as briefly as possible." He sat down, took off his gloves, and reached inside his coat. He leaned over to Burrowes's desk, took the butane lighter that was holding down a stack of papers, and lit a cigarette.

"The transfer of ownership from the Globe Corporation tonight is proceeding without the full consent of the Crown. Nevertheless it will be done. The papers will be signed and the payment will be made tonight." He took a half puff, blew it out, and continued. "Tomorrow the British will intervene, after the fact, after they have the evidence that our prime minister has taken this action. But it will be over the bodies of Guianese soldiers that they will reverse the transaction. Do you understand?"

Burrowes was perspiring freely, his fingers fidgeting on the leather.

"You are a Communist!" he shouted. "A Castroite!"

"Shut up. I am a Guianese soldier."

"A Castroite! An idiot!"

The soldier was soaked with his own sweat; his hand shook as he put the cigarette to his mouth.

"You are offered the command. If you refuse it you will be arrested." He crushed the cigarette under his wet shoe.

Burrowes was appalled. He leaned forward and stretched his hand toward the mess to see if the beast had ruined his new carpet.

"Get back!" The soldier jumped to his feet, pulled a gun from his coat pocket, and aimed it at Burrowes' large stomach.

"But I . . ."

The captain's hand was squeezing the gun, his finger tightening on the trigger. He stepped back another foot, reached for the doorknob, and fired. Burrowes fell back, slid down the front of his chair, and sat on the floor, the whites of his eyes filling his dark sockets, his mouth gaping, his head resting against the cushion, a black hole burned in his uniform jacket.

The captain wheeled, yanked the door open, and raced down the stairs, across the grass to the helicopter. The Guianese militia was already enroute, crowded into and on the decks of two small lumber ships. They would reach the basin at ten o'clock. He wanted to time his arrival with theirs, to be in charge of this operation, the first in the western hemisphere. It would be a show of strength, of force! *Damn the British!*

Dreier and Gene Tinker were playing cribbage in the communications shack. Tinker had flown down that evening, helped the boss get set up in a spare tent, and then had seen to the Jetstar. It was parked at the far end of the field, ready for takeoff. He had filled the tanks right after landing, a precaution in the event of a turbulent signature party, highly unlikely as things stood. They would have to land at Puerto Rico, their usual stop, but that would be far enough away, and friendly enough should things get bumpy at the basin.

At eight-thirty Podgorsky had arrived in his chartered plane, bringing with him the documents that would be needed by his government, and he had brought a passenger. Stephen Moffit was to be in attendance as a courtesy.

Podgorsky had spent no time at all in his temporary tent but had gone straight to Hawthorn as soon as the little Cessna landed. They had been together for over an hour, sitting in the mess hall, drinking coffee, going over the purchase agreement in every important detail. The signing would be a formality. Podgorsky had already given the draft, made out in the name of the cosigners, to Cheddi Jagan.

And in the field, the lonely pumps were nodding up and down, dryly sucking on moist sand eight thousand feet below. The tanks and lines were full, almost full of the same Venezuelan crude oil they had received in July.

Dreier leaned back in his camp chair and stretched as Tinker moved his pegs. Suddenly he dropped down again.

"Where's Moffit?" he asked quietly.

"In his tent," Tinker replied. "I've been on him."

The big engineer relaxed, stood up, and sidled over to the radio bench. Villar-Cruz was listening to the BBC.

"I can't get Havana," he said, glancing up. "But they're on the doorstep. I think Batista has left the country."

"Your turn, big fella!" Tinker pushed the bulging gun butt away from his rib cage and waited.

The mess hall was empty except for Podgorsky and Hawthorn. They were sitting at a table near the door, white coffee mugs steaming in the cool air. Like a vacant house, the walls, the ceiling, the spare furnishings seemed to absorb the poor light, keeping the dreariness of itself a secret from the outside.

"I have already told you how sorry I am, sir. It is a move I neither endorse nor applaud." He was staring into his cup. "They are making a mistake, in my judgment." He looked at Hawthorn. "In the judgment of my government, Mr. Hawthorn."

"So you said. But I keep hearing what you said aboard that boat, Podgorsky. 'No takeover, pals forever,' that little speech."

"I said it with every honest conviction that these people would be . . . would act with some modicum of intelligence. They have not done so, and we are forced to support them under the circumstances."

Hawthorn didn't reply to that. His mind was on Cuba, his thoughts with his ships. He wanted to know what was happening.

"Ten days. That's all they'll give me to clear out."

"Yes. More time than others have been given in similar cases. Still, it is not much."

Podgorsky was trying to salvage something for Hawthorn.

"The shipping is yours, the refining and the shipping."

"Maybe, Podgorsky. Maybe the shipping, but your comrades in Cuba will take the refining."

They both turned at the sound of the mess hall door as it banged open. Stephen Moffit caught it on the rebound, closed it carefully and slid the small night bolt home, then walked slowly across the five paces to their table. He carried a large radio in one hand and a paper bag in the other. He stood at the end of the long table, between the two men, lowered the radio to the floor, and dropped the sack on the table near Hawthorn's hand.

"Just a few minutes of your time," he said.

The young American sat down on the end chair, Hawthorn to his right, Podgorsky to his left. His leather jacket was zipped closed and he was wearing rose-colored night glasses. He reached inside his jacket and drew out the Luger, placed it on the table, and waved his hand, directing the men to move away.

"Just slide down a little bit, Mr. Hawthorn. You too, Russian. Just a skosh." His hand floated above the gun as they obeyed, scraping their chairs on the floorboards.

"Steve, what the hell . . ." Hawthorn looked quickly at Podgorsky. "Is this your . . ."

Moffit rapped on the table once with his knuckles.

"Please shut up, Mr. Hawthorn. This won't take long." He pulled the paper sack to his chest and lifted it up, then dumped the contents onto the table. Podgorsky made a slight move as the sack dropped to the floor, and Moffit's hand fell to the Luger in a casual motion, his eyes riveted to the Russian's face. His mouth was closed, his jaw set.

He picked up an anode connector, a small silver box the size and shape of a wall outlet electrical box. He held it in his fingers as though he were displaying a fine watch, showed it to them, both faces.

"Now, this is a bomb. See the red button, here? That stays out until I feed it a signal from this transmitter, here." He tapped his foot. "When that red button goes down, this little device explodes."

He was watching them, using his hands and his fingers to fix their attention on the device.

Hawthorn and Podgorsky had their hands on the table. Podgorsky was starting to perspire. Hawthorn had been watching Moffit's eyes, not the demonstration.

"Steve, there's no need for . . ."

"I told you to shut up." Behind the glasses his eyes were barely

221

visible. He set the silver connector, the bomb, back on the table. Next to the bomb were two small Zippo-shaped cases. He took the Luger and, with its business end, he pushed them toward the men.

"Concussion sensors," he said. "One in every device. If one blows, they all blow. Do you understand that? Like dominoes."

His face turned toward Hawthorn; he wet his lips.

"You removed the wire, Hawthorn. That was smart, but I don't need the wire. Those sensors will touch off an explosion that will blow this oil field to kingdom come without the damn wire."

He sat back and aimed the Luger at Hawthorn, the butt resting on the tabletop.

"I have placed bombs on every tank, every pump, every line, every wellhead, and there's one concussion sensor in every bomb. You get the idea, Hawthorn? You get the idea, Russian?"

Podgorsky shifted again. Moffit pushed the gun barrel a few inches down the table, swung now in his direction. He reached inside his jacket and removed a folded piece of paper, threw it toward Hawthorn and kept his eyes on Podgorsky.

"Read it," he said. It was an order.

The letter had landed a foot from his hand. Hawthorn eased his fingers slowly forward, pulled it back, and then, with both hands, unfolded it and began to read. His face betrayed no sign as he looked up, then read it again.

"Magnificent, Hawthorn! Tonight you will get one hundred million pounds for a pile of garbage. But you will not keep the money. You will give the draft to Tinker. He will fly to Geneva and he will deposit it to SB #12 Account 46.A336-42. The banker will contact our gentleman and he will notify me in code that the transaction is completed. He has until noon, Friday, January 2. If my confirmation does not come before then, I will trigger the explosion and we will die.

In addition, if the draft is not deposited by the hour named, a copy of CIA Directive Anr665+2L together with documents related to this hoax will be released to the world press.

In addition, you will not then be able to take advantage of the forced and probably violent seizure of American holdings in Cuba, scheduled to take place on Saturday, January 3, at 8:00 A.M.

I will wait in a secure place with my finger on the switch. I have learned to wait.

A similar message will now be given to Josef Podgorsky, omitting the obvious and outlining my demands from his government.

Finish it right, Hawthorn. It's only money."

It was absurd. Almost absurd. He folded the letter, and folded it again, looked at the small black hole in the end of the muzzle, then raised his

222

eyes to Moffit's rose-colored glasses. What he saw there wiped his doubt away.

Moffit turned his attention to Podgorsky.

"You, sir." He threw another piece of folded paper toward the Russian.

"You know about blackmail. You do what it says on that note and I won't blow up your Caribbean Communist Federation or whatever the shit you call it." He turned his head a fraction, spat out a hair with the tip of his tongue. "You ponemaesh?"

Podgorsky nodded, retrieved the note, and studied the few lines. Hawthorn was holding his note in his fingers, staring at Moffit, incredulous, feeling the rage building in his chest.

"Now, gentlemen, I'm going to say good-bye. May I suggest you behave yourselves like gentlemen this evening and get right to work as soon as possible."

In the communications shack the telephone buzzed. Villar-Cruz leaned across the table, turned down the short-wave receiver, and picked up the radio phone.

"Hello?" He heard nothing, then flicked on the amplifying room speaker.

"Hello?" There was a loud crackling, then a voice.

"I have been . . . shot . . . you see . . . the soldier shot me. . . ."

The others looked up and Villar-Cruz waved them quiet. "Who is . . ."

"Oh . . . Angela!"

"Burrowes! It's Burrowes!"

". . . Get out! Ohh, get out! They will kill you. Castroites . . . Castroiyyy . . ."

"Cubans!" shouted Tinker. "Goddamn Cubans!"

Villar-Cruz was holding his hand up, waving, waiting for more. There was nothing but air noise.

"Get Hawthorn!" he shouted. "Get the boss! Sandy, get the Jeep, go get Schultz!"

Villar-Cruz pushed his chair out of the way and bolted for the door, pushing Tinker ahead of him.

"The mess hall, hurry, Sandy!"

The big engineer vaulted left out of the doorway. Villar-Cruz raced after Tinker, their feet driving hard onto the packed sand. Suddenly, from the direction of the river, they heard a flupping sound.

"*Oh, shit!*" Tinker said in full stride. "Choppers!"

* * *

Moffit eased his chair back, stood, then froze. He listened, heard the beating of chopper blades, heard someone shouting, a man running. He pushed himself away from the table, grabbed the radio in his left hand, swung the gun wildly from Podgorsky to Hawthorn, then at the door as Tinker burst through.

He fired point blank. Tinker flew backward, his mouth open, crashing against the wall next to the door. Moffit wheeled, aimed at Podgorsky as Villar-Cruz flew through the open doorway and took off, his arms splayed out front, his feet off the floor. His shoulder struck Moffit just as the gun exploded in his face. Podgorsky rocked back, fell onto the table, spun once and crashed to the floor, his legs jerking. Hawthorn lunged and grabbed Moffit's gun hand, wrenching the Luger from his grasp. He took one back step, whipped the pistol high over his head, heaved hard, and brought it down with all his strength, striking the top of Moffit's skull with the butt. The radio fell, and Moffit crumpled in Villar-Cruz's arms. The sound of the chopper was pounding closer.

"It's Cubans!" Villar-Cruz shouted. "They shot Burrowes!"

Hawthorn grabbed the radio, stuffed the Luger in his belt, and got himself under Moffit's loose-hanging arm. They both looked at Podgorsky, saw him lying motionless, blood oozing from the side of his head. They shuffled forward, stopped at the door; Hawthorn loosed himself and knelt down by Tinker, then stood and caught hold of Moffit's arm again.

"Let's get outta here," he said.

They dragged Moffit to the door as the Jeep slewed to a skidding stop, Schultz hanging onto the windshield, Dreier holding the wheel with his huge hands, standing on the brake. Villar-Cruz dropped down and grabbed Moffit's legs; Hawthorn threw his weight behind, vaulting the unconscious spy into the backseat. They scrambled in, one on either side of Moffit, holding him upright while Hawthorn jammed the transmitter between his legs.

"The plane! Go for the field!" shouted Hawthorn. Dreier jumped on the gas and spun the wheels, throwing a cloud of dust and sand back. The Jeep leaped forward, careening wildly through the camp.

Dreier looked back. "*Tinker!*" He was shouting over the sound of the chopper, close behind them now.

"*He's dead! Move!*"

Their headlights bounced from the road to the blackness ahead, stabbed the night sky, came back to the road as the Jeep hurtled through the compound. Schultz was half-standing, looking frantically back, lurching as Dreier threw the Jeep hard right, skipping a steel drum with his left fender.

"*Faster, Sandy!*" Schultz cried, shouting above the mounting roar of the approaching helicopter. The horrendous beating swooped over their heads, they felt the hurricane wind, blinding dust in their faces, saw the huge black machine swing, start to settle sideways to the ground. Dreier's hands were chasing themselves on the wheel; they skidded as his foot hit the brake and slammed them to the left. He swerved right, jammed the gas again, spun rubber against dirt, aimed his lights at a mound, and hit it hard. The Jeep took off, flew twenty feet across the ditch, and landed on the runway, throwing heads forward, Schultz belly-bent against the windshield.

Crack! The windshield shattered. Now Dreier was standing, his full weight on the gas pedal, bullets whining overhead, chunking into the ground. He saw the plane, poised for takeoff at the far end of the field.

"Get the door! Somebody get the door! I got a gun!"

Behind them was the firecracker sound of guns, rapid fire, hot lead blasting apart as slugs hit the body steel.

Dead ahead, fifty yards. Dreier aimed for the wing, stood on the brake, and spun the Jeep on two wheels. Before it rolled they were on the ground, Schultz on his feet and racing for the door.

Dreier fell to his knees next to the Jeep, his gun drawn, firing into the dust cloud with his automatic. Hawthorn and Villar-Cruz ran with Moffit slung between them, reaching the open door as holes spit black in the fuselage near their heads. They heaved together and threw Moffit inside, Hawthorn scrambling over his unconscious body, flying for the cockpit.

"Sandy! Now! Now!" Villar-Cruz was scuttling through the door, shouting over his shoulder. He turned and saw the big engineer lying flat on the ground, spread-eagled, bullets spitting into the dirt, into his lifeless shape. Villar-Cruz reached for the door lock.

Hawthorn had spun himself into the copilot's seat, flicked the start switches, hit the fuel, battery, and ignite toggles with one sweep of his hand. He jammed the thrust levers around the horn.

"Go! Go!" Villar-Cruz slammed the door shut, twisting the lock. Schultz was heading for the cockpit, saw Hawthorn waiting, teeth clenched, watching the dials, helpless as the mob surged on.

The ignition lights were glowing red. The slow winding sound was a mounting scream. Hawthorn reached for the flap switch, drove the thrust levers forward to the stops. They began rolling, slowly, too slowly, the soldiers caught in the plane's lights, crouching, running at the jet as it picked up speed. Flaps down with his right hand, his left on the throttles, Hawthorn dropped his right; a bullet ripped through the pilot's side and tore through his knuckles, splattering bone and blood into his face. Ahead, the huge black tanks loomed, rushing at the plane. He jumped hard on the rudder; the nose swung wildly left. The yoke was like mush! Faster, *faster!* They ran over a soldier, the jolt felt on the pedals; Hawthorn was holding the yoke with his arm now, his left hand forced against the thrust levers, back . . . back . . . solid pressure. *Back!* He gripped the yoke with his bloody hand. *Back! Back! Get up, damn you!* Too far to the right. His screaming attack was aimed straight for solid steel. Ninety knots, the vibration was shaking the plane apart, the noise was deafening. *Now!* The wheels were off the ground, a second more! He choked the yoke with both hands, slippery with blood, tighter, urging it left, his leg a piston rod jamming the rudder; the nose jerked up, violently left, the right wing leapt high, the plane crabbed sideways, the wing light shattered as it kissed the steel tank. And they were flying, climbing away, up and away.

On the ground, where the plane had been parked, a young soldier picked up the transmitter and shook it, fumbled at the knobs, then looked for the switch to turn it on.

It was as though the universe had exploded, as though all the stars in the heavens had fallen and crashed on that spot in a world-shaking, thunderous, billion-colored, ear-shattering Armegeddon. The tanks burst with the first charge, then the light oil, released to the fury of the intense heat, boiled instantly along the exploding concussion line and burst into an inferno, sending flames and orange-red black smoke thousands of feet into the sky. The shore tanks at the harbor disintegrated, and their captive oil, afire before it ever felt the air, spewed out in great waves of crashing, burning, billowing death that poured into the river, rushing across the water like an enormous molten tidal wave, setting barges, lines, everything in its wake into a boiling, blazing sea of flame.

The Jetstar, seconds past the black field tanks, was swooped up with the blast, its nose streaking to the sky, its belly thrown against the blazing night. Hawthorn dropped the yoke, kicked the right rudder, eased back again, found the dark horizon, and held the plane level, feeling the thrust of her powerful engines, hearing them in their screaming escape from the holocaust below.

And now the ground behind them was the hell of Hamburg, the fire storm of war.

Hawthorn touched the wheel switch, relaxed the yoke, and raised the flaps. He dipped his right wing and did not look back as they turned to the north.

CHAPTER 16

When things began to get hot in Cuba Admiral Duncan Barnes ordered the usual operations at Guantanamo Bay canceled. Carrier qualification training, gunnery, night formation, rocket practice, all were canceled. On Christmas Day he called back the units of his Western Atlantic Command to the central Caribbean to be on station in the general vicinity should there be a need for their services.

Two destroyers and the U.S.S. *Antietam*, a canted-deck aircraft carrier that had seen its last war days and was used for training and goodwill missions, were steaming toward Cuba from one such exercise off the French island of Martinique. The captain, James J. Cooper, himself a veteran aviator, had been on the bridge a good part of the evening, listening to reports of the Cuban development. He had been advised by COMAIRLANT that he was to take no action of any kind; his command was to continue monitoring all normal frequencies as usual.

As he went below at 0020 hours he checked their position. The *Antietam* was at longitude 66.0 and latitude 16.0, crossing the lines at that moment, a thousand miles from Havana and nearly one hundred fifty miles south of Puerto Rico. The men were having a party below, on the hangar deck, without booze as far as he knew, and he wondered how that was possible. He decided to go down and see for himself.

Two hundred miles from the *Antietam*'s position the Globe Jetstar was cruising at seventeen thousand feet, heading in the general direction of Puerto Rico, flying on automatic pilot. Schultz and Villar-Cruz had done what they could for Stephen Moffit, lying now on the foldaway bed in the rear cabin. He had not recovered consciousness, was dealing with a probable concussion, perhaps a skull fracture, and a small caliber wound in the back. Villar-Cruz, with some training, feared a lesion near the renal artery and subsequent, rather swift death from internal bleeding, but the man was still alive, making sounds, uttering words in his dark battle.

Reinaldo had gone forward immediately after their escape from the camp, when the plane had found its straight and level in the aftermath of the explosion. The best he could manage for Hawthorn was cleaning of the hand, removal of the skin and bone shards and pieces, a tight bandage and ice. The hand rested in Hawthorn's lap, numb and useless.

The fuselage was badly torn in a dozen places, limiting their altitude and compelling them to manage their conversation as best they could in what amounted to a cyclonelike howl throughout the plane.

The bullets had not spared the cockpit instrumentation. Even with a full panel Hawthorn would have had a rough time bringing them to safety. He was in some pain, had lost a good deal of blood, and his instrument training was practically useless in this aircraft, fitted with radio aids and communication devices that were totally strange to him. Now even those primitive skills he had were limited. There was no gyro compass, the pitot tube had been shot away, and they had no altitude or air-speed indicators.

By magnetic compass and by feel he had taken them north, over the coast and over a cloud layer that sat at four thousand feet for as far as the sliver of a moon would allow him to see. They were riding above it, in the clear, but the ground was completely shrouded by the stratus cover below.

To his left, an hour out, he thought he saw a lighter patch, Trinidad, and as he made his easy turn in its direction he fumbled again with the radio switches and dials, trying every combination he could think of to make contact, to receive, to transmit, but he could not even manage to raise air noise on the cockpit speakers. And the light below had disappeared. A large ship? Grenada? Could he have gotten so far off course that he had seen Barbados?

Hawthorn was lost. Without an air-speed indicator, with no ground speed reference whatsoever, with no visible landmark to guide him, there was no dead reckoning, and Hawthorn was reduced to his sense of their position in flight by the poor compass and by the light of the North Star, which hung above the horizon at one o'clock.

For a while Villar-Cruz had sat in the cockpit with him, proving only that he knew less about navigation and radio than Hawthorn himself. His training had not included communications, though he knew code and could handle a key and a ground set, useless skills now. And Villar-Cruz was suffering pain as well, his hand resting in a sling, a bloody bandage holding his left arm together.

Hawthorn leaned to his left, dropped his arm to the fuel transfer switch, and tried again. He watched the gauge. The belly pod showed empty, the wing tanks showed empty, though he had used neither of them. The barrage of bullets had taken its toll on their fuel as well as their bodies.

They were flying now across that great empty space of water called "the Devil's Pool," where land in any direction was too far away: too far for the schooners and the frigates, for the pirate buccaneers and the Spanish galleons that were caught in battle, or in a storm. And too far for modern aircraft that were in trouble. At that hour, the Jetstar was in serious trouble.

It made no difference now who the marauders were, Cuban or Guianese or Russian, or for that matter, bandits from a neighboring country. Hawthorn had described the scene in the mess hall, Villar-Cruz had embellished that with his account of the Burrowes call, and there were bullets aimed at their backs. The bargaining platform had become a hot plate.

Villar-Cruz came forward and leaned between the seats.

"Moffit's talking," he said. "Something about the Philistines. King David."

"That's helpful."

"I put ice around him. His temperature is down, I think."

"Maybe he can come up here and fly this thing to San Juan."

"How much longer, sir? How much fuel?"

Hawthorn grimaced, pulling his hand to his chest and adjusting the ice pack. "I don't know," he said. "Less than an hour, maybe an hour." He glanced at the panel. "The main tank gauges are moving back and forth. I don't know what that means."

"He's awake, sir! Moffit's awake!"

Schultz was standing behind Villar-Cruz, poking his head up front. Hawthorn made a move to turn, winced, and flopped back. Villar-Cruz stepped into the cabin, kneeled beside Moffit, and used a wet cloth to wipe his face.

"Where's Tinker?" Moffit coughed.

"He couldn't come."

"I shot him."

"You sure did." Villar-Cruz dipped the cloth in cold water that had melted from his bed ice.

"Goddamn tha's cold." Moffit said. His words were slurred, drunken sounds. "Where's the Russian?"

"He's dead, too."

"He's dead. Good. Tha's good. Tha's good."

"Take it easy, mister. You were hit pretty hard."

Moffit closed his eyes. "Who's flyin' this thing?"

"Mr. Hawthorn. He's trying." Villar-Cruz glanced forward, saw Schultz sitting in the pilot's seat, holding a chart.

For more than a minute Stephen Moffit stared at the light over his head.

"I was shot," he said finally. "I'm dying."

"I don't think so. Not yet."

"My father knows it."

Villar-Cruz leaned closer to his mouth.

229

". . . an' my father . . . knows it . . ."

"Hang on. I'll be back."

He stood up slowly, went forward, and leaned on the seats again. "He's only semiconscious."

His observation was lost in the small space, his voice a poor whisper against the jets, the competing wind.

Schultz touched the yoke, tapping it with his fingers.

"When we run out of fuel this plane will drop like a rock. Is that what you said, sir?"

"Not quite," Hawthorn said. "We'll get some glide out of her." He hefted his hand, dropped it again. Dead weight. "We'll keep the instrument lights on with the battery and make a water landing, then hope for the best."

Hawthorn turned his head. "Better start now, men. Go strap Moffit in, tight. Get the rafts, set them in a seat and tie them down, remember where they are. Then you get yourself . . ." He stopped, his mouth half open, his eyes fixed to a spot in back of Villar-Cruz's head.

"Outta the way, mister." Moffit had a hand on Villar-Cruz's shoulder, pressing him to the side. He was stooped, soaked from sweat and ice, his face ashen in the poor light.

"Move outta there, Schultz. Lemme in that seat."

Schultz turned himself, stepped over the middle console, and squeezed past. Villar-Cruz leaned in, helped Moffit into the pilot's seat, laid the strap across his legs.

"Forget that!" He brushed Villar-Cruz's arm away.

Moffit looked across, saw Hawthorn watching him. Then he looked away, out the side window.

"You don't look so good." Hawthorn said it loud enough, but Moffit made no reply. He settled his body into the seat, dropped his hands to his lap, and stared at the instruments. "How bad is it?"

Moffit was blinking, his eyelids barely drawing open. "Where are you?"

"I don't know. Over water, two hours out from Georgetown, a little more."

Moffit reached down and turned the fuel selector, watched the instrument panel.

"I know," Hawthorn said.

"Trouble." Moffit looked across. "What happened?"

Hawthorn could see Moffit's face clearly, even in the dim light. A line of dried blood ran down the side of his face. He looked half alive.

"Somebody screwed up," Hawthorn said. "It's all over. Can you operate this damn radio?"

Moffit turned his head to the left, looked at his reflection in the small window on his side, saw the dim face there, and looked beyond into the darkness.

"How did they do it?" Moffit was speaking to the window. Hawthorn saw his lips moving but barely heard the question.

"How did they kill Captain Chou?" Moffit said.

"He was tortured and shot," Hawthorn replied.

Moffit was silent, staring at the glass and through the glass at the black, screaming wind inches from his face.

"It was Podgorsky. Podgorsky did it," Moffit said.

"Yes," said Hawthorn. "It was Podgorsky."

"Who are the Philistines?"

The sound of the bullet-hole wind muffled his question. Hawthorn leaned closer, but in that moment Moffit looked forward again, and closed his eyes.

Above the cyclonic howl, the constant sound of the twin jets was almost comforting. Moffit eased his hand to the thrust levers and made a small adjustment, evening out the power on both machines, smoothing the roar. He brought his hand back to his lap and sat motionless for a few seconds longer. Then he reached forward with his left hand, pressed a circuit breaker, found another button below the console, reached to the ceiling radio panel, and flicked switches, turned cranks. On the UHF panel he wound a tuner and thumbed the volume dial. The cockpit was filled with static. He fine-tuned again, then took the microphone on its coiled wire, brought its ribbed face to his mouth.

"Mayday, Mayday, Mayday, and again I call Mayday. This is Globe Jetstar four-niner-three-seven-seven and I call again Mayday, Mayday." His voice trailed off. He let the mike fall to his lap and he closed his eyes again. They listened, heard nothing but soft static.

Hawthorn brought his microphone up and repeated the message. The clouds had cleared below, and they could see the water, doppled and black, satin with silver flecks where the waning moon caught the wavetops.

"Mayday, Mayday." Moffit again. "Globe four-niner-three-seven-seven, Mayday." The words were flat, lifeless.

Again the soft static, an empty world. They were alone in their empty world, with the wind and their broken bodies and the red glow of their instrument lights.

"Globe four-niner-three-seven-seven, this is the U.S.S. *Antietam*. We acknowledge your Mayday. . . . I say again . . . we copy your Mayday. . . . State your problem. Over."

Hawthorn's stiff lips broke into a smile, a grin. Moffit went about his business, casually, correctly, painfully.

". . . Thank you, *Antietam*, this is Globe. We have estimated eighteen

231

minutes fuel; I don't know where we are, I don't know my altitude but I guess about twenty thousand. Did you copy? Over."

"Roger, Globe, *Antietam*, we copy. Give me ten seconds transmission and five off then ten more for a fix, over."

"Roger, *Antietam*." Moffit counted slowly to ten, released the button, then transmitted a count to ten again.

"Confirm, Globe. I think we have you bearing one-eight-five and thirty-seven miles at seventeen thousand. What is your intention, Globe? Over."

Hawthorn wanted to intervene, to help, as he wanted to help when the pumps were laboring in slow motion, knowing it was a futile want. He was watching Moffit, seeing him slump then recover, saw his eyes close and open slowly, a stuporlike expression, a wax mannequin.

"We can't make it on the water, *Antietam*. We got pods and she won't make it. *Antietam*, I'm starting a vector to your position. Help me with the heading, please. We have no gyro on board."

"Globe, I understand no compass. Turn right now. . . . Continue your right turn. . . . Hold your heading. . . . Come right five degrees. . . . Hold your heading. . . . Globe, you are on a closing vector oh oh five degrees. Begin your descent at two thousand feet per minute and hold your vector."

Hawthorn took his mike. "*Antietam*, this is Gregory Hawthorn, the plane's owner. I have urgent and top-secret information for the captain of your ship. I must talk with the captain. Over."

"*Antietam*, roger. Stand by."

There was a pause, lasting not more than fifteen seconds. The captain must have been alerted with the Mayday call.

"Globe Jetstar, this is Captain Cooper, U.S.S. *Antietam*. Say again your name, owner."

"My name is Hawthorn, H-A-W-T-H-O-R-N, and my message is urgent and top secret for Admiral Barnes in Guantanamo. Please relay the following: The Globe project in British Guiana is finished. It has been destroyed by fire. The Globe project has been destroyed. Hold all ships offshore, repeat, hold all Globe ships offshore. Look for hostile action Saturday morning. Will you relay that message to Admiral Barnes? Over."

Moffit looked across at Hawthorn. He held his own mike, added his message.

"Forget the hostile action, Skipper. That part was a lie."

"Globe, this is Captain Cooper. What the hell is going on with you? Over."

Hawthorn again. "Captain, will you relay that message, all except the hostile action segment. Will you relay that immediately. It is very urgent, sir."

"Roger, Mr. Hawthorn, Cooper, I will relay that message. But Hawthorn, if this is false or treasonous or felonious in any respect, you are in serious trouble. Over."

Moffit came on, his voice weaker than before.

"Captain, we're in trouble now." He released the key. He blinked several times, and a shiver passed over the muscles of his face. "I'm a Russian . . ." He stopped, sat straighter, looked out the side window. "Hawthorn is an American operative . . . and . . . I'm . . . I'm . . ." He could get that far, no further. He lowered the mike, closed his eyes. Hawthorn was ready to take over, to handle the communications.

Suddenly Moffit tightened his fist around the black microphone and he spoke again.

"I'm a naval aviator with eighty-nine carrier landings, sir! I can bring this plane aboard your ship." Now his eyes looked as though they had been washed, the lids locked open, wetness in the corners.

Silence. Then, "Stand by, Globe."

They were on manual control now, Moffit guiding the plane down on an approximate heading that would take them close to the carrier. The pitch of the jets was lower, their descent allowing a decrease in power. Hawthorn glanced at Moffit.

"Can you? Can you do that with this plane?"

"You're damn right." His head fell forward, jerked back.

"Say your name, pilot. Over."

"Moffit, Stephen . . ." He lowered the mike, stared ahead. ". . . Jonathan Moffit." The last part was lost in the wind.

"Roger, Lieutenant Moffit. Stand by."

He blinked. His lips moved. ". . . Lieutenant . . ."

"Globe, this is the *Antietam*. Lieutenant Moffit, have you ever landed on a canted deck?"

"Negative, *Antietam*."

"Roger, Moffit. We copy." Dead air. "Moffit, are you OK with night operations? Over."

"Roger, *Antietam*, forty landings."

"We copy that. Have you ever gone into the barrier? Over?"

"Negative, *Antietam*."

"Roger. We copy that information. Stand by, Globe."

The silence lasted longer this time, half a minute. The two men waited, each with his own thoughts. Behind them, Villar-Cruz and Schultz were crowding the passage, leaning forward to listen.

"Globe, this is Combat Information Center." A different voice now, a businesslike voice. "Continue your vector oh oh five and slow your rate of descent to five hundred feet per minute. Report when you have the ship in sight. Over."

"Roger, *Antietam*. Five hundred FPM and report sight."

"Does that mean they'll take us?" Hawthorn said.

Moffit turned his head, wagged it slowly. He was leaning back, his hand on the yoke, his eyes focused on the windshield in front.

"They'll get us close and . . . uuuhh!" He touched his side.

"Steve, this is Don Bryant. I'm your LSO. Over."

"Well damn! Well damn!" Moffit coughed. "Hullo, Bryant. What the hell."

"Welcome home, Steve. Listen, I'm OK with you up there. You're the best. But this won't be easy. You'll make one pass, that's all, and I've got a canted deck down here. She's not lined up with the ship's wake. You copy? Over."

"Roger, Don. I copy. I land this thing on an angle."

"Not like the old *Ti*, Steve. You've gotta cross the ship's wake, hit the flight deck centerline and follow that. Forget the wake. It's too dark to see the damn thing anyway. Steve, I'm headin' down now. My flags will be lighted, boy. Watch my flags. I'll catch you on the downwind. Out."

Don Bryant. A name from the past, the man who had watched Moffit's old flight come home on a day in July without Cocksure 309, had waved the others aboard then gone below, watched them put red tape across Moffit's locker.

He would fly the Jetstar parallel with the ship, on its right side, a mile off the right side, then turn left to cross the ship's path, keep turning until he was flying back again, parallel with the ship, heading the opposite way. Abreast of the ship's bow he would start his left turn, descending slowly, keeping the ship in his left windshield, seeing it plow ahead while he turned toward its stern, seeing the angle correct itself until he was chasing the big carrier, running its centerline . . . but this time, this time he would have to cross the wake to get to that good line.

The Jetstar was trimmed perfectly, descending toward the U.S.S. *Antietam*, finding the approach altitude. Moffit didn't need a dial on the panel to tell him his space above the water. He could feel it. His right hand was on the thrust levers, his left on the yoke. His face was wet with perspiration, his shoulders were sagging forward, his eyes were trying to stay open. From his seat, Gregory Hawthorn could see ahead, could see the horizon dimly, a line that crossed darker below, a shade lighter above.

And there, just below the horizon, seen by the light of a universe full of stars and a crescent moon, the U.S.S. *Antietam*, a speck in the vast ocean, a place for them.

The carrier was moving at twenty-five knots now, heading into a wind that was blowing at a fine, steady twelve knots. It would give them thirty-seven knots down the centerline, more than enough under even the worst conditions. A nylon barricade had been rigged across the flight deck, rising twenty feet off the deck plates like a giant tennis net, with vertical nylon webbing running from the top cable to the bottom. It was flapping, waiting, a strong net for an errant bird. The Jetstar had no tailhook.

The plane would come across the threshold at a relative speed of seventy miles per hour, hit and bounce, then crash headlong into the net. There was no guarantee that even if the pilot found the centerline, got the right speed, found a wedge of vertical space maybe ten feet deep, and was headed down the middle of the deck, they would get aboard. The gear could fold, send them crashing in any direction, the plane might hit the net sideways, or miss the net and hit the superstructure, or miss in the other direction and scream across the deck and plunge into the sea.

Every man aboard the ship knew what was happening, but few of them were allowed topside. Those who were on the flight deck had to be there, and they were secured behind something solid. Don Bryant, the landing signal officer, was standing near the spud locker, that broad, fat brace of steel that formed the trailing edge of the landing platform, nicked and blackened from near misses, spots where the tail hooks of fighter planes too low in the grove had hit and bounced, then caught a wire down the deck. Bryant wore his cloth headpiece, the microphone winding to the outside, earphones bulging inside. To his right as he faced the wake of the ship was his net, two strides away in case the pilot miscalculated. This night, Bryant was ready to make the dive. His signal flags were lighted, the modern approach ball a useless aid for a pilot who had never used it. Moffit knew the flags. He knew them very well.

Firemen in asbestos suits were stationed nearby, other men on the recovery team ducked behind turrets, ready.

Now the sidelights came on, very dim, hardly seen by the deck crew, Christmas bulbs outlining the tiny rectangle for the pilot.

"*Aooooooooooooga! Aooooooooooooga!*"

The carrier was ready to receive Lieutenant Moffit, who was now barely conscious, who could scarcely see the instrument panel, who hadn't seen an aircraft carrier in over five years and who had never seen a canted deck in his life. The wake behind the great ship was silver and full of froth, and Moffit would have to cross it to land.

* * *

235

"*Antietam*, this is Globe. We have you in sight, over."

"Roger, Globe. This is carrier controlled approach. Turn now to heading oh one five and begin your upwind leg one mile out at niner hundred feet. Over."

"Oh-one-five-and niner-hundred. Roger."

The carrier was only a few miles off, and they were seconds away. Moffit eased the plane right, found the upwind leg and intersected it perfectly. Below them, the water had become a living thing, moving, swelling under their wings, waiting.

When the ship moved to his seven o'clock, he lowered the left wing, as from a thought command. He kept turning, crossed a mile in front of the ship's bow, turning, until they were heading back.

"Globe, this is CCA. You have turned onto your downwind leg and I am handing you over to the LSO. Good luck, sir."

"OK, Steve. You're looking good. Don Bryant. Report now, Globe, report flaps and gear at the final and start your final at the bow. Say back."

Moffit tried to talk but his lips were parched together. He dropped the microphone and nodded at Hawthorn.

"Roger, LSO. I'll answer for the pilot. This is Hawthorn."

"Roger, I copy. I have you in sight. Gear and flaps . . . confirm your gear and flaps. Over."

"OK. Gear and flaps coming down."

Moffit dropped his hand to the console and flicked the gear lever. They heard them grinding down, felt the plane begin to shudder. He added power. Now his fingers found the flap control and they came out, down. The sound of the engines was deafening, the nose was so high Hawthorn could no longer see the horizon, could barely see the ship from his side. The panel light came on as the gear pins snapped and locked.

"Our landing gear are down, full flaps," Hawthorn reported.

"Roger, Globe. Begin your final turn when I give you the mark. Get ready, Steve. . . . Five . . . four . . . three . . . two . . . one . . . *Mark!* Do not answer back. I will talk you in. Keep the stern in your left windshield. . . . You look good. Your turn is good. . . . You're high . . . all right, good, nice correction. . . . Keep your eye on my flags and look for my cut. . . . Come left, come left . . . dammit! Look at my flags and come left! . . . good. You're at the wake and crossing . . ."

Moffit saw the wake, running sideways. The turbulent silver river ran at an angle. He was gripping the yoke with his fist, strangling it. Racer disintegrated. He crossed and he burned. *Forget the wake! Fly the*

236

centerline! The howling engines, the screaming, the howling engines, the plane was standing on its tail. Nose down, turning, too fast! . . . Ease back on the power. Now the ship was ahead, the centerline was dead ahead, the plane was chasing the ship, running over the black water, the deck lights were flat, coming fast, too high! *Too high!* The barricade loomed, the LSO standing feet apart, flags at arms' length straight out. . . . *Cut! Cut! Cut!* Moffit's hand pulled back on the thrust levers, he held the yoke for an instant, then he let go. They crashed straight ahead, and the nose wheel sheared; the wounded Jetstar ricocheted and careened forward on its chin for half a second, sparks flying. It hit the barrier, the tail swung high, stopped, then settled slowly back to the deck. The nose was thrust half through the nylon webbing, trapped there like a wounded beast.

Before the tail dropped, even before the plane was dead on the deck, ten men in yellow shirts were around it, and men with asbestos suits were at the engines, hoses ready. Other firemen were at the wing tips with canisters and foam nozzles, but there was no fire. There was only smoke, billowing back from the tailpipes, black carbon thrown out from sand-dry, exhausted burner nozzles.

Moffit knew his hand was reaching forward to turn off the ignition, that it was rising to the ceiling to find the other switches. But it was so quiet. They were below him . . . far down below. He saw the plane below, and the men, and he was floating above them all, light and serene, and he was smiling at them.

The door was torn off, and a man in a navy-blue flight suit was standing on the deck, a flashlight beaming inside.

"Which one is Hawthorn?" he shouted.

Villar-Cruz was helping Schultz to the door. "In the cockpit. Get somebody to help up there!"

Two men were inside in a moment, helping them out; another moved quickly to the cockpit and pulled Hawthorn, helped him to the cabin, then onto the flight deck. More men came and hurried into the plane.

The officer threw him a salute.

"Are you Hawthorn?"

"I'm Hawthorn."

"Thank you, sir. Please follow me, and bring your people."

They walked a few feet behind the officer, the brisk wind rushing past them. Hawthorn looked up at the island tower and saw men at every rail, in every lighted window. The tower rose up and up, as high and as strong as any structure he had ever seen, dark and overwhelming.

Then he saw the row of seamen making way as they crossed to the island hatch, fifty men, smiling. One of them began to clap, then another, and on the bridge others joined in until there were a hundred men, a thousand men. Applauding.

From deep within the belly of the carrier there was heard another sound, the ship's own sound booming across the water:

"*Phoooooooooo'a.*"

Moffit's bleeding body was carried to the ship's hospital where it was laid on an operating table. Doctors were there, ready, but within the flaming dimensions of his mind, he felt himself leaving the room, then drifting back inside to look at them, at himself. He felt his body shrinking, then growing heavy and huge, then shrinking again, and he heard a man's voice talking to him. He knew the voice, deep and warm. Was it his father? There was a brilliant light. Then the light grew dim, and the voice faded, and the colors grew dark, and he died.

EPILOG

Two hours is usually more than ample time to allow for the drive from Heathrow International to the tiny village of Maldon, but Gregory Hawthorn allowed three. That would give him an hour to stop along the way and smell the air, walk through the spring clover, feel the freshness of the channel breeze. It had been a long time since he felt like doing that, and it was nice. Now it was May 1960, time to get ready for another war.

The Globe Corporation had been under constant fire since the events of New Year's Eve 1958, legally, financially, and politically. Gregory Hawthorn had been charged by the United States government with conspiracy to commit sabotage against a friendly nation, but the charge was eventually dismissed when it was shown that Globe's operations in British Guiana were in every sense legal—if disgracefully foolish—and that the destruction of Globe's facilities was the result of a minor local uprising in which Hawthorn was in no way implicated.

The Globe fleet was never discovered off the coast of Cuba, so there was never a hint of a possible connection between the Guiana incident and the Cuban revolution, though several newspapers carried a story that attempted to tie them together, using Globe as the ball of twine.

There was no blockade, no melodramatic destruction of Cuba's ports, no sabotaging of the refineries. But there were other effects, some of them as devastating in the long run as any that had been contemplated by the visionary Commission.

Hawthorn had watched the scenario unfold in British Guiana from his penthouse in Baton Rouge. First came the stages of blame and accusation, then the denial and the protestations of innocence relating to the fire and explosion, the death of thirty-four soldiers and civilians and the shooting of the military commandant, Jeffry Burrowes. No one was proved guilty, but a deputy minister and an Army officer spent time in prison and were forced to resign.

Then came the rebuilding, the invitations to bid on the rights to the lease that Globe had relinquished, and finally the drilling by a group formed in Trinidad. When they made their pathetic announcement in July that there was no oil in the ground, that further searching in the region was futile, the billion-dollar hoax was ended.

Through it all Hawthorn had maintained a vigorous stance of silence, confirming nothing and denying nothing. The worst he could be accused of was incredibly bad management, the penalty for which would be the disintegration of his reputation. Those in the industry who knew the man sought in vain for better explanations.

Probably the most satisfying development from Hawthorn's view-point was the refusal by American corporations to refine Russian crude oil in their Cuban refineries, followed eventually by their ouster from the country. It wasn't their exodus that satisfied him so much as the alternative that Fidel Castro chose. Cuba signed an agreement to exchange a mere five million tons of sugar for ten million barrels of Russian oil, a few months' supply. Hawthorn, and a host of others, wondered if Mother Russia had perhaps miscalculated—based on "other suppositions"—and was having misgivings about the adventure. It was a certainty that sugar alone would never begin to pay the bill.

Then came the crowning triumph. With a startling urgency, oil prices started to soar, the Suez closure forced shipping costs to record highs, and Russia, now committed to supply Cuba's petroleum requirements, was forced to lease one hundred tankers from Stavros Niarchos, "The Golden Greek," at least twenty of which were pressed into emergency service to ply between the Black Sea and the island of Cuba. The exercise was costing Russia millions of dollars a day, and it would get more expensive as the price of oil continued to soar and as Cuba forged ahead into the era of military industrialization.

Hawthorn's entire fleet had been sold at auction, along with Globe's domestic operation. A west coast retailer reportedly paid cash to close the deal.

Of almost passing interest to many observers was the fact that, while Western investors were gobbling up concessions and rights in the Middle East, the Russians had been conspicuous by their absence. Until now. One by one Russian negotiators and diplomats were filing into Tehran and Baghdad and Bahrain, arranging purchases of crude oil to supply their friends in other lands. The superabundance they had claimed was not enough.

It was a beautiful day in May, and all of that had gone on for more than a year.

Hawthorn stood at the side of a brook that sounded very busy, enroute probably to the Chelmer River and thence to the sea. He had traveled this way before, many times, but always in the company of someone else, never alone. The glade air and the fragrance of spring flowers reminded him now of a time long ago, before British Guiana, before Globe. He had left the hospital, gone to the parking lot, and driven for two hours before he was aware that life was continuing. There had been a place like this, a place they used to know.

He took a last deep breath of air and trudged back through a thicket, up a small incline to the road, and squeezed himself behind the wheel of his rented MG convertible. It was nearly teatime, the reunion hour at Alan Drinkwater's country estate.

He stayed on the main road for a mile, then turned off onto a gravel road and followed it past birch, hickory, and ash trees that crowded the shoulders. He drove slowly, thinking he might be hearing the sound of the ocean but hearing instead the chattering of chipmunks and birds in the forest.

He slowed as the path widened, saw the cottage nestled among the oak trees, and absently recalled the many times he had come to this place before. He parked in the driveway, climbed out, and walked up a step to the front door. It opened before he could drop the lion's head knocker.

"Mr. Hawthorn. How glad I am to see you again."

"Hello, Reinaldo. It's been a long time."

"I say it has. Come in, please."

He held Hawthorn's arm as he led the American through the foyer and into the large, comfortable library. They found places near the warmth of the fire, the room having a spring chill not yet gone out of the walls with summer.

"A long time. A lifetime," Hawthorn said. He was taking in the beauty of the room, the stained-glass windows in the garden bay, the bookcase with its worn volumes. He had dreamed of such a room, but could never own or occupy one like it. There was a sense of finality here, a feeling of eternal retirement that would have complicated his balance.

"It was one of the hearings, I suppose, the Senate investigation last summer. We had lunch afterward and didn't know whether to laugh or cry."

"I don't know about you," said Hawthorn, "but I felt more like crying at the time." He looked toward the door. "Where's our illustrious host?"

"You won't believe this," Villar-Cruz replied, "but he went to the village to buy a new hat. Took his lady with him."

Hawthorn smiled. Yes, he would. He would believe that.

"I suppose you want to know what happened, Rei. What really happened, I mean."

"As opposed to what we told them? Yes, I suppose I would. There were no informants among the pigs and sheep in Campoalegre. I never heard a thing except what was said at the hearings."

Hawthorn stood and crossed to the heavy wooden mantel above Drinkwater's fireplace. He leaned on it and looked down into the burning embers. *Snap!* A charred bit shot out and lodged in the screen, hissing blue and orange.

"All right." He frowned, then faced the diminutive Colombian. "How much do you know about Howard Barry?"

"Howard Barry." Alberto answered quickly. "He set fire to his house and shot himself. You pointed out the article in the *Post* on the day of the hearings."

Hawthorn moved away from the mantel, sat down in a rocker. The old wood protested as he leaned back against the Haitian wicker.

"No. Let's begin someplace else." Hawthorn eased his foot up, rested it on an ottoman. "If you were to assign the whole project a grade, how would you score it?"

"Score it? You mean against the original directive?"

"The directive, right."

Villar-Cruz thought for a moment. "I suppose I could give ourselves a C minus for the Caribbean part and maybe a B plus for the Middle East." He waited, watching Hawthorn for a reaction to his judgment. "Did I score us too high or too low, sir?"

"I don't know, Rei," Hawthorn replied. "We didn't slow Fidel down very much, but from what we know at this point it's not surprising. As for as the rest of the Caribbean, their federation sure fell apart. Was that our contribution? I don't know."

"How about British Guiana, then?"

"See for yourself. The coalition won't stand for Jagan. The PPP is finished, for all intents and to all purposes. As far as the Persian Gulf is concerned, what should I believe? It's not too late for the Russians to buy from the Middle East producers, but I think they missed the boat when they didn't get in sooner. Did we foul up their forecasting? Sure. I think so. Did we delay their plans? You're damn right we did."

It was quiet in the room for a moment. Then Villar-Cruz turned to Hawthorn again. "OK," he said. "Who was Barry?"

"Howard Barry was a member of the Communist party. He taught biology at Dunwoody Junior College," Hawthorn said. "He was also an agent for the CIA. They used Barry to keep track of doubles and singles, people like the ones Yu Hsin Chou sent over from China.

"Chou was responsible for the education and the training, the preparation of agents over there. In some cases he just let them pass on through and do their duty to Mother Russia or to China, like he did with Moffit. No tricky double stuff for the student spy to learn. In other cases, he would let the Podgorskies think they had a live one, a really solid agent when in fact they had a damn tennis ball that bounced from one court to another and gave all the points to the CIA.

"But the interesting thing about Barry was that he was on the receiving end of those reports from both kinds. Barry didn't know who was a double and who was a single. He just did his job.

"He acted as a mailbox. He received the stuff, whatever it was, took pictures of everything, and sent the original material on to his connection. Then sent the same material in duplicate form to the CIA."

Villar-Cruz sat motionless, his hands on his knees. "OK," he said softly. "What now?"

Hawthorn examined his hands, idly scratched at the scar tissue.

"Now Mr. Moffit discovers what we're up to in British Guiana. Don't ask me how, because I don't know. He writes a report and sends it to his contact, Howard Barry.

"How much money do you think a biology instructor makes, Rei? Ten thousand a year? Maybe that much. How about a full-time CIA operative? I'll give you twenty thousand plus expenses. Guess what a damn mailbox makes."

It was all over in any case, Gregory. God knows! I didn't plan this from the beginning, but when I saw how futile it all was . . . good heavens, man, the thing was decided by the time I got to Fidel. He knew exactly what he was going to do by that time. You were under budget in any event, you see.

"Barry decoded that report from Moffit and he probably collapsed right then and there. For years he's been reading crap about some prime minister cheating on his wife, a hundred pistols going to the chief of police in Bolivia, a conspiracy to overthrow the sardine monopoly in Argentina, I mean really heavy top-secret stuff. Now, all of a sudden, he hits the jackpot. The biggest hoax ever perpetrated by one nation against

242

another, and he begins to add up the cost of that masquerade. He sees the enormous implications of a possible leak."

It never even occurred to me, never, to use my position in this way. Nor did I consider using my information to the advantage of Russia, selling myself as it were to the Communists. I trust you will credit me with that much integrity at least.

"Barry wasn't a field man, Reinaldo. He didn't have a fake passport, he didn't know much about travel secrecy. When it was all over we checked with the British down there and found out that he entered Georgetown on a freighter from Suriname on the fifteenth of June, several weeks before we even had the crude oil transfer completed. He met Steve Moffit in a bar or someplace, and talked him into the blackmail idea. That would leave him, Barry, clean as new snow.

"But Moffit didn't want the money. You have to understand the guy, Al. He was like a kid in the schoolyard whose cap got swiped off his head by a bully. All he could do was wave his fist and say, 'I'll get you for that!'"

Please forgive the revolver, Gregory. I'll put it in my pocket, so. To become a prince, that's what he wanted. The boy wanted to sit on a throne next to the monarch and look at the heads of the poor people below him, on the streets. He was so poor himself, you see, in spirit.

"It seems Moffit wanted something the Russians couldn't give him," Hawthorn continued. "He wanted, I don't know . . . prestige? Whatever it was, he wasn't getting any in British Guiana. He saw no future for himself there, or even in Russia, no matter how sharp he got, no matter how good he became at his trade."

"So." Villar-Cruz was nodding, seeing the direction now. "So he made a deal with Barry to contact the Cubans, Castro's people. Moffit could trade his information about the project in exchange for a place in their sun."

"Right, but Howard Barry wanted cash. He didn't give a damn about living high in the sugar cane. He wanted the sweet green, a piece of the pie intended for Fidel."

It was logical, their plan. Do you recall our conversation, Gregory? A revolution needs people, energy, and money if the new form is to endure? But when they told me how much it was they had in mind, to use as barter, I immediately reduced the figure to a sum that was feasible. For young Moffit, of course, it wasn't the idea of money as much as the other thing.

Hawthorn sat at Drinkwater's mahogany desk, fidgeting now. He wanted a cigarette, could almost feel the acrid smoke coursing down his throat, into his lungs. But he was on his third day, the worst day of quitting. He closed his fingers behind his neck and squeezed, then relaxed.

"Barry thought he knew his way around the network, so he went to Havana, set up a meeting with a man he knew was close to the generalissimo, and he made the guy a proposition. 'Look,' he said, 'you people have a nice revolution here, but you need lots of money. I can get you a couple hundred million bucks, right in your own private account.' He said something like that. Then he said, 'And I can tell you a little secret about that oil deal, keep you from makin' asses out of yourself when you march into the city.'"

Hawthorn was tapping a pencil on the desk. He continued. "Then Barry named his price. He said, 'Just hold out a million for me, and find a nice, cushy job with lots of class for my friend here.'"

I am a man who needs recognition, Gregory, but a man in my position is never recognized, not really. There was never a desperate need for money in my home. I always had enough until I purchased the manor . . . but now, now, you see . . . when there is no recognition, when there is the danger of losing even the little we have, the small estate we have . . . a man becomes obsessed with the idea that he has failed in his living, he is suddenly afraid. It was awful, being afraid.

Hawthorn opened a desk drawer, found an old tissue, a few tacks, pencils, paper clips, and pipe tobacco but no pipe. He slammed it shut again.

"But Barry connected with the wrong man. Isn't that amazing? This smart agent for the CIA, this Howard Barry made his little speech to a limey tennis ball, one of the *Commission's* agents, and that guy bounced straight back to . . ."

"Alan Drinkwater!"

"Himself."

I find it extraordinary, don't you? One is placed in a position of enormous trust, with full authority to spend millions upon millions, and has not the personal resources to maintain his own home. It seems somehow inequitable, Gregory. I have nothing else, you see, no friends to speak of, no wife to see me through these last years.

* * *

"And when the other thing came up," Villar-Cruz said, "the purchase deal with a one hundred percent negotiable check for one hundred million pounds . . ."

"Change in plan. Why screw around with a few hundred million dollars when you can play the same game and win a lot more? And safer! Sure, it took Drinkwater twenty minutes to make the calls from Guantanamo and it took Moffit five minutes to type up a new note for me."

I would never have let them use that directive, Gregory. It was a chance I took. He suggested three compelling reasons for you to consider when he gave you the note: You would stay alive, you would maintain the secrecy of the mission, and you would have an opportunity to avenge Cuba's outrageous act. It was really quite clever. Don't you think so? You would have gone along with it, I'm very sure of that!"

Villar-Cruz touched his nose, strolled to the window.

"Where is he now, do you think?"

"If I had to guess, I would choose one of the Canary Islands. I expect he bought a little house on the beach with whatever he could scrape up, maybe rents a room to weekenders."

It must have been a big car. The sound of its engine lumbering to a stop in the driveway made the bay windows rattle in their frames.

He paraded in first, his very thin wife trailing behind. She wore a flowered silk dress and a floppy hat, and she carried an umbrella, her skinny legs stuck into a pair of pink high-heeled pumps. He was elegant in tweed trousers, a rough wool sweater with patches on the elbows, and a new glengarry, replete with ribbons at the back.

He came to a halt inside the door, surveyed his library from wall to wall, and grinned broadly. He doffed the cap, swept it grandly toward his guests, and introduced the lady.

"Madam," he said, the magnificent black wart riding proudly on his forehead, "these are my friends from America."